# PEONIES AND PO

*Audrey Herbert*
*Hong Kong 1988*

EX LIBRIS

# PEONIES AND PONIES

## HAROLD ACTON

HONG KONG
OXFORD UNIVERSITY PRESS
OXFORD  NEW YORK  MELBOURNE

Oxford University Press

Oxford London New York Toronto
Kuala Lumpur Singapore Hong Kong Tokyo
Delhi Bombay Calcutta Madras Karachi
Nairobi Dar es Salaam Cape Town
Melbourne Auckland

and associated companies in
Beirut Berlin Ibadan Mexico City Nicosia

First published by Chatto & Windus in 1941
First issued, with permission, as an Oxford in Asia paperback in 1983
Second impression 1984

ISBN 0 19 581593 9

OXFORD is a trade mark of Oxford University Press

Printed in Hong Kong by Ko's Arts Printing Co. Ltd.
Published by Oxford University Press, Warwick House, Hong Kong

*To Michael and Anne Rosse,*
*whose laughter and whose sympathy*
*refilled my fountain-pen.*

## Note

Since 1928, when the Chinese National Government moved to Nanking, *Pei-ching* (Northern Capital) has been called *Pei-p'ing* (Northern Peace), commonly spelt Peiping, and still referred to as such by the loyal, in spite of Japanese efforts to re-christen it *Pei-ching*— hence variations in the following pages.

# Contents

*

# Contents

# CHAPTER I

## In the Pavilion of Longevity

"PEKING's such loads of fun. Jugglers, fortune-tellers, acrobats, puppet-shows, temple tiffins, treasure hunts and Paomachang picnics—not to speak of costume jamborees, galas and fancy-dress affairs—always something original ! Home-made natural fun, not imported or artificially manufactured as in Shanghai. And there's always a delicious spice of the unexpected. Just think of this quite perfect little gathering . . ."

Mrs. Mascot surveyed the group as if it were part of a mirage. Herself was real enough ; there could be no doubt concerning her own solidity. She was a violin-shaped woman, flat, with hips. Her eyes were limpid, but their would-be soulful effect was crudely counteracted by irregular equine teeth. She was allowed to babble on to her heart's content. Mrs. Mascot's memory was short-lived, and her present audience had heard her *obiter dicta* too often before.

Was that all Peking meant to the woman : loads of fun ? Reverently Philip Flower tried to think of what the city had meant to him. Since his return after the war he had but left it gingerly, for occasional trips to the Western Hills and one almost fatal August of ptomaine poisoning at Peitaiho. His face was strangely contorted ; for Mrs. Mascot had prodded his most delicate membrane. He felt about Peking intensely, as certain poets have felt about their mistresses, but unlike Mrs. Mascot he had no specific desire to communicate his emotions. Perhaps he feared they would be lost in the

I

B

difficult effort of communication, like the nameless *Tao*, or
"Way," of his favourite Chinese mystics. "Those who
know do not speak ; those who speak do not know " . . .
Sufficient to know and be profoundly grateful, to realize that
he was as far as it was possible to be from post-war politics
and the general jumpiness of Europe while comfortably
within the orbit of its dubious civilization, imbibing serenity
from the geometrical quietude of China's ancient capital
And everything about him still remained supernatural,
brought grist for pantheistic reverie and wonder.

What were the feelings, so copiously aired, of a Mrs.
Mascot, in comparison with his ? What right had she here ?
She and her polypus type were profaning all his sanctuaries.
Had he not seen her with a party of tourists, who had
motored, actually hooting their horns, up to the very Temple
of Heaven ! When he thought of the spiritual isolation of
those walled precincts, the lapis-lazuli tiles above the cypresses,
the marble circles of the altar where he had often stood alone
in ecstasy, so close to earth yet in the very midst of heaven,—
when he thought of all this and then, as with a nightmare
jump, of the tartarized teeth, the viscous stream of Mrs.
Mascot's still flowing saliva, while she sprinkled her vicinity
with specks of chewed-up cheese, Philip Flower, a mild
middle-aged Londoner with neat grey eyes and greying hair,
sympathized whole-heartedly with the most ruthless and
fanatical of Boxers. Neither blistering labour in a chain-
gang, nor the most exquisite refinements of torture, seemed
adequate penalty for so barbarous a basilisk.

Mrs. Mascot twitched, not because of any psychic inkling
of the gruesome trend of Philip's reflections ; only a wanton
breeze had brushed her sharp shoulder-blade.

It was Elvira MacGibbon's virtual At Home day. People
dropped in continuously, a high if not very animated average
of Peking's foreign community, and " anybody who was

anybody" was encouraged to bring friends and acquaintances, especially if they were recent arrivals.

Everything in Elvira's garden, a characteristically Chinese
arrangement of gnarled trees and pseudo-mountains of super-
imposed rockery, seemed saturated in sky-fluid to the point
of being glazed and brittle. For it was also Spring.

This particular group was lounging in an open pavilion.
The ideograph for longevity was cut in the marble floor,
through which a trickle of water twisted its way from a small
cascade at the back. Formerly a light goblet would be
floated along this significant channel ; by the time it had run
its course each guest was expected to improvise a poem.
Those who failed were mulcted in wine. Philip Flower
regretted he had not seen Peking in those palmy days. Now
the pavilion was marred for him not only by the presence of
Mrs. Mascot but also by the rattan rocking chairs of Western
design and cocktail paraphernalia, his æsthetic objections to
which did not deter him from swallowing the " Gloom-
chaser " in his frosty glass and accepting another. So far he
had been silent. When the cocktail-shaker tinkled out a tune
from some Broadway musical comedy, he raised his voice
and hands in gentle protest : " My word, Elvira, isn't that
going too far ? Jazz, in the Pavilion of Longevity ! "

Captain Gulley guffawed. Poor old Flower, he must be
getting soft in the head. People who went in for Chinese all
got that way . . .

" I simply love it. Do play it again," whooped Mrs.
Mascot viciously.

" I am sure your pet Manchus would dote on it," said
Elvira. " What about those musical clocks in the Palace
Museum ? Those were the latest gadgets once, you know."

" I'll bet Ch'ien Lung would have fallen for Elvira's cocktail-shaker," said Captain Gulley, who in his spare time, as a
hobby, was tinkering at a book about that emperor's military

campaigns, and liked to remind people of the fact. When the atmosphere was a little bit different from one's own, one had to show a sort of passport now and then . . .

The Captain's innocent remark, reinforced by another " Gloom-chaser," reminded Mrs. Mascot that she had by no means said all she intended to say on the subject of Peking. But would she ever ?

" It affords one so much scope. And it helps us to discover our real selves," she now asserted, " talents we never suspected were tucked up inside us. You, Captain Gulley, illustrate my point : before you came to Peking you never dreamt of becoming a historian, did you ? Now you'll have your niche next to what's-his-name."

" And be buried in Westminster Abbey," chirped Philip.

" As for me," said Mrs. Mascot, disregarding the interruption, " I have so many new strings to my bow . . ."

More indeed than she cared, at the moment, to remember. The strings in Mrs. Mascot's bow were getting rather mixed. It was a hard life, for ever trying to foist things on people who did not want them, summoning all the powers of suggestion and auto-suggestion, tactfully persuading Mrs. X. that the entire colour-scheme of her Park Avenue drawing-room would be nil if she failed to invest in some rare specimen of Ming *cloisonné*, and Mrs. Y. that she had found the only jade pendant in the whole wide world for her individual bust. And between the coming and going of globe-trotters she was busy breeding Tibetan lion-dogs, supervising a beauty-salon, a lending-library, and an Olde Albion Tea Shoppe. Beside these activities, she was president of the Ladies' Inner Circle for the Appreciation of Hopei Crafts and Arts. Oh, it was a hard life, and she had only herself to blame if she often tottered on the brink of a nervous breakdown, but she faced it manfully, determined to convert everything, eventually, into terms of riotous fun.

" But we're not all like you. You're a magician," said Captain Gulley gallantly. " I often wonder what we lads of the foreign brigade would do without you. I honestly believe the whole social merry-go-round would come to a full stop."

Mrs. Mascot tried to be coy, at Elvira's expense, about the Captain's tribute. Elvira stifled a yawn and looked up at the sky. The dust-storms were over. Layer on blue layer of luminous enamel, and more blue flooding the ether beyond, a flawless infinity of azure. But Spring in Peking, even more than that season elsewhere, brought with it an insidious and penetrating lethargy.

" I have to reserve my energy for sculpture," she said, " *ars longer*, you know."

Her hands were so small that it was not easy to visualize them hammering at some uncouth block. Nobody had ever seen her wrestling with her medium. Her theories were uncompromising. Any attempt at realism she despised. Consequently her work involved a lot of cerebration. To begin with there was a long flirtation with the substance ; wood or stone was only selected after a frenzy of self-debate. An interval of dreaming followed. Elvira would lie on her back fanning the fugitive breeze of visual fancy ; ideas would soon buzz helter-skelter through her brain. The gramophone helped her to sort them out. Stravinsky, de Falla and, more recently, certain records of Balinese gamelans, had played their part in focusing her projects and straightening her line of vision. Finally she shook off languor ; the sculpture shaped itself in a sudden access of brawn.

" My husband pined for babies," she said. " At all hours of the day and night he would ask me : ' When are we going to have a little stranger ? ' It was too pathetic. Slowly I had to break it to him that that kind of motherhood could never be part or parcel of my consciousness. My children

5

would be giants of stone and bronze, vast abstractions for the future to gaze upon. So he left me. It was a mercy for both of us. From the first minute of our honeymoon he was insanely jealous of my art . . ."

Cool to call it art, thought Mrs. Mascot ; if that was the issue no wonder her husband had left her. It couldn't take much time to produce her stuff. A trunk of wood was bequeathed a pair of breasts and one was told that Diana of the Ephesians had reappeared in Elvira MacGibbon's studio. Even those who pretended to know something about this modern sculpture were apt to mistake the rockery in Elvira's garden for her latest experiments.

There were times when Elvira herself, contemplating her garden, suffered from vague pangs of doubt and discouragement. Why sculpt, when nature could achieve such marvellous abstractions ? At present she was in one of her " supine periods " of inspiration, but her gramophone records had lost their efficacy. This afternoon she was waiting for some new stimulus. She wondered what would turn up next. If only she could hustle Time ! Everything in Peking seemed to borrow its pace from those camels, which sauntered and sneered and sat about on their necks.

Like Mrs. Mascot, Elvira enjoyed the unexpected. She almost lived for it. She said things that were calculated to bring out what clandestine effervescence there happened to be in people. She had left Paris determined " to penetrate another unexplored reality." For ten years she had been experimenting with all sorts of 'isms, and from Dadaism to Surrealism they had left her exasperated and unsatisfied. The long-prophesied " new shivers running through the intellectual atmosphere " had failed to trot in her direction. Tired of waiting, she closed her studio and caught the Trans-Siberian express without saying good-bye to anybody. It was in spite of herself that she fell headlong into a popular tradition—among those who come to spend a fortnight in Peking yet linger on, often for the rest of their lives.

She could not explain how it had happened : within a few days of her arrival she found herself engrossed in revolutionizing the sanitary arrangements of an old Chinese mansion in the north-east quarter of the so-called Tartar city. With her utter contempt for symmetry and balance, such scruples as first assailed her for settling down in the most formal of rectangular courtyards were soon dissipated by the adjacent garden. At once she felt it had been laid out for her, an ideal background for her personality.

Attractive in a striking way, thought Captain Gulley, but all the same, a wee bit cracked. Why was she living by herself in a house of paper windows when there were quite decent European houses of solid masonry to be had in Peking for the asking ? These women gallivanting about on their own in the Far East, he suspected them of secret vices, unhealthy hankerings after new sensations. He would like to get to the bottom of it.

Captain Gulley had never tasted the spell of the East. "It's all very well to say Peking's such fun," he objected, "but can't we get the same sort of fun at home, and more of it ? "

"Treason, Captain ; you know jolly well we can't. Not for the prices we pay here," said Mrs. Mascot. "And at home there's none of the additional excitement of feeling you're in China. Sometimes when I'm snug in bed I hear the watchman go by with his rattle and I say to myself : I'm in China, the land of the Dragon. It's positively eerie ! Though I'm an Old Resident, I still manage to get a thrill out of it."

" But most people here don't want to feel they're in China ; they certainly don't behave as if they did," said Elvira. " Wealthy widows like Mrs. Rashbaum come all the way from Buffalo to devote their entire time to bridge and cocktail parties. They seldom budge from the Legation Quarter."

" I see what you mean," said Captain Gulley, " the South of France is nearer home, and that's where they belong— among the casinos. It's not as if there were any gigolos about. I wonder what makes them do it ? "

" You're far too modest, Captain," said Mrs. Mascot with a leer. " You're underrating your own fascination."

" Those widows are a pack of sadists," said Philip. " They turn up hoping for another Boxer rising. I'd like to stage one for them. It would clear the air a bit."

" Excuse me, Mr. Flower, but Mrs. Rashbaum is a par- ticular friend of mine." (Friend and client were synonyms to Mrs. Mascot.)

" I wasn't referring to her. In her case it's just plain snobbery behind it, the satisfaction of bragging when she gets back to Buffalo : I always winter in Peking. It sounds so glamorous. One can imagine the faces of her poor relations."

Mrs. Mascot bit her lip. The odious little earwig : she would have to think out some crushing retort. Mrs. Mascot wanted nothing better than to feel that her life was glamorous, and it was her heart's vocation to induce others to feel that their lives were glamorous too. And what was Philip Flower but a shoddy sentimentalist, one of those all too apt to " go native."

" Speak for yourself," she hissed.

Captain Gulley proceeded to explain that he had to make the best of his job here : his heart was in Peebles. In the sublime segregation of the British Legation his notions con- cerning the Chinese in general were quite Gilbert and Sulli- van : quaint chaps with a penchant for opium and a relish for rats and cats and puppy-pies. He still pictured them with pigtails. The same things that roused Philip Flower's wonder and awe made Captain Gulley chuckle. It was true that since he had been in Peking he had undergone a process of metabolism. Recently he had become aware of a yearning for a gentle companion. Only at the back of his mind though. The picture was vague : no special eyes or clear-cut features ; just an amalgam of youth and competence and healthy colour. He was now in the prime of life. No doubt the right sort would tootle along in time ; he didn't have to worry. In England there were droves of women only too eager to be hitched on to such a sound piece of military manhood.

Elvira MacGibbon impressed and interested him ; he had never known anyone remotely like her. He supposed it was because she came from that other world—the world of Art. He had been both flattered and abashed at their first meeting ; Elvira had said to him in her pensive, drawling voice, as if weighing the words in her larynx :

"You give me a feeling of power : your eyes are very brave and innocent. I feel we should harmonize, we should be friends."

No woman had spoken to him like that before. That had been at least six months ago. He had even gone so far as to tell her about his chest measurements. Nothing had come of these expansive bursts. He was always hoping to find himself alone with her; but she was continuously besieged by others, most of whom he managed to tolerate without approving. And as he looked at her now, rather piqued, he was inwardly sizing her up : attractive, yes, but like most arty folks, a wee bit cracked.

Elvira, of course, had quite forgotten her disturbing utterance. Elvira was so spontaneous. Rapid coitions of sympathy were followed all too soon by indifference, if not oblivion. She was like a cigarette that required continually to be lighted again. And Captain Gulley could not provide the necessary spark. Had she kept a diary and, turning back its leaves, noticed the phrase about a feeling of power as applied to the Captain, she would have smiled incredulously —the good old comfortable collie !

Mrs. Mascot, Philip Flower and Captain Gulley had turned up early on purpose. Mrs. Mascot, because she could not afford to miss potential customers ; Philip and the Captain because each had looked forward to a soothing *tête-à-tête*. For Philip it was a tonic to confide in Elvira periodically. But Mrs. Mascot spoiled everything. Each was beginning to feel frustrated.

Elvira herself was getting bored ; there were no new faces and the talk was becoming vapid. At this rate she would have to discontinue her At Homes. She decided it was time to make herself felt. So she began to tell them how she could become a starfish at will.

" You should try it. It's wonderful exercise. Soon you find yourself floating, floating round the room. All obstacles vanish. You melt among cool currents. You get in tune with the infinite. I'm a starfish every morning before break-fast. It makes all the difference in the world to my solar plexus. . . . "

" I should be afraid of peeping Toms," said Mrs. Mascot.

" After you have done it once or twice you're afraid of nothing. You can begin as a palm-tree : you merely stand and concentrate on a root. Soon you feel the sap rippling in your veins and the tender leaves beginning to sprout. The starfish stage comes later. Eventually you're so limber you have the choice of being a kangaroo, a skyscraper, a bubble, all sorts of lovely things ! I prefer to do it to the gramo-phone, but it can be done without. This morning Wang (the Number One boy) came in while I was floating round with-out a stitch. I told him to wind up the machine. ' O.K.,

Missy,' said he, not the least bit dismayed, just as if I had all my clothes on. You see I felt fully robed—as a starfish, of course."

Captain Gulley could not prevent the blood from surging upwards. His neck was crimson. By Jove, he wouldn't have minded standing in Wang's shoes. . . .

" I'm sure if it was me I could never confront my Number One again. But there are boys and boys. Most of those in foreign service become pretty thick-skinned. Take my imperturbable Chang . . ."

Philip Flower was wincing. When amahs, Number One boys, squeezes, mafoos, losses and gains of " face," constituted the topic of conversation, he took his cue for departure. It was another of Mrs. Mascot's depressing inevitabilities that she should steer any discussion towards the scullery and let it stay there. Moreover the invasion had begun in earnest ; the Trumpers and the Aspergills were approaching. . . . Poor Elvira, he thought, still to depend so much on Western contacts. It betrayed the real weakness of her armour.

Evening was gathering fast as he shook hands and bade farewell. How much cleaner simply to bow, like the Chinese ! After Mrs. Mascot had dropped a humid paw into his, he instinctively sought his handkerchief.

The rigid garden swayed in the green aquarium light. Rocks melted into mythical animals ; headless torsos and posturing skeletons mingled with the foliage. An amber glow came filigreed from semi-translucent paper windows. Sometimes a pedlar passed in a neighbouring *hut'ung*, leaving the air in faint anguish with his remote, shrill, melancholy cries. Probably it was only bean-curd or dumplings that he was peddling. Yet the cries seemed fraught with fatalism.

Philip Flower remembered the cockney chirpiness of news-

11

boys amid the steady roar and reeling lights of Piccadilly Circus—the exacerbation of unformulated desires of a spring evening in London. With the blitheness of Charlie Chaplin he preened and shook himself before stepping into the narrow lane outside Elvira's house. Promptly he forgot Mrs. Mascot and other *bêtes noires* ; he had left the jabbering circle of Europeans like Darby returning to his Joan. For all her devotion, she refused to accompany him to certain houses. Yes, he felt as if he were married to Peking, and this marriage was to be an inexhaustible adventure.

He sniffed the faintly stale, lukewarm odours—the indescribable special effluvia of an average Peking *hut'ung*—and they were to his nostrils as ozone. Soon he was in the street dubbed after Dr. Morrison of *The Times*, now sprinkled with sparkling bulbs like gay nocturnal tulips. Fra Angelico-blue gowns fluttered past on bicycles ; rickshaws moved soundlessly towards their destinations, lanterns bobbing beside them. On the pavement passengers wandered with calm, unhurried gait, or stood smoking, or squatted at corners. Minute children toddled with breeches open behind, partially bare to the breezes. Huge mongrels quested for garbage, tail in air.

Philip Flower, too, was in an admirable humour with life. As he strolled, his consciousness blurred into happy incoherence ; he became a stranger to himself and to the passage of time, buoyant, almost ethereal. He was on his way to buy goldfish at Lung Fu Ssŭ.

A succession of sounds more or less painful suddenly assaulted his ears. A small crowd blocked the pavement near the Salvation Army headquarters. In their midst, a drum, a trombone and some other strident instrument were strangling out the strains of " Onward Christian Soldiers." Philip quickened his pace but failed to get out of earshot. He tried not to think. " Marching as to-o War. . . ." Alas, Peking was doomed ; dying piecemeal of every sort of Western blight. The only thought that gave him solace was that he had already purchased his own burial-ground in a secluded corner of the Western Hills.

# CHAPTER II

## *Elvira's Salon*

ELVIRA'S At Home was soon in full swing, but it became too chilly to linger in the Pavilion of Longevity. Cocktail in hand, watching her step, Mrs. Mascot followed the fun indoors.

A newcomer might have been puzzled to hear spinsters and matrons prattling about " my temple " in the Western Hills. Did they preside over some religious community ? Did they ponder the nature of Buddahood and study the sūtras ?

No, these temples merely provided an occasional change of décor. It was pleasant to pretend, as if one were in London, that one had to escape from the wear and tear of City life. The Trumpers rented one in which they had patiently tried to produce an illusion of their Surrey nest, for the walls were covered with Cecil Aldins and the furniture with a chintz of flouncing cabbage roses ; one felt sure that lamb and mint sauce were on the sideboard. Monsieur Lefort had banished the Eighteen Lohan to install a cocktail bar in his temple, with modish appurtenances in surgical steel. He called it *Le Bœuf sur le Toît.* It only lacked Jean Cocteau. . . . The Aspergills—but why expatiate ? Even Mrs. Mascot managed to tear herself away from her metropolitan activities for a Sunday-to-Monday retreat. Her temple was somewhat smaller than the others but far cosier in consequence and, she honestly believed, " more Chinesy " ; each room a rendezvous for unexpected patches of colour. And the whole place reeked of joss-sticks, for Mrs. Mascot had her reputation

to uphold as past-master, or mistress, in the creation of just
the right Oriental atmosphere.

" At last I feel I'm in China," her visitors were wont to
exclaim, after partial asphyxiation. It was the China of " Chu
Chin Chow " they were thinking of.

The men were discussing the races. Captain Gulley and
the Trumpers had been out early that morning to watch
their ponies train. Captain Gulley and the Trumpers had
been out early every morning for months to watch their
ponies train.

A " Gloom-chaser " too many had made Mrs. Mascot
maudlin. Forgetting her original thesis, she now began to
lament the changes that had overtaken Peking in the last few
years. It was becoming more and more provincial. The
Japanese were ever rumoured to be on the verge of seizing it.
And the Japs (though she loved " Madam Butterfly " and was
not averse to the idea of Geishas) had little sense of fun. The
empty palace had become an empty museum. Even Paomachang wasn't quite what it used to be ; many a bungalow
near the race-course was now forlorn. Round-the-world
cruisers seemed fewer and further between, and the tourists
they disgorged had developed a tiresome tendency to count
small change.

She peered about. Hullo, a new face . . . But it was
only another novelist in search of local colour.

" Do his books sell ? " she asked Poppy Trumper with an
affectation of nonchalance.

" Like hot cakes, dear. Don't you remember *Yashmak* ? "

" So it's *the* Lancelot Thistleby ! "

In a jiffy she was plumb beside him, simpering all over :

" I'm thrilled to the core to meet you, Mr. Thistleby. It's
so seldom a literary genius comes our way. So you are an
authentic person ! " She dared not confess her delusion that
he was a woman writing under a *nom-de-plume*.

The novelist's expression was discouraging, but she continued : " To think of all the wild ideas you've put into the heads of innocent girls ! Me, for instance. You used to make me pine for Morocco."

" Turkey," the novelist gently interposed.

" I mean Turkey, of course. Ah, now it all comes back to me, the blue, blue Bosphorus ! Yes, I've eaten loukoum with you, and sniffed the roses of Ispahan. It was *Yashmak* that first attracted me to the Orient. I can't express how deeply indebted I am."

" So many are ! " said Lancelot Thistleby, with a comic gesture of resignation. Mrs. Mascot refused to register surprise. " I am so glad," she said, " that you have decided at long last to switch your attention to China. We need you, Mr. Thistleby, with your unique understanding of atmosphere. I am sure your next novel will make the whole world pine for Peking."

" My last. I've only come here to put in the finishing touches. My next is about Bali."

" How long do you expect to stay ? "

" In Peking or in Bali ? "

Mrs. Mascot was beginning to get muddled when Elvira whisked the novelist away.

" West must meet East, Mr. Thistleby," said Elvira. " I must introduce you to Doctor Li Ssŭ ; he is the greatest living Chinese thinker, and he writes his philosophy in English. Such an advantage ! Altogether a divine person."

Philip Flower's diagnosis was wrong. Although the sight of new faces agreeably rocked Elvira's imagination, although she was always leaning with desperate intensity on the depths of each new creature's possibilities in the hope that some word, some gesture would astonish and illuminate her, Elvira was no slave to Western contacts. She was in Peking to grasp a new attitude towards China. She wanted to " get at " the Chinese, to enter the penetralia. Above all she desired a *salon* for the New China to congregate in and friends who were Chinese to the core, mentally as well as racially *pur sang*. But this apparently simple ambition had suffered many a set-back. The " pukka Chinese " grew suspicious at the sight of her. Such a female had no counterpart in Chinese life : they failed to comprehend what she was driving at. Why this perpetual combustion at their expense ? They exchanged polite indifferent smiles across a separating ocean. A few ventured into her house because they were sometimes smitten with nostalgia for the West, but these could scarcely be classi-fied as thoroughbreds.

Christopher Columbus Lo and Lincoln Pan, for instance, whose heroes could be detected in their nomenclatures, were natives of Honolulu and San Francisco. Y.M.C.A. Rotarians, they wished to make China safe for American democracy and frankly despised the culture of their ancestors. Neither could converse in any of China's dialects, and both identified their aspirations with the West, as an outward and visible symbol of which they preferred plain succotash and pumpkin pie to all the delicacies from land and sea which ivory chopsticks conduct into the mouth. Doctor Li Ssŭ, although a missionary-product and a Rotarian, was more com-plex. Since he could express himself in tolerable journalese and his disyllabic name was easy to remember, he enjoyed a considerable reputation among foreigners as " a philosopher." A Chinese Vicar of Bray, alternatively he strove to be all things to East and all things to West : in Chinese circles he spoke of Westerners as " the only barbarians we have failed to assimilate " ; among Anglo-Saxons he would denounce the " rickshaw civilization " of China and laud his " gallant missionary friends " for all they had done to emancipate Chinese womanhood, though what that was he never

C

specified.   Presumably he referred to foot-binding, but it was
no secret that he preferred cramped feet to natural ones, and
that his wife's poor " lily hooks " had never been unbound.
He posed as the inveterate enemy of Confucius, yet he owed
what measure of talent he possessed to his surreptitious study
of the Confucian classics.   He enjoyed impressing those foreigners he inwardly despised, for he found it much easier than
trying to impress his compatriots.   Hence Elvira could
generally count on Doctor Li.

Steering the author of *Yashmak* towards him, she said :
" You two must have a talk.   I'll listen in.   That is, if you'll
allow me to."   Then she settled herself in a lacquer throne
beside the divan she had propelled them to, craning an ear
for conversational pearls.

Mrs. Mascot, however, was not to be baulked ; if pearls
were to be dropped, she was determined to grab a few.
Scarce had the lions' lips begun to murmur when she fluttered
up like a lapwing.

" May I join the intellectual coterie ?   You won't mind my
eavesdropping, will you ? "

" Why should we mind, dear ? "   Elvira shrugged her
shoulders with ill-concealed irritation.

" I'm naturally reluctant to poach on your preserves, but
this is such an exceptional occasion."

As both women leaned forward to listen, eager for the
novelist's first impressions of Peking, " Scratch, scratch,
scratch," said Thistleby in an undertone.

" I beg your pardon ? " queried Doctor Li, wondering if
he had heard aright.

" I fear that the dust of Peking has got into my whistle,"
said the novelist aloud.

Doctor Li, still puzzled, observed : " It comes from the
Gobi desert."

" Like the dinosaur eggs," said Thistleby.

" And is this your first visit to Peiping, Mr. Thistle ? "

" My very first, Doctor Li."

" The impressions of a noo-comer are always noo and instructive. I shall be vurry interested to hear your slant on our Chinese institootions. Our old culture is dying. Let it die ! A more virile culture, a finer creativity, is quickly taking its place. We are living in a period of national renascence, Mr. Thistle. The whole of the Chinese nation believes in progress now. We love and revere your H. G. Wells, your Bertrand Russell, your Sinclair Lewis. We study their writings with affection and happy anticipation. Now that you have come to our cultural capital I rejoice to bid you welcome. I hope you will give us a talk at the Mo-têng University of which I am Chancellor, Rector and Dean. When I tell my students about you they will all be vurry anxious to hear your viewpoint."

" You are very kind, but I'm afraid I haven't yet had time to register a viewpoint. I have just opened a porthole so to speak, to fill my little cabin with draughts of the Great Unknown. The result is rather bewildering. I have a feeling, for instance, that the intimacy of my little cabin is gone, that my pet canaries have flown away. . . ."

" I can see that you are a poet, Mr. Thistle : you talk just like one. I am also a poet. Under a practical exterior most Chinese scholars are. We love and revere your Hemans, your Whitmans and your Longfellows. We are also fond of birds. I am sure you will feel yourself at home here mighty soon, Mr. Thistle. When you have formulated your viewpoint, we shall expect to hear from you at the Mo-têng University. And you may take it from me, Mr. Thistle, that the whole faculty as well as the students will embrace the privilege and opportoonity of listening to you."

Elvira puckered her brow. This sort of thing was not worth her attention. She decided to surrender her celebrities to Mrs. Mascot, who promptly booked them for a dinner, which she promised would be small but quite select.

Elvira glanced impatiently round the room. Where was Alice Tu ? Alice was the pivot of her diminutive Chinese circle and something had to be done about the girl. . . . She went over to Fêng Chung-han, the young man Doctor Li had introduced as " a poet with a future."

" Do you know Alice Tu ? " she asked.

He didn't ? All the better. As in a flash of second sight, it struck Elvira that this might be the young man she had been looking for, the very one to help Alice over the stile in escaping from her family. She told him so, and she told him about Alice. It was a long story, and in the telling she relived the early scenes of her friendship with that remarkable young woman.

Alice, whose Chinese name was Tu Yi, had appeared to her in Paris two years ago. Apparition was the word. Among the plush and Sèvres of Doctor Vigneron's dark, stiff, stuffy sitting-room in the Rue du Bac, on a November afternoon, a face more round than oval, skin the surface of shelled almond and eyes like black diamonds ever so slightly slanted. A slender figure, at a first glance you would say brittle, Miss Tu was the first of her race with whom Elvira had come in contact.

That this flower transplanted from extreme Asia should have mastered the Parisian idiom in almost every sense—chic, intonation, a familiarity with Paul Valéry and the ephemeral currency of intellectual small-talk—dazzled Elvira and filled her with delight. But when their acquaintance ripened Elvira became aware of an impenetrable obsidian hardness at the core of her apparently fragile young friend. They could frankly discuss Gide's " Corydon " and Proust's " Albertine "; but Miss Tu's attitude was disappointingly objective. They never got very far.

Even after she realized that Miss Tu was withholding her-self, Elvira took infinite pains. She tried to view their friend-ship as a union of two great civilizations ; she perpetually plied her with questions about her sensuous experiences and physical reactions. Alice merely laughed ; the slanting black diamonds sparkled with a disconcerting mockery.

" Nearly every girl in the world," said Elvira, " is waiting for a chance to shine. I can give her this chance, help her to shine among the lights of Paris. It will test my own calibre as well as hers . . ."

She gave several parties for her. Alice remained undemon-strative, arriving late and leaving early, but even so she glittered. She eclipsed Elvira at her own parties. *La petite Princesse des Pagodes*, they called her. Without being jealous, Elvira became exasperated.

" Are you happy here ? " she asked her. "*Mais oui,*" she replied, without conviction, and again sent off a peal of irri-tating laughter ; for it was neither gay nor nervous, rather it sounded contemptuous and hard.

" *Pourquoi pas ?* Come, let us look out into the twilit street. Aren't those chestnuts being roasted over there ?— just like Peiping, in winter. Perhaps we can even smell them, if we open the window. Let us go out and eat some. . . ."

This just after Elvira had introduced the girl to all her most exclusive geniuses ! Wasn't it enough to dishearten any-body ? Off they had gone and bought a packet of roast chestnuts, which Alice tore open and started to nibble there and then in the street, splitting the chapped lips of the chest-nuts open, dropping them on the pavement.

Elvira, always accustomed to manipulate those moving within her aura, began to sense that Alice was deliberately evading her. After several months of intercourse she had never once been allowed to penetrate the invisible reality. Impossible to divine what lay behind the porcelain mask, what

Alice was really thinking as she chirped along in her clear, neat, over-polished French. Elvira became resentful. But she was not one to admit defeat.

Then she received a thin volume entitled *Stances*, printed in Bodoni type on soft and silky paper, numbered (for the edition was discreetly limited : six *exemplaires sur Japon nacré* ; thirteen on *Papier Montval*, and the remainder on *Vélin D'Arches*, *Vélin Pur Fil Lafuma* and *Papier Vert Lumière*), signed both in Chinese ideographs and Latin script. Nicolas Trompe-l'œil of the *Académie Française*, whom Alice had met at Elvira's, had contributed one of his characteristic prefaces, a string of aphorisms with stars between each jewelled phrase. It was the last word in precious Parisian typography. But Elvira was far from delighted with her gift. Though she was not superstitious, she did not relish receiving number thirteen on *Papier Montval*, and she was piqued because the book had come as a surprise. Alice had never mentioned it. Apart from these considerations, the poems themselves were quite impersonal ; the themes restricted to wild geese, cranes, the moon half-concealed by clouds, a sprig of jasmine, a lonely fisherman, a bamboo-grove and dawn's reflection on a desolate lake. Wild geese : tame emblems. Of what ? Of something boring, such as conjugal fidelity. Nothing personal, real, direct. Never a word about human contacts or social aspirations.

Elvira read them with disillusioned eyes and increasing irritation. They seemed to her as empty as the crescent-shaped smile of some archaic goddess.

Elvira did not quarrel with Alice—one might as well quarrel with a peacock ! They drifted apart, to meet again.

In an environment which could not have been stranger, by contrast with Doctor Vigneron's sitting-room, for it was on the occasion of Elvira's first visit to a Peking theatre, they met again. Deafened by the thunder of gongs, blinking under the kaleidoscope of colours, Elvira was sitting limply beside Philip Flower in a private box. On the stage, sumptuous heraldic personages were wailing lustily against a pink embroidered curtain. But another performance, among the congested audience, entertained Elvira more than that on the stage ; attendants were hurling hot napkins from the gallery to the pit and vice versa, all aimed and caught with amazing precision ; others ran to and fro with teapots and trays of strange edibles. In a neighbouring box, a bevy of Chinese matrons were blandly nibbling melon seeds. It intrigued her that such neat, Nonconformist-looking dames could sit through this cacophony without quivering an eyelash. As if she wanted to hear it more distinctly, one of them was picking her ears with a long jade hair-pin. A demure girl in flowered black satin walked in and greeted them.

" Why, it's Alice ! "

As soon as Elvira recognized her, she stretched across the partition and kissed her effusively. Philip Flower was hardly less astonished than the matrons, whose beady eyes peered up at her in panic. Perhaps this impulsive foreigner would kiss them too ? Alice introduced Elvira to her female kin, not one of whom could speak a foreign language.

" How deliciously Celestial you've become ! " Elvira exclaimed. " I never realized how Chinese you were till now."

The Parisian accent was perfect still, but she had forsaken all vestige of Parisian costume. Her dress had a stiff high collar : it reached to the ankle and was slashed on either side of the skirt from the hem to just above the knee. Elvira wondered if her character had become as demonstrative as her legs. Decidedly the rouge on her cheeks and lips was louder than before. She had dropped the name of Alice, and asked Elvira to call her Yi.

" Are you happy to be home again ? "

This time Yi answered her directly. " I am sorry I did not stay away longer."

The bitterness of her tone was disarming. She had seldom looked more incapable of strong emotions.

" My poor child," said Elvira, " we must change all that."

" Impossible. You do not know China," she replied.

" That's what everybody tells me. But I mean to know it yet," said Elvira.

At last the borderline into friendship was crossed, and Elvira began to learn something about Yi's actual existence.

During her three years' sojourn in Paris Yi had forgotten the restraints of her original environment. On her return, the sharp reality of these restraints, and the strict notions of her parents as to the conduct she should observe, had been swift to administer a disagreeable shock. Her grandfather, a retired official of the old school, who still burned paper on which ideographs were written, decided that it was high time for little Yi to be married. The enlarged photograph which was all she had seen of the fiancé chosen, filled her with repulsion. But his wealth and influential connections were the main consideration. For once Yi openly rebelled. So strenuously did she object to the match that her family was forced to cancel it. As a result her behaviour was branded as unfilial and Communistic. She was now in disgrace.

" I love my parents," Yi repeated every now and then, as if to persuade herself of a fact in which she did not quite believe, " I do love them truly, but they can be very difficult sometimes . . ."

" Worse than difficult," said Elvira. " Why did they send you to France if such a marriage was all they had in store for you ? It seems so illogical."

" You do not know China," said Yi again. " My family considers itself progressive, but in essentials it remains conservative. What does it matter if the bride's sedan-chair is

replaced by a motor-car ?   Underneath it all the conventions
are the same.   In China, progress is measured by motor-
cars."

" You mustn't allow it to affect you," said Elvira.   " I
mean, you must never allow yourself to be delivered like a
parcel to an utter stranger."

" How can I prevent it from affecting me ?   After all, I am
Chinese."   And she looked hopelessly resigned.

To escape from her family she taught French at one of
Peking's fifty-two universities.   It was only a partial escape,
but she was pleased to discover that she had it in her, without
effort, to exert a considerable influence on the students.
Possibly it was due to sex-appeal : her classes were crowded.
Thus the French symbolists acquired a vogue in pastures new,
and their verses, transcribed into the Peking vernacular, were
murmured by many an adolescent couple of the black-haired
race.

Much of this Elvira communicated to Fêng Chung-han,
who had listened to every word with studious concentration.

" Ah, there she is ! "

Cedric Aspergill, of course, had pounced on her as soon as
she had arrived.   Cedric considered himself the Don Juan of
the Diplomatic Corps : as such he felt it his duty publicly to
pounce on every Chinese girl within range.   He rarely
pounced in private.   At the moment he was wearing cordu-
roy trousers ; the open collar of his lemon shirt revealed the
pronounced curve of an Adam's apple which he fondly
believed to be graceful.   His fair hair seemed as pink as his
gaping nostrils (so sensitive, in his opinion), as pink as his
hands (so shapely, so tactile ; one was pressed to his hip in an
orgasm of self-consciousness).   You would have sworn that
even his eyes were pink : in point of fact they were blue.   It
was evident that he was supremely anxious to hold Tu Yi's
attention.

25

Yi would have been remarkable anywhere, for she possessed distinction as well as beauty. Among the blowsy women at Elvira's her slim figure, moulded supply from ankle to chin by her light Chinese gown, appeared as a fine-grained porcelain vase surrounded by terracotta. Her delicate fingers reduced all others to badly rolled cigarettes ; they truly tapered. Even now Elvira felt that she had never been quite real to her.

" Come here, *ma belle*," she called, " I've found an Adonis for you ! Cedric, don't be selfish : you can't expect to monopolize her."

Fêng's cheek-bones were flushed a feverish tint, like ivory faintly rouged, although he had refused a cocktail. His jetty eyes emitted sparks of enthusiasm and he wiped his horn-rimmed glasses, as if they had been misted by the vision of Tu Yi.

It was with a rare tingle of satisfaction that Elvira introduced them to each other, these clever, comely and modern children of Han. Again she was living in the sheer moment, bringing, she hoped, a proton and electron together—manipulating fresh young human contacts. The consequences would rest on her shoulders. She gloated over them with a quickened pulse. As they conversed in the vernacular she could not understand what they were saying, but after the impact of so many who had failed to stir her imagination, she was exhilarated by the sight of this Chinese couple who had never met before, physically refreshed, as by a shower. Doctor Li and Lancelot Thistleby might have disappointed her expectations —celebrities often did—but now she felt sure that her afternoon had not been frittered away.

The assorted tit-bits of toasted cheese and red caviar had been devoured, save for a triangle here and there which seemed to lisp : " I have been left for Miss Manners."

Elvira, remembering her duties as hostess, swept the stragglers into her dining-room. The repast agreeably broke the rhythm just when it threatened to become monotonous. Inconsequential phrases hovered about attractive salads and cold meats. There was a haggard perambulation of the buffet with variously stacked plates. While knives and forks were busy, other problems vanished except, in a different sense of Mrs. Mascot's well-worn phrase, that of boundlessly enlarging one's contours. They did not vanish for long. For Captain Gulley and the Trumpers were soon grumbling in a corner about " those Aspergills."

" They should never have budged from Chelsea," said the Captain.

" Quite," snapped Poppy Trumper. " I can see him with his hair marcel-waved over his collar, mincing about a studio in velveteens, and her inventing futuristic dadoes on the floor. Why, look ! She's on the floor now. Why can't she sit in a chair like other folk ? Here they are fish out of water, poor things. They made their biggest howler, of course, to begin with—not leaving a single card. I said to her myself : ' Peking has manners, Mrs. Aspergill, even if Mayfair hasn't . . .' "

" And what did she say to that ? "

" The cheek of her ! She said (and Poppy Trumper tried to mimic her drawl) : ' How quaint ! You make me feel I'm in Surbiton.' "

" Rank outsiders," said Archie Trumper, and sharply blew his nose.

Thus were the Aspergills dismissed by the Trumpers, who regarded themselves as pukka representatives of Peking's Old Residents, with snorts of indignation. They could not swallow that serene indifference : it was a menace to all they stood for. For the Aspergills' rudeness was seldom calculated : it simply had not occurred to them to leave cards. They lived in a restricted world of their own, in the British

Embassy compound but not of it, as the Captain said, since they never went near Paomachang. Their lack of punctilio did not offend the Captain; it was their lack of exercise which he regarded as a personal affront.

"What do you do about exercise?" he had asked Cedric, and Cedric, annoyed by the Captain's public-school voice, had replied:

"Sometimes we play croquet, but our exercise generally consists of a leetle trot with Heliogabalus in the Central Park," —Heliogabalus being a "wonk" or pariah-dog, which he had saved from starvation and cured of divers canine ailments, last but not least of which had been the mange.

"Good God," exclaimed the Captain. "The Park is full of natives, isn't it? I've never set foot inside it."

"You don't know all you've missed. The adorable Chinese girls. I can specially recommend it when the peonies are in bloom. I'm afraid Veronica and I prefer peonies to ponies, Captain Gulley."

Hence he had sent the Aspergills to Coventry. That last riposte had rankled.

To rescue conversation from torpor over coffee there was a summons for music.

"It is time you obliged us, Cedric," said Elvira, "do play something of your own."

He had been working miracles with Chinese music, she explained, adapting it for Western ears.

Recently he had written a series of *études* inspired by Peking street-cries, and had transcribed such phrases as had struck his fancy in the course of desultory visits to Chinese theatres. His wife assisted him. "We get at the spirit of the thing, the quintessence," said Veronica, "by popping into any old theatre for half an hour at a time. One can't stand too much of it . . . gives one the collywobbles."

"Chinese music gives me gooseflesh," said Elvira, "like

listening to an electric drill.  God knows I've tried hard to appreciate it.  I suppose it's too minor for me."

" I quite agree," said Mrs. Mascot, " a little goes a long way."

" Sorry," said Cedric with a temperamental sigh, " I'm not feeling in the right mood."

" No hanky-panky," said Elvira.

" Really, I've never been able to interpret my own compositions at the best of times," he half-apologetically drawled, " as I am far too lazy to practise.  Besides—my finger-nails just now are a wee bit long."

" Long and artistic," sneered Captain Gulley, *sotto voce.* (The word " artistic " evidently had some unpleasant private connotation in the recesses of the Captain's mind.)

" But you know you have the touch of an Ariel, darling," pleaded Veronica, while Mrs. Mascot shouted :  " Be a sport ! "

All he needed was urging.  He loved to be coaxed.  He hesitated, waiting for further pressure, before he decided to surrender.  Then, smiling like a bride on the way to the altar, he said :

" I've just finished a pictorial pastiche called ' Pagoda glimpsed through gingko trees.'  I'm afraid I'll hardly do it justice, but here goes ! "

There was a hush.  After a ceremonious removal of rings, Cedric's fingers flourished and pirouetted over the piano—a preliminary canter.  The audience, expectant of something queer, shifted nervously as at a spiritualistic *séance.*

What had Elvira let them in for ?  What havoc would be wrought by those soft white hands besprinkled with orange hairs ?

But only a thin, watery dribbling of scales followed, sonorous drops, interspersed with occasional discords, discreetly pedalled.

A few minutes of this and everybody felt safe on *terra firma*, for Cedric Aspergill had successfully conjured the atmosphere of Sunday afternoon in a London concert-hall.

" Witchery," cried Mrs. Mascot, " how you have managed to recapture the rusty gorgeousness of Old Cathay. Sheer witchery ! You definitely made me hear it all, the tinkling temple-bells, the swish-swish of bamboos . . . Cedric, congrats ! "

Which set the ball rolling, so to speak, and gave Cedric the impetus to proceed with his repertoire.

There was something in his nonsense after all, thought Poppy Trumper. Politely the chords bowed, slowly the piano-keys simpered under his touch until they were muffled. Wanly the musician smiled.

What instrument can be so polite as the pianoforte ? Certainly, as manipulated by Cedric, it neutralized his incivility in other directions. One felt one should be wearing evening dress.

Fêng Chung-han laughed quietly to himself. That in so far as his country was concerned most foreigners could see little beyond their own big noses he already knew, but that their ears could be thus deceived was a startling discovery.

The music that Cedric supposed he was interpreting will never, perhaps, be accurately described by an Occidental, but it was the very reverse of these pallid genteel strains. Oscar Wilde wrote of the mad scarlet music of Dvořák. By what hue would he have characterized the shrill notes which Chinese musicians have trumpeted down through fabulous centuries ? By his favourite vermilion, or by a piping, parrot green ? Against the sober hues of Chinese life, the uniform beige and blue, these notes rise, flash and fall like iridescent rockets. To some their dissonances have recalled Hogarth's picture of the Enraged Musician. In the theatre are gongs and cymbals to deafen thought and chafe the nerves, to prepare for the pageantry of painted masks and towering plumage, for the prancing of warriors to the staccato rhythm of instruments stranger still, mechanical insects, magnified cicadas, pieces of wood that are clicked like super-castanets, a two-stringed fiddle of bamboo, so slender that you would hardly guess its capacity for contending with the highest falsetto and surmounting it, and a clarinet producing tones which lead one to surmise : even so may the pterodactyl have beguiled his mate.

Even when vocal, this music transcends the ordinary joys and sorrows of humanity ; it is immeasurably ancient, yet fresh and unadulterated, like gushes from the throats of tropical birds. It has retained its youth, for its ringing rhythms are still, as by magic, imbued with the phenomena of nature. The Oriental musician seeks to escape from time and he achieves his ends by repetition, plunging his listeners into a state of beatific detachment not unlike intoxication. Often he acts directly on the sensibility without touching the intellect. But the Western ear is swaddled in harmonies of its own. These harmonies are intellectual, hence anti-magical ; they bring the listener in contact with an objective reality.

Aspergill's compositions fell between two stools : they appealed neither to the sensibility nor to the intellect. Maybe this fact accounted for the general applause. "You have never played so well," his wife assured him. Was it because he fancied he had made a hit with that slit-eyed minx ? she wondered. He had carried off the whole bag of tricks with a nonchalance altogether unusual. . . . But the minx had left the room as soon as he started to play. Veronica would remember to tell him that.

Mrs. Mascot conducted the claque. "Sheer witchery !" she chimed. "Bravo, Cedric !"

"Ta-ra-ra-ra boom de-ay !" scoffed the Captain. "Now for a drop of Scotch."

\*         \*         \*

Fêng Chung-han and Tu Yi had slipped into the garden. They wandered through a moon-gate on to a pathway by a miniature lake where willows were drooping sentimentally. It was a relief not to hear the piano, that absurd mockery of the music in their blood. Then, as in sympathy with their inmost thoughts, the sound of a *hu-ch'in*, sharp and vital, vibrated from a neighbouring house. A familiar tune see-sawed happily towards them on the perfumed air.

Yi, a Yi who might never have left Chinese soil, was suddenly moved to sing. It was a strange voice to issue from one who seemed so fragile ; and its metallic resonance might have acted somewhat acidly on Occidental nerves. But it acted like fire on the simmering susceptibilities of the young man beside her. He was lapped by musical flames.

What was this enchantment falling about him ? The song was not a dreamy song. The music of this voice had nothing ghostly about it—no delicate film of breath upon the surface of a mirror. It was a song that had never died, that had lived through countless evenings such as this, in such gardens, at such moments even, when it had touched the deepest chords of listeners as now it caused Fêng's whole being to throb, tenderly desirous of the singer. To utter any word after this would require more self-mastery than he could muster : speech would sound false, unworthy of Yi—sentences, as if strung together like a necklace of chilly beads. How futile was the ancient game of controlling one's emotions ! Yet all his life he had been trained to obey the rules of this game, and so thoroughly, that he could not bring himself to break them now, while more than anything else in the world he longed to enfold Yi in his arms, and murmur all the passionate words that were trembling on his lips. Terrified of talking nonsense, he goaded himself to insipid utterance.

" At last," he said, when the song had joined the highest of the stars, " I feel I'm in contact with reality—the reality of our

China. You may think me foolish, but surely our meeting this afternoon was as strange as it was unexpected. With all those foreigners about me it was hard to realize I was in China. I felt lost, stupefied. You see, I know very few foreigners ; I had never been here before or met our hostess. And as soon as she saw me she began to talk about you ! "

" What did she say ? "

" She seems very fond of you ; but perhaps I had better reserve what she said for the next occasion we meet."

" Do tell me now ! "

" To be quite frank, her account of you alarmed me. I imagined you were another of our brilliant expatriates who lose their nationality abroad . . ."

" Am I ? " she smiled.

The question was not answered, for the distant *hu-ch'in* had begun to quaver again, more loudly, a high, taut, abstract air : it might have been composed to cheer the solitude of Ch'ang Ô in her Palace of Ice and Snow.

And while this modern couple listened, they were entering another realm of consciousness. And instinct told them, in clear imperious accents, that they should never allow themselves to be duped by that Western civilization. Borrow from it, by all means, delve plentifully in the ore ; but the fundamental magic was not there. Deeper, subtler were the perceptions of the Chinese people, the inherited wisdom of the race. Whatever new type eventually emerged, heredity would triumph : the vital factor would remain loyal to the ancestors. They would recover from the shocks of Western oppression as from barbarian tyrannies of old, and because they were bequeathed a knowledge of racial sorrow, fighting the same war over and over again through the long, relentless, systolic centuries, they would learn the highest and richest forms of joy.

Fêng sighed : " If only we could stay here always, just

D

where we are ! Must we go back into that zoo ? Let us stay here a little longer, in the China that is ours."

He pressed Yi's hand and neither spoke : there was more than physical understanding in that mute moment's pressure.

\*     \*     \*

" I've always abominated cats," said Mrs. Mascot. " They send cold shivers running up my spine."

Turning to Elvira she asked : " Did you hear that ghastly caterwauling ? "

" No," said Elvira. " Where ? "

" I fancy it came from the garden. You should keep a dog, dear. Why not get one of my Tibetan lions ? Of course I would make a special price for you. It was a wonder to me how Cedric could keep his mind on the piano."

The sound of the *hu-ch'in* entered Elvira's salon. Like a cicada announcing the airless heat of summer, it was disquieting. But what really disquieted Elvira was the sense, which this piercing instrument seemed to accentuate, that China was outside her : she was never beyond the fringe of the magic circle. By hook or by crook she determined to force her way through.

" Some Pekinese troubadour," said Poppy Trumper brightly, " serenading our Elvira."

" I wish it was Toselli's," said Mrs. Mascot.

" That's the stuff," said Captain Gulley. " *O Sole Mio. Funiculi-funiculà.* . . . Come, let's strike up. A serenade for Elvira. Are there any glee-singers in our midst ? What about you, Archie ? You've always been a keen member of the Choral Society. . . ."

Nobody took up the challenge, except Mrs. Mascot.

" I know some sweet negro spirituals," she faltered. " *All God's chillun.* . . ."

"Not just now, dear," said Elvira somewhat sharply, for she had no wish to be unduly depressed. All at once she was swept by a wave of fatigue.

Yi and Fêng were standing by the open door. Figures on a silk fan, thought Lancelot Thistleby, just wakened from the doze into which Doctor Li Ssŭ's platitudes had sent him. The hour was late, and the Aspergills were afraid they must be going, or rather Veronica said so, on seeing the eyes that Cedric rolled at the Chinese girl in the doorway. She had cause to be apprehensive. Cedric was absurdly susceptible to these Oriental hussies.

# CHAPTER III

## The Seeker of a Dream

IN spite of Fêng Chung-han's reputation as " a poet with a future," his Muse had been silent for more than a year. His reputation rested on a volume of experimental verses in the vernacular and certain fables with a flavour of Rabindranath Tagore, brief colloquies between peasants and paddy-fields which had mystified the critics and even, in secret, mystified himself. Innumerable Cultural Advancement Associations had thinned his blood ; he had spent far too much of his time at their inauguration ceremonies, conferences and assemblies. He had edited half a dozen advanced periodicals and played an active rôle in the literary renaissance ; he had dabbled in student-union politics, helped to organize much propaganda, and devised some dramatic slogans, when he was not suffering from sick headaches, in the intervals between.

No doubt the aims of these Associations were high, but few of them outlived their manifestoes. Albeit admirable " to cultivate the spirit of the Chinese race among the people to-day, so that the nation could be developed into a stronger state to meet the present crisis " ; albeit necessary " to promote a scientific and creative spirit among the people," the funds for all this cultivation and promotion could never, alas, be guaranteed for an appreciable period of time. Idealistic flashes in a series of unpractical pans, that was what they generally amounted to. Under the endless torrent of speeches, discussions, fresh publications and formulations of rules, Fêng failed to notice it. But he began to notice that

36

his preoccupation with these diverse activities was killing his own creative spirit. Among his papers there was a fragmentary translation of *The Waste Land*. Then there was also Miss Jessie L. Weston's *From Ritual to Romance*, which he had not finished reading. . . .

He tried to console himself by saying that his Muse had languished for his own good, that all serious art must have a social revolutionary core, that perhaps the paths of Beauty led nowhere, that Keats was mistaken, Beauty was not Truth. . . . Nevertheless he felt uneasy about it all.

He had a still more serious reason to feel perturbed. Recently his mother had come up from Amoy, which was a long journey for a Chinese matron travelling alone, with the sole object of persuading him to take a wife as soon as possible. She had attained the age of fifty and, in spite of a robust physique, considered herself on the brink of dissolution. Now she had but one desire in life, to dandle a little grandson. Beneath his bright mail of modern opinions Fêng's conscience pricked him ; he suffered from a secret, atavistic shame because he was still a bachelor.

His mother was making herself ill with worry. Yet his gorge rose at the prospect of yoking himself to any mere instrument of procreation. As a poet, he wished to exhibit himself in a modern, which to him signified a romantic, light. He tried to explain that he was in search of a soul-mate. But his mother failed to understand. She said : " It's all because you read foreign novels and go to the Cinema."

In her opinion the relation between the sexes in China had been perfectly sane until the foreigners had come and made a mess of it. What dangerous nonsense, this gabble about a soul-mate ! Eventually such notions would put a stop to marriage. Chung-han told her that she was old-fashioned. Pity she hadn't been when she had brought him up ! Her other son, dutiful but unlucky, had had five daughters in succession ; it was now Chung-han's turn to try and produce a male heir.

When her husband died in straitened circumstances she had received no assistance from the rest of the family, ostensibly because she sympathized with that " crack-brained theorist " Sun Yat-sen. After selling most of her property she had managed to send her eldest son to study in Tokyo and Chung-han to Shanghai, incurring the further enmity of in-laws by sending her children to modern schools, infected with the new ideas from the West. For how had the old scholarship materially benefited her *hsiu-ts'ai* [1] husband ? More than most women she deserved to be considered progressive. And yet—oh penalty of progress—Chung-han now dubbed her old-fashioned because she could see no sense in his pursuit of a soul-mate !

He had just left her in tears for a committee-meeting, when Doctor Li Ssŭ remarked upon his pallor and suggested a change of environment. " I'm afraid the board is over-working you," he said—referring to the board of the latest Cultural Advancement Association, of which, as usual, the eminent Rotarian was passive president and Fêng most active member. Doctor Li could not afford to lose so valuable and modest an assistant, the man who drafted most of his famous speeches. He decided to take him along to Elvira MacGibbon's, confident that there he would be able to find some salutary diversion. " It is almost as instructive as a journey to Europe," he said. And there, at a glance, almost at a word from Miss Tu, Fêng's aspirations promised to materialize. Perhaps Miss Tu was the sister-soul of his quest. That she had burst into song now seemed auspicious. How wise he had been to wait ! He had met her at the crucial moment of his career.

A last glimpse of her hatless, her slender figure enthroned

[1] Rank given to successful candidates at first Imperial Examinations.

in a private rickshaw, assured him that she was made to be worshipped. She sat erect like a goddess, but the rickshaw was an anachronism : she should have been in a gorgeous palanquin.

For a while he stood gazing after her, as if to etch her image on his mind. As soon as he got home, within twenty minutes of that last glimpse, he sat down and composed a letter. Composed, for every sentence was lingered over : so much that had failed him in her presence now struggled for expression, and he wished to set it forth in poetical prose.

Since chance brought us together [he wrote], my heart has throbbed with an invincible new emotion. . . . What struck me most, without your mentioning the fact, was that I knew you found this world, especially this corner of it, insipid. Although I do not entirely agree with you, I sympathize too deeply for words.

Formerly, night after night, my tears would fall like rain. But I gritted my teeth ; whatever happened, I would never let a sigh escape me. For if one allows oneself to be invaded by pessimism, far better commit suicide at the earliest opportunity. Of what avail to sob and moan in contemplation of such a life ?

We were born to struggle. Let us then declare war on " destiny " and " nature," regardless of success or failure. If you allow yourself to grow discouraged you will become a mere plaything of fate and, eventually, a victim of chronic melancholia. And in this condition how will you ever achieve anything, with all your blend of Chinese and European culture ? I cannot but feel you were intended for high achievement.

The meaning of life is to be found in conflict. Optimism and pessimism, fortune and misfortune, all are illusory. Perhaps you will tell me that I do not sufficiently understand your thoughts and your background to hold such a definite theory. I enclose a poem entitled " The Seeker of a Dream." It is addressed to you, with an earnest hope that you will manage to derive some consolation from it, since that was my sole aim in committing the lines to paper.

Oh, Miss Tu, already I am ardently hoping that you will write to me as often as possible. Above all, I need your advice. Dare I imagine that you need mine, and that we shall remain companions of heart and soul forever ? . . .

The fountain-pen—he did not write with a brush—dropped from his fingers.

Actually " The Seeker of a Dream " had not been written. For many months Fêng had intended to compose an allegorical poem with this title ; he intended to do so now, under Miss Tu's immediate inspiration. But he suddenly felt exhausted. The flesh was weak ; it had been a tiring day, and for all his strength of will, he could not repress a succession of shattering yawns.

Did Miss Tu really find the world insipid ? Pure guesswork that. Of a certainty his own existence had been insipid until he met Miss Tu.

He let himself be wafted on the wings of illusion. Powerful aeroplane ! Their correspondence would begin with philosophy and end with passion. One day it would be published ; each would select a subtle pseudonym. For the time being nobody would be aware of it : it would remain a precious secret between themselves until . . .

The wooden reverberations of the watchman in the deserted lane reminded him that the night was being slowly trodden away.

Unable to keep his eyes open another minute, the seeker of a dream sank on to his couch and slept quite dreamlessly. In any case it was something far more tangible than a dream that Fêng Chung-han was seeking.

# CHAPTER IV

# *Jade*

Elvira's last At Home had been no sterile function. It soon bore fruit on many a swaying bough. The leaves clustered thickest, perhaps, about Mrs. Mascot. Gaily she hummed while arranging multi-coloured bon-bons in lacquer bowls. Those bowls had been real bargains ; admiring their dragon design she remembered precisely what she had paid for them. She felt sure that they had been given fifty coats at least. Poppy had moved heaven and earth to find a set exactly like them, the sly old copycat, but why surrender one's professional secrets ? She smiled maliciously as she recalled her rival's futile machinations, how Poppy had even sent her husband to bribe her Number One boy for the shop's address. " Fifty coats, fifty coats, fifty coats of lacquer," she sang to the refrain of an old ballad.

Then : " Chang," she called.

" Yes, Missy ? "

" You'd better have a key ready, in case cook's nose starts bleeding again."

" Righto, Missy."

Of late the cook's nose had developed a tendency to bleed at dinner-parties, perhaps because Mrs. Mascot's was a difficult house to squeeze in : he was too notorious to find a lucrative job elsewhere.

" Have you put stockings on the cocktail glasses ? "

" Me no forget, Missy."

She was referring to the small slips of Szechuanese embroidery which prevented alcoholic rings from spoiling the table-varnish.

Mrs. Mascot was on tenterhooks. Only the *Peiping Star Bulletin* was in the know ; she had sent the social editor a list of her guests, a dazzling galaxy. For she was to give this dinner, quite unofficial, of course, in honour of Princess Joachim XVIII of Dummstadt, better known as the former Blanche Biggs (heiress of Elihu Biggs, the mouth-wash magnate), who had arrived in Peking at three o'clock this afternoon. And—*pace* Poppy *et al* !—it was rumoured that Her Serene Highness was interested in jade. Mrs. Mascot had great expectations.

Lotta Beal, who had sent the letter of introduction, would expect a stiff commission, but that was all in the day's work. Mrs. Mascot re-read it, in case there was any hint she had missed between the lines.

> Princess Blanche, as her intimates call her, is travelling with Miss Crocker, her private secretary, who is the master mind. At any rate the Princess's final decisions always rest with her.——

(Another to be squared, sighed Mrs. Mascot ; she would have to marshal all her tact.)

> —Both of them have a decided penchant for the unusual. I have told them all about your carved walnuts, the cricket-weighing machines and the Buddhist prayers written in lama's blood, which you mustn't forget to show them. They were thrilled by my account of your temple. . . .

Why was there not a single reference to jade ? Perhaps Lotta was getting absent-minded. Or was she also a scout of Poppy Trumper and the jade " ring " ? But if the ring went on widening for ever the game would hardly be worth the candle. It was a feather in her cap to be the first in Peking to entertain the Princess, whatever came of it.

Restlessly she roamed the room, lighting sticks of incense and rearranging brocaded cushions on the divans, which she effected with many a punch and pull. Having also invited the novelist-in-search-of-local-colour, she had to assure herself that the atmosphere would be up to scratch. Mrs. Mascot could never sit and wait. She had to keep in motion.

She switched off most of the lights so that only dim bulbs emitted a glaucous glow from niches in the walls, which were occupied by contortionist idols of multiple members and fearsome aspect. They writhed in couples ; but with so many arms and legs their licentious activities were somewhat camouflaged. Such an effort was entailed upon the eye to disentangle them that nobody had ventured to criticize their presence in a respectable drawing-room.

" Chang ! " she shrilled again.

" Here, Missy."

His approaching puffs, despite the incense, were powerfully fetid.

" Haven't I told you time and again not to eat garlic when I'm receiving guests ? You had better chew some cloves. Has Mr. Ma brought the jade ? "

" O.K., Missy."

" And those brocades I got this morning, put them in the Korean cabinet. We'll be looking at them after dinner."

Chang did not need to be told. He had already put them there.

Lancelot Thistleby was the first to arrive, with a vaguely distraught air.

" Am I dreaming ? " he murmured. " I was wondering if I had the right address, when lo ! your vermilion portals opened. To walk from a sordid alley into this house of many mansions : it's positively unreal. One feels like Aladdin. I shall have to cancel my ticket to Bali and re-write *The Thirteenth Concubine*."

43

Mrs. Mascot beamed. " I hope that means you will prolong your stay. But why re-write your novel ? Why not
begin another ? I can provide you with the data. I've
enough ideas for a dozen Peking novels. Of course I shall
expect you to dedicate it to me in return. I am Peking, Mr.
Thistleby, at least so many people have told me so that I've
come to believe it. I've a moral certainty that I was Chinese
in a former incarnation."

" You Peking, Mrs. Mascot ? That seems rough justice on
you. I hadn't noticed that you exhaled garlic, though I
fancied its fumes did follow me into this room. No, I'm
impressed by the peculiar neatness of everything about you,
the sheen of rugs, the lustre of damask, so picturesquely
ordered, yet spick and span. Yes, it's very impressive after
seeing the rest of Peking."

" I'm disappointed in you, Mr. Thistleby. By unreal, I
thought you meant like a page out of the *Arabian Nights*.
After all, you did say you felt like Aladdin."

" And still mean it, in so far as your place is concerned.
I hope you won't mind my saying so, but it has the atmosphere
of my *Thirteenth Concubine*. Peking, unfortunately, hasn't.
That's my trouble. I had depicted Peking as . . ."

The novelist's fancies were interrupted by a yapping of
dogs.

" Here comes Her Serene Highness."

Mrs. Mascot's eyes leapt from their sockets and in her
excitement she dropped a curtsy to Miss Crocker.

" We don't stand on ceremony, Mrs. Mascot. The Princess prefers travelling incog.," Miss Crocker quickly explained. She was the taller and ampler of the two ladies :
her *décolleté* revealed shoulders that would have done
credit to a Life Guard. Beside her the Princess looked
shrivelled.

" Lotta did us a real good turn," said the Princess. " Delighted to meet you, Mrs. Mascot. We've heard so much about your Chinese home."

" It gives one an entirely new integration," said Flora Crocker. " You see, the Princess and I have been deep in Marco Polo, Mrs. Mascot, and our first impression was that this spot had deteriorated a whale of a lot since then. But now," she smiled most graciously, " it promises to be quite the most vivid item of our travel-programme."

" Lotta was right, I guess this place is getting me," said the Princess, pausing in front of a licentious couple of idols and producing her lorgnette.

Miss Crocker never allowed the Princess to enlarge upon her utterances. " We've been visiting with Mrs. Trumper, and the Princess and I feel quite worn out after looking at that wonderful collection of hers. . . ."

" We darn near didn't come," said the Princess.

" I'm so glad you decided to, after all. I've invited a great English novelist and a great Chinese philosopher to meet you. Try some of this jasmine-tea. You'll find it soothing. It was given me by one of the Empress Dowager's ladies-in-waiting : I hope you will meet her ; she's a perfect gem, and very popular socially," said Mrs. Mascot all in a breath, her worst fears suddenly confirmed. Then : " Which collection," she asked, " if I'm not being indiscreet ? "

" The jade. Do you mean to say that you live right here in Peking and don't know about Mrs. Trumper's wonderful jade ? "

" I'm afraid I had forgotten," said Mrs. Mascot. " In Peking we all have collections. One simply has to collect, you know. . . . It's in the air, an epidemic that catches everyone sooner or later. . . ."

(Lancelot Thistleby made a mental note for the benefit of interviewers : Peking is not a city, it's a virulent microbe.)

" Such a tragedy poor Mrs. Trumper has to part with hers,"

Miss Crocker continued. " We've been feeling so sorry for her."

" You needn't," said Mrs. Mascot. " Poppy Trumper has parted with a good many collections. She must be getting used to it by now."

Miss Crocker and the Princess were visibly disappointed, and Mrs. Mascot felt she had allowed her tongue to run away with her.

Lancelot Thistleby sipped the lady-in-waiting's tea without relish. All gammon, this talk about fragrant China tea ! Just an infusion of bird-seed, he thought, sprinkled with a few drops of cheap scent. Give me honest, brown, belly-warming Mazawattee, he almost said aloud. But the women appeared to enjoy it.

Fortunately Chang came in with cocktails ; the jasmine tea had been but an atmospheric prelude, so to speak. Doctor Li Ssǔ, in an impeccable evening suit of Western design, followed. He always fortified himself at several Chinese banquets before proceeding to a European meal. This was betrayed by his breath.

Doctor Li undoubtedly possessed what was known as presence. A spiritual frock-coat, and the pompous aura of long sessions at public conferences, clung to him at all times. The Princess and Miss Crocker were captivated at once by his bow. He inquired if this was their first visit to Peiping and, as soon as he was answered in the affirmative, assured them how much he looked forward to hearing their first impressions. Eloquence was his natural vocation, and Mrs. Mascot congratulated herself on securing his company. The novelist was an unknown quantity as yet. As for the Doctor, he liked Princesses all the more if they happened to be American ; it helped him to feel that progress was authentic. This Princess was so simple and unassuming, so wistfully hungry for culture. Mrs. Mascot has got hold of a real sucker this time, he thought, but he failed to account for Miss Crocker.

Lancelot Thistleby had escaped his memory, and it amused the novelist to hear the Doctor spouting to the ladies in the same strains as he had spouted to himself at Elvira Mac-Gibbon's. H. G. Wells, Bertrand Russell and Sinclair Lewis, the speech was almost identical.

During dinner Mrs. Mascot tried to draw him out on the subject of jade. But the Doctor was too full of an article he was penning on the political situation to discourse on other subjects. The gist of this article was that Doctor Li Ssŭ felt sincerely sorry for his Japanese neighbours.

" Sorry for them, Doctor ? I don't quite get you."

" Don't you feel sorry for people who disgrace themselves ? They have shown their culture to be a hollow and a sham. Their *Bushido* is only another word for big-scale burglary."

" I feel much sorrier for those who are burgled," said Miss Crocker.

" You take the shorter view," he smiled, " but eventually the burglars will have to eat bitterness, as we say in China. Even if the rest of the world allows a nation of bandits to go scot free, there is a law of historic justice. . . ."

" Optimist," said Lancelot Thistleby.

" I am an optimist and proud of it," said Doctor Li sententiously. The novelist could see nothing to be optimistic about, but he refrained from saying so.

" What has happened," the Doctor continued, " has been summarized in a nut-shell by our eminent philosopher Doctor Hu Shih : China has suffered a new shame and gained a new inspiration."

Mrs. Mascot wondered if they realized that it was Asti Spumante she was serving. . . . How slowly the Doctor talked. It was like the launching of an ocean liner. Deeper and deeper by slow degrees it sank, which was disappointing after the preliminary rites, the baptismal champagne. It was obvious that the Doctor had received a thorough Yankee training. The Princess and Miss Crocker had to keep their eyes open to remember that he was not a compatriot.

"Human nature can be pushed just so far," he said ; "Japan is forcing us to fight."

"Remember you are talking to pacifists," Miss Crocker demurred. "The Princess and I are inborn pacifists. We refuse to believe that there isn't some other solution ! "

Dramatically the Doctor paused and shook his head before he wound up his peroration. "The greatest crime that can be charged against Japan is that I, and the intellectual leaders of New China, once inborn pacifists like you, have now become earnest advocates of war. Yes, boldly we proclaim it. Rather than accept a humiliating peace, we will fight like beasts at bay. Our jaws are set."

"Bravo ! " said Mrs. Mascot, "I like your spirit."

Lancelot Thistleby was disgusted at the way these women prostrated themselves, wonderstruck, before this nickel-pated windbag, merely because he happened to be Chinese. The author of *Yashmak* sat like a player with an unsatisfactory hand at cards. He was not used to others monopolizing the conversation, and tried to communicate his resentment by maintaining a frigid silence and looking down a supercilious nose.

Doctor Li sighed. It was a sigh of deep self-satisfaction. Yes, that article had been an effective bit of work. He could afford a night off : he felt he richly deserved it. Indirectly Miss Crocker's undulating outline had stimulated carnal thoughts behind that parchment brow. Indirectly, for Doctor Li had wondered what sort of figure she would present in the nude. He came to the conclusion, as he watched her manoeuvring a fragment of chicken towards her open mouth, that the spectacle must be gruesome. He felt little but distaste for white womanhood. Yet he owed no small measure of his

international success to such repulsive anthropological specimens as Miss Crocker. His mind's eye compared her with
little "Jade Lotus-bud," and while Miss Crocker fancied he
was manifesting sympathy for herself, he was inwardly
chuckling at the contrast. He decided to visit "Jade Lotus-
bud" tonight. The older the civilization, the more complete its mask. Who would suspect this solemn orator of
dalliance in a brothel?

"Are you occult?" Miss Crocker asked him.

"A cult? I guess I am. But only with the younger
generation."

"How strange! I felt you were: I felt it in my bones.
We must arrange a *séance*."

"I hope you ladies will come to my Cultural Advancement
Association: I shall be lecturing next Wednesday on 'The
Mother-Soul of China': I invite you all as my guests of
honour.... You know our headquarters, Mrs. Mascot.
And now I regret I shall have to leave you: an urgent Com-
mittee Meeting calls me...."

"The Doctor leads such an arduous life!" said Mrs. Mascot. "I count myself lucky to have persuaded him to join
this little party."

"Listening to you, Doctor, has been a proud privilege and
a rare inspiration," said Miss Crocker earnestly.

Princess Joachim XVIII of Dummstadt echoed: "It has,
indeed."

"I knew you would enjoy meeting Doctor Li," said Mrs.
Mascot. "One should see China as the Chinese see it."

His early departure suited her plan. For the Chinese, when
confronted with antiques picked up by Westerners, are apt
to communicate their own suspicions. What do Westerners
know of Chinese art? The question is plainly printed on their
features; even if they refrain from comment, a smile suffices
to say: this is a fake. Mrs. Mascot could now get down

E

to work, her work (although so brightly camouflaged as play).

" Since Poppy tired you out with her collection, I'll show you my bric-à-brac some other day. Enough is as good as a feast ! But I think we ought to take a peep at some tribute silk which a friend of mine, a Manchu Prince, brought in this afternoon. The poor dear Prince is in desperate straits. They're so thriftless, the Manchus, I suppose it accounts for their charm ! But I don't want to exhaust you. Are you sure you're in the mood ? "

" I can't imagine a pleasanter post-prandial occupation," observed the novelist, who had now recovered his good humour.

" At any rate, it's thoroughly Pekinese," said Mrs. Mascot.

" Let's all be Pekinese then," said Miss Crocker.

So Mrs. Mascot summoned Chang, who nonchalantly spread some brocade at their feet.

It was as if fireflies had suddenly flown in through the window, forming elaborate live patterns on the floor.

" The field of the cloth of gold," said Thistleby.

Mrs. Mascot instantly betrayed more animation. " From the Forbidden City," she said, in a tone that was quiet but nevertheless emotional. A hush followed.

" I guess it would liven up our cabin on the steamer," said Flora Crocker, " but there is far too much gold in it for my taste. I have the silver bias, I'm afraid. Silver is more spiritual, and spirituality is just another word for beauty."

" Flora, you make me tired. I think it's swell," said the Princess.

" From the Forbidden City," Mrs. Mascot repeated, patiently and persistently. " We may never look upon its like again ! "

" ' Quoth the Raven : Nevermore ! ' " said Thistleby.

" Feel the delicacy of this material," coaxed Mrs. Mascot.

Everybody started fingering the fine crisp texture. Miss Crocker fingered it and remained obdurate : " If only the gold could be turned to silver." But of course it couldn't. The Princess attempted to defy her companion by declaring : " It's gorgeous just as it is."

" You've all got a silver complex in America," observed Thistleby, " but isn't this carrying it too far ? "

" Where's the tribute silk ? I want to see the tribute silk," said Flora Crocker, unmoved.

Chang brought in some rolls of damask and a couple of mandarin coats.

" What an orgy of colour ! " said Thistleby.

Mrs. Mascot flushed with pleasure. He always stepped in with the right word. " A *palace* orgy," she added. " But you haven't had time to see the palace yet. . . . Too bad, it's a mere shell of what it was. . . ."

" Life," said Thistleby, " should be patterned like this brocade."

" I dare say, but it looks brand new to me," said Miss Crocker. " Besides, it would never do for a dressing-gown, would it, Blanche ? We've been wanting some stuff for a dressing-gown, but this is too stiff."

" I can't help it. I like it," the Princess all but whined. " I think it's swell."

" You're always carried away at first sight," Miss Crocker scolded. " And you always regret it later on. We must look at these by daylight. Could you send them to our hotel to-morrow morning ? "

" I can't send them later than to-night, I'm afraid," said Mrs. Mascot. " The Prince will be coming round in the morning. He promised me the first refusal. I suppose he's been gambling again. They're all such gamblers, the Manchus."

" How tiresome of him to be in such a hurry," said Miss Crocker. " I call that bullying."

Mrs. Mascot was taken aback. She had met her match. It was no use trying to argue with Miss Crocker.

"Would you care to see a *K'o-ssŭ* panel embroidered by K'ang Hsi's mother ?"

"Let us be quite frank, Mrs. Mascot. The fact is, Princess Blanche and I are only interested in jade. We got over the textile fever way back in Bombay."

"Flora, how could you be so rude ? I'll have to apologize for you."

"Please don't. I welcome frankness : and it's always fun to discover an affinity. I have a passion for jade myself, but I try to keep it secret. Jade is so intimate. It's the aristocrat of precious stones. The Chinese regard it with reverence : so do I. As I was telling Mr. Thistleby, I'm sure I was Chinese in a former incarnation."

Miss Crocker came straight to the point. "Have you any jade we can see ?" If not, she all but added, we had best be going.

This was too good to be true. Mrs. Mascot held her breath. But she shilly-shallied splendidly.

"Are you sure you haven't seen enough for to-day ?"

"We are always ready to look at jade," said Miss Crocker.

"I happen to have a few exceptional pieces," said Mrs. Mascot.

"Why didn't you say so before ?" exclaimed the Princess. "I'm all keyed-up. I can hardly contain my excitement."

Neither could Mrs. Mascot. With a "Will you walk into my parlour ?" expression, she conducted her guests to her "jade boudoir."

"I always light a little incense before looking at jade. It makes one feel properly reverent and rarefies the atmosphere. Jade is not for the carnally minded."

" How right you are," said Miss Crocker. " That's what I always tell Princess Blanche ; it's blasphemy to wear your jade when you go to the movies."

As soon as the incense was smouldering Mrs. Mascot drew back the panels of a vast lacquer cabinet, where ingeniously illuminated symbols of heaven and symbols of earth, archers' thumb-rings, amulets, seals, snuff-bottles and mythological monsters, chicken-bone white, mutton-fat white, sea-weed green, lavender grey and russet (stained by contact with putrefying bodies), some dull and wax-like, others sharp and vitreous, were ranged as in a shop-window.

Mrs. Mascot scanned the faces of her guests and saw that they were blank. Of course they proffered polite remarks, but they failed to respond with the true collector's glow. The Princess picked up a seal ; Miss Crocker toyed with a mutton-fat lion ; both seemed listless. Mrs. Mascot sensed that she was wasting her time. The novelist was trying to adjust various archers' rings to his fat little thumb without success. At last one fitted, but once on he could not get it off ; it had caught against the knuckle. His forehead all beaded with sweat, he asked : " What am I to do ? "

" Keep it," said Mrs. Mascot, informing him at the same time that it was one of her most ancient pieces, maybe three thousand years old.

" I couldn't possibly do that," he said, still desperately twisting. His thumb was beginning to swell.

These objects were more archæological than practical, Miss Crocker decided. There was nothing here that could be worn. The Princess required another necklace for herself, and had promised Flora a pair of ear-rings.

" Have you no jewel-jade ? " she inquired.

" Let me see," said Mrs. Mascot, " I have a necklace. And its history is unique. It belonged to the last Empress Dowager, the one who suffered from Bright's disease."

" Don't bother about its history just now. The jade's the thing. May we look at it ? "

" If you don't mind browsing alone for a few minutes. It's in my safe."

She blessed her lucky stars that she had sent for Mr. Ma. Patiently that gentleman had been waiting outside, recumbent on her Number One's brick bed, an emerald-green jade necklace ensconced about his girdle. But as soon as Mrs. Mascot set eyes on him, she knew there was a hitch.

" So very sorry," he murmured, " afraid no can sell."

" Nonsense," Mrs. Mascot rapped out brusquely. " Why ? "

" My friend "—(there was always a friend hanging about at the back of the stage)—" he want too much money. Very much money. Sure no can sell."

Mrs. Mascot flushed impatiently.

" You told me distinctly that your friend wanted six thousand five hundred dollars, last price," she said.

Mr. Ma gave her a melancholy smile, as if it were really not his fault ; his friend was so unreasonable. But he only repeated : " So very sorry."

" I should jolly well think so," said Mrs. Mascot, cursing the Chinese and all their ways from the very ventricles of her indignant heart. For this was no time to prevaricate. The proper course was never to act hastily ; but the Princess was waiting to see the necklace, and she did not feel at ease about Miss Crocker. Perhaps she had already come to terms with Poppy Trumper. The spirit of competition had been kindled in Mrs. Mascot's breast.

" How much does that friend of yours want now ? " she asked. " Last price ; and by last price I mean last price."

Mr. Ma's smile was even more deprecating. " I tell my friend too much. He say : number one jade, no matter.

My friend plenty money, no hurry sell. . . . He got motor-car."

" How much ? " insisted Mrs. Mascot.

" Eight thousand dollars." Mr. Ma's shrivelled fingers clawed an octave out of the air as he articulated the words.

Mrs. Mascot heaved a sigh. It was a hard life. She felt like sitting down and having a good cry ; at the sight of those eight claws she pulled herself together. Strange that after years of highly profitable transactions Ma still indulged in the tricks of petty dealers. He would keep her haggling up to the last gasp. On this occasion she saw she would have to surrender. However faint-heartedly, she put on the usual bluff to save her face.

" Nothing doing," she said. " But I want another look-see. Savvy ? Have you got the necklace with you ? "

He hesitated, thought better of it, and fished it from his girdle. The beads were wrapped in puce-coloured silk. A deep translucent green, they were like cabochon emeralds, as he dangled them amorously against the light. For a second Mrs. Mascot's orbs were blurred ; she nearly staggered before the Niagara-vision of what she could do if Princess Blanche's interest in jade materialized. The beads had a devilish glint, as if the whole of her future depended on a casual tourist's whim.

" I'll think it over ; you stay right here," said she, " I go show it to my friends. . . ." Deftly, before Mr. Ma had time to respond, she snatched the necklace from his fingers and skipped away with it.

" I'm so sorry to have kept you waiting."

" We've been absorbed in getting the ring off Mr. Thistleby's thumb," said Miss Crocker.

" And it's off at last, Mrs. Mascot. There was a nasty moment when I nearly burst a blood-vessel."

" All's well that ends well. The ring was obviously meant

for you, and you must keep it. Perhaps you wore it in a former incarnation."

"What about the necklace, Mrs. Mascot? Have you brought it? Otherwise I fear we shall really have to be going. . . ."

Mrs. Mascot fixed her guests with a hypnotic eye, and never uttering a word, produced the necklace from its silken placenta.

"Why didn't Lotta tell us? We'd have come straight here from the railway-station, instead of wasting our whole afternoon. . . ."

Mrs. Mascot stood watching her audience. The conjuring trick had succeeded. Petrified bubbles of some sea unfathomably green, the cold beads glittered, the only light and colour in the room.

"This alone," said Princess Blanche, "would make our trip worth while."

"Sure, it's a beauty," Miss Crocker grudgingly assented. "But remember, honey, Mrs. Trumper promised to show us a special necklace to-morrow. You may decide you like that even better."

The Princess turned a deaf ear. "I haven't seen anything to beat this," she declared, "not since we left New York."

"It was an imperial heirloom," said Mrs. Mascot, "and has a remarkable history. During the Boxer trouble . . ."

"Oh, never mind that now, Mrs. Mascot. Will you let me try it on?" Mrs. Mascot assenting, she hung it round her neck and posed before a mirror. Amazing what jade did to one: wrinkles ceased to matter. "I'm every inch a Princess now," she mused.

"Some people bring jade to life," said Mrs. Mascot; "it is human, you see . . . Absolutely! But it can go through long periods of hibernation. There are people whose personalities don't suit it. Many a Manchu princess has begged

me to wear her jade for a day or two because I've the knack
of bringing out its brilliance. I am sure, Princess, you
also have that knack. It's probably a question of spiritual
magnetism."

" The necklace actually seems to be smiling," said Lancelot
Thistleby, with his tongue in his cheek.

" Now that you say so, it does," said Miss Crocker crypti-
cally. " What are you asking for it ? " she whispered to Mrs.
Mascot.

" You surprise me, Miss Crocker ! It had never entered
my mind to part with it. But if I did, I couldn't let it go for
less than ten thousand dollars. It must be worth far more.
I doubt if I could find another like it. . . ."

Miss Crocker swallowed hard : " Ten thousand dollars !
I reckoned that jade would be much cheaper in China."

" It is only in China that the true value of jade is understood," said Mrs. Mascot firmly. " This necklace would be
a bargain for ten thousand dollars."

" I don't think the Princess is prepared to pay so much.
Nowadays there are such wonderful imitations."

A cry from the Princess interrupted them. She had broken
the clasp and the beads were pelting all over the floor.

Mrs. Mascot at once went down on her hands and knees.
While the Princess stood by like a pillar of salt, exclaiming :
" Oh my ! oh my ! How ever did I do it ? " Miss
Crocker and Mr. Thistleby helped to collect them.

Mrs. Mascot moaned, " I had them strung by Cartier.
And now I'll have to send them back to Europe. Jade is the
only thing I'm superstitious about. This may bring me years
of bad luck." Tears welled into her eyes. " I'll never feel
the same about my necklace again."

" Never mind," said the Princess. " You must let me
pay."

The beads had managed to roll into the remotest corners of

the room. The novelist gave Mrs. Mascot a handful. " My beautiful necklace ! " she sighed, and started counting them. They were incomplete, however, and the search began again. As rugs were pulled back, more truant bubbles glittered into view. When these were counted : " But one of the biggest is missing ! " wailed Mrs. Mascot. " What can have happened to it ? " Every crevice was explored in vain.

Then Mrs. Mascot had a brain-wave. " Would you mind looking into your shoes ? There's just a chance it may have got into one somehow. . . ."

Mrs. Mascot took off her shoes ; the others followed suit and lo, it slipped from one of the Princess's.

" Well, I declare ! " said Mrs. Mascot. " It was in your shoe all the time and you never felt it there."

" It is very mysterious," the Princess laughed, " I hope you won't think I tried to get away with it. My, would you believe it, Flora, it's nearly twelve o'clock ! We must really be thinking about bye-byes. What a thrilling day this has been ! And we're to see another necklace at Mrs. Trumper's tomorrow. I'm afraid it will be an anticlimax after this. It was simply swell of you to take so much trouble. Whenever you come to New York you must let us know."

Mrs. Mascot made no comment. Then—" Have you a cheque-book with you ? " she demanded.

" No," Miss Crocker gasped in astonishment. " Why ? "

" The Princess offered to pay, and perhaps, after that awkward little incident . . ."

" What do you mean ? "

" Don't embarrass me, Miss Crocker. The Princess herself remarked that it looked—well, peculiar . . ."

Miss Crocker could hardly believe her ears. " What *are* you suggesting ? Why, this is an outrage ! Blanche, I won't hear of you paying. It's nothing less than a hold-up."

For a minute Mrs. Mascot's features hardened. " There are others who might not view it in that light.   Mr. Thistleby will be my witness if necessary," she said.   " And since you assume this attitude, I feel I may have counted wrong.   Perhaps you had better undress to make quite sure.   Or would you prefer me to call in the police ?   At any rate, I shall feel it my duty to warn Mrs. Trumper."

" But surely you will take my word," said the Princess. " I said I would pay for having it restrung."

" Those were not your first words, Princess.   You distinctly said, ' You must let me pay for it.'   I've come to think that that is the only solution.   I shall never feel the same about my necklace again."

" Sheer blackmail," said Miss Crocker.

" I'm sorry, Princess," Mrs. Mascot continued.   " Your friend puts a different complexion on things.   Why did she ask me the price to begin with ? "

" Did you, Flora ? "

" I sensed it was for sale, as of course it was . . ."

" Oh, Flora, it would really save trouble to pay for it right away.   I feel completely pooped."

" But she's asking ten thousand dollars.   It's a regular ramp . . ."

" Others might not view it in that light," Mrs. Mascot repeated dryly.   " The clasp was strong : how did it get broken ?   How did that bead get into the Princess's shoe ? What prompted Miss Crocker to ask me the price of the necklace ?   This isn't a shop.   Please put yourselves in my position.   I am a woman of modest means and you ask me to show you my only treasure.   I doubt if I could find another like it in all the length and breadth of Peking.   The Princess goes and breaks it and says she will pay.   Then it turns out that she only means to pay for having it restrung.   I think I am entitled to demand a cheque before further complications arise. I consider myself most fortunate in having an eye-witness."

"The whole thing's just a ramp. I'll tell every soul I know," fumed Miss Crocker. "I'll shout it from the chimney-pots."

"My, this is like stepping into a melodrammer," said the Princess, "but I'm feeling so dog-gone tired. For my sake, Flora, do go round to the hotel and fetch my cheque-book or I can see we'll never get to bed."

Mrs. Mascot told Chang to escort Miss Crocker to the hotel. "And perhaps you had better bring your passport," she suggested.

She herself kept guard over the Princess. "Will you help me to count the beads again," she said, "just to make doubly sure."

After a *mauvais quart d'heure* Miss Crocker appeared with passport and cheque-book. The Princess made out the cheque. Mrs. Mascot compared the signature with that on the passport and wrote a receipt.

The beads were packed in a padded box of imperial yellow brocade. "I'll send you back the box first thing to-morrow," said the Princess.

"Please don't bother," said Mrs. Mascot. "Now that the necklace is yours, I am sure you will never regret it."

Miss Crocker supported the weary Princess to the door. "I'll see that you live to regret it," she shouted back.

Mrs. Mascot turned to Lancelot Thistleby. "I am so sorry about this unpleasantness. I hope I am absolved from blame."

"By Jove," he said, "you were magnificent. Let me congratulate you!"

Mrs. Mascot pretended not to understand. "One can't allow oneself to be imposed upon," she said, "if that's what you mean. Do you think the Princess is a kleptomaniac? I once knew a baronet who could not resist sugar-tongs : he always went away with a pair in his pocket. One had to make allowances. But there's a difference between sugar-tongs and jade. And what about Miss Crocker ? They both behaved pretty oddly. . . . I am glad you were there," she continued. "I needed a man to protect me. Women of Miss Crocker's type are apt to become violent. My nerves have seldom suffered such a strain. I didn't know what she was going to do or say next."

"There was certainly an element of surprise. But you showed a remarkable presence of mind, and I must thank you for a memorable evening."

"Don't forget your thumb-ring."

"May I really keep it as a souvenir ? "

"It claimed you from a distant incarnation. Besides, you deserve it."

"It is I who should present a ring to you. I admire you enormously. Do you know that I feel sorely tempted to propose to you ? "

"Unfortunately I have a husband. But don't forget, you're dedicating your Peking novel to me. And don't forget this, Mr. Thistleby ; I am Peking."

"Of course, I shall lay my novel at your feet. My Lady Peking, good night ! "

Mrs. Mascot extended a freckled hand and Mr. Thistleby stooped to brush a protruding vein of it with his lips. As soon as he was out of the door, she scrutinized the cheque and held it against the light, precisely as she had held the jade necklace. For a panic moment the thought flashed upon her that there might be something wrong. No, the date was all right. "Halleluia," she exclaimed.

"Yes, Missy." Engrossed in her cheque " Missy " had not noticed that Chang was standing behind her. His presence reminded her that Ma was waiting. Ma was wont to appear depressed, as if he were the loser, at moments of reckoning.

It was part of his technique. He never expected prompt pay-
ment from Mrs. Mascot. At sight of her cheque, although
it was post-dated, for eight thousand dollars, although these
were in local currency, he permitted himself to beam.

" I shall expect a nice little present from your friend with
the motor-car. It is twice as much as he ever dreamt he'd
come in for. . . . He ought to be very grateful."

" You no buy to-night, Missy Trumper buy to-morrow,"
he replied.

" Now no can do, Mr. Ma ! " she said archly. " Definitely
no can do ! "

Mr. Ma tuskily shared her merriment. Poor old Poppy,
she said to herself, this time I've given you a great big tit for
many a tiny tat. And so to bye-byes !

\*　　\*　　\*

To-morrow Mrs. Mascot would have to be at the bank as
soon as it was open. That night she could not sleep a wink,
for the cheque had released a torrent of new projects which
kept her eyes wide open, staring into the darkness. If only
the tourist industry were in her hands ! Her dream might
still come true : she would open a travel bureau of her own.
She would flood the world with illustrated pamphlets. Already the phrases cantered through her brain. . . . " Dance
to divine Slavonic orchestras 'neath the shadows of age-old
walls vibrating with barbaric grandeur of forgotten emperors." The Japs and Mount Fuji would have to look to
their laurels !—the tourist-stream would give them the go-by.
Peking would be the centre of attractions, and she would be
the intellectual pivot. She'd keep the whole caboodle whirl-
ing ; she'd begin with a casino—the Hall of Imperial Silk-
worms might serve for Roulette (or had Chemmy become
more popular ? she would have to ascertain), there would be

a foreign restaurant and a grill-room attached, a roller-skating
rink and a jazz-band, a floating barge for dancing on the Pei
Hai ; the enclosure of the Temple of Heaven she visualized
as a dirt-track, the Temple of Agriculture as a canidrome. . . .
Peking, the home of culture, the home to boot, of universal
sport. As for culture, she'd adapt old Chinese styles until the
Chinese themselves would be surprised—give them the Real
Thing.

Not since the night before her marriage had Mrs. Mascot
experienced such elation.

# CHAPTER V

# *Goldfish*

THE goldfish stirred like erratic red torches in liquefied black velvet. Their *mise-en-scène*, a series of tubs densely populated with vivacious animalcules, quivering clots of slimy substance, gobs of anonymous spawn-jelly, intensified the scarlet shimmering of their copper goitres, as a rippling arpeggio of visible scales caught a ray of sunlight. Thickly they steered towards the surface, goggling upwards to survey that fraction of the universe above them. Some appeared to be suffering from indigestion : they wheezed out gaseous bubbles ; they lolled, all paunch, half-paralysed, or heaved about, yawning, the very picture of somnolent satiety. Some trailed long floating whiskers, elaborate and cumbersome : through spectacles with very powerful lenses they peered and veered in retreat—a filmy train, as of some disappointed dowager, swept back into the depths. So swift a disillusion ? A glazed momentary glance had sufficed. Whatever they had seen would soon be dismissed. It was evident that they preferred their own milieu : the microscopic animalcules wriggling among them were far more interesting than their biped visitors.

No doubt they were entitled to their supercilious airs. Now that the weather was warm, inquisitive spectators would wander daily from tub to tub, making personal remarks about them.

A vague smile hovered over Yi's face as she paused with Fêng Chung-han. Since their meeting at Elvira's, Fêng had sent her a letter every day. But this was their first rendezvous. All week she had been teaching at the University and conscientiously correcting French compositions at home ; so she had suggested a change of air in the Central Park.

" Fins or wings ? " she asked idly. " They really might be either."

" These specimens," said Fêng, who knew something of pisciculture, " happen to be without any dorsal fin.—But what is the point of it all ? "

" Art for art's sake, I suppose," said Yi.

Recently she had been lecturing on Mallarmé and Huysmans, and now these goldfish made her wonder why. What had the French Symbolists, nay, what had any foreign literature to communicate of value to the Chinese ? From prehistoric times her people had cultivated the rare, the artificial. Men with the temperament of Mallarmé had flourished while Europeans inhabited crude caves : the elements of *A Rebours* could be found in chronicles going back two thousand years before the Christian era. Did not Chou Hsin, last of the Shang dynasty, build a pleasure-palace underground, hang the trees of his gardens with dainties, and dredge a lake to fill it with wine ? He was Gilles de Rais and Des Esseintes and Nero rolled into one. . . . Why waste time over these *nouveaux riches* ?

" Precisely," Fêng was saying, " art for art's sake, as exemplified by the culture of insignificant carp. Let us alter the natural forms of these vertebrates at all costs, expend our ingenuity on transforming them—until they have no dorsal fin, et cetera. Let us develop their eyes until they project like electric-light bulbs. Superb ! That's the way we Chinese choose to triumph over nature. And the rearing of these abortions is still quite a lucrative business. Doesn't it exasperate you, with China in danger of national extinction ? "

Fêng was out to impress her this afternoon, but while he

65

F

was borne away on the pinions of his eloquence, Yi was only half listening. She was thinking of her father.

There had always been goldfish at home and she had scarcely noticed them. They led cool protected lives behind rocks and ferns. At the proper seasons their spawn had to be carefully removed or the greedy males would devour it ; and they were hatched in shallow bowls by the heat of the sun. Her father would stand before his various specimens, lost in contemplation. He was an unhappy man, a follower of K'ang Yu-wei—a liberal of the old régime. But he never talked about himself ; he preferred talking about his goldfish. Doubtless they were a consolation for many disappointments.

Yi admired her father's reticence. There was too much talk in China. She began to wish that Fêng were less garrulous. His remarks were out of keeping with the light-headedness, the faint delirium of the spring weather. She caught at a spray of blossom, cherished it for a moment, then carelessly cast it away. Fêng wondered if she would deal with him likewise.

" After all," she said, " the rearing of goldfish cannot make much difference. What are a few small fish in the immensity of China ? "

" I see that you are of the Taoist persuasion," he answered. " I never would have guessed it. In that case you are hopeless : it is no use arguing with you."

" If you're referring to *laissez-faire* and Lao Tzŭ's doctrine of inaction, aren't we all Taoists ? Before you know it, you will prove to be one yourself ! "

" Never," said Fêng, " I am a Chinese-American Pragmatist—a pupil of Hu Shih and John Dewey and William James. . . ."

" What alternative employment do you suggest for those who rear goldfish ? Should they join the militarists, or manufacture explosives ? A thousand times no. Let everyone cultivate his own garden in peace, as I think Voltaire said—or was it Confucius ? " she smiled.

" By garden meaning goldfish ? "

" Why not ? At least it is a harmless occupation, and the result is positive, however small the scale. Let us work without moralizing : it is the only way to make life bearable. As soon as we lay down our tools we start moralizing, and then we never stop. It is all very eloquent, but where has it led us ? "

" Where, indeed ? " thought Fêng dismally. He had never intended the conversation to take such a turn. He had wished to steer it towards more intimate things, to make Yi talk about herself. Then he could talk about himself. They would look into each other's eyes and their two selves would meet : her soul would be mirrored on his retina, his soul on hers. That was how he had visualized this meeting, in anticipation. And, for once, time had become incredibly precious. He wished he had the courage to say so. Yet he heard himself saying—he almost wondered how : " At least talking has prevented us from signing. We have not negotiated with the enemy. We have stood firm."

" Taoist ! " said Yi, " Do nothing, and all things will be done ! "

Fêng heard himself laughing, but he had lost confidence in himself. Yi was too clever. He remembered what Elvira had told him about her life in Paris. He must seem terribly parochial. In the suit of Western clothes he had donned for her benefit he was feeling uncomfortably hot.

The Central Park had an air of elation. Soldiers sauntered like happy children, hand in hand : the struggle with the " dwarf bandits " forgotten. A squadron of doves, armed with whistles, shrilled overhead, flashed in the sun, and disappeared into the blue. Buxom schoolgirls in " gym " costumes strode past with sturdy legs and tennis rackets.

Fortunately those who adopted such garb were in the minority. Their sisters to whom the national dress still clung made the avenues more beautiful, as if the slender willows to which poets eternally compared them had decided to take a stroll. The peony-beds were invaded by elderly gentlemen who examined their petals minutely, as if they were oracle bones, while wives and concubines stood by at respectful attention. For the "king of flowers" had begun to chuckle; his petals were opening. Soon he would burst into laughter and full bloom.

Yet Fêng could not forget his country's plight, and of all people it was Yi who should have helped him to forget it. The three eastern provinces had fallen, and still the government blundered on without a definite policy. Whether politicians favoured resistance or non-resistance the calamities continued. The frequent visits of Japanese aeroplanes reminded one all too crudely of that fact. Yi was right. It had been a pyrrhic victory at Geneva. Mukden, Shanhai-kuan, Jehol had fallen among mere words. The government drifted like goldfish.

Fêng's bitterness and indignation rose. Could he do nothing? Was he, too, one of those carp without a dorsal fin? For all the sunlight on the peonies, he felt as if there were grit in his eyes; his muscles ached; hopelessness and despondency descended upon him. Yi had not given him the sympathy he longed for. Perhaps she despised him. But was he not expecting too much? How could she read his thoughts? He suddenly realized that this was only their second meeting. They must get away from these accursed goldfish, put them out of mind. He was determined to make the most of this afternoon with Yi.

A dumpy foreigner in a prim grey suit approached them, bowing like an old-fashioned Chinese official, only more so. Fêng looked astonished. Who was this ceremonious clown?

" It's that English curio, Mr. Flower," Yi explained, " at Elvira's they call him the Manchu Maniac. Everything about him, even his servants and dogs, must have a Manchu pedigree. . . ."

Sublimely unconscious of what this attractive girl was telling her companion, Philip Flower stepped up and greeted her. He did not shake hands, but in Chinese style, only a little more so, he shook his own. " *Nin hao, nin hao !* " he ejaculated in suave parody of his Chinese teacher's voice.

" This is an unexpected pleasure," he proceeded in English. " I have just been reading your poems, Miss Tu. Elvira lent them to me. Charming ! I envy your mastery of French. I particularly appreciated the lines about *Pei-ching*." (Philip Flower refused to call the city Peip'ing), " I even tried to commit them to memory :

> *Je m'attriste devant la terrasse de Yen,*
> *Le bruissement des feuilles évoque le passé.*

But you must forgive my accent. I know it is vile. The past : yes, everything here evokes the long-ago—best of all the leaves. I have a gingko in my courtyard, Miss Tu. Orthodox Buddhism, you know, admits that certain dewas or spirits reside in the body of trees and speak from within them. My gingko tells me the most romantic tales. I'm never tired of listening. So you see I've caught your meaning, though I'm no good at French. The study of *Kuo Wên* has absorbed my paltry modicum of talent."

" You are too kind to say such things. But I shall have to scold Elvira. Those verses were youthful indiscretions. I am quite ashamed of them, and Elvira knows it."

" You needn't be, you needn't be," Philip earnestly assured her, " even in English that's a splendid line : the rustling of the leaves evokes the past."

Yi was embarrassed. She had not mentioned these literary

efforts to Fêng. After a banal exchange of remarks about the weather, Philip Flower was struck dumb. To judge from the severity of his countenance, Miss Tu's companion was annoyed. It struck Philip that the couple might want to be left to themselves ; perhaps he was intruding. But he could not suddenly break away. Besides, he was interested. He was anxious to exchange ideas with " young China."

The trio stood staring at each other with strained polite smiles. Philip Flower never knew what to make of the Chinese who had been educated abroad. They were so cynical about their ancient customs, and they seemed to regard his enthusiasm as a tiresome affectation. But he liked to be with them : it satisfied a streak of vanity in his nature to be seen in their company, which he undoubtedly preferred to that of his compatriots. Hence his frequent bouts of loneliness. Self-consciousness prompted him to say something, anything.

" I must pay my respects to the goldfish," he said.

He was aware of a flicker of indefinable ridicule. There ! now they were laughing at him. I've gone and put my foot in it, he thought. He could have bit his tongue but it wagged on to conceal his growing uneasiness.

" Such gorgeous creatures," he continued. " I rather envy them their clean, fresh, noiseless lives and conversations."

Now the young couple laughed out loud. He winced under their mockery. Or was it because of some private joke of their own ? He had not intended to be funny.

" Some of them are pretty enough," said Fêng, " but how futile ! "

Philip took offence. He refused to be crushed.

" I can't agree. Nothing is futile that helps to make our lives a little brighter." He assumed a paternal tone. " You young people are far too practical. That makes you intolerant. I dare say you think me an old fogy. Be that as it may,

I swear my ideas are not nearly so old-fashioned as those of the younger generation. I suspect you are a reader of Herbert Spencer. A fig for Herbert Spencer, Mr. Fêng ! When you reach my age you will be grateful for every speck of colour life can yield. A common or garden bee has more to teach us than Herbert Spencer : it sees more of life to begin with. That man had no visual apparatus, Mr. Fêng."

"But why a bee, Mr. Flower ? Because it can gather honey ? Because it can sting ? Or because the bee is a sort of Communist ? Are you in favour of Communism ?" For a moment Fêng looked interested.

"Oh dear no ! Of course it must be nice to gather honey, but apart from this talent a bee can distinguish colours invisible to man, small, intricate patterns in ultra-violet. Just think of the tapestry on flowers and the wings of butter-flies invisible to us, the patterns within patterns, quite in-dependent of those we are able to enjoy ! Insects move in a world of beauty beyond our feeble vision. Yet a bee's eye is apparently simpler than ours. In your salad days you scarcely give colour a thought, you have so much of your own. You can afford to wallow in gloom ; I suppose that is a privilege and luxury of youth. So the bright little gold-fish are beneath your contempt. When you get older, you may learn to appreciate them. I'm sorry for you if you don't."

Fêng betrayed his impatience with a carefully contrived yawn. He had hoped to discuss Communism. Was there no escape from this old bore ? He looked despairingly at Yi. He scanned the clouds.

They were back among the goldfish again.

"How is your father, Miss Tu ? I clean forgot to ask you. It is difficult to visualize the connection between you, if I may say so—the Confucian scholar and his Parisian daughter. . . ."

" Thank you, he is very well.  I did not realize that you were friends."

" Although I am one of his numerous tenants, I seldom have the pleasure of seeing him.  Please give him my warmest regards.  Perhaps you will do me the favour of bringing us together more often.  It would be a mutual benefit, for we have much in common.  I might almost be his younger brother.  Ah, Mr. Fêng, you should see Mr. Tu's goldfish !  They might induce you to change your mind.  We'll convert him, won't we, Miss Tu ?"

Fêng glowered at the neat, middle-aged symphony in grey beside him.  So this stranger bragged of his familiarity with her father as well as with her poems, while he had seen neither !  Annoyed in the first place because the bore had barged into his precious rendezvous, he deeply resented what he mistook for the patronizing tone of a British Imperialist.  He knew the genus !  Nothing else to do but dig up unnecessary information about the history and habits and heaven knew what else of his people, concentrating on the very details that lowered them in the esteem of civilized moderns, absurdities better buried and forgotten.  Self-styled sinologues who could not see China for that past into which their myopic eyes were forever prying.  Why didn't they stay at home and dig up facts about Druids ?  They gushed about their " love of China."  Porcelain was generally what they meant. . . .  A lot their League of Nations had achieved !

Meanwhile the object of this mental tirade, gazing at Yi, continued imperturbably to discourse on goldfish.

" Look at this, for instance ! "  Philip designated a creature floating towards him in a nebulous tulle of tails and fins.  " Is it not like Salome dancing the dance of the seven veils ? "

" Then you," said Yi, " must be Herod."

" How I wish I were.  And I should like to think that the worms which fed on me would finally feast these beauties.

# Goldfish

But come, let's be serious ! Salome is dancing for us.
Admire the variety and originality of costume displayed by
that chorus, the mannequin with crimson corsage and silvery
train, and this one in moiré silk, which in certain lights
becomes a mantle of diapered gauze. When you were in
Paris, Miss Tu, did you see such dresses in rue de la Paix ?
Never, I warrant. How remote are these bejewelled courtiers
from their European cousin, the pathetic little *carassius
auratus* blinking in his bowl, the very image of suburban boredom. And those pocked and freckled voluptuaries, what
a wealth of imagination has gone into their composition !
I have a theory—don't look askance, Mr. Fêng, 'tis a poor
thing but mine own—a theory that the great poets of China
have recreated carp, each in the image of his dreams ; it is
by these poets that I can distinguish them. In fact I call this
the Chinese Poets' Corner."

A mocking smile played over Fêng's pursed lips. Philip
took no notice. He seized Yi by the hand. "There goes
Ch'ü Yüan," he continued with voluble eagerness. "The
slander and intrigue of jealous rivals have not yet sapped his
position at Court : he is still in his prime. And that wistful
one in black, she is evidently Li Ch'ing-chao. Her lips are
parted ; she is reciting the poem Judith Gautier translated as
*Mes Yeux Fixes.* . . . 'Restless and fevered under my crimson
coverlet, I cast it off and suddenly I rise. But I lack the
courage to complete my coiffure ; the comb weighs heavy
on my weariness. The dust still gathers on my dressing-
table ; I let it gather . . .' These poets are in perpetual
motion. Did not Nietzsche say that poets make their water
muddy that it may seem deep ? In this case, alas, it would
seem to be true. They like their water thick with weeds
and particles, pips and grains of mechanical matter ; who
knows what rôle these animated commas play in their lives ?
I decline to believe it is purely digestive. Personally I wish

they preferred more clarity, but it would be ungrateful to grouse : one can't have everything. Do you see Tu Fu ? He's over there, with all the gold of sunset in his scales. Li Po's just beyond him, glittering like a cascade in the moonlight. I suppose you will deny, Mr. Fêng, that Li Po was drowned in his gallant attempt to embrace the moon's reflection."

Fêng nodded, but Philip would not let him interrupt.

" Well, well, sir, it's a moot point," he continued.

" Decidedly moot. There's no denying, however, that the Moon was his Muse :

> *The Moon sheds her rays*
> *On my goblet and me,*
> *And my shadow betrays*
> *We're a party of three.*

Giles hit that off to perfection—there's never been a translator like old Giles ! "

" The poet I love best," said Yi, " is T'ao Yüan-ming. Is he included in your Poets' Corner ? "

" I'm afraid not."

" Why not ? Without him it is surely incomplete."

" The essence of T'ao Ch'ien is simplicity," said Philip. " The simple carp which has escaped cultivation does not belong here. His quiet grey would form a soothing contrast with his scarlet progeny, but it would be inconsiderate to force publicity on such a lover of retirement. ' Length of years and depth of wine ' were what T'ao Ch'ien desired ; and if we substitute water for wine and don't interfere with him, the carp fulfils these desires. He thrives at the bottom of my humble pond. If you want to catch sight of him you must come along before he is fed : unless I beat his dinner-gong he seldom rises to the surface. Which reminds me that these fish possess the virtues of punctuality and obedience to a remarkable degree . . ."

" Purely negative virtues," snapped Fêng.

" You are not yet qualified to appreciate them," Philip retorted, and forgetting his own celibacy, he added : " When you are married you may think otherwise."

The pleasantry jarred on Fêng, but Yi laughed gaily, the small teeth glistening between her raspberry lips.

" In any case I defy you," said Fêng, " to pick out a poet here with a social message."

" As well you may ! In trying to eke various kinds of messages out of Chinese poetry many an honest scholar has run amuck. Your greatest poetry is essentially free from such dross."

" Do you dismiss the *Book of Odes* ? Or don't you consider that poetry ? "

" The *Shih Ching*," smiled Philip, " just happens to illustrate my point. Generations of commentators have shown that it is possible to find fantastic meanings in the simplest ballads. No poetry was ever so crystalline, yet your pundits remain suspicious, and will read a scathing political satire into some rustic's lament. Social messages are purely arbitrary, and the folk-song is the unhappy hunting-ground of those who hanker after them. Doctor Hu Shih, with a moral earnestness we would call Victorian were it not Confucian, discovers a condemnation of the Chinese marriage system in a folk-song about a lass who is married to a hunchback. Hunchbacks may prove excellent husbands, bringing out all the finer fibres of the female nature, the richest maternal instincts—but that is beside the point. The last stanza of this ditty runs :

> ' *Good neighbours,*' pled the little wife,
> ' *Scoff not at my wretched life !*
> *Preordained was such a mate.*
> *How can I contend with Fate ?* '

If there is condemnation here, surely it is Fate that is being condemned. But there is more of resignation than condemnation. No, Mr. Fêng, we shall find few social messages among the goldfish. But they still have something to teach the younger generation. Good manners, for instance. When deportment becomes a lost art, people may have to take lessons from goldfish. Confucius said : ' A gentleman is calm and spacious : the small man is always fretting.' Goldfish can teach us how to be calm and spacious. Their very movements tell of a more leisurely and a more honest age than ours."

" We don't require such teachings. We Chinese are far too placid as it is. A gentleman cannot be calm and spacious when he sees his country going to the dogs."

" You and I seem agreed to disagree," said Philip sadly. " But I shall convert Miss Tu, for she is a poet. When I first set eyes on these fish I felt that they, apart from all else in the Middle Kingdom, were worth the long journey from England. They are the aristocrats of the piscine world, they are the living rubies and fire-opals. I think it was your father, Miss Tu, who told me that they are sometimes reared in egg-shells. A masterly device ! The spawn is transferred into an empty shell and the hole sealed up. Then the egg is returned to its nest ; the hen sits on it for a few days, after which it is reopened, and the spawn put into tepid water, where it soon hatches. They have their specialists too, physicians who can treat their ailments with subtle herbs. I have even heard of goldfish tattooed with ideographs. When these were marshalled into ranks you could read antithetical couplets in the water. Beauty must always be fostered by such careful processes. Ah, Mr. Fêng ! Even in the gorgeous East, the colours of life are fading, and I fear that the West is to be held responsible. We should cling to goldfish before they vanish too. I would certainly regard their disappearance as a dire calamity. But I am maundering.

Forgive me. You have more serious matters to think about."

"You are right," said Fêng, "I have . . ."

"Matrimony—the League of Nations?"

Fêng blushed. There was something uncanny about this Philip Flower. Perhaps, with many foreigners, he shared the superstition that Chinese people have no nerves. Fêng wished he could treat him to an exhibition of his own at this moment, and give the old fool a ducking among those goldfish for which he affected so singular a passion. Yi saved the situation.

"Why don't you write about China?" she asked Philip. "If you write as well as you talk, everybody will be reading you, especially now that China is in vogue. . . ."

"Yes," said Fêng, "it's a shame that your erudition should be wasted on us . . ."

Gingerly the cloud had passed.

"I love China far too much to write about her. It would seem like an act of betrayal. And China is too vast for a Lafcadio Hearn."

"You must be Peking's Lafcadio Hearn." Yi smiled maliciously. Seeing her smile, the earth grew springy under Fêng's feet and he became light-hearted. It was as if he had been relieved of a burden and a fragrant breeze were wafted against his fevered senses. . . . The foreigner had ceased to mean anything to him. He was just a peg for a suit of grey flannel. A jabbering peg. Why listen?

"Let us sip green tea under the green trees," said Philip. "How's that for a poetical theme, Miss Tu?"

But Philip Flower was talking to himself. The couple had vanished.

## CHAPTER VI

## *A Solitary Flower*

" I AM not really unsociable," Philip mused, "but the barrier of being British separates me from the Chinese, and I am too Chinese for the foreign community. Moreover I am getting on in years. I came here too late. Had I been able to marry poor Patricia . . ." His thoughts returned to his youth, but he could find nothing to sentimentalize about, not even his cousin Patricia, who had died in a sanatorium during their engagement. An untilled field sloping down to a quicksand of war, a few emotions choked by surrounding thistles—but no passion until he had reached Peking. He loved the city to distraction. Then why did he suffer from these bouts of solitude ?

For nearly an hour since Miss Tu and her companion had left him he had not shifted from his point of vantage, a tea-table under an artificial hillock whence he could contemplate the passers-by. They are passing me by, life is passing me by, he mused, and here I am in the very midst of it.

The tea lay cold and bitter in the cup, a saucer of winking melon-seeds beside it. To and fro the men and women streamed, laughing, talking, joining acquaintances at other tea-tables, like moths, like swallows, like pleasure-seekers at a fair. They seldom looked in Philip Flower's direction. If only somebody would come and sit beside him ! A miracle so easily performed, yet one and all moved on. . . . From his solitary table he ogled them in vain.

The twitter of birds had beguiled him from his books and the old scholar who daily instructed him in the art of Chinese calligraphy. For once those strokes had seemed meaningless, —pitiful sterile devices. For once his carefully organized leisure had palled. Almost he wished that he might lose himself again in the impersonal activity of a London office.

Why blink the fact which his recent encounter had suddenly brought home to him? His Chinese friendships had been a failure. He had been too assiduous, perhaps, in his cultivation of any Chinese that had come his way. I'm just like Elvira, he thought. But that was not true : he was no social seeker after sensations. Drudging at the Chinese Classics, sometimes past midnight with a wet towel about his forehead, always he hoped for new light on the elusive spirit of the Chinese people and new guidance for the direction of his life in the land of his chosen exile. He wanted to meet the Chinese on their own ground and be accepted as one of them. He would have liked nothing better than to be adopted by a Chinese family, and in his reveries he fancied himself performing the Confucian rites, setting forth on Ch'ing Ming, or the Festival of Pure Brightness, to sweep the ancestral graves—forgetting that his nearest, if not dearest of kin, were mostly sepulchred in distant Croydon.

Alas, too often the motives of those Chinese who had taken up the challenge had been narrow and crudely transparent : curiosity about the West, combined with opportunities for practising and polishing their English, rather than a desire to establish any deep enduring sympathy. All his expense of intellectual effort and accumulation of lore had not assisted him in his quest for a Chinese friend. A dilettante he would remain to the scholars of an older generation, while impatient youth eyed him through horn-rimmed spectacles in blank amazement. The idea of anyone wantonly wasting time on the *I Li*, the etiquette and ceremony of the Chou dynasty, in this age of television ! To all and sundry he seemed at best but an amiable crank.

He had had little truck with the foreign community. Elvira served as an occasional contact-maker, and she had startled him about the reports which grazed his blameless bachelordom—rumours of opium and concubines, and since he had been guided by enthusiasm for the Manchu days of yore in his choice of servants, had even been indiscreet enough to boast that his entire staff, including the rickshaw-coolie, was of pure " banner-man " stock, descended from those who had formed the Imperial Household brigade, a recent rumour had gone so far as to endow him with a male seraglio. This had been traced to Poppy Trumper, and Philip Flower was determined to get even with her. Perhaps he should consult Elvira now. But each visit meant picking his way through the malevolent group that hemmed her in—he exaggerated their malevolence—and usually, after he had said his say, he departed feeling like an empty grapeskin. Alone with Elvira, he was apt to talk too much, surrendering unconsciously to her magnetic hunger for the secrets of other souls, he would tell her more about his inner life than he could tell himself. She subtly encouraged these confessions while taking him to task for being so self-centred.

" For a professed Confucianist you sublimate too much," she had said. " Do try to be a trifle more *terre à terre*. Find yourself a fleshly mate, if only for an occasional rough-and-tumble. Fill yourself up with cocktails and forge ahead ! "

" If only I could ! " he murmured helplessly. " I'm afraid it's not in my line. . . ."

" Your line ! " she echoed in tones that seemed to say : " You're not a eunuch, are you ? " Elvira could be disarmingly masculine. " What's in a line ? You mean a groove, I suppose. Nonsense ! I'm waiting to hear of your seduction. I'm not a crystal-gazer, but I can see that it's not far off. Promise you'll tell me all about it when it happens. You know I can be trusted."

But no seduction had occurred. . . .

The scent of green leaves was stabbingly sweet. The park had become an oasis of silence amid the hum of the city, whence hawkers' cries emerged, plangently, distantly, and a single strident horn, as if blown by Neptune from some ocean's coral bed, warned the tent-like houses that the sky was already on fire : the sun would soon be setting, and the upturned roofs would melt in darkening blue. Old men were beginning to escort their birds home, back to the incoherent noise and dust of streets, after inhaling this vegetable vitality. The petals of the peonies were closing.

Perhaps I should join those elders, thought Philip ironically, invest in a singing-thrush or two to keep me company on my excursions.

According to Chinese standards he was already old. Yet he felt he was still in the prime of life. What would he feel like ten years hence, when he began to grow old in earnest ? Philip caught sight of his shadow, appealing against its loneliness.

In the London hurly-burly he had suffered occasional pangs of solitude, but his life had not contrasted so forcibly with those around him. Here he was isolated, and his isolation increased with evening. His precious years were smouldering in a brazier of indifference, which was worse, in the long run, than hostility : more petrifying. But it was too late : this was the life he had chosen ; against death he had selected the site of his tomb in a grove of white pines among the Western Hills. He would never leave Peking.

As if some goddess's eyelash had fallen and been arrested in its flight by a detachment of stars, a fine bright curve of phosphorus, the young moon made her *début*. Philip shivered : the cooler wind penetrated his thin grey suit like a premonition of winter, dead leaves, death. Why was he

81

G

thinking of winter, now that it was spring ? Morbid. He really must be moving.

Outside the park there was a clamour of rickshaw-pullers. He found himself in the midst of a scrimmage for fares, which a policeman tried to settle with his truncheon. The constable gathered momentum and increased in ferocity as he belaboured his less fortunate fellows. One of them was whacked repeatedly ; evidently the petty officer enjoyed exhibiting his earthly powers before the assembled crowd. The coolie merely grumbled. Another whack was followed by a groan. Philip walked briskly up to the policeman, dealt him an effective blow on the chest, and called the staggering brute a turtle's egg. His own man-power vehicle sped him in a trice from the scene of mimic slaughter. A tram outsped him, scattering green sparks from the cables, and he outsped a party of American marines. They sprawled all over their rickshaws, legs a-dangling : happy men, they sang of Dixie at the tops of their voices.

He stopped outside the Tung An Market. Buildings within buildings, it comprises a city in itself, with four main avenues, bazaars and gateways, pullulating, crammed with merchandise. He passed through an alley where the constant click of abacus balls, the clink of coins, the clatter of copper pans merged with mutton-fat, garlic and sesamum oil into a Rabelaisian bouquet which affected all senses simultaneously. Bare torsos were bending over steaming pots. From a restaurant issued gusts of joyous belching. " A bath of multitude "—of the Chinese multitude—this was what Philip's nerves required ; and it was in the theatre that the multitude was most compact. A play was in shrill progress. He hesitated at the door. The beating of the gong decided him. As in a dream he was conducted to a stall in the twelfth row. At first he could only make out blurred shadows of green and scarlet above the rows of craniums. Live figures soon came into focus, figures of warriors magnificently painted, who pranced towards each other, feathers bristling, like super-chanticleers.

Again, with a shock of surprise, he realized what a completely different world the Chinese inhabited. He scrutinized the tense expressions of the audience : yonder he recognized his tailor, transfigured by his absorption in the play, his commonplace features sensitized by strains which, even though Philip had heard them repeatedly, failed to convey more than a strident noise to his own dull tympanum.

Why should such a note hang on like a trapezist, suspended airily at such a moment ? All this remained puzzlingly exterior, outside his instinctive notions of harmony. He knew the story of the play. Yet the queer jerks and quavers of falsetto distracted his mind from it. He remembered the voice of a peasant among the Ming tombs—an oriental counterpart to Wordsworth's solitary Highland lass. For that song had been evocative of " far-off things and battles long ago " ; and the Chinese labourer, too, had sung as if his song could have no ending. Yet Philip could not for the life of him remember the tune ; evidently it had one, but there was nothing, as in an English ballad, to catch hold of. A mysterious rhythm of their own these people possessed, a magic circle into which he could not enter. Sometimes he fancied he had caught the " hang " of it ; then, just as he was beginning to enjoy and possibly to understand, the song would stop, clipped for no reason his ear could discover, and he returned to his bafflement.

Meanwhile the audience in which he longed to merge, vociferated in applause. Why ? As by Miss Tu and her companion, Philip felt he had been left in the lurch. He was determined to catch up. Avidly he concentrated on every gesture. Did this languid boneless body belong to a man ?

He turned to the programme and learned that the name was Yang Pao-ch'in, an actor he had never heard of.

"*Ch'ing wên, shih nan-ti, shih nü-ti?* (May I ask, is it a man or a woman?)"—he asked his neighbour. As usual he had to repeat the question: so few Chinese are ready to believe their ears when addressed by a foreigner in their native tongue. After this unexpected query had been properly digested, his neighbour answered with a hearty guffaw: "Undoubtedly it is a man!" And when, after hiding his face behind yards of sleeve, the actor's eyes first peeped upon the audience, there could be no doubt of it. Perfectly the timid little steps mimicked the gait of a girl whose feet had been pinched into the tiniest of slippers, but those eyes were animated by a hard flame of lasciviousness that was scarcely feminine. "For a' that and a' that, a man's a man for a' that!"—— Perhaps his falsetto was too penetrating to please the audience: much of the applause was ironical. But it was Yang Pao-ch'in's imperfections as an actor that appealed to Philip's imagination—the fact that he retained some accent of virility while giving so plausible an imitation of a young bride. He had a feeling that this youth was an intelligent critic and observer, too intelligent to achieve complete success as a female impersonator: it must be by some mischance that he was now tripping in this faintly ludicrous rôle. Evidently he was trying to make the best of it. His silvery hair-trinkets sparkled; his voice ascended like a rocket, and Philip was stirred by an intense curiosity.

As soon as the play was over he sent the actor his card with a request for an interview. He was an Englishman, he explained, pressing a dollar into an attendant's paw, interested in the Chinese theatre in general and in Yang Pao-ch'in's performance in particular. He was on the verge of retreating in panic, overcome by his own rashness, when the attendant beckoned him to follow. The green-room was packed

84

with mummers in many attitudes, awaiting their turns. One stalked to and fro reciting his lines ; another, throat back, emitted a few acidulous cascades, spat and bubbled on in a clearer key ; aged supers stood about in dingy robes ; a warrior with a scarlet face was sipping tea ; from the sweating mask of live lacquer his eyes rolled glassily at the dapper foreign devil in the light grey suit, a strange and unaccustomed sight, a sparrow from the world of skyscrapers, plunging and pecking his way between these stragglers from China's historical pageant. Philip's nostrils were overpowered by alternate whiffs of musk and burning tallow.

The air was very dense, as in some catacomb lighted by acetylene, for last but not least among the odours was that of garlic. Was a thunderstorm brewing ? The drums on the stage were ominously rumbling. Philip felt shaky about the knees ; his lungs were oppressed nigh to suffocation. The figure briskly fanning himself by a narrow wooden staircase he recognized as Yang. All the softness had gone out of him : he looked stocky, a promising athlete. Now that he was so near the object of his pent-up curiosity he longed to withdraw. His powers of speech were threatening to desert him. This really wasn't in his line ! He halted and gaped at the compact reality : in this saffron light the female impersonator's head appeared to belong to the crudest of freshly painted dolls Triangular patches of peony-pink almost monopolized the face, the rest of which was streaked with a chalk-white so inhuman that it seemed to offer a clue as to why that pigment had been chosen in China for funerals. The finest tributes to dentifrice—and Yang possessed fine teeth—became old ivory in comparison. There was no escaping that smile. Philip bowed : " Have I the honour of addressing Mr. Yang Pao-ch'in ? "

" That is my humble name," the actor replied, with a stiff little bow.

Philip scattered a few ready-made compliments, which cropped like mushrooms out of his subconsciousness. " I enjoyed your performance vastly, even more than Mei Lan-fang's," he said.

" Ai-ya ! You're too polite by far. I am only a poor beginner." The actor smiled with pleasure, and it was no mere lip-smile : dimples and eyes were a lustrous part of it, so charmingly natural that it was an anachronism in that artificial mask. Philip went on to express admiration for his costume.

" Such costumes are mighty expensive. This one costs over five hundred dollars. But it doesn't belong to me : I had to hire it," the actor explained with disarming *naïveté*. In return he praised the foreigner's fluency in the Peking vernacular : he could actually understand every word he was saying ! " You must have spent many years in the Middle Kingdom."

" Not nearly long enough," said Philip. " There are so many things I want to learn. I know very little about the theatre, for instance. After your performance I wished to know more, and I felt that only you could help me. Will you instruct me, Mr. Yang ? "

" I would not dare to be so presumptuous."

" Don't stand on ceremony. I hope you will have time to look me up. My address is printed on this card. When are you free ? Let us make an appointment now."

" I am free the day after to-morrow," Yang replied after some hesitation, " but I fear you will not recognize me without my make-up."

" I would recognize you anywhere," said Philip.

The actor chuckled unexpectedly from the abdomen and bowed him out of the stage-door.

There was a new jauntiness in Philip's step. That brief interview had been a stimulating adventure. But he could not understand how it had all come about. He was amazed at his own urbanity ; as if everything had been prepared in advance his words had issued pat ; and Yang, fingering his printed card, had said yes, the day after to-morrow, so simply. He had forgotten that anything could happen quite so simply.

# CHAPTER VII

## Domestic Interlude

" **M**ASTER come back ? "

Mrs. Mascot was alarmed. Three years had passed since she had set eyes on her consort, three strenuous years of ups and downs, culminating in her lucky transaction with Princess Joachim XVIII of Dummstadt. Evidently he had got wind of her recent *coup* and had come to share the booty. She would have to brazen it out. Not a penny would he extract from her. She refused to look as alarmed as she felt, braced herself and said : " Show Master in."

" Well, here I am ! Home again, my love ! " He surveyed her with bloodshot eyes. " Still your old self, I see." Bluff, loud, cheerful, he might have just padded in from a shower bath.

" This is a pleasant surprise, Dick."

She tried hard to sound matter-of-fact, but certain wrinkles betrayed her anxiety. For Dick was quite capable of putting a spoke in her wheel, which had seldom turned so smoothly.

" Just arrived this morning."

" Where from ? "

" Why ask ? " he maliciously smiled.

" Well, all I can say is, you might have dropped me a line, if only for old sake's sake. It would have been slightly more considerate."

" I wasn't sure of anything up till the last minute, waiting for a windfall. And I know your aversion to wires. How goes it, Deborah ? "

" Hush, Dick, I've changed my name. Deborah never

suited me. I'm Sheila now. It has rejuvenated me no end. Besides, it's more poetical : Sheila ! " She uttered it with a Swinburnian inflection.

" You'll always be Deborah to me, old girl. Mind if I smoke ? "

" If it's a cigar, I do."

Deliberately he bit the end off a fat Havana, pensively he lighted it ; and the flame illumined a face that was full of guile, although, like that of most Old China Hands, it looked as if it had long been soused in hard liquor.

" How's the shop ? " he inquired. He always called a spade a spade. She had to lump it.

" Not doing so well this year. Fewer tourists and greater competition. I have been waiting for a windfall too."

" Poor old Deb ! Sometimes I think the palmy days we knew have gone for ever. It beats me how you can stick in this hole year in year out the way you do. Honestly, you deserve a gold medal."

" Platinum," said Mrs. Mascot.

She was visibly relieved. But if he had not come to touch her for money, what had he come for ?

" It's a hole one wants to return to, all the same," he continued. Mrs. Mascot became anxious again. " I suppose we'll both die in it, and be buried side by side."

" That's comforting," said Mrs. Mascot acidly. " I'm sure you haven't returned on my account."

" Why not ? Let me take a good look at you. Just the same old Deborah. The same sweet smile, same dinky mole on your cheek."

When Dick grew wistful Mrs. Mascot knew she had to keep her wits about her.

" Stop calling me Deborah or I'll scream," she cut in, repelling his impulse to cuddle her. " I suppose you've been drinking. Why must you always drag in the past ? "

Dick Mascot was a material reminder of what she had been, of all she had become. He had served as an efficient stepping-stone. Her memory shunted, as through a series of tunnels, back to her father's vicarage in Gloucestershire. Dick had come to help her pater with the parish. Not the lily-livered curate they had expected, but a tousled, beefy young Christian Socialist. In those days he had yearned to convert the Congo. They had prayed and bicycled together, and fallen in love with each other's vitality.

Their married life had been one of storm and stress, entirely canalized, at first, by zeal to propagate the faith. Dick had so saturated himself in literature about the dark continent that dreaming and waking he was as much haunted by totems and tomtoms and poisoned arrows as a later generation was to be haunted by African jazz. Once she had almost broken off their engagement on this account.

" You must think of me as a gorilla," he had said on that occasion, half squeezing the life out of her. " And I'll think of you as a dear little chimpanzee. It will help us to acclimatize ourselves to jungle conditions."

Deborah was a great devourer of Kipling, and she communicated this enthusiasm to her husband.

Through Deborah's and Kipling's influence Dick's African obsession was superseded by an Asian one. Next he dreamed of converting misguided maharajahs and fakirs : decent Gothic spires would spring where unsavoury temples to Siva had spread their tentacles. . . .

The Reverend Richard Mascot and his wife were to land much farther East ; at last they were called to Peking. It was here that Dick began to question his vocation. He, so proud of his breezy personal magnetism, had made no converts after a year's hard work, and he discovered that his seniors were rarely more successful : in some places their ministrations were limited to salvarsan. If anything, the heathen he came in contact with were more virtuous than his Gloucestershire parishioners : concubinage was at any rate more normal than incest, and he had not encountered a single case of bestiality. He could detect no flagrant vices. Their chief drawbacks seemed due to inertia, conservatism and lack of hygiene. By airing such views he quarrelled with his fellow-workers, whose bread and butter depended on a firm belief in the preponderant sinfulness of Sinim. Things came to a crisis one evening at the Mission. Dick was fond of an argument ; so was their guest, the Bishop of Lu-chou-fu. The argument on this occasion had turned upon the sex of the Almighty, Who, Dick maintained, was bi-sexual. Mrs. Mascot had made matters worse by telling the Bishop's wife that she considered Mary Baker Eddy a modern saint. Both of them had been struck by one particular phrase in Mrs. Eddy's writings : " Will you doff your lavender-kid zeal, and become real and consecrated warriors ? " To this clarion-call they decided to respond. They had had enough of lavender-kid zeal. . . .

For Dick the revolution broke out in the nick of time : he was about to lose his job. His chance had come. A man of action, he dashed into the zone of revolutionary conflict, leaving his spouse behind. Home-life began to irk him, and his intervals of absence became more and more prolonged. Evangelist, gun-runner, dealer in high explosives, adviser to upstart bandit-generals, Dick Mascot had all the material for an exciting autobiography, but he was solely interested in the future. The past was in the cigar he puffed at now and then, in the rings of smoke that drifted away from him.

A fuzzy little dog ran up and sniffed his ankle.

" Another disappointment," sighed Mrs. Mascot ; " the Tibetan lions haven't caught on this year."

" I never imagined the missus was in such a bad way.

Maybe I can come to the rescue. I'll have to think it over. Always the collector, I see. You're a wonder, Deborah. What haven't you collected in your time? I wouldn't recognize the old place. To think we used to take Sunday School in this room!"

And everything, he noted, had been transformed into something practical, old stirrups into ash-trays, gilt idols into standard-lamps. Sections of a Ningpo lacquer bed had been reconstituted as a mantelpiece. Opium-smoking paraphernalia emphasized the exoticism of the central divan; but innocent throat-drops lingered where once the drug had lain. Yes, Deborah was a capable woman: she might yet go far. Having failed to convert the heathen, she had succeeded in converting a ramshackle Chinese compound into what could be described as "a singularly charming freehold residential property," and all on the cheap. He remembered the place when they had first camped in it—the fleas and scorpions and general discomfort; dampness oozing through the walls in summer; the all-penetrating dust at other seasons; the lack of running water. He remembered the cumbersome missionary furniture, the biblical texts in Oxford frames, the oleograph of the Light of the World. It made one rub one's eyes. . . .

While Dick admired the energy behind it all, he would have hated to live in it. He preferred existence in some up-to-date hotel; a lift to whisk him down to the bar, and up to his bedroom; an orchestra to play classical music at dinner and dance music afterwards; the entrances and exits of flotsam and jetsam one could strike acquaintance with; above all, that stimulating sense of flux which had become essential to his enjoyment of life. A house in Peking—no thanks! It was sheer stagnation. One might as well set about preparing one's coffin, like the Chinks. But he would not hurt the missus's feelings.

" A high old spot for a honeymoon," he remarked.
" What about a drink ?  I'm getting thirsty."

Mrs. Mascot ordered some tea.

" I said a drink, not a laxative.  Whisky and soda for me."
Then raising his tumbler, Dick boomed :

" Bung ho !  Here's to the classiest show in Peking and
the brave little woman who runs it."

" It's a flop, so what's the use ?  I've toiled and moiled
and about reached the end of my tether. . . ."

" Nonsense, Deb. Keep up your pecker, my girl. If
there's a fly in the ointment, we've got to turf it out."

" It's because I don't hit it off with the degenerates.
They're getting the run of the place. Take Elvira Mac-
Gibbon ; she keeps open house for them ; they fairly
swarm around her. I dare say she's tarred with the same
brush."

" Times have changed," said Dick, " but people are much
the same. You've still got the missionary touch, Deb.
Perhaps your methods are too obvious, you go at them too
hard. I'll bet they get a wind up when they catch that
gleam in your eye."

Mrs. Mascot fetched a sigh. " I can't compete, I can't
compete," she moaned.

Dick puffed at his cigar in silent speculation. " Eureka ! "
he crowed. " I've found the bug. I've been wondering what
was wrong with this place of yours. It's too much like a
museum. I don't deny its glamour ; but it lacks a *sine qua
non*—I mean conviviality. Why not introduce a human
element ?  Make the eyes of those Buddhas sparkle. Bring
in a few lassies to help you entertain. I could put you in
touch with a pal of mine who specializes in this sort of
thing. . . ."

" What sort of thing ? "

" Don't be dense !  Entertaining globe-trotters. What

else have we been talking about ? You waste too much time on the women. You should concentrate on the males : they're always more generous. Henpecked husbands, most of them, dragged round the world when they'd sooner go round a golf-course."

" Are you proposing that I'm to turn my home into a disorderly house ? "

" I'm not proposing anything. I'm throwing out a suggestion. You may take it or leave it. You can't rely on windfalls, but you can rely on the gratitude of henpecked husbands. You need only provide them with bridge-tables, or the girls could teach 'em mah-jong in tip-top Chinese style. After a sociable and exotic evening it'll be easier to palm off a few souvenirs—apart from the profits on breakages and bubbly. And talking of bubbly, I have some excellent stuff in tow. As agent, I could let you have it dirt cheap. . . ."

" That's all very well, Dick, but I'm afraid we don't see eye to eye."

Mrs. Mascot was an ideologue, but she liked to think that her ideas were respectable. And she liked to think that she was the sole pivot of attraction in her own domain.

" Don't fool yourself," said Dick in a sudden huff. He liked quick decisions. " This place of yours has a future if you'll listen to me. Here you have a fine stage without any actors. A few girls would freshen up your outlook ; and I could help you to get the show started. I've made you a sporting proposition. If you accept it I'll back you to the limit with first-class bubbly. If you don't, I'm through. I've got some mines to attend to in Manchukuo."

" Hadn't we better change the subject ? " said Mrs. Mascot with an affectation of weariness. " You must give me time to think."

Chang came in and announced Mrs. Trumper.

"Lord, is that Poppy? If it is, I'll hop it," said Dick.

"Just rushed in to congratulate you, dear."

Poppy Trumper was near-sighted. She always talked before she saw, and her words jumped breathlessly on top of each other. "You're in the money now. You must be rolling!"

"I don't know what you mean," said Mrs. Mascot.

"Well I never! The turtle-doves together again. A domestic scene. It's like a good old-fashioned romance. Now that you're here, Dick, I hope you'll stay and keep an eye on Sheila. She's far too clever for us all—up to all sorts of tricks. It was simply heartless of you to run away. . . ."

"She seems to have managed pretty well without me."

"You don't know whom you've married, Dick; you've never done justice to your better half. She runs Peking. We're all at her feet. But we've sadly missed excitement since you left us. I'm sure the Martinet would be glad of a pow-wow. He's just in from Paomachang. I'll ring him up instanter."

The Martinet was Archie Trumper.

"I haven't the slightest wish to see the blighter," said Dick, as soon as she was out of earshot. "I'm sick of horse-flesh. About those girls, send me a chit with Yes or No to the Club. So long."

And off he swung before she could detain him, seized his preposterous sun-helmet and was out of the house.

Poppy consoled herself for his flight with the fact that she had News. She could tell Peking she had witnessed the truant missionary's return, had even caught the Mascot pair in an embarrassing position. And when Poppy set news rolling through the foreign community, unlike the rolling stone in the adage, it would gather masses of moss.

# CHAPTER VIII

## A Visit from Yang Kuei-fei

SINCE Philip Flower's encounter with Yang Pao-ch'in, his most casual actions seemed fraught with significance. Last night he had dreamt of high weird pheasant-plumes, and now that he was expecting a visit from the actor he found himself tracing the character for *Hsiao*, the cardinal Chinese virtue of filial piety. The thought struck him, why not adopt a son? He would need a companion in his old age. . . . The brush quivered : his wrist was less steady than usual : he could not concentrate. Why had he never thought of it before? A joyous tremor thrilled him through and through.

The thin dry ticking of the clock insisted that Yang should already be here. What if he failed to turn up? He would have to begin all over again. That fragmentary conversation in the theatre might lead to nothing after all. Philip had nothing tangible to reassure him, whereas Yang at least had his card. Would he recognize the young actor without his make-up? How complete had been his disguise? There could be no mistaking the possessor of those disquietingly small expressive hands, the cynical glitter of those almond eyes. Philip hoped he would appear in a long gown of celestial blue silk : it would form a pleasing contrast with his furniture, the heavy tables and inlaid screens and stiff ebony chairs. His rooms were too austere, like his existence. Yang would introduce a human colour-scheme. . . .

Thus was his fancy roaming when, in brilliant blazer and checked plus fours, his visitor arrived. Yang marched into the room and, instead of bowing, gripped Philip's hand and shook it *con brio*. His hair was closely cropped and the proportions of his face were considerably reduced by enormous horn-rimmed glasses. This was so unlike the visitor his imagination had anticipated that Philip for a moment stood speechless. The mutation from celestial blue silk to checked plus fours had been far too abrupt.

"You were right," said Philip, "I'd hardly recognize you in these clothes."

Yang seemed delighted. "I have put on my first foreign garments to visit my first foreign friend. Do they become me well? Would you take me for an American?"

"I am flattered that you should have put them on for me, but to speak truth, I would prefer you in Chinese clothes. Were I not English I should never wear anything but Chinese clothes myself."

"You must be joking!"

"I assure you I am not."

"Well, I have plenty of Chinese clothes, but I only possess one foreign suit. I thought you would like to see me in it. Besides, now that the weather is neither hot nor cold, this is far more convenient, and it's in the very latest fashion, isn't it?"

"I suppose it is," said Philip tactfully. "I know nothing about the latest fashions. But why do you wear spectacles?"

Beneath the horned bridge his nose looked absurdly small, like the bone of a humming-bird. Behind the lenses his sharp eyes glittered like beads of black amber.

"Because I want to be modern."

"It's a pity to spoil such eyes. We foreigners only wear them when we cannot see without."

But Yang was unwilling to remove them. "My best photograph," he continued, "was taken in foreign costume: I had to borrow it for the occasion." He rummaged in his

97

H

pocket-book and handed Philip a picture-postcard. It portrayed him in full evening dress, sitting in a cathedral chair that might have been designed by Pugin. His bright infant's face had almost disappeared into a stiff high collar such as was worn by pioneer bicyclists. The left hand had been thrust into a trouser pocket to look *dégagé*, the right sleeve had been jerked back to display a liberal expanse of cuff, while the starched shirt-front bulged like the breast of a pigeon and vivid clocks claimed attention to the socks.

" A splendid photograph," Philip agreed.

" My teacher has an enlargement in beautiful colours. You would never guess it was a photograph. Some day you must see it. Some day I hope to buy a suit like this. But it costs so much money. . . ."

Philip fancied he heard a sigh, but soon the boy cheered up and asked : " Have you got one, too ? "

" It has probably fallen to pieces by now—so many years have passed since I have worn it."

" Do show it to me, please," Yang implored.

This will never do, thought Philip. A bad beginning, a bad beginning. But he sent a puzzled servant to fetch his tails, which had long been buried in a camphor chest. He also ordered tea.

" Do foreigners drink tea ? I thought they always drank brandy (*po-lan-ti-chiu*) ! "

" I am only half a foreigner," said Philip.

" How's that ? "

" My body is foreign but my soul is Chinese. I have lived so long in Peking that I am fast forgetting the customs of my native land. Those of the Middle Kingdom are far more sensible, in my opinion."

Yang smiled incredulously. He knew better. Everything that was foreign must be good. Of course he was too polite to contradict his host. He was an ardent votary of the foreign

98

cinematograph, which had opened his eyes to a Western world quite as marvellous as that of the *Hsi Yu Chi*. Indeed each visit to the films was like T'ang San Tsang's pilgrimage to the West, but instead of Buddhist scriptures he brought back visions of Tarzan and Frankenstein, of rodeos and sky-scrapers. There was not a little of Sun the Monkey in Yang's composition. It was under the inspiration of Harold Lloyd that he had procured his goggles.

" How long, then, have you been in China ? " he asked.

" Fifteen happy years. And this year promises to be even happier."

Yang was quick of comprehension. Nevertheless, with feigned *naïveté*, he asked Philip why.

Philip could barely restrain an impulse to hug him.

" Because I have found a certain young friend who is as charming as he is clever. And his name is Yang Pao-ch'in."

" I am unworthy," said the boy. " But after fifteen years of absence, won't you soon be going back to your family ? "

" I have no family," said Philip. " I am alone in the windy dusty world."

Yang thought this very strange. " You mock me," he said. " In England you have a wife and many sons and grandsons."

" Indeed I do not deceive you. I am alone."

Yang pondered a minute. " If you go back, you will take me with you, won't you ? "

So earnest was the tone of this supplication that Philip was disarmed. " Perhaps," he said. " But why should you ever wish to leave Peking ? You may travel far and wide, but you will never find a city so beautiful, so complete. As soon as you leave it, you will long to return."

" I'm sure I shan't. I never think of Peking, except that I want to get out of it and see the world. . . . Mei Lan-fang returned from America full of riches and honours : without passing any examinations he was even made a ' Promoted Scholar.' Perhaps the same good fortune will come to me."

" You must first make a name for yourself in China," said Philip. " Peking is the home of Chinese theatrical art."

Yang was not listening. He did not appear to be interested in Chinese theatrical art.

" Have you any pictures to show me of Western lands ? "

" I'm not sure that I have, but I'll investigate."

He managed to produce some old copies of *The Illustrated London News*. Yang was enchanted with them. He scanned each page, each picture, firing off questions which were none too easy to answer. These pictures of ski-ing, of parachutes, the Lord Mayor's Show, ice-hockey, cathedrals, dreadnoughts, exploding shells, power-stations, airwomen, champion swimmers, coal-mines, and Queen Mary handing the traditional leek to the Welsh Guards on St. David's Day, these advertisements even—how interpret the significance of Johnnie Walker still going strong ?—each required such a wealth of explanation that Philip became more and more involved in his efforts to simplify the various technicalities concerned. He began to see these things as he had never seen them before. The pages he had turned so casually became extraordinary documents of Western enterprise, invention and achievement, and of the sports and conventions which accompanied them. He was suddenly amazed to think that he, Philip Flower, belonged to a race of such energy and organizing genius : it was portentous. He marvelled as Yang marvelled at the vastness and complexity of this world reflected in *The Illustrated London News*. His head swam, his eyes ached, and he felt utterly insignificant, a wayside weed.

What was he doing, explaining to a Chinese boy these things he had never explained to himself ? Should not the sight of them impel him to instant action ? But then what sort of action ?

He sat like a child listening to thunder. The thunder was distant, thank God ; and he soon emerged from his brainstorm. When he thought of the private lives of these " enterprising men, restless in the search for new industries, alert to the march of invention and quick to realize their opportunities and to profit by changes of fashion," and then of the gingko in his courtyard to which he could turn so easily, with which he could almost converse, he was quite satisfied to remain where he was, a gentle nonentity. The pages of *The Illustrated London News* clouded over like those portions of an X-ray photograph which spell disease. To Yang, however, they were the vehicle of fabulous daydreams ; he ski'd and parachuted and played ice-hockey and climbed cathedrals while gazing at the paper reproductions ; he was splashing across the Channel when tea was brought in.

" If you would prefer brandy, I have some," said Philip, " but you must promise me not to leave a drop in your glass."

" I should like to know what it tastes like."

At sight of the tumbler he was alarmed, but his eyes declared : " I'm game." Philip poured out an infinitesimal quantity. Yang sipped it and puckered up his face.

" Ai, but it's hot ! " he exclaimed, " it tickles the tongue and throat, it burns the lungs ! "

" Mind you keep your promise," said Philip with mock severity.

Yang took a gulp and began to giggle. Then the long-neglected tails arrived in invisible clouds of camphor. Yang examined them as if they were python ceremonial robes of the T'ang dynasty, caressed them with his fingers. His eyes were gleaming with a strange soft light. At last he said : " Will you allow me to try them on ? "

" On one condition."

The actor looked upset.

" That you remove those monstrous spectacles."

This interview was getting out of hand. Things were not shaping themselves as Philip had expected. Not at all ! Curiouser and curiouser, he muttered. He watched the actor wriggle into his old tail-coat, which of course was much too big for him. Nevertheless he was pleasantly exhilarated, wondering what his young friend would do next. It suddenly occurred to Yang that a top-hat was necessary to complete the costume. Philip only possessed an antiquated opera-hat, but Yang urged him to rout it out. The collapsibility of this quaint headgear compensated for its lack of lustre ; after bouncing it up and down a few times Yang cocked it on his head, which it fitted to perfection. Either the brandy or the hat, perhaps the combination of both, had intoxicated him : Yang cleared his throat and began to trill.

Never had Philip's quiet study heard such piercing strains. The very tassels on the lanterns trembled, and Philip dropped his tea-cup. Sparks flickered before his eyes ; his ears were on fire ; his insides were melting away. One of his servants standing by the door forgot himself so far as to ejaculate " *Hao* "—Bravo !—and fled in fear of a scolding.

Completely oblivious of his whereabouts the young actor was posturing in a dance. The coals of his irises blazed in a mask of abstract passion. This was another Yang—Kuei-fei, the most artful of China's four historical beauties. Had the imperial favourite ever foreseen that one afternoon she would be transmigrated into a young actor clad in such outlandish togs ? Here was a transmigration of body as well as of soul. While Philip watched this figure swaying and drooping to subtle wine-laden rhythms in high falsetto, he forgot the alien clothes : the tails had become long silken sleeves and the opera hat a tiara of quivering kingfisher's feathers. He was in the Pavilion of a Hundred Flowers. Then the dancer drooped down to the carpet ; the song was ended, the vision shattered. The brief period of Kuei-fei's transmigration was over : Harold Lloyd's admirer sat breathless and panting on the floor.

So swift was the transition from the T'ang Dynasty to the Machine Age that Philip was tempted to believe in witchcraft. Was this boy a medium, possessed now and then by beauties dead and gone ? Forgetting that he was a boy, Philip helped to raise him from the floor and poured him out a cup of tea. Yang mopped his forehead and smiled a far-away smile. The smile changed focus, became roguish. The eyes too, as they surveyed him interrogatively, were the eyes of some sinister little animal, ardent and egoistic.

" Is it true that you never wear this costume ? " he inquired.

" Why should I ? " said Philip, " it is neither comely nor comfortable."

" Will you give it to me ? "

Philip was somewhat taken aback, but he nodded. "Since it seems to afford you so much pleasure. . . ."

" The hat also ? "

" Oh thank you, thank you ! And now I am afraid I shall have to leave you."

" So early ? That's hardly fair, you know. You have told me nothing about yourself, absolutely nothing ! There are so many things I wish to hear. I feel that we might still be strangers."

" It is getting late. At six o'clock I have to eat my rice."

" Why don't you stay and sup with me ? "

" My teacher is expecting me. As it is, I have not thought of an excuse. You see, he does not know that I am here."

" Why didn't you tell him ? "

Yang hesitated before replying. He was obviously embarrassed.

" My teacher would not like me to become acquainted with foreign . . ." He was about to add " devils " but paused in the nick of time.

" Surely it won't matter if you return a bit late ? "

" My teacher is very strict. He will punish me. Besides, I shall get no rice unless I arrive on time."

" Punish you ?  How ? "

" He will beat me."

" At your age !  How old are you, by the way ? "

" Seventeen."

" Old enough to be my son !  Well, how are you going to account for the suit I have given you ? "

" I shall have to conceal it."

" Then it won't be much use to you, will it ? "

" Later on I can pretend that I borrowed it, and then, after I have worn it a few times, he will forget about it. He forgets everything in the end."

" Won't this make it difficult for you to visit me again ? Now that you know where I live, I should like you to come and see me often."

" I am hardly ever free.  My teacher is so strict.  He is just like a father to me. . . ."

" I am sure it could be managed if I go and call on him."

Yang was unable to write, so Philip went to his desk and jotted down the teacher's name and address.  The ideograph for " filial piety " caught his eye.  A son. . . .  He looked at Yang and wondered.

Yang had an afterthought.  " Would you please lend me one of those foreign illustrated papers ? "

" You may take the lot," said Philip.

What would he ask for next ?

" You are very kind.  I shall look at them to-night before I go to sleep and think of all the things you told me and of this happy afternoon ;  then I shall have wonderful dreams.

My teacher smokes opium. These will be my opium. While he lies smoking I shall be wandering through the streets of great Western capitals among crowds of red-haired people with bright blue eyes. And even if they stare at me I shall not mind. I have been thinking, sir, what a pity it is that your hair is not red and that your eyes are not blue."

" Why ? You surprise me more and more."

" Because I had always imagined most foreigners were thus, and I wanted to get accustomed to it. Perhaps it is true what you said : you are only half a foreigner."

Swept by emotion at these words, Philip clasped Yang to his breast and implanted a fervent kiss on his close-cropped cranium.

" You are a foreigner after all," said Yang. " That is not a Chinese habit. Do you really like me very much ? "

" I suppose I do," said Philip.

" Aren't you sure ? "

" That depends on how you behave. Will you let me keep your photograph ? "

Yang was reluctant to part with such a precious record of himself in all his Western glory, but Philip reminded him that he had not kept his promise to finish the brandy.

" I should like something much better than this, but it will have to suffice until you give me one in Chinese dress. You can tell your teacher that you have met a foreigner capable of instructing you in the art of writing Chinese characters."

" He will not believe it."

A happy inspiration. Philip put the character *Hsiao* into an envelope and said : " Then give him this with my compliments. And if he remains sceptical, tell him he may come and watch me while I wield the ink-brush."

" My teacher," said Yang, " is only impressed by good dinners."

Philip noted the plural. "I shall invite him entirely for your sake."

Yang took his leave with the suit wrapped up in a parcel. What a world of unnecessary complication the Chinese lived in ! Nothing was ever direct : always the roundabout way. However Chinese Philip fancied he had become, this disdain of short and simple cuts exasperated him, though he would have been the last to admit it and so betray the Anglo-Saxon bedrock of his character. He consoled himself by reflecting that nothing worth while was easily attained. Though he had failed, in Elvira's pet phrase, to get in touch with Yang Pao-ch'in's vibrations, he was not altogether disappointed. His ears had been opened to the beauty of Chinese music. He examined Yang's photograph : it was as baffling as the Sphinx, as the smile of Mona Lisa. The stocky youth with close-cropped hair was hard to reconcile with the delicate beauty he had become, full of strange feminine ardour. Mere theatrical skill and a strenuous training failed to account for the mystery.

Philip's ruminations were disturbed by Yang's brisk re-appearance. But he had only come back because he had forgotten the opera-hat.

## CHAPTER IX

### *Philip Dines Out*

PHILIP FLOWER was wont to sup on Vita-weat and malted milk and retire to bed at nine. "Plain living and high thinking" was his motto. But if he was ever to adopt Yang he foresaw that he would have to make certain concessions, at least in so far as plain living was concerned. Without the co-operation of Yang's teacher he would achieve nothing, and the teacher was partial to good dinners : neither Vita-weat nor malted milk would fit into this category.

Mr. An responded readily to Philip's invitation. Since the Englishman professed ignorance of Chinese culinary matters he asked Mr. An to choose his favourite restaurant and order his favourite dishes in advance. They met in an upper room of the "Unbounded Virtue and Felicity" restaurant, every detail of which, from the tea-pot with the purple pansy on it to the strawberry-pink spittoons, impressed itself indelibly on Philip during the half-hour he had to twiddle his thumbs before his guest's arrival. Mr. An was not in the least apologetic for having kept his host waiting.

Clad in a time-worn gown of claret silk and a round black satin cap with a bead of coral on top, his aspect was picturesque but far from prepossessing. A semi-wen demi-mole on his dewlap, whence trailed a thick long wisp of hair, imparted a goatish character to his head of pock-marked mahogany. His cadaverous form bulged unexpectedly at the paunch. And his frequent expectoration, in spite of loud warnings from the preliminary clearance of his gullet, was very trying to the nerves : Philip always had a hygienic

horror of human spray. Nor was Mr. An a genial guest.
He disdained the warm wine with which Philip replenished
his cup ; on the other hand he did ample justice to the sharks'
lips, bears' claws, orchidaceous tripe and other dainties that
appeared in rapid succession. So fast and so furiously did he
gobble these down that it did not look as if he would ever
cross the meridian of polite platitude to float on the lagoon
of friendly conversation. He congratulated Philip on his
capable manipulation of chopsticks and came to the rescue
when delicacies were evasive, but he manifested no inclination
to broach the subject which had brought them to the restaurant of " Unbounded Virtue and Felicity." Instead he subjected Philip to an intensive catechism. So Mr. Flower had
not come to China on business of any kind ? He had no
offices in Peking, no affiliations with the British Embassy ?
Mr. An failed to understand why a foreigner should choose
to live so far from the land of his ancestors without some
remunerative occupation ; surely there must be something up
his sleeve. Though he knew well enough that Philip took
an interest in his pupil and even guessed that he must
have some proposal at the back of his mind, he decided
to keep away from the subject until his curiosity was fully
satisfied.

" So you live here merely for pleasure ? " he asked in
incredulous tones.

" For pleasure and instruction," said Philip. " If ever I am
allotted another existence, in a future reincarnation, I hope
that Peking will be my birthplace."

Mr. An grinned ironically.

" By then it will cease to be recognizable," he retorted.
" It is changing rapidly from day to day, and not for the
better. . . ."

" I agree that it is not for the better," said Philip, " but so
long as Coal Hill and the White Dagoba stand, I think I shall

recognize the ancient capital, and love it if only for the sake
of what it was."

This launched Mr. An on a sententious oration. Philip
had often listened to its like : the virtue of China was exhausted ; Mr. An could only see perdition ahead ; only the
faces of the younger generation were Chinese, their hearts . . .

" Are the hearts of Western barbarians," concluded Philip,
somewhat to Mr. An's surprise. " I believe that I am more
of a son of Han than they ! ' "

But a sense of humour was not among Mr. An's attributes.
As if his host's remark were the last straw that breaks the
camel's back he fetched a sigh of infinite melancholy, shook
his head, and helped himself to another spoonful of luscious
sea-slugs. There was no further discourse till Mr. An rent
the air with appreciative belches. The dinner was over
without a reference to Yang. Mr. An gargled and rinsed his
mouth into a spittoon and then said curtly : " Thank you.
I must be off. See you some other day."

Although he had but pecked at snippets, Philip left the
restaurant feeling bloated. Resentfulness followed discouragement as he stood stirring bicarbonate of soda in his
bedroom. Confound the man, why had he not come to the
point ? Some other day, forsooth ! Philip wilted at the
prospect of more " good dinners."

Soon, however, Mr. An became a frequent caller at Philip's
house. Too soon. Next morning at half-past seven he sat
smoking a cigarette in Philip's study. Philip strained every
nerve to be civil after a sleepless night. They exchanged
remarks about the weather and their respective state of health,
and Mr. An revealed that he had not visited the privy for a
week. Philip suggested a simple remedy, but Mr. An had
no opinion of Western medicine. He believed in nature
taking her course. Some of his friends, he said, were even
longer " absentees " ; as yet the heat of his intestines did not

greatly perturb him ; in another week's time perhaps it would . . .

Philip's expressions of polite concern were rewarded with a promise that Mr. An would do him the honour of rejoining him that self-same night for dinner. In view of his costiveness Mr. An suggested that they should dine on lenten-fare at the restaurant of " Abundant Merit." Concerning Yang he remained provokingly reticent. He took his leave with a polite " pray don't bother to accompany me to the door." Philip returned to his beloved bath with a sigh of relief and lay there soaking until his troubles all seemed to dissolve. Later he was astonished to discover that Mr. An was still on the premises, chatting familiarly with his servants, who seldom had much else to do. The teacher was determined to find out all he could about Philip before entering into negotiations.

That evening Mr. An broke the ice. Evidently his curiosity had been sated. " So little Pao-ch'in has taken your fancy ! That's scarcely to be wondered at. I have brought him up from the age of seven. The lad has a fine voice. Never a false note, never out of harmony. And his movements, so graceful ! How he can twirl a spear ! You haven't seen him in a military rôle, have you ? Oh, he will be a star yet, one of the first magnitude. You may take my word for it. . . ."

" I do, Mr. An, but you must forgive me for suggesting that others may not. The audience did not go wild when I heard him in public."

" He has now reached the most critical stage of his development," declared Mr. An, " and his voice is somewhat unequal. Mine was too at his age."

" Yours, Mr. An ? I did not realize that you were an actor."

" I might have been the foremost of the Pear Orchard ; in female rôles I could have made my fortune. But in those days it was not considered a gentleman's profession. My father was a duke. So I was forced to remain an amateur."

" *Noblesse oblige*," said Philip, breaking into French. "Then you are a Manchu ! Why didn't you tell me so before ? "

The fact that Mr. An was a Manchu changed Philip's attitude completely. His exterior ceased to seem unprepossessing : Philip already began to view it through rose-coloured spectacles. He noted the distinguished hands, the long literary nails.

" I should have guessed you were a Manchu from your unusual name. You behold a great admirer of the Manchu dynasty and race, Mr. An."

" A man is not always known by his looks, nor the sea measured by a bushel," he observed complacently. " My misfortunes began with smallpox. Then came the revolution. My family lost everything ; what we did not lose was embezzled by Chinese stewards. I knew nothing of finance, since we were brought up to consider ourselves above material things and depended on the Emperor's bounty. I could only turn to the theatre for a living. My voice was very fine, so fine that my face did not matter. It is still worth listening to. Yes, even now."

To prove it he sent for a two-stringed fiddle. Rare is the restaurant without this light and potent instrument. Mr. An passed the bow between the two strings. After tuning it to his satisfaction, his falsetto soared through the matchboard wall partitions. The diners in adjacent rooms stopped their shrill clamour. He sang the air of Princess Yü from " Pa Wang's Parting with his Favourite " :

> " *Within the tent my lord is sleeping in his coat of mail.*
> *I shall creep out alone to soothe my sorrow.*
> *Softly I move, and pause beneath the stars,*
> *And start to see the icy wheel above.*

*The clouds roll slowly by till heaven is clear,*
*The moon swells like a wave upon the night.*
*Ah, splendour of this night of tranquil autumn !* "

Philip was deeply moved by the tragic power of this old music.

"The other day Yang sang to me from ' Kuei-fei Drunk with Wine ' : it was a revelation. Now I can understand why he sang so well. At best he is but an echo of his wonderful master ! "

"You do me too much honour ! "

"I am not exaggerating. That your diction should excel your pupil's goes without saying. But your voice also surpasses his. Even if I never hear it again I shall feel indebted to you. While there is such music in China none can complain that the virtue of China is exhausted."

"You may be right." Mr. An scratched his head. "Sometimes I think Yang is not progressing as he should. . . ."

Here is my chance, thought Philip. If he is not cut out for a stage career, what objection can there be to my adopting him ? But I must move warily. It isn't the moment yet to show my hand.

As if he were reading Philip's thoughts, Mr. An's physiognomy was lit by a portentous leer. "But he will never become a star," he added, " if his mind is taken off his work. He must stick to his present régime. . . ."

"Even so he needs some relaxation now and then. Who doesn't ? " Philip tried to render "All work and no play will make Jack a dull boy " in the vernacular ; having failed, he said : "A change of air, you know."

"Every morning early he must exercise his vocal chords at the Temple of Heaven. That gives him all the air he needs."

"I fear you are a hard taskmaster, Mr. An."

" I have to be," he replied with a chuckle. " I do not want to see my efforts wasted."

Nor did Philip. Entertaining Mr. An was distinctly an effort. He was about to let the whole thing drop and return to plain living and high thinking when he received a message from Mr. An, requesting his company at dinner. Since this was Mr. An's first invitation and the dinner was to be given at a private residence he decided, mainly out of curiosity, to accept. Perhaps Yang would be there.

He was surprised to find that the residence was in Tudor style. Mr. An came out to welcome him at a lych-gate reminiscent of an English churchyard. " This is not my humble abode, nor is it that of my friend and former pupil Mr. Wang Chin-hsin, who is holding this banquet in my honour," he explained, introducing him to a matronly figure in dove-grey silk who glided forward with cere-monious salutations.

Philip had only seen him on the stage. His celebrity would have equalled Mei Lan-fang's except that he had never been abroad. As one of China's leading interpreters of feminine rôles, his name was a byword for all the charm and extrava-gance coupled with the profuse strains of an art which had been premeditated for generations and brought to perfection by himself. When that art was not specifically concerned, it was apt to be pronounced with an ambiguous smile. For the mosquito press made the utmost of every malicious zephyr touching this hero-heroine of the buskin : if two generals came to blows outside the theatre where Wang was performing (as indeed they did), they were represented as having battled with regiments behind them ; a daring theft of pearls from Wang's Shanghai residence was magnified by journalists into a theft of something far more precious than concretions of the succulent bivalve. Wang's life had not only been threatened by gangs of terrorists. Ever since he

I

was kidnapped from a scissors-grinder at the age of four it had maintained a consistent level of lurid melodrama. But all this defied credulity when you were confronted by the avuncular blandness of the double-chinned protagonist.

" Really, Mr. An, you should have told me about this beforehand. I had not the faintest idea that such a celebrity was to be my host this evening. Being a nonentity myself, I don't feel comfortable."

" My friends are Mr. Wang's friends. When he heard about my new English friend, remembering the words of the Sage—' If friends come from afar, should we not rejoice ? ' —he begged me to invite you."

Although Philip was disappointed not to see Yang, he could congratulate himself in one respect. In this respect he was definitely a snob. His bosom swelled with pride and pleasure at the thought that he alone should have been singled out from the foreign community in Peking for invitation to this banquet. I am not looked upon as a foreigner, he reflected.

Some of the party were peeling fruit, others were sipping tea. Before all formal Chinese dinners there is a heavy atmosphere of fumbling and uncertainty, and this waiting for guests who have scant sense of time provokes innumerable platitudes. Cocktails, however deleterious to the constitution, have helped to solve the pre-prandial problems of Westerners ; punctuality, too often pronounced a bourgeois virtue, has also helped. Mr. An told Philip that the house belonged to a lady known as *Hsiao Hsi Shih*, one of the most famous of Peking's professional beauties, and that Wang had rented it for this single dinner-party, disbursing a thousand dollars for the privilege.

" Surely Mr. Wang possesses a mansion of his own ? "

" Many mansions ! But it saves trouble to get the prettiest woman in Peking to act as his hostess."

So far as he could see she was the only woman in the room, and she impressed Philip as brazen rather than beautiful, as if she were capable of clinching a very hard bargain. There was a five minutes' ordeal of polite pushing and scrambling before everyone was settled at the dinner-table. Wang and Hsiao Hsi Shih sat at the other extremity from Philip, after pouring wine for their neighbours. Mr. An did the honours for his vicinity. Philip sat on his left, and while he was glowing at the prospect of a purely Chinese evening— he had refurbished quite a thesaurus of polite formulas and literary phrases in anticipation—his other neighbour yapped out : " I guess we haven't been introdooced : I'm Mr. Lincoln Pan, of 'Frisco. Mighty glad to have you know me."

Philip's face fell. He had seen this person at Elvira's and had purposely avoided him. An epitome of all that was nasal, even if he was not chewing gum his mouth gave an impression of chewing it, and his hair stood back in quills like a pomaded porcupine. Mr. Pan divulged that it was he who took care of the famous actor's publicity and foreign investments.

" So you're genu-winely interested in our theatrical busi-ness—honest injun ? " he added.

" I am profoundly interested in your theatrical art."

" Say, who's the gal ? "

Seeing that his question and wink were disregarded and that Philip stared frigidly ahead of him, Mr. Pan concluded he must be deaf. As through an ear-trumpet he shouted : " Funny we never got acquainted before. Peking's so social, if you know what I mean. I just can't make it out."

" Try a little of this," said Mr. An, helping him to a gelatinous mass of what resembled frog-spawn. " It will fortify you for the pleasures of life. At our age we need fortifying."

Did Philip look so decrepit ?    Since advanced years would account for his desire to adopt Yang, he did not protest.

" We must be about the same age, you and I," he continued.    " What is your honourable age ? "

Philip hummed and hawed over his calculations, trying to make out under which of the twelve animals he was born. He decided it was under the sign of the Rabbit.    As Mr. An had first seen light under the sign of the Tiger, he was delighted.    This augurs well, he thought ; the Rabbit is overcome by the Tiger.    And Philip was thinking : why not humour them, these sweet old superstitions ?

Though more dishes accumulated in bewildering profusion, Mr. An dedicated himself to gormandizing unabashed : his chopsticks were everywhere.    Mr. Pan played " fist-game " ; voices soon became strident.    The dense air seemed to have a hectic flush.    Girls began to trickle in, and Mr. Pan greeted each arrival with cheers and war-whoops.

" Is there any particular dame you would like to send for ? " he asked Philip.    " I guess you must be feelin' lonesome."

" I am afraid no dame would make much difference to me."

" Well, if you care for any of these, just tip me the wink. A rendezvous can quickly be arranged.    I'm always ready to oblige a friend."

Philip noted with approbation that the turn of each beauty was brief ;  a substitute for liqueurs, a fragrant aid to digestion, so evocative, so subtle !    Either she exploded into song —five minutes in an aviary—or perched beside her admirer like a parakeet.    For women in China still have a tendency to assume ornithological forms.    Even when their feet have not been subjected to compression, they do not appear to walk with ease : earthbound spirits, you feel it would be more natural for them to fly.

*Mao-mao Yü* (" Delicate Drizzle ") was the popular ditty of the evening.    The words were sentimental.    A girl is awaiting her lover in wind and rain. " Ah," she sighs, " how green are the budding willows ! I do not want your gold, my dear ; I do not want your silver, dear. I only want your heart "—a desire which, since the singer's price was notoriously high, evoked much merriment. And when the song was repeated, it was here that many joined the chorus,

*Hsiao ch'in-ch'in, pu yao ni-ti chin.*
*Hsiao ch'in-ch'in, pu yao ni-ti yin.*
*Nu-nu chih yao ni-ti hsin.*
*Ai-ya-ya, ni-ti hsin !*

" Perhaps he is ill," she falters ; " Perhaps he has met with some calamity. What am I to do ? " In the last stanza, of course, the lover turns up—the song ends with her joyful exclamation upon his appearance.

Almost an English ballad, thought Philip, when it is translated—" Cold blows the wind on my true love. And a few small drops of rain "—" Green grow the willows, o ! "——

Yet how thoroughly transmuted in the singing ! All sentiment was stripped from it. Incredible that the words should be so sentimental, incredible that gramophone records of this naïf ditty should be forbidden !

" I can't listen to that without getting hot all over," said Mr. Pan. " I guess that's why the local government has gone and banned it, 'cause it makes the boys so hot. Say, Mr. Flower, do you like our Chinese gals ? . . . Maybe you find them a bit phlegmatic. Most foreigners do. That's simply because they don't know the right way to get around them, even when they know the lingo. It needs a special vocabulary I'm telling you ! Soft words, words of passion, are required to make red-hot mommers of 'em. For instance—shall I teach you a few flaming words of passion, Mr. Flower ? "

Mr. Pan's long submersion in the U.S.A. seemed to have melted that reserve which is almost a racial trait. His tongue behaved like a carburettor. While he was offering Philip unsolicited advice on the technique of a Chinese love-affair, which differed not a whit from the generality of such transactions, Mr. An was offering him snuff. He sprinkled it from a crystal bottle on a tiny ivory saucer. Philip levelled it to his nostrils and sniffed.

"Where is Yang?" he demanded, after a thorough sneeze.

"He has gone with a troupe from the school to Shanghai."

"When do you expect him back?"

"That depends on their success."

Suddenly Philip realized that he had ceased to enjoy himself and that he did, as Mr. Pan had suggested, feel lonesome. The sirens were goading their gallants to eat and drink more; the one on Mr. Pan's knee had seized his chopsticks, and with a lot of spilling and giggling was popping small black mushrooms into his mouth. The fringe which nearly concealed her eyes reminded Philip of Mrs. Mascot's Lhasa lions.

Neat piles of silver dollars were stacked in front of the host. Each singing girl was presented with five of these ere she departed leaving a trail of scent behind her, and each accompanist with one. The piles never seemed to diminish. But Philip had had enough of this entertainment; thus far but no further. He vowed that unless Yang's teacher began to exert himself on his behalf he would have nothing more to do with him.

The final flakes of rice had been shovelled down; the guests had risen; many took their departure, in Chinese fashion, immediately after dinner. Philip looked for Mr. An, but he had vanished.

"Is there anything I can do for you?" piped Mr. Pan.

Philip explained that he wished to say a few parting words to the old teacher.

" I guess he's having his smoke. Just follow me."

Mr. Pan opened an imitation wardrobe which led into a small adjoining den. It was pervaded with an aroma like burnt caramel, and monopolized by a massive *k'ang* or heatable brick couch. And on that couch, twisting the tip of a long needle over a small blue flame, was Yang. Beside him the teacher reclined, eyes glued to the needle, watching the brown pellet as it was kneaded, watching it sizzle and swell. But it was not docile yet : Yang had to knead it again in his palm before the teacher could inhale. They were far too preoccupied to notice the intruders.

Philip was struck dumb by the quiet intensity of the scene. He felt he was intruding on some secret rite. Mr. An ingurgitated with such ferocious concentration that the bamboo pipe looked as if it must follow the opium into his lungs. When, with a spasm and grunt of satisfaction, he had extracted the quintessence of the drug, his glazed eyes roved, languid and remote, and settled on the foreigner. Almost too spiritual to look at a mortal, he smiled benignantly. But Yang vouchsafed no sign of recognition.

" So Yang returned from Shanghai while we were eating our dinner," said Philip. " His season must have been brief. I hope that doesn't mean it was a failure."

Mr. An placed a phosphorescent hand on the boy's head. " Little Yang has a filial nature. He played truant, since he could not bear to be parted from his teacher. Forgive me, will you smoke ? "

For a moment Philip was tempted to recline and be ministered to by the actor, inhaling the drug and losing himself in visions of China under the Empress Dowager. But he was angry with Mr. An, and angry with himself for being fooled. Besides, having had no experience of opium, he feared it might make him vomit. Already the stale fumes were beginning to affect him after the gargantuan meal : he was feeling queasy and a little faint.

" No thanks," he said, " I've come to say goodbye. It has been an unforgettable evening. Good-bye, Yang. I doubt if we shall ever meet again."

Mr. An's languor left him with a jerk. He sat up, sobered and perplexed. But Philip did not give him time to ask questions. Through the imitation wardrobe he retreated with Mr. Pan, who whistled athwart his teeth.

" So that's why you are interested in the Chinese theatre ! "

" You're quite a detective, aren't you ? "

" One doesn't have to be. Back of most everything in life there's a simple human cause."

" Well, then, a psychologist."

" I should say I am, sir, being in the theatrical business. Maybe I can give you a word or two of advice. I'll grant you that Yang's a pretty good kid. He's quick as lightning; always picking up ideas. But as an actor he's a flop. He'll never catch on."

"I don't follow your argument, if he's as quick as you say."

" He's got no stage-allure, Mr. Flower, no personality. Even on the stage of old Cathay it's personality that's half the battle."

" You amaze me. Yang's personality struck me as his principal asset."

" Off stage, perhaps. His heart isn't in the business. Mr. Wang swears there's nothing to be done with him, and Mr. Wang is invariably right."

" Mr. An assured me he was a rising star. And Mr. An, as his teacher, ought to know."

" Banana oil ! The old man's going blind."

Philip began to take a liking to Mr. Pan. Just now he found his crudity refreshing.

" You'll think me a sentimental old duffer," he confided, " but I was drawn to Yang the moment I set eyes on him. He appealed to my imagination. I'd do anything for him. Don't ask me why : I hardly know myself ! I suppose it's because he is a living symbol of China, and I'm in love with China."

" It does me good to hear you say that, Mr. Flower. I wish more foreigners felt that way. You are in the minority."

" China has cured all my ills. During the war my life became a desert. And Peking has made it blossom as the peony. Well, I really must be off. I have enjoyed our little chat. But before I go, Mr. Pan, perhaps you will explain something which has been puzzling me all the evening— Mr. An's attitude towards myself. I came by his invitation, you know. He realizes that I take a special interest in Yang, yet he hampers me in every possible way. My hands are tied if he prevents me from seeing him. At dinner he told me that Yang had gone to Shanghai."

" Didn't you say Mr. An believes in his future ? He is jealous of your influence, afraid that you will cut in. But that would be best for the kid. If you want to help him, it must be along some other line. He'll never make good on the stage."

" I can do nothing for him while Mr. An takes all the wind out of my sails. Could I—could I rely on your sympathy and co-operation ? "

" I'll say you can, Mr. Flower."

They shook hands, as after a business deal. Mr. Lincoln Pan had a tight grip.

Though the banquet was over, Mr. Wang Chin-hsin still sat amid its hovering effluvia dispensing silver dollars to singing girls. Champagne, sweet and sour and warm, was passed in cocktail glasses. " To Yang, the future son of my adoption ! " said Philip, and clinked his glass with Mr. Pan's.

" To your Chinese family," retorted Mr. Pan. " May you have a succession of honourable sons, as the old folks used to say."

Miss Hsiao Hsi Shih had exchanged costume with a batrachian banker who was reputed to be her lover. In a blatant pullover, panama hat and Oxford bags, she was posing for a series of flashlight photographs. The banker, plastered with cosmetics, thrust a skinny arm through hers. Completely feminine were his legs in the beauty's open-work silk stockings and his feet in her high-heeled shoes, but his face was like the offspring of a bullfrog. Miss Hsiao Hsi Shih urged Philip to take her other arm.

" I would be sure to break the camera," he protested. But the beauty seized him and Philip, furiously blushing, completed a trio which Mr. Pan facetiously dubbed " The Three Musketeers."

Philip corrected him : " You mean the Three Brothers of the Peach Orchard."

" Never heard of the guys," said Mr. Pan, " but have it your own way."

When the ordeal was over he whispered : " Did you notice the down on our hostess's arms and her peculiar odour ? "

" I cannot say that I did. What makes you ask ? "

" She is supposed to have a touch of the fox in her composition, a fox-fairy, you know. But I'll tell you more about that when we meet again. So long ! "

The sweet champagne on top of all that Chinese wine has proved too much for him, thought Philip. He did not realize, until he stumbled on getting into his rickshaw, that it had proved too much for himself.

" Serves me right," he groaned, " I approached the party in the wrong spirit. I shouldn't have gone."

# CHAPTER X

## *Inspiration*

WITHIN a month Mrs. Mascot had six adopted daughters, and her establishment thus augmented, its courtyards capering and echoing with feminine twitter, had thrived to such an extent that she decided to embark on a new venture. Soon she was announcing the inauguration of a night-club. The strange word " whoopee " having recently swum into her ken, she decided to christen it *The Whoopee Hop*.

Her first instinct had been to decorate the place in scarlet and gold with dragons and palm-trees everywhere, and masses of lanterns like lotuses and herons, such as are displayed at Chinese festivals. But Cedric Aspergill had persuaded her to restrain the colour-scheme for once :

" Let's paint the town red by all means, but not *The Whoopee Hop*. We want to get away from the exotic. No palm-trees, please ! You must give us the illusion of, well, somewhere in the neighbourhood of Piccadilly. I suggest beige." After some argument in favour of mauve—mauve alcoves with tables for two—Mrs. Mascot surrendered to Cedric's passion for beige, not without misgivings, because she felt that Cedric was the sole representative of London's Bright Young People in Peking.

" My outlook," she confessed, " has been so steeped in visions of the Orient that I'm afraid I'll get all out of focus by dabbling in the Occident : I'm out of touch, hopelessly out of touch. . . ."

"Don't be morbid, Sheila. We'll make things pop all right. I've just composed a rousing tune for the opening."

Cedric promised to be one of her best clients ; he had made himself astonishingly useful. Since the advent of her girls he had become a daily visitor at the Mascot mansion ; in the evenings he made a point of coming in to play mah-jong.

"They are perfect gazelles," he exclaimed. "I should like to elope with the whole bevy."

Mrs. Mascot did not discourage him : whatever his detractors might say about Cedric, he had both feet in the British Embassy. She was thankful she had always stuck up for him. When Captain Gulley sneered, she said :

"One day you'll find you two have a lot in common. One always does, in Peking. Look at me and Poppy Trumper. We were bitter foes to begin with, and now two schoolmates couldn't be more chummy."

"That's as may be," the Captain had retorted, "but Aspergill is radically different from the rest of the human species. Why, he takes no exercise ! He even prides himself on being a slacker. He surely can't be normal."

"I don't agree. A woman can usually tell if abnormality's in the air. Remember he's a married man."

Whereupon Mrs. Mascot had eyed the Captain so darkly that he had felt quite uncomfortable. No, Cedric had his fads but he was a ladies' man. Forgetting his prejudice against Paomachang, he had even taken her girls to the races. This last excursion had created a mild sensation, since his preference of peonies to ponies had long been a byword in the Legation Quarter. Everybody had exchanged significant glances. Captain Gulley and the Trumpers were dumbfounded at the apparition.

"I'm blest if he hasn't brought his peonies with him. My word ! Six of them ! Wherever did he pick them up ?"

Cedric's Basque beret, baggy plus fours and bright suède brogues composed a parody on the open-air life.

"I see seven peonies," sneered Captain Gulley, perhaps too

conscious that his own puttees and breeches were so very pukka.

"High time the F.O. recalled him," said Archie Trumper. "I call it a bit too thick. And I've always been broad-mindedness itself, haven't I, Poppy? But I mean to say, for a chap from our Embassy, who's got a wife, to come and flaunt his vices in the midst of our decent community—I feel it's letting down the Raj. He's a rank outsider; I won't go back on my word."

Mrs. Trumper could not take her eyes off them. She borrowed her husband's binoculars.

"Why," she exclaimed, "they are Sheila's adopted daughters. I saw them buying buns in the Russian bakery. I call it awfully sporting of Sheila to look after Dick's wild oats. I knew he was up to mischief as soon as I set eyes on the rascal."

Captain Gulley whistled.

"Do you mean to say . . ."

"Yes, Sheila's a brick. Archie could never persuade me to do such a thing."

"Come, come, old girl, you're not comparing me to Dick Mascot, are you?"

Poppy rather wished Archie had something she could find to compare. In her heart of hearts she still had a weakness for Dick, and thinking of their brief affair, which had ended on the rocks at Peitaiho as suddenly as it had begun, she almost said aloud: There was a man!

For Cedric Aspergill the prospect of helping to run a night-club spelled salvation. He was fed up with Peking and fed up with Veronica. He had been married two years, a year in London which had passed all too quickly, followed by a year in Peking which had all too definitely dragged.

At first he had enjoyed concentrating on the four tones of the Mandarin dialect, exploring the restaurants and theatres and collecting Chinese musical instruments. Cedric tried to persuade himself that he had a vocation for sinology and Veronica did her best to humour him : she shared his lessons and sat up half the night with him trying to memorize Chinese characters. But after six months the characters became blurred ; an immense physical effort was required to bring them into focus. Cedric struggled, but it was all he could do to conceal these symptoms of ennui from Veronica. He groaned when his teacher was announced, and half way through his lessons would take refuge in the novels of Mr. P. G. Wodehouse. Eventually Mr. Wodehouse monopolized his lessons entirely. The sinologues, he decided, were wasting their time. Of course they would never admit that they'd been bamboozled after years of strenuous study. He had read the Chinese classics in translation, with a profound pity for the translators. He lost interest in the Chinese musical instruments ; he abandoned his piano. At night he pined for the Kit-Cat Club or whatever had taken its place, while Veronica pined for those Bloomsbury parties where one sat on the floor and discussed Soviet films to the accompaniment of the latest " swing " records—it was at such a party that she had become engaged to Cedric.

Both of them were disappointed by Peking but neither would confess it. Their friends in England envied them. What a gorgeous opportunity to study conditions in China ! They would come in contact with such heaps of intriguing people ! But " conditions in China " were as vague in Peking as in Bloomsbury. And as for people—those who enjoyed a local reputation as " intriguing " were mostly mountebanks, and the capers they cut were a fatigue and a deception. Somehow it wasn't easy to make Chinese acquaintances in the Legation Quarter. There was always Elvira to fall back upon, but having met her in Paris and London they did not associate her primarily with Peking.

In the main, outside the Legation Quarter, there were worshippers of the past, like Philip Flower, and exploiters of the past, like Mrs. Mascot. The exploiters outnumbered the worshippers. Betwixt these extremes were those who eyed the past dispassionately : maybe it was worth inquiring into ; at any rate it provided one with a hobby, something to do when one found oneself at a loose end : poking one's nose into the rag and bone shops one might pick up heavens knew what priceless object "for a mere song, you know," and practise the vernacular by bargaining with the shopkeepers.

Cedric had caught the collecting measles too, and one day, for no particular reason, had purchased a scroll of precipices and pines, all tangled and jammed on top of one another. He and Veronica generally agreed about pictures, but this rock-scape caused the first rift in the hitherto harmonious lute of their ménage.

"You must have been out of your senses to buy such a thing. Why it's just a stale old platitude ! You cannot admire that and admire Picasso."

Fundamentally that was what she had come to feel about all things Chinese, even at best they were glorified platitudes. Yes, she agreed with Tennyson : "Better fifty years of Europe than a cycle of Cathay." And now she had blurted out just what had been bobbing in Cedric's own mind ; she could not have expressed it more bluntly. Cedric had bought the scroll against his better judgment, but merely out of pique he hung it over his desk until he could bear the sight of it no longer.

Trivial on the surface, that incident rankled. He could not forgive Veronica for being the first to declare herself. Obscurely he had hoped that if he came to like the rock-scape, he would come to like Peking, but Veronica had precipitated the failure of this test. Hitherto they had hardly ever exchanged a wry word : suddenly Cedric's nature began to undergo a disagreeable transformation. She discovered that he could be horribly sullen and snappy. One of their worst scenes had started because she had referred to Queen Victoria as Vicky.

"I never knew you had it in you to be so monstrously insensitive," he had said. "I suppose you call Tz'ŭ Hsi Old Buddha, and Elizabeth Good Queen Bess. Or Gloriana . . . You've given me a very nasty shock."

She strained every nerve to keep him amused, organized treasure-hunts by rickshaw, and engaged sing-song girls when they had dull colleagues to dinner. She even gave a Christmas party for Heliogabalus the Wonk, to which all the canine pets of their acquaintances were invited, a party memorable both for the dogs and their owners : at sight of the Christmas tree with bleeding chunks of meat and gorgeously beribboned bones affixed to the branches, all the quadrupeds, irrespective of pedigree, leapt, yapped and made an orgy of it. Fido ! Bromo ! Scruff ! Scotty ! Bibbles ! Bijou !—they snarled, scrunched, gorged and quarrelled without restraint, deaf to the commands and entreaties of masters and mistresses ; it was difficult to induce them to tear themselves away. When the Lhasa lions decided to leave visiting cards, windows had to be thrown open and the party broke up. Mrs. Mascot enjoyed it immensely, but Cedric's colleagues had frowned. In the sudden blast of ventilation several caught bad colds. As for those Old Residents who had not been invited, they were rabid about " these antics of the Bright Young People."

After this Cedric and Veronica decided to rest on their laurels. The odds of a fossilized parochialism were too heavily against them. They felt they had done their best to wake Peking, but that ancient sleeping beauty continued to snore. Evidently Cedric was not the right Prince Charming, and he expressed his resentment with various projectiles : ash-trays, salt-cellars, tea-spoons, anything handy he flung at Veronica. Nothing daunted, she tossed them back. It became a diversion, a release of pent-up steam, and no day seemed complete without some fulmination. Rather consciously they behaved like the couples in Noel Coward's plays. The climax came when, in the course of a tussle, Veronica slipped and sprained her ankle. In the bedroom they enacted a scene of reconciliation which even Noel Coward could not have bettered. And they threw the blame entirely on Peking.

" Oh to be out of it all ! " said Cedric.

" Oh for the friendly aroma of a tube-station ! " sighed Veronica. And between kisses, they wailed in a chorus loud enough for the whole neighbourhood to hear :

" We're so bored, bored, bored—so fiendishly, hellishly bored."

The sprained ankle set a new precedent for Veronica. Henceforth she retired to bed whenever she felt in the mood, and the mood descended upon her at all times and seasons with greater frequency, though there was little the matter with her constitution. The bedroom was a haven of refuge from Peking, and it had a wonderfully soothing effect on Cedric. Here Veronica had marshalled her resources with a technique worthy of a classical courtesan. In her mauve lamé pyjamas, with yellow-backed French novels scattered about her, she knew that she was irresistible : she looked her softest and frailest, almost ethereal, melting against a mound of pillows. A bunch of lustrous grapes and a goblet of crystal water on the eighteenth-century night-table beside her were just marred, as a still-life composition, by the intrusion of a trite bottle of aspirin tablets. The air was discreetly perfumed ; the settee was occupied by a couple of Pierrots, the fur rug by Heliogabalus the Wonk ; but it was chiefly the assortment of cosmetics on the dressing-table, the lotions

K

and creams and skin-foods, which lured Cedric into the room and kept him on his best behaviour. Even when Veronica was not there he would steal in to dally with them, sprinkle a little Cœur de Jeannette on his handkerchief, the purely ornamental one with the triangular monogram, and sniffing it the while, would stand fascinated before his reflection in the mirror. For Veronica's dressing-table commingled, as in a kaleidoscope, fleeting sensations of Bond Street and rue de la Paix which filled him with nostalgia for Europe.

Sometimes Cedric felt he was attached to Veronica less for her physical self than for the general atmosphere of femininity her belongings diffused. His mind could even rove more freely when she was not present in the flesh. Alone in her bedroom, he could foster the illusion that he was back in Europe. Veronica had helped materially to build up this illusion. She knew its value as a marriage bond. Except Heliogabalus there was not a single object to remind him of Peking : everything Chinese had been banished. The walls were hung with French engravings after Moreau le Jeune, delicate scenes of eighteenth-century abandon evocative of *Manon Lescaut*, Cedric's favourite novel. And a gramophone was there to serve up the castrated forms of jazz which Londoners relish.

For a time the bedroom had admirably served its dual purpose. Cedric and Veronica declined all dinner-engagements, read Restoration comedies together and devoured freshly-imported *foie-gras*, gloating on their successful evasion of the boredom outside. Yes, the flounced silk curtains effectively shut off Peking for a while. Too often repeated, however, such evenings wore thin. To maintain that lovely sense of playing truant they should have attended classes now and then. What had begun spontaneously, as a result of Veronica's sprained ankle, became self-conscious ; and the bedroom became as much a part of Peking as the city walls. Cedric felt gloomy and curiously empty, more aware than ever of the long year that loomed before his furlough, and that neither he nor Veronica could devise a way of speeding up the time. He even talked of resigning from the Service.

At this juncture Mrs. Mascot stepped in, bursting with enterprise, and swept Cedric off his feet with her night-club project. Evening after evening he would leave Veronica alone with her thoughts : he seldom returned before three o'clock in the morning. When Veronica called from the bedroom he would thump on the piano ; she appealed to him in vain.

Mrs. Mascot's girls had inspired him to a frenzy of composition. He spent whole days at the piano. Tunes came at his beck and call, one after another. The words were the difficulty. . . .

> " *Mating in the trees,*
> *Mating on the breeze,*
> *Mating ev'rywhere*
> *But I don't feel at ease*
> *Somehow—somehow !* "

Had he caught the right note of wistfulness ? Veronica's anguished voice appealed again. Much depended on the crooning ; he might croon it himself. . . . Should he call it *Mating* or should he call it *Somehow* ? That was the question. Veronica started beating on the bedroom wall.

" What the hell do you want ? " he shouted back.

Her voice returned to him faintly :

" I've got such a splitting headache."

Usually he tiptoed into her room when she was thus afflicted ; now he rushed in with as much noise as possible and slammed the door.

Veronica lay back wearily among the cushions and uncut

French novels. Heliogabalus was sprawling on the rug. A new perfume from Molyneux pervaded the room : Veronica had hoped that this would make a difference. It lingered desperately, insistently : it was like an aphrodisiac which had failed. Keen as were his nostrils, Cedric did not deign to remark upon it. The Wonk shifted and grunted as if some dream of succulent bones had been disturbed. With one kick Cedric drove the yelping, cowering animal from the room. Veronica looked on with frightened blue-rimmed eyes while he took up his position by her bed. Formerly his eyes would blink and he would gnaw his quivering lips when he was angry, but now he stood like a pugilist, his whole face rigid and determined.

" It's about time you put a stop to this tomfoolery," he snapped.

" I don't know what you mean. Haven't I told you that I've a ghastly headache ? " Her words came out in gasps.

" I've witnessed this performance once too often. You had better get up. We're dining with Elvira and going on to *The Whoopee Hop*."

One by one he swallowed the grapes that were to constitute Veronica's supper and spat the skins on the floor while she protested. Then, pocketing her aspirin and peering at his watch, he said :

" You've nearly an hour to dress in, and if you're not on time I'll thrash you within an inch of your life."

Never had she seen him so virile. She nestled herself winningly against him ; he pushed her roughly on the bed.

" This can't be you," she cried. " Cedric ! Darling ! " her voice implored. But she looked at him with a new respect when he marched out of the room. Then she burst into tears—too late. She realized that the game was up. The spell she had woven with such delicate art was snapped. Back to that Gehenna of stifled yawns and attempts to be polite to impossible people : back to those laborious conversations which invariably commenced with Pearl Buck, since all at least had read *The Good Earth* and the Aspergills were vaguely supposed to be " literary."

And Veronica remembered a sentence of Virginia Woolf : " It's not catastrophes, murders, deaths, diseases, that age and kill us ; it's the way people look and laugh, and run up the steps of omnibuses." There were no omnibuses in Peking, but the truth of that sentence, in its application to the foreign community, now struck her as profound. Above all it was the way these people looked and laughed and stepped into rickshaws that filled her with unutterable gloom, that had driven her into the fortress of her bedroom.

Resignedly she rang for the amah to prepare her bath. She would have to jog on somehow, for Cedric's sake.

Cedric was in great form at the piano again. This time the words came as fast as the tune.

> " *Nuts to me and nuts to you,*
> *I've got a gal in Tim-buc-too !*
> *Eyes of blue—*
> *Bright tattoo—*
> *Fig-leaf—noo !*
> *Parley-voo . . .*"

There could be no doubt about his inspiration since the Mascot girls had come to town. Cedric was a new-made man, what, what !

# CHAPTER XI

## *The Whoopee Hop*

PROMPTED by her theory that everybody, consciously or unconsciously, contributes his mite to the general merriment, Mrs. Mascot had issued invitations even to her bitterest foes. Of course they all turned up.

Elvira brought her coterie ; Paomachang and the Legation Quarter were amply represented ; archæology and sinology, by Hector Pilchard, of " Fecundity Symbols " fame ; and Literature had sent its emissary in the portmanteau-like person of Rosa Hawkweed, whose luscious romances about life in Ningpo were remarkable inasmuch as the authoress had never been within a hundred miles of the milieu she had chosen (on account of something intimate in its name) and sprinkled so liberally with passional, in lieu of mere local, colour. Poor Lancelot Thistleby had had a stroke at the eleventh hour. Rewriting *The Thirteenth Concubine* had proved too much of a strain. For a whole week he had not been able to get beyond : " In the Jade Canal the frogs were croaking, croaking . . ." Doctor Dunlop said they would have to go on croaking for some time ; what Mr. Thistleby needed was a rest-cure and a properly trained nurse.

The only Chinese visible, apart from the Mascot girls, were Fêng Chung-han and Tu Yi. Fêng had been prevailed upon to attend against his will. In these days of national crisis, he said, it was heartless and unpatriotic to patronize dance-halls : such frivolous distractions ought to be discouraged. They were not suitable for the Chinese people, and were liable to become a menace to social welfare. But Elvira waived his objections aside with : " I assure you that Mrs. Mascot is running the place for foreign devils only. You will enjoy seeing them go to the dogs, I know you will. You and Yi can come as observers, watching our antics from a higher plane."

He finally assented because Yi would not second him. His quick black eyes, apprehensive of meeting a Chinese acquaintance, made a lightning inspection of the cabaret. There was just a chance that Doctor Li Ssŭ might put in an appearance. But so far the coast was clear.

Mrs. Mascot greeted her guests effusively. More than ever, as mistress of revels, she allowed her irregular teeth to express themselves. " Boo ! " she cried, charging at Yi with a laugh that was positively hirsute, " I'd love to kidnap you. I'm adopting daughters, you know. You'd be the perfect seventh, and seven's always been my lucky number."

She reeked of gin. Yi recoiled from her as from the tentacle of some loathsome octopus.

Turning to the entire assembly, Mrs. Mascot continued : " We must bear in mind that we shall soon be in the merry month of May. Mr. Aspergill is going to contribute his syncopated version of ' Here we go gathering nuts in May ' to the fun of the fair."

" *And* may, not *in* May ; the hawthorn-blossom, not the month," said Philip Flower. " Why not give us the correct version ? "

" Order, order ! " said Captain Gulley. " No pedantry here, Mr. Know-All."

Mrs. Mascot drowned their arguments. " Friends, Romans, Whoopee Hoppers ! " she shouted. " Hush ! Mr. Aspergill is about to give us a delicious treat. He will now conduct his latest composition. . . ."

When the band was in full swing under Cedric's baton, Mrs. Mascot diverted her attention to Elvira : " I do hope you approve of the colour-scheme. I hadn't a moment to consult you, dear, and it's been on my conscience. Everything was done in a frantic hurry : I've never been nearer collapse. My heart was set on something more exclusive—a pavilion in the Pei Hai with a floating barge of our own, but that fell through. This was Cedric's arrangement—I left it to him, so don't go blaming me ! I've always felt so sorry for the boys here. There's not a single decent place for them to go to—for a romp after supper, I mean. It was up to somebody to do something about it. Somebody had to tell Peking how to have a good time. Peking needs it. We all need it. . . ."

Seldom had she soared to such evangelical heights. " Whoopee, boys and girls ! Dance your feet away. Put some pep into it and swell the chorus :

> *Nuts to me and nuts to you,*
> *I've got a gal in Tim-buc-too !* "

Mrs. Mascot articulated the words without singing them, so sedately that the nuts were converted into prunes and prisms. Captain Gulley repeated them with gusto.

Fêng, who had spent the afternoon at a dreary educational conference, was more depressed than usual by this fresh evidence of Occidental inanity. He was appalled by the indifference of these people to the land they were exploiting, to the dire poverty within a few yards' radius. He thought of the consumptive chests and aching feet of rickshaw-boys outside, lingering all night for a miserable fare, and this environment seemed pestilential. Elvira had deeply offended him into the bargain : during dinner she had made the sweeping assertion that the sculpture of savage African negroes was quite as fine as that of the Wei dynasty and finer than anything China had since produced.

The world was too rotten. But since Yi was beside him,

the incarnation of all that was precious to him, unsullied and shining in the midst of the rottenness, he could not go away. Yi's indifference it had never entered his mind to criticize : it was that of a comet.

" Cheer up ! " said Mrs. Mascot. " Don't damp our evening as well as yours. Try a little of our special fizz."

" Jig up your liver," said the Captain, " do you a world of good. You look as if you want exercise."

Fêng did not seem to hear. He only had eyes for Yi, and Yi's eyes were elsewhere. Elvira was purring over her proudly, like a sleek white cat over its yellow kitten. Veronica Aspergill had gone to bed, complaining of migraine.

The throng increased ; it was impossible to hear what anyone was saying. Mrs. Mascot's *soi-disant* adopted daughters, who managed to look demure in dresses like bright striped sugar-candy, were distributing nosegays and buttonholes, balloons swollen with every sort of suggestion, and multi-coloured pellets and celluloid balls for the release of superfluous energy. Eagerly Philip snatched as many of the latter as came his way ; to the refrain of " Nuts to me and nuts to you," he looked like a squirrel hoarding them. But to hoard them was not his intention : in a moment he sent them flying at Poppy Trumper, one after another, with a speed and precision that surprised Elvira and quite surprised himself.

" It is rather early for such exuberance," Elvira interjected, " you had better save a few for later on."

" Make hay while the sun shines," said Philip. Mrs. Mascot's red nape presenting itself as an irresistible target, he could not restrain himself ; he had to release another.

" I bet that stung," he observed complacently. Lest Mrs. Mascot discover the identity of her assailant, he looked the other way. His surmise was correct. Tough as she was, Mrs. Mascot stopped the further distribution of celluloid balls.

" Aren't you being rather unkind ? " Elvira reproached him.

" I thought you wanted me to let myself go. . . ."

" Not that self, Philip.—Do look at Fêng and Yi : wouldn't they look adorable in an old-fashioned Chinese bed ? "

They were dancing as smoothly as if they had done it all their lives. Elvira could not take her eyes off them. It will come out right in the end, she thought, little Yi shall be saved from the clutches of her family.

Captain Gulley had a sense of being, as usual, left out in the cold. Why did Elvira pay so much attention to that couple of Chinks ? What was it she saw in them ? They looked and talked as if they had jaundice. What was her mysterious bond with Philip Flower ? He was rightly called Flower—a regular pansy, somewhat the worse for wear. A frost-bitten pansy. She did not appear to take much interest in anyone, apart from that unwholesome trio. Captain Gulley began to wish he had joined the Trumpers. But he was as wax in Elvira's hands. He'd sell his soul to dance with her, cheek to cheek. It was a rum world. . . .

" Let's have a shimmy."

There was a canine eagerness about his posture ; his eyes moistened with invitation. Two wide nostrils, thought Elvira, if I were to sculpt him : two warm wide nostrils, and I should colour them magenta.

" Later on," she murmured. She could not face being breathed upon just now : her make-up might not survive it.

Little did she guess the power of the blow she dealt him. Ever since he had exercised his pony at six o'clock that morning he had been hankering for this moment ; his entire day had been a preparation for it. To have her secure in his arms ! He had fully resolved to take the utmost advantage of that temporary closeness, to express the long-frustrated emotions surging within him at every step, if not with words, at least

with the significant pressure of his palm. Why was such bliss
denied him ? More passionately than any other man in the
room, Captain Gulley desired to dance. Miserably he con-
templated Elvira's features one by one, features which had
been described on her passport as regular. They baffled the
Captain, he could neither describe nor analyse them. When
she was silent, they set into a hard conventional mould which
might have belonged to any well-dressed model of up-to-date
womanhood. Yet they inspired the Captain with a deep
sense of feminine mystery. Why should Elvira be more
desirable to him than any other woman in Peking ? Was
he in love with her personality, with her voice, or with her
cosmopolitan accent ? She had a Parisian way of rolling her
r's. Perhaps it was cultivated ; perhaps it was due to her
French-Canadian extraction, but it gave him a thrill to listen
to it. To-night her voice was husky, Garbo-ish, from too
many cigarettes. The Captain had not approved of women
smoking until he met Elvira. She smoked with such grace ;
cigarettes enhanced the curve of her mouth, the delicate poise
of her fingers between each puff. He still nourished the
delusion that it was Elvira who had made the advances to
begin with. Did she wish to play the cat and mouse game
with him ? His heart ached from the false hopes she had
aroused. What a fool he was to be so vulnerable ! Why
didn't he get up and leave her now ? But he could not bring
himself to do anything so drastic. Poppy Trumper was leer-
ing across the room at him. He knew the significance of that
leer,—there was plenty doing there,—but she failed to interest
him in that way. What a curse this sex-business was !

Elvira's lips had a vicious little curl while she gazed at the
erect, calm figures of Fêng and Yi through wreaths of cigarette
smoke. Fêng's wrists were almost as tiny as his partner's, and
when he removed those horn-rimmed spectacles he resembled
a Buddhist novice, austerely treading to some tempo of his

own. They were like two ivory figures set in motion, two neat, elaborately constructed automata. You could not tell if they were enjoying themselves : they were so perfectly detached from the others, and so solemn, as unaware of Elvira's scrutiny as she was unaware of the mournful Captain beside her. She envied these two diamonds sparkling with detachment. They needed no setting. Alas, one had to find somebody to be detached with. Hitherto, she reflected bitterly, she had not found a soul.

The champagne which Dick Mascot had supplied was flowing at every table. Saccharine-sweet and topaz-tinted, it was chiefly consumed because it quelled a thirst created by tobacco-fumes and absence of fresh air. Whatever its consistency, its effect was alcoholic. By keeping an eye on empty bottles, Mrs. Mascot calculated the mellow moment to introduce the star of her variety show, Nadja of Harbin, whom Dick had also supplied. This flaxen giantess twirled a delirious solo in a dim light, tearing off her few trappings and scattering them among the audience, the size and propinquity of which somewhat restricted her leapings. One bit of muslin flopped on Philip Flower ; another near Doctor Pilchard, who was stuffing it into his pocket to keep as a souvenir when all the lights were switched on. But this petty larceny passed unnoticed, since a gnome-like figure had crept from behind the band and with a violence which could hardly be connected with such slight physique, seized the enormous Nadja, and carried her struggling and kicking one knew not whither. A table was upset in the offing. The applause was terrific.

Only Fêng and Yi retained a Confucian composure.

" What did you think of that, Mr. Fêng ? " Philip inquired.

" The maiden's energy was admirable but surely misdirected. She seems to have studied her Havelock-Ellis and catered for what he calls fetishism. Personally I am not

stimulated by bits of stray clothing ; and muscle repels me
in a woman. And I would level at her performance the
same objection that you foreigners level at our drama : it
lasted too long and was far too noisy."

" Hear, hear ! " said Philip. " For once we see eye to eye."

" Now don't start grousing, dearie. You know it's just
what you expected ; the decline of the West, et cetera. I
don't like you when you're the ethical professor. Nor does
Yi." And turning to Yi, Elvira added : " You don't mind
my saying so, do you, darling ? I think he should be warned
for his own good. It doesn't suit him."

But Fêng was in combative mood. He had seen in that
flaxen giantess a symbol of Western civilization. " As I remarked at dinner," he continued, " you foreigners bring with
you the wrong influences. I am glad there are not many of
our people here tonight. Callow youngsters who look to
the West for enlightenment might think there was something
in it, might search for a message behind all this nakedness and
wriggling. It's bad enough for them to see models of the
Venus of Milo exhibited in our stores. . . ."

He had forgotten the plaster Venus on his roll-top desk.
Captain Gulley frowned and said nothing. The colossal
cheek of it ! he thought. It was the first time he had ever
listened to such criticism. How dared the coxcomb talk in
such a tone, after all the West had done for China ? What
on earth could have happened to make us lose prestige to such
an extent ? All those White Russians, no doubt, and the
failure of the League. . . . And the damnable thing was that
there happened to be some truth in it.

" Why worry ? " said Elvira cheerfully. " Chinese girls
don't look like that."

" Not yet, but in the near future they may. The missionary schools are producing a new type of Chinese girlhood,
with minds and muscles like that Russian dancer's."

Philip had taken to exploding balloons with his cigarette. Mrs. Mascot and Cedric were trying to organize musical-chairs. It was not easy, for the pseudo-champagne had affected many people so that they were unwilling to move. Perhaps they distrusted their legs. Then Veronica appeared : Cedric made off as at the sight of a banshee, and the musical chairs were interrupted. " We'll have a rumba, boys," Mrs. Mascot commanded the band.

Pale and dazed, Veronica threaded her way mistily between the crowded tables. " Have you seen my husband ? " she asked Mrs. Mascot.

" I can't keep track of everyone, dear. He was here some time ago. Why didn't you come earlier ? "

" I had one of my headaches."

" You poor lamb," said Mrs. Mascot with affected concern. " You're not looking yourself. Try some of our special fizz."

But Veronica sheered off to explore the lavatory. Being near-sighted, she peered to right and left—" Just like a lost soul," said Poppy Trumper, " I'm beginning to feel sorry for her, she must be quite unbalanced." After a fruitless search she returned to Elvira's table. Elvira coaxed her to sit down.

" There was no aspirin in the house," she explained. " Cedric took it away from me. And I simply couldn't get to sleep with these shooting pains in my head. I felt I couldn't bear to be left alone another minute."

Exhilarated by the hope that she was about to assist at a domestic drama, Elvira switched her full attention to Veronica. It was evident that she was trying desperately to control herself. Her eyes were dilated and deeply underlined. Perhaps the headache was a euphemism. Elvira scrutinized her figure. No outward signs yet.

" You should take a holiday," said Elvira. " Go to Mongolia. Leave Cedric to his own devices. Why bother about

him ? Is he worth it ? Is any man worth it ? It's wonderful
what Mongolia can do to one, I'm told."

" I could not leave Cedric alone in Peking. It's Peking
that makes me bother. I wouldn't have cause to elsewhere.
He doesn't know how to take care of himself."

" Don't delude yourself, my dear. Come, come ; must
we be tethered to men's braces ? "

The rhetorical question was answered by a hyena-like
whoop from the saxophone.

" You," she continued, " are vividness itself. With those
eyes of yours you can live by your own flame. You'll soon
discover men are only moths. The clumsy things will flap
up against you and bore you to death if you don't look out.
Serve them right if they singe their whiskers ! Go to
Mongolia, my sweet."

Inner Mongolia happened to be one of Captain Gulley's
subjects. " You'll like the place and you'll like the people,"
he declared. " When all is said and done, they've produced
the finest emperor China ever had."

Warming to his theme, he proceeded to explain that the
ponies were real ponies and the men real men, who understood ponies, enjoyed good mutton, and had plenty of back-
bone, after centuries of clean living in the open air. The
country wasn't like England, of course, but still one could
feel comparatively at home there. Speaking for himself, he
had felt far more at home with the Mongols than with the
Chinese.

" But isn't the whole place ridden with unmentionable
diseases ? " Philip queried. " I've heard that before touching
food and drink, one has to rouge one's lips with some bright
scarlet disinfectant. Do you, Captain ? "

" I'm neither a doctor nor a missionary," said the Captain,
" but the tribes out there looked hale and hearty enough to
me. If unmentionable diseases give a fellow grit and make

a fine upstanding man of him, I'm all for 'em. Let us have more of them, say I, and this world would be a jollier place to live in."

Veronica had never troubled to be passably polite to Captain Gulley ; of all her neighbours in the Embassy Compound she had regarded him as her natural antagonist, the most Philistine of Philistines. In the stifling atmosphere of *The Whoopee Hop* he suddenly appeared sympathetic, like a first glimpse of the dear white cliffs at Dover. The health that was in him beckoned to the health that was at the core of Veronica, temporarily reduced, by Peking, to a mere sediment. For Veronica had none of the adaptability of the more masculine, hard-riding, happy-go-lucky type of Englishwoman who haunted Paomachang. Though she did not think of herself as such, she was purely insular ; when she felt energetic her voice was like a cool whiff from an English cottage-garden, when she was tired, like lavender mixed with pot-pourri, ladylike however indistinct. Her charm, her humour, her gush—sentences lavishly sprayed with superlatives—her insouciance, her smartness ever on the verge of dowdiness, that irrepressible temptation to add a necklace of moonstones at the eleventh hour ; her thin pointed face and manner of parting her hair ; the whole amalgam was of the kind that thrives in England and runs to seed elsewhere. *The Whoopee Hop* did not agree with Veronica and Captain Gulley, but like brass filings they endured it on account of Cedric and Elvira, their respective magnets. Their distress was mysteriously signalled to each other.

"Let's jig up our livers," said the Captain. It was his slogan for the evening.

Veronica assenting, they were swept by a rumba-wave into the centre of the room. The Captain whirled Veronica round as if she was a top ; when he slowed down for lack of space he footed it so awkwardly that she ventured to steer him.

His awkwardness was rather endearing ; it seemed to empha-
size his dumb animal pathos. Struggling through a rumba
relieved the tension of these fellow-sufferers.

" Elvira's right about Mongolia. It's just the place if
you've had too much of Peking. But I was forgetting ;
you don't ride, do you ? "

" Who said so ? "

" Well, why don't you ever come to Paomachang ? "

" It's one of Cedric's phobias." Veronica tried to be
tactful.

" You should come out on your own. I'd lead a dog's
life here if it weren't for Paomachang."

It struck Veronica that one mode of escape might serve as
well as another, and that Paomachang might play a corre-
sponding rôle in Captain Gulley's life as the bedroom, with
its French novels and engravings, in hers ; both were substi-
tutes for Europe. The music stopped, Veronica disengaged
herself with a sincerely murmured, " Thank you."

" I wish we could see more of each other," said the Captain.
" Hang it all, we're neighbours."

" The fact is, Cedric and I are pacifists. We're scared stiff
of the army."

" And I," he admitted, " have always fought shy of artistic
folk."

Captain Gulley wagged his tail and they made friends.
But there was Elvira, reminding him that he had something
to worry about. " *À la bonne heure !* " she exclaimed.
" You seem to have livened up a bit."

A Chinese officer in uniform walked up to Yi and invited
her to dance. Elvira asked Fêng who it was, but like herself,
Fêng had never set eyes on him before. Both were surprised
when Yi waltzed off in the stranger's arms. He was exceed-
ingly smart for a Chinese officer, taller and more athletic in
build than Fêng, and yet—surely there was something odd

L

about him ? Surely his hair was rather too long and glossy for a militarist ? It retreated from the forehead in a wave of blue-black lacquer. And that satin epidermis had never been mown by a razor : the chin and upper lip were without a trace of stubble. But so were Fêng's. In China the sexes often seemed to get a bit confused. When the officer un-covered his pearly teeth in a smile, Elvira decided that there could be no further doubt about her first conjecture. "That's not a man," she said. Certain masculine tricks, a conscious swagger, still kept her in puzzled suspense.

Fêng had imagined that Yi would give very short shrift to anyone who attempted to thrust himself into terms of in-timacy at first sight. But she had responded to this stranger's invitation as eagerly as if she were a taxi-girl. There seemed to be a masonic understanding between them. It was almost too painful to watch. He loathed the way this officer smiled at the pure Yi whom he had called his sister-soul. It was a cool glittering smile of appraisal, and it evoked uncomfortable suspicions. As he escorted Yi back to her table he talked with considerable animation.

Yi introduced him as her old room-mate, Captain Yuan. A bomb might have dropped at Fêng's feet. Even Elvira gasped. Captain Yuan shook hands all round.

"Gee, this is great," he said, "I didn't know there was such a dive in little old Peking."

Captain Gulley inquired : "Are you stationed here ?"

"Golly, I wish I was !"

The music struck up again. "Oh boy !" exclaimed Captain Yuan, "this tune is irresistible. Come on, Yi, we mustn't miss it." And off they glided.

Elvira was displeased. For her a cabaret was a place where one sat till dawn, discussing art and life, and she had chosen her guests with that aim in view. Jazz made one feel reckless, broke down one's inhibitions : it was stimulating to gossip about the things that made life worth living in competition with a saxophone. Remarks which could not be whispered elsewhere could be shouted in this atmosphere. "Let us take a little intellectual exercise," her eyes were pleading. But her guests eluded her. They plainly preferred to exercise their legs. . . .

Her precious Yi, Veronica, Captain Gulley, all had joined the dancers ; Cedric had deserted her party to conduct the band ; and Philip's head had been turned, first by the celluloid balls, then by the balloons—he made a bee-line for every balloon within his orbit, only to explode it with a cigarette. When Elvira expostulated, he merely repeated : " Self-expression first."

Mrs. Mascot had triumphed. But Elvira would not leave before she had learned more about this mysterious officer. Fêng sat beside her, dumb, consumed by jealousy. At last the couples fell apart, and the Chinese Captain swaggered back to Elvira's table.

"You folks must pardon me for cutting in," he said.

"Why on earth shouldn't you ? Do join us in a little refreshment, Captain Yuan." He sat down, crossed his legs, lighted a cigarette from Elvira's case, and ordered a lemon squash.

"Call me Ruby," he said. "Why be so formal ? Everybody calls me Ruby . . ."

"But that's a woman's name," said Captain Gulley.

"Say, what do you take me for ? " Captain Yuan burst out laughing. "Maybe I don't look my sex in this uniform. Yi and I were at Primary School together. Didn't she tell you we were room-mates ? "

"I rejoice to hear that there are still amazons in China," said Philip. "So far I have only seen them on the stage."

"I'm not much of an amazon. I'm just one of General Pao Tzŭ-lu's liaison-officers."

Fêng recollected scandalous tales about this schoolmate of Yi's. In this case the term liaison-officer could be taken quite literally. Fêng wondered if Elvira understood its manifold implications. For General Pao was the notorious stallion-bandit, and " Captain " Yuan was said to act as his procuress. The girls she had been instrumental in ruining were legion ; those who were not in brothels had committed suicide. One of the latter had earned posthumous fame for a poetical account of all the horrors she had suffered. And this school-mate of Yi's was responsible. She should be boiled alive ! How could he save Yi from her clutches ? General Pao happened to be living in semi-retirement at present, but that would not mitigate the danger. Perhaps this she-monster would introduce her to the bandit. Fêng would fight to the death to prevent it.

" You're the first soldier of our sex I've had the pleasure of meeting, Captain," gushed Elvira, leaning towards her with all the collector's curiosity which made her so agreeable to newcomers.

Captain Ruby said she had just arrived from some place Elvira had never heard of, doubtless in the interior : Chinese names were all alike to Elvira and geography was not her *forte*. " The only foreigners there were some Swedish missionaries. As the General set fire to their church on a former visit, they weren't very friendly. I was afraid I had forgotten my English, but you've made it all come back. And Yi has just reminded me that I can dance. What about this one, Yi ? "

" She promised it to me," Fêng interposed.

" Ladies first," said Philip.

" Not if they're dressed like men."

" Do stay and talk to me," said Elvira. " I have been tremendously intrigued by you all the evening. As a school friend of Yi's, I hope you will consider my home as yours."

148

But the amazon did not respond. She was watching Mrs. Mascot's girls, who were now distributing rolls of paper ribbon. She questioned Elvira about them, and showed an interest that struck Elvira as disproportionate on hearing that Mrs. Mascot had recently adopted them.

" Are you a friend of Mrs. Mascot ? " she inquired.

" That's rather an embarrassing question."

" I guess you're not. Then I can tell you the truth. Those are the runaway concubines of General Pao. I've come to fetch them home."

And she bade Elvira good-night and *au revoir*.

Philip was up to mischief again. Perceiving that some pellets still remained, he opened hostilities against the Trumper clique. Many a remark of Poppy's had rankled : he decided to make her tingle in return. He kept a male harem, did he ? Ping ! Let her take that, and that, and that.

The Martinet was bristling. " One more," he growled, " and I'll give that cad a hiding he won't forget." But many more continued to hit the mark, and the Martinet sat tight. Poppy tried to retort in kind, but she expended altogether too much energy. The harder she hurled them, the wider her missiles fell of the target. Meanwhile the paper streamers wound themselves about the necks and legs of dancers, tangling them up in a cobweb of brilliant colours. One of them caught in Poppy's coiffure. Flustered and furious, she tore it off, undoing her elaborate bandeau in the process. Strands of false hair floated into the false champagne. Poppy burst into tears.

" I'll give him such a licking for that," said the Martinet. " One day he'll get the fright that's coming to him ! "

But Poppy refused to be comforted by such vague promises. She called loudly for Mrs. Mascot. " Either he apologizes straight away or you order him out," she insisted. " He did it wilfully, maliciously. I have never been so insulted in my

life. Never. Unless," she added, " you want my husband
to give him a public thrashing."

Mrs. Mascot found herself making excuses for a creature she
cordially detested. She would have certainly turned him out
but for the risk of offending Elvira. She had to pocket her
pride to keep in with the woman. She went over to Philip
and begged him to apologize.

" I'll be damned if I do," said Philip.

" That's not the way to speak to a lady," said Captain
Gulley.

" Never mind him, he's plastered," said Elvira.

" I'm by far the soberest person in this assembly."

Veronica broke in : " Where is Cedric ? That's what I
want to know."

" As I told you before, I haven't the ghost of a notion."
Mrs. Mascot spoke with some acerbity.

" Liar," said Veronica, and slapped Mrs. Mascot's face.

Elvira's expression brightened. At last something was
happening. After an hour among the overcoats, Cedric
decided he would rather face the music. He had under-
estimated Veronica's obstinacy.

" I am extremely sorry to find you here," he said. " I
thought you were in bed, where you belong. I apologize for
her, Sheila. Veronica isn't herself."

" You have all my sympathy, Cedric. Be brave ; and
keep smiling. That's my motto, you know. Every cloud
has a silver lining. Remember the silver lining and "—
Mrs. Mascot designated Veronica—" forget the cloud !
As for me, it is ' on with the motley ! '—Laugh, Sheila,
laugh ! "

And Mrs. Mascot laughed : her irregular teeth flashed in
the absinthe light.

Elvira strained her ears. Amid the din of the orchestra she
could not make out all they were saying. She caught some-

thing about a cloud with a silver lining and sighed. Altogether too Anglo-Saxon. Why couldn't people play up, make thorough rumpuses, and let themselves go?

Cedric urged Veronica to leave. " You've disgraced both of us. If you were a man I'd call you a cad. I hope you're satisfied."

" It was your fault for stealing the aspirin."

" Come on, or there'll be trouble."

" Run off to your Mrs. Mascot. I have a matter to discuss with Captain Gulley. We're planning a trip into the wilds." She knew that would baffle him.

The Captain chose this moment to renew his invitation to Elvira. " What about that dance I've been waiting for ? "

Disregarding the entreaty in his voice, Elvira snapped : " Sorry, not in the mood."

Something went pop in the Captain's brain. " Well then, I'm not in the mood to stay. Good night."

" Early to bed and early to rise, I see. Sleep tight, bless you. It's bad for chocolate soldiers to sit up late. . . ."

Grinding his teeth, munching his moustache, the Captain strutted towards the door. Mrs. Mascot caught him by the sleeve : " Don't leave us now. The fun is just beginning ! "

" Polo tomorrow," said the Captain.

Thank God he knew where he stood. No more fooling. Polo tomorrow, and Elvira be damned.

Mrs. Mascot gazed after him. What had come over everyone ? A wave of hysteria seemed to sweep the room. There was Poppy Trumper behaving like a ruffled hen and Captain Gulley like a turkeycock. Cedric was twisting Veronica's arm in an effort to drag her away. Only Rosa Hawkweed's table was an oasis of calm. Rosa was holding forth to her spellbound guests. Or were they all asleep ? Mrs. Mascot drew nearer. Yes, their eyes were glazed ; one of them was snoring. But that never deterred Rosa.

" There is something about Peking that keeps one questioning. What is it, I am always asking myself. For all my
command over words, my power of analysis, my long experience of the Middle Kingdom—(I cannot think of China as a
Republic)—I have never been able to find the answer. I
don't care for the climate : I never cared for it. I don't care
for the natives : I never cared for them, except from a
picturesque and professional point of view ; yet here I am, I
always return. When I'm away I pine for my maisonette,
tucked away behind Marco Polo Street among my sleeve-
weights and snuff-bottles. . . ."

It was said that Mrs. Hawkweed had been vaccinated by a
gramophone needle at birth. But an extra loud snore interrupted her disk. Seeing Mrs. Mascot, however, she proceeded : " Yes, there are only two places in the whole wide
world for me—Peking and Menton. Menton *chéri* ! It
was there that I wrote *Fiery Noons* and its sequel *Effigies of
Pain*, also my trilogy *Coral Dust, Vanward Clouds* and *Thorns
in the Gale*. Peking, of course, provided the inspiration for
*Gangplanks to Buddha-land*. But I shall always have a sneaking
fondness for *Fiery Noons* ; it is so intimately bound up with
the happiest, most exalted moments of my young girlhood.
But here I am baring the hidden calyx of my soul. . . . I
wonder what makes me feel so confidential ? "

She held a fan widespread across her bosom. Her eyes
were full of soul.

This time it was Hector Pilchard, the sinologue, who interrupted her. " And where did you write *Nipples of Nippon*,"
he queried.

" I beg your pardon."

" N for nuts, i for imps, p for pips, another p for puddles,
l for lollypops, e for edible, s for saucy sow. Nipples, in
brief."

" It is sadly evident, Doctor Pilchard, that you are the unfortunate possessor of an erotic imagination. I never wrote such a book."

"No offence ! Somebody else must have written it, or the name wouldn't have stuck in my memory."

Hector Pilchard was exasperated beyond endurance. For Mrs. Hawkweed, sure as an opiate, had sent his only possible audience to sleep. There was nobody to give the signal for silence, to spread the news that he, Hector Pilchard, was now fully prepared to address the Whoopee Hoppers. Just as Captain Gulley had looked forward to dancing with Elvira, he had been looking forward to the moment when he should rise and make his speech. That moment seemed to have passed. With the hall a tangle of paper streamers and people who never stopped dancing, he wondered if order would ever be restored. He fingered his little notebook and peered at the headings of his speech : *Sodalitas* ; memories of Mrs. Mascot's hospitality ; Old Familiar Faces ; Peking Past and Present— (but for Mrs. Mascot he regretted to say that he was personally *a laudator temporis acti*)—*Mores Mutantur* ; *Carpe Diem*, and the key-quotations he had selected with such care :

> *I taste a liquor never brewed,*
> *From tankards scooped in pearl ;*
> *Not all the vats upon the Rhine*
> *Yield such an alcohol !*

How neatly that applied to the champagne he had been drinking this evening ! He pictured himself raising his glass to " mine hostess " with old-world courtesy while he intoned the lines. He had always made a point of quoting American poetesses ; the next key-quotation was from Edna St. Vincent Millay : " My candle burns at both ends, It will not last the night. . . ." That always went down well. " But ah, my friends, and oh, my friends ! It gives a lovely light. . . ."

Doctor Pilchard glanced at the revolving rush of people,

all involved in the morbid, self-destructive quest of physical pleasure, and then at his austere little notebook. How rich, how spiritual was the latter in comparison ! The cream of a lifetime's experience had gone into those jottings. The speech, he decided, would have to serve for a more favourable opportunity, when he was among people who had attained a higher cultural grade. But the applause of past speeches insistently rang in his ears. He tugged at his tie ; he pulled out his cuffs ; he looked about him with a frenzied eye. "Ladies and gentlemen," he murmured to himself. No : it would only be casting pearls to swine. What was happening to Peking ? Surely these people must realize that no assembly was complete without a speech from Hector Pilchard ! The success or failure of every gathering could be gauged from an item in *The Peiping Star Bulletin* to the effect that Doctor Pilchard, " in a few well-chosen words, had, as on so many convivial occasions in years past, addressed the assembly and evinced once more his remarkable prowess as a speaker." Tomorrow the readers of *The Peiping Star Bulletin* would search its columns in vain. . . . The atmosphere wasn't right for Emily Dickinson. All the same, the fact that nobody had invited him to speak had cast a gloom over him which no amount of Mascot champagne could dispel. Freud had hit the nail on the head : repression was bad for one. He could not relinquish his notebook.

Mrs. Mascot immediately whispered something to Cedric, and the stalwart saxophonist intensified his activities. She had observed the speech-gleam in Hector Pilchard's eye, the notebook in his hand. That must be avoided at all costs ! Since those missionary days she was so anxious to consign to oblivion, this ghoul had pursued her with tactless homilies. Not even Dick had been such a thorn in her side. Uninvited he had crashed into her cocktail party to celebrate the opening of the Mascot Beauty Parlour and inflicted an oration about old friendship on her.

" *Beautiful and rich is an old friendship,*" (he had quoted)
" *Grateful to the touch as ancient ivory . . .*"

There and then she had decided to put a stop to it. For Hector Pilchard was the last man she would allow to touch her, and she deeply resented the comparison to ancient ivory. Of that speech he had sent a *résumé* to *The Peiping Star Bulletin*, rendering her doubly ridiculous in print.

The saxophonist, who had been in the American Marines, now broke into Cedric's wistful refrain :

" *Mating in the trees,*
*Mating on the breeze,*
*Mating ev'rywhere,*
*But I don't feel at ease*
*Somehow—somehow !* "

Hector Pilchard arose.

" Ladies and Gentlemen . . ." he pushed back his chair and coughed his well-known cough.

Through the rattling and banging of the band his vocal organs plunged and he boldly said his say.

" As I survey this festive scene, I cannot help contrasting the Peiping of today with Peking as it was when I first stepped into it, a raw young archæologist, inordinately proud of his bushy side-whiskers. But I am not here to tell you of my pilgrimage in quest of that primeval symbol or emblem of all fecundation, generation and creation, which, I believe, is beginning to regain its rightful position in literature, nor to narrate my numerous misadventures after I had explained to the high Manchu authorities the purpose of this pilgrimage. I am here to express our common gratitude to another symbol. I refer to my perennially vivacious friend, Deborah Mascot.

This centre of love and light, this brave little lady who is our hostess tonight, stands for a link with the past. Wonderful changes have overtaken this city of great distances. These distances, as Alexander Michie has observed, used to conduce to stay-at-home habits and segregation, which, like mast— ahem, most habits, it required some energy to overcome. . . ."

Except to Rosa Hawkweed, who sat beside him, all this and the more that followed remained inaudible. Hector Pilchard went the whole hog. He quoted Emily Dickinson, and he quoted Edna St. Vincent Millay.

" Hear, hear ! " cried Rosa Hawkweed in the wilderness of cacophony.

" Old Pilchard at it again," said Philip Flower, and looked about for more balloons to prick.

Encouraged solely by Rosa Hawkweed, Pilchard's baritone contended with the band for three-quarters of an hour. The strain had brought tears to his eyes. Mrs. Hawkweed filled him a glass which he raised to toast the health, wealth . . . But his voice at this moment gave way. Mrs. Hawkweed roused her slumbering neighbourhood by tapping hither and thither adroitly with her fan.

" Wake up ! We're toasting Sheila Mascot. ' For she's a jolly good fellow.' "

" Who's a jolly good fellow ? "

" Sheila Mascot ! " said Teddy Furlong.

" I didn't think of her as a fellow exactly. Can women be called fellows ? "

" Of course they can, you nitwit. Never heard of a bedfellow ? "

" Oh Ted, you *are* a wag." The Paomachangites roared.

" Behave yourselves, boys. Remember where you are. I repeat : For she's a jolly good fellow."

Rosa's bust commanded respect where little else could have done.

Standing at obedient, if unsteady, attention, they repeated, glass in hand. " Here's to Sheila Mascot ! For she's a jolly good fellow . . ." Seeing them stand, others stood also ; the words were echoed, the dancing stopped, and soon everybody, even Philip Flower, was turning to his neighbour and singing : " For she's a jolly good fellow."

Mrs. Mascot was overwhelmed by coyness. She fluttered her hands and giggled in deprecation. But a party of Paomachangites, led by Jim Croft, Tom Cressy and Teddy Furlong, hoisted her shoulder-high, shouting with all their lungs :

> *And so say all of us, us, us,*
> *And so say all of us."*

It was half-past two, and many were departing. Already the chill of dawn seemed to have crept in among the dancing feet. Mrs. Mascot wondered what had happened to her girls ; it struck her that she had not seen them for an hour. Had Cedric been as good as his word and eloped with them ? No, Cedric was still there. He had at last, thank Heaven, got rid of Veronica. Elvira's party had gone ; just as well, she thought. There was no knowing what that rat of a Flower would do next, and the Chinese couple had not been much of an asset. Her exertions began to tell on Mrs. Mascot : she hankered after bed, but that hall, those shuffling feet revolved round her. It was she who had caused them to revolve. She was afraid to leave without her girls. Perhaps they had already gone home, taking companions with them. Perhaps —why had she listened to Dick ? Experience should have taught her. She cursed her folly when Chang came up saying : " Missy ! Missy ! the Kuniangs they all go 'way by motor-car."

" Go away where ? "

" No savvy."

" Call the police ! "

" The girls have fled," she told Cedric. " I must go home at once. I suspect robbery, if not arson. You stay here and see that all's quiet on the western front."

Mrs. Mascot rushed home. Everything was intact. They had taken nothing, not even their own clothes. Relieved and bewildered she let her coat slip to the floor and sank on to the nearest bed. How her feet ached, or was it her head ? For the first time in her life she admitted her exhaustion. She must be getting old. The thought of the future began to alarm her : would it be a continual struggle to keep up her pecker against increasing bouts of weariness ? This time she had bitten off far more than she could chew. But it had been a triumphant evening : *The Whoopee Hop* had been launched in splendid style. No matter how tired she was she resolved to keep going. A dash of cold water, and she turned back to *The Whoopee Hop*. There was still a pyrotechnic display to crown the diversions.

# CHAPTER XII

## *Exit Mr An*

OVER-STIMULATED by *Whoopee Hop* champagne, Philip had not slept soundly.

After a few hours' fitful dozing, he was awakened by a violent stream of noises. Was he still in Mrs. Mascot's cabaret? Was the saxophone still braying? No, it was really too inhuman. Cedric shouldn't be allowed. " Nuts to me and nuts to you ! " In Peking this sort of thing was an outrage. The Foreign Office should put a stop to it. He would write them a stiff letter ; if they paid no attention he would write to *The Times*. The deleterious activities of our diplomats in China. He would quote " Mating in the trees." It was obscene. . . .

More piercing even than the saxophone, the noises continued. Philip unglued his eyes and sat up. His mouth had never been so dry ; his tongue was like old blotting-paper. Yawning, he wrapped himself in his dressing-gown, a mandarin robe magnificent with embroidered phœnixes and dragons, which made him look puny but gave him an inexplicable feeling of importance. Maybe the ceremonious spirit of its departed owner still clung to it. Thus accoutred, he strutted into his courtyard, cocking his ears, wondering muzzily what had happened. Had the Son of Heaven been restored to the Dragon Throne, or was it another revolution ? Ah, if the Manchus were restored, Philip, their devotee, might play a rôle in history !

A desperate squeal interrupted these musings. It was too much to hope that the squeal emanated from Mrs. Mascot, yet his fancy toyed with the idea, pictured her squealing in precisely that note. Since he was usually asleep at this hour, he had forgotten that pigs were being driven to slaughter near Lung Fu Ssŭ. His house was more than a mile away, but the acoustics were capricious. Magical waves of porcine sound were relayed to his calm courtyard as if by radio. His ears could almost distinguish between the stages of each animal's decline : now some struggling hog was being dragged to its doom ; the fatal stroke, the " dying fall," followed in the crisp twilight. Philip stood and listened to these agonized wails, smiling till the chorus subsided. For there still seemed a chance that Mrs. Mascot, the Trumpers, Rosa Hawkweed and Hector Pilchard were receiving retribution.

The old watchmen with rattle and gong were still doddering on their rounds. Click-click, plong-plong, at regular intervals, reverberations indispensable to some folks' slumber : the sharply defined rhythms assured the dreamers on their *k'angs* that they could safely dream on. Philip gazed up at the rectangle of sky that belonged to him, and was as near as *Homo sapiens* could be to purring. The scent of the lilacs flattered his nostrils. He half-expected a phœnix to swoop down on his *wu-t'ung* tree—the only tree whereon a phœnix will deign to alight—and Philip was proud to possess one. He was astonished to be alive. We do not realize, he thought, what a miracle life is. He made a resolve to rise with the dawn in future, if only to listen to the murmurs of the slowly wakening city and dabble in the dew. The ever-wonderful *Book of Changes* would amply serve to occupy the rest of his existence. He was about to take up his studies of the sixty-four *kua* when he heard a loud knock at his front door. His servants were still asleep. Who sought admittance at this early hour ? The knocking continued ; he decided to go and answer it himself.

## Exit Mr An

Yang Pao-ch'in was standing at his threshold.

"Come in, come in!" said Philip. It was indeed astonishing to be alive.

"Please forgive me for disturbing you," said Yang.

"Disturbing me? Not in the least. I'm delighted! But does your teacher know? Isn't it very bold of you to venture here alone, and aren't you afraid of a beating?..."

"My teacher, that's just the trouble—oh, it is too terrible! Three weeks ago he was arrested and he has been shut up in the *yamen* ever since. Perhaps he will be shot. I have come here to beg you to save him."

"Shot? Why on earth should they shoot him?"

"He had gone to buy some opium. He was caught in a police-trap...."

"Surely they cannot shoot a man for that!"

"He had been warned many times. His name was registered as a smoker. He had even gone through the cure. Yes, this time they will shoot him. Only you can save his life. Mr. Wang Chin-hsin can do nothing for him; he has tried in vain. It is well known that my teacher is a Manchu, and that he hates the Kuomintang. All his relations followed P'u Yi to Manchuria, and he is therefore suspected of being an agent of the Japanese."

"You say he was arrested three weeks ago. Why didn't you come to me before? If his life is in such danger perhaps it is too late."

"Mr. Wang has much influence and many friends. He felt sure he could save him. But Mr. Pan, who was to have arranged everything with the police, disappeared with the money, after forging letters from the Bureau of Public Safety. Nobody knows where he is. Perhaps he has gone back to America. It is certain that Mr. Wang has been badly duped. Now only you can save my teacher's life. Will you please come with me to the *yamen*?" Yang clutched

M

Philip's hand and tightened on it ; he looked at him beseechingly. " Promise that you'll save him ! " he cried.

" Since it is you who ask, I'll do what I can. But I scarcely know your teacher, and what I know of him I do not like. He has not been frank with me. Well, well ; first let me put on some clothes."

Philip roused the servants, sent for a taxi, and was soon on the way to the *yamen*. Yang nodded beside him. Poor child ! He too was feeling exhausted after a sleepless night. Philip's mind was now resolved. Even if it was within his power to bribe the old rascal out of prison, it would have to be on one condition, that Philip should have custody of Yang in future. Since the banquet at Hsiao Hsi Shih's extraordinary domicile Philip had tried to dismiss all thought of adopting a son. That last vision of Yang among the opium fumes, as Philip had made his exit through the wardrobe into an aviary of sing-song girls, had melted into fantastic unreality. But the photograph of Yang in foreign evening dress was no fleeting fancy. Sometimes it seemed to speak to him out of the twilight. " I shall return to you," it seemed to say. And Fate had willed his return. Mr. Pan had kept his promise ; though Philip could not approve his methods, he *had* co-operated. It was ironical that Fate should have chosen such an instrument.

In front of the *yamen* a hawker was doing a brisk trade in fresh steamed bread, which reminded Yang that he was very hungry. Philip bought some and they breakfasted on it in the street. The policemen on duty were much intrigued by this foreigner's visit ; they all clustered round him, jabbering and examining his card. Finally he was conducted into a dismal apartment with a few battered chairs, a marble-topped table in the centre beneath an elaborate mid-Victorian chandelier, and the ubiquitous enlarged photograph of Doctor Sun Yat-sen on the wall. Tea was brought in, and Philip explained the purpose of his mission to half a dozen people, who repeated it to others loitering inquisitively outside. Yang proceeded to harangue them with considerable eloquence about the unlimited wealth and power at the disposal of this foreign gentleman, who was determined that his friend Mr. An should be set at liberty, while Philip blustered and snorted to conceal his nervousness. For he was awkwardly aware that this was no concern of his ; it was even an impertinence to interfere with the workings of Chinese law and order. He had little sympathy for Mr. An, who must have known the ropes. The new laws pertaining to the sale and consumption of drugs were stringent enough to put every smoker on his guard. Yet he found himself extolling the virtues and high scholarship of his " esteemed old crony," whose feeble state of health made him depend on regular doses of the forbidden drug. He was listened to with deference.

Chou Shu-chang, who was in charge of the *yamen*, had not yet arrived. But his secretary assured Philip that all would be well, if he was prepared to go bail for him. Philip distributed a few five-dollar notes so that Mr. An's small comforts should be attended to. In the courtyard outside some twenty men and women were on parade ; their feet were fettered and their hands were tied ; their grey-green faces were pinched out of all expression. The secretary explained that these were singularly ungrateful specimens of heroin addicts, since they had returned to their dope after being discharged from hospital as cured, and that their lives were already as good as finished. Whereupon the secretary retired, and Philip was left alone with Yang. Now and then a constable would peer in at the door.

" How much longer am I to be kept waiting ? " said Philip.

" Chou Shu-chang will soon be here."

Two hours dragged, and it was just as if a pebble had been

dropped into a stagnant pond, the ripples of curiosity subsiding, nothing happened.

"It looks as if we shall spend the rest of the day here," said Philip. Gloomy as it was, the room, the whitewashed walls of the courtyard, Philip was inwardly glowing. Yang sat at the marble-topped table ; all of a sudden he began to sob, his head in his hands. Philip bent over and tried to comfort him. He could feel the body trembling ; the sobs, which at first were very quiet, grew gradually louder. The poor child had restrained himself so far. Now he had come to the end of his strength. He slipped down from the chair and knelt at Philip's feet, clasping his knees. His wild black eyes were full of tears. "If anything happens to my teacher," he moaned, "what shall I do ?  What will become of me ? "

"Don't worry," said Philip softly, as he raised him from the floor. "I'll do all I can. I shall look after you, whatever happens. With me you may follow whatever career you choose, and if you are willing I shall adopt you as a son."

A gleam of joy came into the gypsy eyes.  "I think I must be on the pillow at Han-tan," he said, "dreaming the Yellow Millet Dream." Philip was deeply touched by his reference to the charming old legend.

It seemed as if the urgency of his errand had been forgotten. At last when Captain Chou turned up, it was only to inform him that Mr. An had been removed to another *yamen* in the East City, which was beyond his control. "I am extremely sorry, sir, that you have been kept waiting. My foolish secretary should have explained. Being an honourable stranger, perhaps you are not aware of the facts. The case is a serious one. This An is a hardened offender : he does not only smoke opium, it has been proved that he sells it. Doubtless you did not realize this. If we had charge of him here, I might be able to oblige you. I always attempt to be lenient. As it is, I am sorely afraid that you have come too

late. It is already three weeks since his arrest, and his case
has been thoroughly investigated. . . ." He turned to his
secretary. " We will telephone, just to make sure."

A fresh pot of tea was brought in and a tin of *My Dear*
cigarettes. Mr. An's case was dismissed as an unfortunate
affair not worthy of discussion. It was as if Philip had come
to claim a lost mongrel. Captain Chou plied Philip with the
usual polite questions, while Yang sobbed quietly to himself.
Philip's nerves were on edge, but he tried hard to remain
civil. The secretary reappeared. " Excuse me for a moment," said Captain Chou. After a long conference he
returned. " It is as I feared," he said. " The prisoner has
already been sentenced. He is now on his way to T'ien
Ch'iao. There may still be time for you to witness his
execution. There will also be a bonfire of narcotics. It is
very regrettable, but after all it is necessary to teach the
people. One should think of those he has poisoned and led
astray. He must be made an example of. . . ."
Captain Chou shrugged his shoulders.

" But surely the penalty is excessive. There are others
with money and power who have done more harm to the
people than this feeble old man. He is poor and defenceless.
It is barbarous to shoot him." Philip forgot his customary
patience and suavity ; all his British blood was on the boil.
He puffed and glowered while Captain Chou nodded with
affected sympathy and said : " It is the law. We cannot
allow our people to be poisoned."

Yang now fell on his knees and kotowed to Chou
Shu-chang.

" I am very sorry," he repeated. " There is nothing
more I can do."

Yang wailed, " Have mercy," while Philip tried to prevent
him from battering his head against the hard brick floor.
He had to exert his utmost force to pull the boy to his feet

again. " Come, come," he said, " that will not help your
teacher ; we had better be going."

" If you wish to witness the execution, I can send some of
my men along with you to clear the way."

" Thank you. I have no desire to see anything so painful."

" You surprise me. I thought foreigners were entertained
by executions." If sarcasm was intended, his tone was inno-
cency itself. But Yang broke in : " I must take leave of my
teacher before he dies. What will happen to his body with
nobody there to claim it ? "

" My men will remain at your disposal, Mr. Fu, in case
you change your mind. They will arrange for you to have
the body. Beyond that I can do nothing."

These words afforded Yang some consolation, and he
promised to burn a brazier full of incense by way of thanks-
giving.

" Never mind that ; you have no time to lose. You had
better start at once." Captain Chou sealed the necessary
permit, granting Philip the corpse of Mr. An. " I regret I
shall be unable to escort you myself," he said.

Beyond Ch'ien Mên the crowd was so dense that the car
had to slow down ; half the population seemed intent on
seeing the show. Now and then the car was brought to a
complete standstill. After various futile attempts to clear
the way, the police became ferocious with their truncheons.
A bicycle squad assisted them with vigour : the heads and
shoulders of all in the vicinity were made to suffer. There
were growls of protest and shrieks of pain. Philip implored
them to desist, but apparently they were enjoying this
unwonted muscular activity.

Yang peered out of the window for a glimpse of his teacher.
" Chou Shu-chang was not mistaken," he said. " There are
many foreigners here. Who is that old lady waving and
beckoning ? Do you know her ? "

Philip's heart sank within him. The old lady was Mrs. Mascot. Lancelot Thistleby, still hot on the trail of local colour, sat beside her. Hers was not the only foreign car ; there was a line of them, packed with the tourists Mrs. Mascot was shepherding. No doubt they were hitting two birds with the same stone, and would visit the Temple of Heaven, a stone's throw away, immediately after the spectacle. The execution would serve as a pungent appetizer for shopping in Jade Street.

Philip's taxi came close behind the open waggons conveying the condemned—emaciated, terror-stricken creatures with their arms tied behind their backs to which narrow boards, inscribed with their names and crimes, were affixed. Some of the spectators cursed them. " Turtle's eggs ! " they bawled. " Where is your courage now ? Why don't you show some pluck and give us a song ? "

" I want to get out of this. Turn back," said Philip in sudden panic to the driver. " Turn back, I tell you ! "

But the taxi was caught in the current. There could be no retreat from this multitude. Yang seemed to have regained his composure ; he gazed dispassionately at the human tide. Could they be called human ? Philip's last illusions withered, for of all created beings the Chinese were the gentlest by nature, the most innately civilized ; yet there were moments when even they could behave like this ! Humanity ! it was like the philosopher's stone. He had survived the European war still believing that somewhere it could be found. And he fancied he had found humanity in China. It was as if darkness veiled his eyes and an ominous drumming beat upon his ears. Was he about to faint ? Was he, too, among the condemned ?

Yang seized his hand and cried, " There he is ! An *Lao-pan*—my teacher ! "

Philip would never have recognized that skull. To and

fro it swung, like a pendulum, to a drunken hysterical tune.
For he was singing. His falsetto just pierced the hubbub of
the gaping crowd. Cracked solitary phrases stabbed the
stifling atmosphere. Some of the mob applauded as in a
theatre : *Hao !* Bravo ! As the taxi drew nearer he shut
his eyes and burst into another flight of song. This time
Philip could hear distinctly : it was the air of Princess Yü
from " Pa Wang's Parting with his Favourite " :

> *Within the tent my lord is sleeping in his coat of mail.*
> *I shall creep out alone to soothe my sorrow.*

The very air he had sung at the restaurant of " Abundant
Merit." That seemed only yesterday. Now the voice became a scream. This was nightmare in broad daylight.
Yang leapt out of the car and tried to break through the
guard : if Philip had not tugged him back he would have
been badly mauled. An's eyes remained tightly shut. He
had seen nothing of his pupil's effort. Soon there would
be the whizz of bullets ; his troubles would be over. Misery
or ecstasy, it was difficult to tell which predominated ; his
facial muscles were set in a trance out of destruction's reach.

Mrs. Mascot's car again caught up with Philip. " Fancy
seeing you here, after last night ! " she shouted. " Don't you
dare call anyone a sadist again : it's just the pot calling the
kettle black. I suppose this is your morning pick-me-up.
Against doctor's orders, Lancelot insisted on coming to take a
few notes. . . . The Oriental attitude towards death is such a
mystery, so different, I mean to say, from ours. In the old
days prisoners were decapitated. It was more gruesome
but more picturesque. What was that you said ? I can't
hear . . ." Mrs. Mascot thought he said : " Go to Hell."
But she couldn't be sure. The crowd was making such a din.
One could hardly hear one's own voice. Really this was
not nearly so colourful as it used to be, when there were

blue-hooded Peking carts instead of motor-cars, and all the men had pigtails—not nearly so dramatic. " I hope you won't be disappointed," she said to Lancelot Thistleby.

There was a trampling of innumerable feet. The mob, which had coagulated into separate disconnected groups, soon merged into one colossal wave. As the wave advanced towards the clearing where the condemned stood up against a crumbling wall, stout soldiers jabbed it back with bayonets. Thus checked, straining and swaying in a semicircle, each crest of the wave was a glitter of oblique excited eyes.

When at last the volleys rang out, Philip was hardly aware of what was happening. He only knew he was ravenously hungry. He was so jostled and pushed that it was all he could do to keep on his legs. His feet were damp and cold. Even had he desired it, he could not have seen much. It was quickly over. Except a small band of onlookers who lingered as if hypnotized by the dead bodies, the mob dispersed, the soldiers marched away. The chatter and laughter and excitement were over. They had watched some of their fellow men, on the verge of death and immediately after. Doubtless their curiosity was assuaged. Gloomily, silently, they padded away, staring straight ahead of them. Perhaps the transition had been too abrupt. Perhaps they had expected a different kind of thrill.

A constable from the *yamen* steered Philip and Yang towards the straggling remains of Mr. An : dark blood still trickled from his emaciated chest, and the dry grass drank it in. Yang fell on his knees, and while he stayed watching over the corpse in a daze of grief, Philip went off to purchase a coffin and grave-clothes, and rent a room at a neighbouring temple for storing the coffin. Coolies attended to the rest. Just before the lid was closed on Mr. An, a curious thing happened. Yang possessed a single piece of white jade, carved like a minute peach of immortality. This he proceeded to force into the dead man's rigid mouth. When the coffin was nailed and every chink of it filled with wax, Philip took Yang home.

Wholly immersed in his sorrow, Yang was too exhausted to get to bed alone. Philip helped him to undress, coaxing him to swallow a little rice congee, and soon his eyelids closed, he fell asleep. Gazing at the sad pale face, Philip wondered what Mr. An had meant to him. Granting the Chinese reverence for teachers, could Mr. An as pedagogue inspire such deep affection ? It was hard to believe the old scoundrel had been a father to him ; comrade or brother he certainly had not been. Perhaps the boy had never had another friend. At the thought of the hardships he must have endured, the beatings and privations and even worse, Philip quivered with indignation. What would have become of Yang had Philip not crossed his path ? Where were his former associates ?

After the agitation of the last few weeks, he lay calm in Philip's bed. And as Philip stood over him a delicate mist came into his eyes, and like Robert Louis Stevenson he admired and bowed his head before the romance of destiny.

## CHAPTER XIII

## *No Escape*

To escape from his foreign friends was Fêng Chung-han's obsession since that evening at *The Whoopee Hop*. His distrust of Elvira had curdled into active dislike.

But it was not easy to escape with Yi, for she was still under Elvira's influence. Whenever Fêng and Yi were together the conversation inevitably returned to Elvira, or they would encounter one of her familiars, like Philip Flower : it seemed impossible to break away. It was only in letters that they could freely exchange ideas.

As soon as they parted, each had an imperative desire to sit down and write to the other. Meetings which had almost passed in silence begat long explanations on flowered letter-paper. They dreamed and analysed the state of their hearts in black and white, yet when it came to meeting in the flesh they were reticent and dazed. At sight of Yi, Fêng never ceased to be filled with newness. It did not seem as if quite the same selves had been in correspondence. They talked impersonally and watched each other shyly. Sometimes Fêng would start writing a letter to Yi half an hour before they were due to meet, and would continue it as soon as he had left her. New questions, new phrases, would occur to him even while she sat beside him, but he reserved them for his next epistle.

At first he had been in raptures over her replies, which were none the less tender for being discreet. But as their correspondence increased, Yi's discretion became more apparent than her tenderness. A carping note crept in ; she criticized what she called his verbosity.

"You are too impressionable," she wrote, "and not sufficiently reflective."

Fêng retorted with a quotation from Conrad : "It is better for man to be impressionable than reflective. Nothing humanely great—great, I mean, as affecting a whole mass of lives—has come from reflection. On the other hand, you cannot fail to see the power of mere words ; such words as Glory, for instance, or Pity." And, he added, Love. Had the word Love no power over Yi ?

Yi argued that this power of mere words was an evil. Had he forgotten his Pragmatism ? How could he hope to affect "a whole mass of lives" merely with words ? The Taoists perhaps had exaggerated the futility of language. She would not go to such an extreme as Lao Tzǔ. Besides, she was no mystic. She capped Fêng's quotation from Conrad (whom Yi had never read) with a quotation from Rémy de Gourmont (whom Fêng had never read) : "Language is a great cause of deception. It evolves in abstraction, and life evolves in the most concrete reality ; between the word and the things indicated by the word there is the distance between a landscape and the description of a landscape."

Reading between the lines, Fêng wondered if this were a plea to make love to her physically. He was puzzled. There was a European aspect of her nature which he could not fathom, inviting and repelling all at once. He blamed Elvira for developing it, Elvira with her predatory instincts, Elvira whom he had come to identify with the most danger-ous type of aggressive imperialist. Notwithstanding Yi's foreign education, it was here in China that she truly belonged.

In this state of sterile suspense Fêng's nerves became un-strung. He could not sleep for the voluptuous visions that assailed him. He remained, as on the first day of his meeting with Yi, " the Seeker of a Dream."

His mother noticed the change in him : his pallor, his pre-occupation, his lack of appetite. Since he was always writing letters, she deduced that he had fallen in love. The old lady became more cheerful. Buddha would answer her prayers. But Chung-han was very secretive : she could get nothing out of him for all her questioning.

He was particularly wretched because he felt that Yi had sided with the foreigners against him at *The Whoopee Hop.* She had attacked him for disapproving of Ruby Yuan. She had accused him of narrow-mindedness, and had called him a prig.

" Can t you see that Ruby's different," she said, " you should not judge her by ordinary standards. Her sole reason for joining General Pao was love of adventure. She never had a thought of personal gain. Ruby has the makings of a heroine. I won't hear another word against her."

" That sort of adventure is no good to China," said Fêng. " It almost amounts to treachery. Pao Tzŭ-lu is a running dog of the Japanese, an enemy of our long-suffering people. If your friend were to assassinate him, one might regard her as a heroine. As it is, she panders to his vices. If she were poor and did it to help her family there might be some excuse, but she does it to gratify her own senseless egoism. There is nothing to be said for her at all."

" You are making yourself ridiculous," said Yi.

" Do you consider me ridiculous because I love my country ? "

" To tell you the truth," she retorted, " I'm sick of this country. Let's talk of something else."

Fêng did not know what to say. He was cut to the heart. Yi avoided his eyes. That's over, she thought. But she had allowed him to take her home in a taxi. They had sat in silence, side by side, and he had pressed her hand at parting. Her little hand had been limp and unresponsive.

Fêng wrote several ultimatums of which he sent her the mildest :

> I fear that the day is at hand when our beautiful friendship will be broken. Under the influence of hostile surroundings your words have turned into poisoned arrows. The parasites are about to achieve their deadly design. I take up my pen in despair. I am ceaselessly tempted by thoughts of suicide. What sweetness has life to offer when you are against me ?
>
> No misery is greater, said a sage of old, than that of having a dead heart. You are slowly killing mine. But remember this : the heart I offered you when we first met was throbbing and alive. The hearts of those foreigners whose society you prefer to mine have always been dead. They are like corpses shuffling about under our clear sky, polluting our pure air. Alas, you are blinded to their corruption : you cannot see the worms that have invaded them. . . .
>
> If you have leisure next Sunday, I sincerely hope that you will be able to come with me to the Black Dragon Pool. I implore you not to refuse this humble request. I yearn to see you again. Do not condemn me ! But what shall I do, if words still fail to express my profound emotion ?

Fêng's fever was assuaged by her acceptance.

Doctor Li Ssŭ, having been summoned to Nanking for the unveiling of a memorial, had put his impressive streamlined limousine at Fêng's disposal.

At last they left the foreign community behind them. They were impervious to the bumping and jolting and clouds of dust : the countryside in full leaf was a cooling antidote, and the azure of the sky had opened fresh sluices of electric sensation ; their veins were tingling as with ichor, their skin as with a new lustre. The proverb that the sky covers no man in particular was belied, for today it particularly covered

Fêng and Yi. The earth rolled by in tawny waves; there were waves above the houses, and when the undulating roof of a derelict temple was tiled with green and blue the effect of a petrified seascape was completed. A solitary stele, supported by a vast stone tortoise, rose like the stylized mast of a junk from the furrows of a ploughed-up field. The Western Hills that screened the horizon were the highest waves of all.

The fragments of humanity they passed so swiftly gave Yi an unaccustomed thrill. Her thoughts jerked off at right angles; they could hardly keep pace with the vibrations on her retina. These vibrations consisted of buxom geese which, in their peony-pink dye, seemed to emulate flamingos; of children that might have been baked in terra-cotta, gambolling with death (but for the cautious driving of Doctor Li's chauffeur, they would have perished, as naked as they were born, under the wheels of the car); of camels that rose superior to their humdrum duties—no amount of truck with coal could humiliate them!—of platonic willows, intermingling but never intertwining; of a blue-hooded, long-axled, lumbering country cart, and a mule that defiantly tossed its head, bared its teeth and burst out laughing.

But Fêng saw little of these things; his eyes had withdrawn behind their oblique sockets, his inner torment cast a shadow on his sallow face. He held Yi's hand with a convulsive pressure. She disengaged it, asking : " What is the matter ? Your hand seems to be on fire. Are you ill ? "

" I have had such nightmares, since our last meeting. Perhaps I am rather upset."

" What sort of nightmares ? Can you remember what they were about ? "

" I cannot forget ! Don't laugh at me, Yi ! Last night it was terrible. I saw you dancing round and round in a circle."

" There's nothing so terrible in that ! "

"You were on a raised platform, and rows of mad red faces were glaring at you. You were not moving of your own free will. And you were tired, so tired ! But still you continued to move in a slow dance, while the crowd made furious deafening noises. Then you staggered, began to stumble. I tried to push through the crowd, but an arm barred my way ; and I felt I was paralysed. Elvira was next to me, her eyes never left you for a moment ; her expression was grimly tenacious. A shadow crept behind you out of the darkness. Elvira beckoned, and it encircled you like a snake. You struggled until you fell in a heap on the floor. Suddenly I pressed with all my strength and through my own paralysed body I leapt on to the platform. I could hear my spine snapping in two and all my bones being shattered like glass. An icy blast of wind had swept the hall : you and I and the inextricable shadow were blown into a rushing river. Yet above the pandemonium of the crowd I could still hear Elvira shouting : ' Give me a piece of his spine, give me a piece of his spine.' ' And I want a bit of his coccyx,' cried Philip Flower. ' Leave something for me. What about a nice couple of molars,' said Mrs. Mascot."

"That will do," said Yi. "I believe you are making it up. Thank you for coming to my assistance, all the same. It sounds as if you had been smoking opium."

Her tone was so abrupt and matter-of-fact that Fêng was startled.

"I shall listen to no more tales of nightmares today. Look at the sun on those yellow tiles ! Let us enjoy ourselves. Why do we never move outside the city walls ? This was a splendid idea. Have you brought your Kodak ? . . . No ? What a pity ! "

She has changed, thought Fêng. For a second she appeared not only commonplace and superficial, but repellent. This was the worst of his nightmares. Could this frigid, hard-

faced, sprightly creature be the divinity he had worshipped ?
Had he brought his Kodak ? The question withered him.

They had reached the hillock of the Black Dragon's
Temple.

" The wistaria may still be out," said Yi. " It is, it is,"
she cried, as soon as they reached the covered gallery. Transfigured with joy, she was beautiful again.

Their eyes travelled through traceries of translucent green
and mauve and rested on the darker pool for which the site
was renowned. Every branch trailed as if it had been
arranged by the hand of an artist, an artist in diaphaneity.

They sat on the sunwarmed steps leading down to the pool,
which was shaped like a mirror of bronze ; but the patina
was ruffled by wistaria petals which floated in great mauve
clots. Smooth lumps of unpolished jade—or were they the
carapaces of centenarian turtles ?—could be distinguished
among vivid water-cress in the depths. Perfect the stillness
of the water, after the delirious dust and dazzling sunlight ;
perfect the joy of being alone with Yi. Fêng felt immensely
refreshed ; his strength was returning. As a student he had
often come here to bathe. Would he dare suggest to Yi that
they bathe here together, slip off their clothes and jump into
the pool ? The water would wash the immediate past away.
It would purify them from the contamination of Elvira and
her clique.

An old man, who served as custodian, inquired if they
wanted any tea. He wore the mousy relic of a queue and
stood gazing at them with a serene paternal smile.

" Tea would be welcome," said Fêng.

The old man continued to stare with benevolent curiosity.

" Didn't you hear me ? " said Fêng. " We are getting
thirsty."

" All in good time," said the old man ; " first let me catch
my breath ! "

N

His presence embarrassed Fêng, and put the thought of bathing out of his mind. As soon as one left the city, the power of tradition imposed itself in one form or another. Now it had assumed the form of this old man. Not that Fêng was afraid of shocking the conventions of an ignorant rustic : he was afraid of being considered a foreigner, no true son of Han. Yet he could not help wishing that he and Yi were foreigners. Then they could enter the pool without more ado. Their flesh would meet in the water : their first physical link would be forged. . . . But he had visited the new swimming pool in the Chung Hai, and the memory of mixed bathers flopping and splashing to syncopated noises from a radio, of gum-chewing Hawaiian Chinese who pelted each other with atrocious Hollywood slang, still set his teeth on edge. Yi was too sacred. Her flesh and his could never meet in such fashion. The Yi he adored might dissolve in the pool : she might lose her secret separate beauty. And after all he could not swim : with awkward feet he would paddle about among slippery boulders, hollow-chested, dripping and absurd. Ecstasy might only turn to farce.

The scent of wistaria was wafted in gushes by scarcely perceptible breezes. From the other side of the raised gallery—a curved wall pierced by fan-shaped windows—Fêng looked over a stream where trousered women squatted over their laundry, pounding it with stones. Accurately irrigated and furrowed fields stretched beyond them—a landscape in which nothing was hard yet everything was precise. The heart, however fast it had been throbbing, could not but relax and beat more steadily to this calm visual rhythm. The pounding of the laundry set the measure. It was a landscape with a Pekinese tang : it spoke in sagacious proverbs.

The pool, on the other hand, conveyed no impression of material reality. Turn your head aside, and it might vanish

in the haze of a moment. After looking at the outer prospect it was a surprise to find it still there. Pounding of
laundry on one side, humming of bees on the other ; but
the bees were like vague half-conscious murmurs inside
Fêng's cerebellum.

How much of all this was Yi sharing with him ? She
seemed absorbed in something far away.

" At last I have you to myself," said Fêng ; " this is the
first time we have really succeeded in escaping together.
This place offers us perfect happiness for a day. It is ours for
the taking. But I can see that your thoughts are not with
me. Tell me what troubles you. Can't you be happy ?"

Yi shut her eyes. " I don't know," she said, very slowly.
" I suppose I ought to, but I don't. What is happiness ? It
is a tremendous question."

Not only was Fêng disconcerted, he was visibly pained.

" Why, why ?" he implored. " Don't you realize that
I love you, that I am ready to die for you ? Does that mean
nothing to you, nothing at all ?"

Her eyes remained closed. There were tears on the
lashes.

" I don't want to deceive you, and I don't want to deceive
myself. Since my return to China the emotional side of my
nature has died a sort of death. I don't feel things as I used
to. I don't even seem to touch things : it is as if some one
outside were touching them for me. While I was abroad I
could only think of China, dream of China : my country was
always uppermost in my mind. I longed for the day of my
return. And all through my absence I felt sure that a great
thing was happening at home—I don't mean politically—I
mean the intellectual awakening of the people, the flowering
of a new consciousness. Like you, I believed in Professor
Dewey, and he had seen this in the Student Movement of
1919, when I was a child. I remember his very words, and

the joy they gave me when I read them. I even felt I was
wasting my time in Europe ; there was so much I could do
at home. Then I came home. . . ."

" Why needlessly torment yourself ? "

" My family soon made me realize that this was all illusion.
I was scarcely allowed to be an individual. There was
nothing I could do, for my family represented China to me.
' You have gone too far,' they said ; ' we can see that it was
a mistake to send you to Europe. The harm it has done you
must be repaired as soon as possible. It can only be repaired
by marriage. We have found you a suitable husband.' You
may imagine the rest, if Elvira has not already told you.
Disappointment after disappointment, cruel misunderstand-
ings. At first I was so unhappy that I turned to Elvira for
comfort. But what had her experience been compared to
mine ? How can anyone sympathize without a correspond-
ing experience ? Her sympathy could not help me. Slowly
I grew numb. Now I'm just indifferent."

" You expected too much. As Nietzsche said, the ideas
which change the face of things come as gently as doves.
Surely and gently the doves are coming."

" If I could only hear the flutter of their wings ! But I
can hear nothing. Here and there a few signs of material
change ; behind them feudalism. Does not Doctor Li sacrifice to Ts'ai Shên (the God of Wealth) during the Moon
Festival at Po Yün Kuan ? "

" Incredible ! "

" My father actually saw him there. Since then he has
risen in my father's estimation. It may be just a trivial
instance ; but I believe that most of the cultural advancement
associations, in spite of all their banners and badges, would be
ready to do the same. Yes, the mayors and directors of this
and that bureau, the prominent local residents, who say they
consider it their duty to discourage feudalism—I can see them,

each dressed up in his *ma-kua*, sacrificing to the dragon that's supposed to inhabit this pool."

"I thought I was the one who suffered because of China. And all the time you suffered more than me." Fêng was naïvely astonished. He remembered her outburst after *The Whoopee Hop* : "I'm sick of my own country." How could he have misunderstood the depths of disillusion whence it had sprung ?

"Were you ever a Communist ?" he suddenly demanded.

"I was," she smiled, "what else could one be before one understood ? It is not only the toiling masses who are oppressed ; it is not only the workers and the peasants. It is we, the intellectuals, who bear the greater burden."

"I, too, was a Communist," said Fêng.

He held his breath as before a plunge. Then for the first time he kissed her on the lips. Of the two he was the paler, his eyelids fluttering, the skin drawn tight across his cheek-bones. Even after he had released her he could hardly control his painful gasping.

He had a strange face, thought Yi dispassionately, the face of an ascetic : the flesh seemed not to exist. She hardly realized what he had done to her, and there he was shivering like an aspen. Was she responsible for this upheaval ? His embrace had only slightly inconvenienced her : she was rather relieved it was over. Sooner or later she had expected something of the sort. But when he approached her lips again she said as kindly as possible : "Not here."

He looked up at her inquiringly.

"I don't know why you should have kissed me when I said I was a Communist," she added.

"Because it told me that we have shared at least one great emotion in this life. Till now I was not sure. You have filled me with new hope. What other emotions may we not share in future ? Of course I realize that Communism was just a phase of youth, ardent and visionary, certain of reforming human nature and re-creating the world. . . ."

"In other words, we have shared certain emotions of youth, and now, in our old age, are stirred by sweet memories?"

Yi laughed mockingly.

Fêng continued : "We have shared the passion of certain certainties. We have shared the pain of no less certain disillusion. But other certainties arise, and on those we may build our future. Now I am certain of nothing but that I am a man and that I love you to distraction, whoever you are, woman or goddess. My certainty that I love you is even before my certainty that I am a man."

A silence followed in which Fêng could hear the pounding of his own heart. The humming bees increased the sense of this silence. Yi did not want to hurt him. She stared into the pool, as if seeking for another certainty therein. Black dragon of the pool, come out and show yourself ! Not a quiver. The stones like turtles or turtles like stones remained in their positions, stolid and dull. After three years in Europe Yi had returned to this : a pool whence the dragon had flown. It had become so shallow that no self-respecting dragon would stay there any more.

Some small soft petals of wistaria fluttered down, ideas for poems. Yi watched them alight like snowflakes on the water's surface. But they did not melt. What did it matter now if no dragon came ?

There was a shuffle of footsteps. The old man had arrived with the teapot.

*       *       *

"For Heaven's sake keep still. Poppy, do give us a sporting chance !"

"Whew, it's grilling here in the sun. My eyes will water, I can't help it."

"Wait a mo. Shade them till I say ready. I don't think I got that last one quite straight."

The camera clicked. "Dash it all, Poppy. I believe you moved again."

Invaded at last. Fêng looked up like a hunted fawn and recognized the Trumpers and Captain Gulley.

"Quick, we had better run," he said to Yi.

But the invaders had caught sight of them.

"Hullo!" they shouted. "Just arrived?... Where's Elvira? Mean to say you've left her in the lurch?... An ideal nook, this... Are you going to Sheila Mascot's? One needs a bit of refreshment after all that heat and dust. Liu! What's happened to the blighter?"

A servant appeared with a hamper and a portable gramophone.

"Out with the drinks! I'm feeling groggy on top of all those bumps."

"Let's take a dip first. It's not only my innards that need refreshment."

They urged Fêng and Yi to join them. "No bathing suits? Pity we can't do without," said Archie Trumper. "Hi, Liu, buck up and put a record on!"

A hoyden clamoured from the machine: "What can you give a Nudist on her Birthday?"

Fêng stood transfixed while Mrs. Trumper wriggled out of her dress. Fortunately her bathing costume, a fully skirted affair, was underneath. She clamped a compact red rubber cap over her head so that no unruly strand of her crowning glory could escape. Then she dallied at the edge of the pool, nervously anticipating the shock of chilly water. Tentatively she lowered an iodine-tinted toe and withdrew it tittering.

Archie shouted : " Be careful, twinkle-toes, it's too shallow for diving."

As soon as the men were ready, hand in hand they all jumped in together, making a considerable splash. This was followed by screams from Poppy and a lot of spluttering from the men. The gramophone record was cracked, and the same phrase repeated itself with maniacal ferocity.

" Is that Western music ? " the old man with the teapot inquired.

Fêng told him that it was.

" *O-mi-t'o Fo !* Who would have thought it ? " said the old man. " The devils must make such noises in the underworld."

Ah, it was fitting that the temple should be closed and that the yellow tiles should fall and flake among the weeds. . . .

Had the dragon flown, or had it been destroyed by parasites, of which triumphant specimens were now wallowing in its ancient abode ? Red and buoyant the Trumpers and Captain Gulley bobbed up and down. Poppy's rubber helmet gleamed.

Archie shouted to Fêng : " I say, old man, would you oblige us by turning over the record and changing the needle."

Fêng pretended not to hear.

" Let us go back to Peiping," he said to Yi.

The old custodian looked up at him in panic : " Going, *Lao-yeh* ?—but you haven't drunk your tea ! And you haven't seen the shrine of the Dragon King. You ought to see that, sir. I have the key : I can open it for you . . . " It was obvious that he dreaded their departure. There was no knowing what those depraved barbarians would do next. A single woman with two men splashing about after her almost naked, and that diabolical music. . . . Trembling, he tottered after Fêng and Yi as fast as his legs could carry him.

\*      \*      \*

Back to Peiping ! " Or are we returning to the spiritless and shapeless region created by those people we have left behind us ? If so, we shall have to give it another name. What shall we call it, Yi ? "

Yi hesitated and smiled. " It isn't Bohemia, for the people are too conventional. And it certainly isn't Utopia, though they live in an artificial paradise of their own. Perhaps it is Babel. I am reminded of Turgenev's ' Smoke ' and the Russians who used to collect in Baden-Baden—I don't mean the political exiles or intellectuals ; just those who were trying to escape from their natural environment. . . ."

" Parasites," said Fêng ; " and all of them fattening on extra-territoriality."

" You must not be too severe," said Yi. " You can't deny that some of them are entertaining. I have a sincere affection for Elvira. She was very kind to me in Paris."

" Merely because she thought you might be useful. You helped to amuse her friends."

" That doesn't alter the fact that she was kind."

" One has to readjust one's entire scale of values and jump into a Western skin if one wants to get on with foreigners. I suppose I need practice. You do it much better than I could."

" It is far more difficult in Peiping than in Paris," said Yi. " Here there are so many ghosts about us, and they come between us and the foreigner. They interfere and tug at one's sleeve and end by tripping one up."

Fêng caught sight of a crumbling pagoda.

" Ghosts," he murmured ; but it was not of his favourite

Ibsen that he was thinking. During his childhood foreigners were commonly referred to as the crudest variety of goblin, but there were more subtly dangerous varieties in China, the formidable and inescapable ancestors, whose cult was still so very much alive, paralysing even those who had thought to render themselves immune by sojourns in western lands and saturation in the western sciences, belittling their activities and filling them with an ultimate hopelessness. Sage ghosts and smug, cramping the soul with their complacent conservatism. They had served their purpose : now they were sterile. They did not realize that they were ghosts. And towering above them all, Confucius, his precepts still on every tongue, so that you felt : it has all been said, all been done, before ; you only belong to the tail-end of the telescope. Yi was right. China was appallingly ghost-ridden.

"The question is," said Fêng, " should we compromise with the ghosts or drive them out ? I am for driving them out. That is the only course I can see if we are to find a new way of life."

They had reached the outskirts of the city.

" Will you come to my house and meet my mother ? She has long been anxious to meet you," said Fêng.

Yi excused herself. " I am too dusty and tired to make a good impression."

But Fêng pleaded with her. " Oh, do come ! I know that Mother is bound to like you. You must not leave me now. Had I thought so, I would have stayed at the Black Dragon Pool, in spite of the others."

" Since you put it that way," said Yi, " I can't refuse."

Fêng lived in a modest house behind Coal Hill. It was furnished with electricity and a telephone but had no bathroom or evidence of Western plumbing ; water was daily supplied, from one of those ubiquitous creaking wheelbarrows whose charms are not revealed until the winter season, when they are festooned with icicles.

The sitting-room was only separated from the bedroom by a screen of woodwork in a zigzag pattern aptly described as ice-crackle, papered between the interstices. Here and there the paper was embellished by a poetical couplet or spray of symbolical flowers brushed on with strokes so lively they still seemed wet. Except for a roll-top desk everything was settled in pairs, even the spittoons and feather-dusters ; there were antimacassars on the twin armchairs and each was provided with its own plush footstool. This modern furniture was quite as rigid as the old-fashioned furniture it had displaced whose lines, at least, had the virtue of pleasing the eye : it might have been confected from late Victorian English models, but the joiners and upholsterers had some-how failed to discover the underlying secrets of late Victorian comfort.

" The *Lao T'ai-t'ai* is still asleep," croaked the amah, who appeared to be half asleep herself.

" Go and wake her up, then bring us some tea," said Fêng.

" But she gave orders that she was not to be disturbed."

" Never mind : you do as you're bid."

The amah plodded reluctantly away.

Yi closed her eyes : the room depressed her. No, she could never live in such surroundings. That certainty of taste which came from having known and loved her father's collection of calligraphy, his paintings and furniture, whose old wood still exhaled the perfume of hewn forests, made her hate and despise this gimcrack stuff. Life would be more tolerable in a bare whitewashed cell. Here she felt as if she were compromising herself—not her æsthetic sensibility, but some profound and essential part of her personal integrity. She could not express this feeling, but Fêng perceived that she was ill at ease. Being quite indifferent to household chattels, he imagined Yi was nervous at the prospect of meeting his mother. It seemed to him a favourable sign. Why should she be nervous unless she too thought this a momentous occasion ?

" My feet are hurting," said Yi ; " would you mind if I took off my shoes ? "

" Of course not," said Fêng. " Shall I go outside ? "

" Why should you ? " And without more ado, she removed the offending footgear.

Mrs. Fêng walked in as Yi was hugging her toes. She bowed somewhat stiffly. Fêng introduced them in a breathless voice.

" Good ! " said Mrs. Fêng. " Now that we know each other, let us not stand on ceremony."

Yi stood up and bowed ; but Mrs. Fêng had been prompt to notice the deficiency, and her face betrayed how shocked and bewildered she was. To expose one's feet before a man ! Such immodesty was inconceivable. Never in her life had she done such a thing. Her own feet, of course, had been bound, but even so. . . . She burned with shame at the thought of it. " Why, what's the matter ? " she stammered. " Your shoes ? "

Yi explained that she had foolishly worn her high-heeled shoes which hurt her after walking.

" Let me give you some powder at once. Why didn't you think of telling the amah, Chung-han ? "

The women eyed each other furtively. Mrs. Fêng found Yi extremely modern and disconcerting ; although she considered herself a woman of the world, she felt shy and awkward in her presence. She had the sensation of being with a complete foreigner. Yi, on the other hand, was thinking, quite at ease, " They are all alike, these matrons, their brains addled with antiquated ideas. What a penance to have to sit in this awful room and talk platitudes to this old bore because she happens to be Fêng's mamma ! She remembered a phrase from a book she had been reading, *Reminiscences of Tung Hsiao-wan*. That paragon of concubines exclaims to her scholar-lover : " When I saw your mother, I felt as if I were wrapped in the clouds of spring or as if I were sated with genial dew." There was little dew and less spring about Mrs. Fêng. Yi smiled as she thought of adequate words to describe her. " I felt as if I were wrapped in clouds of dust or as if I were sated . . ." It was all she could do to restrain her laughter.

She has seldom smiled so serenely, Fêng was thinking, but the old lady had caught the mischievous glint in her eyes. That glint boded ill for Chung-han. . . . It was a bad beginning, and Fêng did not come to the rescue.

" Had I known you were visiting me today, I would have prepared some special sweetmeats. As it is, I've only these common dumplings to wash down the dust with. Forgive my lack of hospitality. You must be feeling tired after your excursion. As for me, I feel tired all day long whatever I do. Since I came to Peiping, I have not been able to sleep at night. The climate doesn't suit me."

" I have tried to persuade Mother to go to a private hospital. She would be properly looked after and I believe she would enjoy the change. . . ."

" Perhaps it's also the different cooking and the water that doesn't agree with me. I have come out in spots. No doubt I'll get used to it in time."

" We have southern cooking at home," said Yi, " and plenty of guest-rooms. It is very quiet except for the birds. I am sure my mother would receive you with open arms. She comes from your province."

But Mrs. Fêng replied in the stock phrase : " I dare not presume."

Suddenly Yi wished she had gone to Elvira's instead. She

had had enough of Fêng for one day. No, she did not love him, she only had a certain affection for him. He seemed at his worst, his most conventional, just now. Tedious as Yi found the puerile questions of foreigners, she was even more bored by the trite conversational formulæ of her compatriots. With Mrs. Fêng she knew at once that she would never get beyond generalities.

"I hope you will think it over," said Yi. "I shall tell my mother to write to you."

"Oh please don't exert yourself," said Mrs. Fêng.

The talk continued ; questions and answers, short sentences isolated between long silences. Fêng gazed at the women and said nothing. He might not have been there. Yi herself became formal, colourless, mechanical. Her head began to throb, as if there were a bird inside it, desperately beating its wings. Her eyes alighted on the cheerless roll-top desk and noticed a small cast of the Venus de Milo. It did not evoke Greece, but Paris and the Louvre. Never until now had she appreciated that big-hipped figure : though armless it radiated physical health, the serenity of limbs un-hampered and strong ; the very life of which Mrs. Fêng was a grotesque negation. What was it doing here among the scrolls with their fusty aphorisms ?

"I see you admire the Venus de Milo," she said.

"Not at all !" said Fêng. "I think it's hideous."

"Why do you keep it here then ?"

"That's what I'm always asking him," said Mrs. Fêng. "I wish he would remove it. I have begged him to again and again. It is really too shameful. Besides, there's no sense in it : no arms, and the dress slipping off ! Perhaps the creature was struck by thunder for being so immodest. It reminds me of the mouth-kissings and throat-noises of the ' electric shadows.' "

Fêng laughed. "All foreigners consider it a masterpiece.

I am trying to understand why. It is a puzzle I have not yet succeeded in solving."

"I am afraid you never will," said Yi. She did not explain why. She only thought : I must get out of this.

# CHAPTER XIV

## *Philip adopts Pao-ch'in*

PHILIP had feared that the shock of Mr. An's execution might prey on Yang's impressionable mind, but repose and nourishment had served as an anodyne. Apart from Yang's eagerness to do everything that was right and proper for his teacher's obsequies, he did not dwell unduly on the past. Philip's apprehensions were unnecessary. Pao-ch'in adapted himself like a happy chameleon to his new surroundings.

Life began anew for the middle-aged Londoner and his Chinese protégé the very morning after Mr. An's dispatch. When Philip tiptoed into his bedroom, Yang was still fast asleep. The sun beamed through the paper windows ; birds twittered in the courtyard ; Philip had seldom risen in such exalted mood. Every colour appeared in its Sunday best. A ray caught Pao-ch'in in the face, but it did not waken him. Philip examined his features with a new interest : they were so pale and tranquil that on the spur of the moment Philip grew alarmed. " What if he were to die ? " But a pocket-mirror registered his breath ; his hand, though limp, retained some warmth, and the pulse beat with reassuring regularity.

Philip leaned anxiously over his resurrection. Suddenly there was a moan, the boy's muscles contracted with a light nervous trembling in the throat. Philip murmured : " What's the matter ? Pao-ch'in, don't you recognize me ? " The eyes were still vague and distant, trying to recover consciousness of the objects and forms around. Those who waken from protracted slumber often have an expression of anguish. Yang had this look, as if he still saw his teacher bleeding on the ground, but it passed instantaneously : he started up and smiled. He did not say : " Where am I ? " He said : " So it isn't a dream ! "

This exclamation came as a precise echo to Philip's own thought : it was like a bell suddenly ringing from the depths of his being.

The boy soon sprang to life. After a few graceful exercises in that type of shadow-boxing known as *wu-shu*, he was splashing about in the bathroom, then scrubbed and ravenous and gay, he broke his long fast by gulping, one after another, four capacious bowls of very hot noodles. Philip beamed benignly as he looked on : already he was feeling rejuvenated. As for Pao-ch'in, he wiped the sweat off his glowing forehead and uttered a series of shameless eructations. Philip decided to wait a few days before telling him that that wasn't done in Europe. Not that he logically objected : belching was, after all, but an innocent, natural expression of satiety. Nevertheless he winced and looked aside. Something told him that he would never get accustomed to that sound, some fibre of Kensington gentility shuddered within him.

After breakfast Pao-ch'in asked where Philip's ancestral tablets were kept. When Philip confessed that he had none, the boy looked perplexed. " How am I to pay my respects to your honourable ancestors ? " he demanded. " Won't you announce that you've got a son ? "

" Of course I shall, but foreigners do these things in a different way."

" I beg you to instruct me. Since you are a foreigner I must learn the ways of foreigners."

" If you wish to please me," said Philip, " you will forget that I'm a foreigner."

" I'll try to," said Pao-ch'in, but he thought, it won't be

o

easy. "In any case," he continued, "please let me perform my filial obeisance now."

"Let us eschew formalities," said Philip shyly. Pao-ch'in prostrated himself with great solemnity. Philip felt obliged for form's sake to show some impatience at the filial salute, but his heart was beating almost audibly and he went a little wobbly at the knees.

"I should give a banquet to celebrate this great occasion," he said. But whom was he to invite? Certainly not Elvira. She'd bring Fêng and Yi, and they would be sure to scoff. His Chinese acquaintance was at present limited to his landlord, Mr. Tu, and his teacher Chou I-min. He could think of no one else. Mr. Pan, it struck him ironically, should be the guest of honour. . . .

"Have you any relations or friends who ought to be invited?"

"I have an old grandmother in Pei-an-ho. It was she who sold me to Mr. An. Please send for her, that we may all share happiness together."

"So you have a grandmother! Why didn't you tell me before? Of course she shall be invited. I'll send one of my servants at once."

How little he knew about this boy he had adopted! But after all, what did he need to know? Yang Pao-ch'in was under his roof, that was the main thing. Philip's desire had been vouchsafed. A Chinese soul had arisen in him: he harboured no fear of death now that he had someone to sacrifice at his grave. Even so he was faintly disconcerted by the discovery that Pao-ch'in possessed a grandmother. An old woman in the house might lead to complications.

Mrs. Yang did not wait to be sent for. The report of Mr. An's execution had reached her through the broker who had effected the sale of Pao-ch'in, then called by the infant name

of Kou-êrh or "Puppy"; with uncanny dispatch she succeeded in tracing her grandson to Philip's abode.  Having
sold him as a child she had no legal claim; she had never
seen him since, but she had reared him from orphaned infancy
until Mr. An had taken him off her hands and, as a Chinese
grandmother, she knew the strength of her position.  She
would in any case ascertain how the wind was blowing.
Kou-êrh could not ignore the ties of flesh and blood, and she
had the first right to any benefits that came his way.  If this
right were denied she was fully prepared to kick up a shindy.
Illiterate peasant though she was, she had it in her power to
make herself offensive.

When Mrs. Yang appeared with all her worldly goods done
up in a pair of blue cotton bundles, Philip's steward sensed
what she had come for.  He faced her resentfully.  He had
a nest of his own to feather : why should he permit outsiders
to poach on his preserve ?

"The Master is out," he said firmly.

"Well, well, I've come a mighty long way.  I suppose I
may sit down and wait."

"It's no use waiting.  I don't know when the Master will
return."

"I haven't come only to visit your boss.  It is my
grandson Yang Pao-ch'in that I specially came to see."

The steward hesitated.  Mrs. Yang dropped the bundles
at his feet and walked straight in.  She wasn't putting up
with any nonsense.  "A fine place you live in, a regular
palace of jade," she observed.  "You may be counted among
the fortunate."

"So may your grandson."

"*Ai-ya*,"—the weatherbeaten leather crinkled into a sarcastic grin.  "My grandson is fortunate, you say, yet you
begrudge these decrepit old bones coming in for a share of
his fortune.  Are you Chinese ?  If so, nobody would sus-

pect it. I know : it's a case of those who are below imitating those who are above ! In the service of fiery-whiskered barbarians you have picked up their bullying ways. . . ."

The crone continued to vent her spleen on the steward in a crescendo of shrillness until Ning propitiated her with gentle phrases, supplemented by tea and cigarettes. Ning always bowed before the inevitable, and Mrs. Yang appeared in this fateful guise. At first he had hoped to frighten her, but now he changed his tactics and tried to win her favour. Since that grandson of hers had stepped into the house his daily routine was entirely disorganized. The master seemed to be taking leave of his wits. Putting up all that money for the funeral of a dope-pedlar ; paying monks to recite the sūtras for him ; consulting soothsayers—this was not the frugal master he had served all these years. Perhaps he was richer than Ning had imagined. Even so, female impersonators were a notorious strain on the stoutest of wallets ; their whole tribe was proverbially coupled with monkeys and quails for ingratitude, and with turtles for moral depravity. Was it likely that this one would prove an exception to the rule ?

Philip's steward readily came to terms with the rustic virago. At any rate with her bound feet she could never pass muster as a Manchu !

Thus when Philip was on the point of sending for Pao-ch'in's grandmother he was informed that the *lao t'ai-t'ai* was just outside, awaiting his convenience.

" How is it you did not invite her to come in ? "

Philip's nostrils detected a potent farmyard odour. As he turned round he perceived that the beldame had already introduced herself ; she seemed about to perform some sort of genuflexion.

" No ceremony, please ! " said Philip. " I'm comparatively young, Madam, and we have never met before. Furthermore, I've no idea what's the degree of relationship between us—I suppose we become related now that Pao-ch'in is my adopted son."

So dumbfounded was the dame to hear a pale barbarian discourse in this fashion that her eyes protruded like copper balls, and she took no notice of Pao-ch'in's inquiries after her health. This was a far remove from the devil-talk she had been expecting. Philip politely urged her to be seated. She looked about for a brick bed such as she was accustomed to ; seeing none she gingerly approached an elaborate lacquer chair, the like of which she had never seen except in an ancestor portrait, and wrigglingly lowered herself into it. Philip asked if she had breakfasted.

" *Ai-ya !* " Mrs. Yang exclaimed. " It was only yesterday that I heard my little Kou-êrh had lost his second father and that you, my lord, had taken pity on his forlorn plight and offered him an asylum in your mansion. As soon as it was dawn I started out from Pei-an-ho with all the speed my donkey could manage, and had I even so much as time to swallow a breakfast ? "

" You must be worn out," said Philip, and promptly gave orders that she was to be served with a hearty meal and anything else she required. " You must also bring some wine of the best quality," he told Ning, " to celebrate the family reunion."

Ning stood at a distance in the Manchu attitude of respect with arms demurely hanging at his sides, approaching his master one foot forward with every sentence until he was plumb in front of him by the time he had finished. Whereupon he bowed and retreated. Mrs. Yang was vastly impressed. But she could think of nothing to say except : " *O-mi-t'o Fo !* How Kou-êrh has managed to sprout ! "

The wine preceded the breakfast, and there were saucers of melon-seeds and salted beancurd " to send the liquor down." Mrs. Yang gulped three cups, and smacking her lips invoked

Amida Buddha. Pao-ch'in only took a sip, and concentrated on cracking melon-seeds. As the liquor flowed through the old peasant woman's veins she relaxed from her stiff position on the edge of the lacquer chair and her tongue was slackened. "Properly speaking," she observed, "this being the first time I set eyes on you, my lord, I shouldn't mention what I have to say, but since I've come from afar to seek your assistance, dear old friend, I have no help but to mention it. . . ."

When she came nearer to the point she began to flounder : her empty stomach rumbled. "I should have waited till I had eaten," she mused. She winked at Pao-ch'in as a signal to come to her rescue. What was the matter with the lout ? Why didn't he say anything ? She was reduced to staring at the barbarian, and suddenly his sharp long nose and bleached, blind-looking eyes filled her with secret terror : words forsook her. Well, if the worst came to the worst he would give her a present and send her back to Pei-an-ho : she could not return poorer than she had come ! Kou-êrh would see she was provided for. . . .

Philip admired the spruce aspect of her tiny compressed feet : they were like the delicate hoofs of a gazelle. The custom had its merits, he decided, and it was said to strengthen the thighs. Certainly bound feet made up for what a plain face lacked, and retrieved a figure from dumpiness. But they were far more than an ingenious corrective. He could well understand that they might become an obsession. Seeing Philip's eyes directed so boldly at her three-inch "lily-flowers," Mrs. Yang was all the more disconcerted. "I have no help but to mention it," she repeated, winking furiously at Pao-ch'in. But her grandson thought she had a nervous twitch and went on cracking melon-seeds.

"Pray don't hesitate," said Philip. "I shall be only too pleased to do what I can for Pao-ch'in's grandmother."

Ning announced that her meal was ready, and she retired.

Philip was not displeased by this turn of events. There was room enough in the house. The presence of Pao-ch'in's grandmother would solidify their relationship, cement it so to speak. He liked the look of her. It was regrettable that she wasn't a Manchu, but that couldn't be helped. She was probably loyal to the Manchu dynasty. No revolutionary nonsense about her !

But what was to be done about Pao-ch'in's education ? At present he could neither read nor write, and he showed no inclination to pursue his theatrical career. The question of his career did not exercise Philip so much as that of cultivating his personality, and all that was most Chinese in it, the sum total of those " pure and virgin apprehensions from the womb " which he had always suspected were subtler in China than anywhere else in the world. Philip wished his protégé to be the embodiment of all that was best and highest in the life of China, to attain to the Confucian ideal of the Superior Man. It was imperative that he should be thoroughly versed in the classics.

As Pao-ch'in was too old to be sent to school—even were he not, Philip would have been averse from exposing him to those Western germs now infesting Chinese academies —Philip found a private tutor for him, a Manchu descended from a famous *Chuang Yüan*, or Senior Wrangler in the civil service examinations, of the Ch'ing dynasty. This Mr. Tun Liang-ch'ing had seen better days as a provincial magistrate before the revolution ; he was now reduced to picking up a livelihood by cutting seals and serving occasionally as a literary ghost. With failing eyesight and a family to support, the tutorship came as a boon.

Punctilious to the point of superstition in all things concerning his precious Pao-ch'in, Philip was careful to consult with an astrologer as to the selection of an auspicious day for the commencement of his studies. He even consulted with a geomancer as to the most favourable locality for a school-room, with the result that he had to move out of his bed-chamber. The corner formerly occupied by Philip's couch was now appointed as a shrine to Confucius. No detail was overlooked. Philip presented his protégé with a gown of claret silk and a short sleeveless outer jacket of apple-green brocade for the grand occasion. What a pity that queues were no longer worn ! A nicely plaited queue, a blue cap with a tassel and scarlet button, and Pao-ch'in's appearance would be perfect. Again Philip sighed over the departed dynasty.

When the propitious day dawned, Pao-ch'in appeared in an old pepper-and-salt Norfolk suit. He turned a deaf ear to Philip's expostulations. "I wish to be modern," Pao-ch'in repeated.

"But that old suit of mine you're wearing isn't modern at all."

"It is more up to date than that apple-green *ma-kua*. Nobody wears such colours off the stage."

"Very well," said Philip testily, "do as you please. I'll wear the clothes I bought for you. At least one of us shall look dignified."

Pao-ch'in smiled and said nothing. This was his first step towards independence.

When Philip participated in the opening ceremony even Mr. Tun had much ado to keep a straight face. Here was a middle-aged foreigner in old-world Chinese garb of vividest hue solemnly burning gilt paper money, lighting candles and incense and prostrating himself three times before the shrine of Confucius, while a female impersonator in foreign togs mechanically went through the same motions with a grin on his face. The actor had a feeling that he was still on the stage. A new name was chosen for him : Pao-ch'in was discarded in favour of the more imposing Hsing-chieh, or "Starry Terrace."

# CHAPTER XV

## Frustration

AT last Elvira had put the finishing touches to her mammoth statue of Frustration. To be strictly accurate, six masons had finished chiselling at the marble version of her rough clay model. Elvira resembled Rodin in that she never carved ; she left that to the craftsmen under her supervision. They had made a very neat job of it, and now the creatress was alone with her creation. Elvira always enjoyed these *têtes-à-tête*.

Something out of nothing, and what a something ! All who had been racked by passions and high ideals (one and the same to Elvira), would recognize a phase of their lives in this abstract form : it was a thing for the men and women of the twentieth century to stand at gaze before as those of the nineteenth century had stood at gaze before Watts's " Hope." It was her mind's most recent triumph over matter.

Would she ever again collaborate so perfectly with substance ? Elvira lived in terror of her inspiration running dry, of lying, as she had lain too often in Peking, limp and idle amid innumerable lumps and worms and pellets of clay. Her hand slipped over what might have been cicatrices tattooed in high relief, caressing them tenderly.

If she had been frustrated during her sojourn in Peking, at least she had turned her experience to account. She felt entitled to rest awhile and loll on the cushions she loved. She lay on the sofa and lighted a cigarette. In Paris she had been wont to achieve an average of one monthly masterpiece, but in Peking, as she had complained to Philip, something had gone wrong with her creative periods. Philip attributed this to the social prominence of the moon in China. And switching from solar to lunar months must inevitably, he averred, affect the equilibrium of one hailing from Europe, since the sun was male or *Yang*, while the moon appertained to the *Yin* or female principle. He exhorted Elvira to make offerings to the moon.

"Being a woman, it is only meet and proper that you should. And since you are a sculptress, why not model an image of the lunar rabbit [1] busily pounding the elixir of life. It needn't be realistic. Just a quaint little personal offering. I'm sure the moon would appreciate it immensely."

Elvira did not know whether to be indignant or amused at the notion—she, the sculptress of colossi, modelling quaint clay rabbits !

"Oh do !" said Mrs. Mascot, "it would be lots of fun. We'll throw a party in honour of the event. I'll have a sweet brer-rabbit printed on the invitation cards. Why don't you adopt it as your crest ? I feel tempted to use it as a talisman myself."

"You're welcome to it," said Elvira.

"At the party," Mrs. Mascot continued, "we can all dress up as rabbits. And I've a wonderful old Scotch recipe for rabbit pie. Sheer ambrosia, my dear, it melts away in the mouth. I'll swear you never tasted anything like it."

"I'm sure I never have," said Elvira without enthusiasm.

Perhaps one took life too easily in the Orient. External stimuli were fewer ; nothing seemed so momentous as it did in Europe. The scale of any achievement seemed greater in consequence. But was China the real Orient ?

On the map only, Elvira decided. One was infinitely more

---

[1] The moon is often symbolized as a hare on its hind-legs pounding medicine in a mortar.

remote from modern civilization in Palestine or Morocco. The mullah, the mellah, the marabout, the mosque, the minaret, all those m's that enveloped the romances of Lancelot Thistleby as in a burnous ; plump odalisques ; the palm-pricked deserts on " Come to Africa " posters ; the general feeling that coconut oil flowed instead of blood—all that was the Orient as Elvira conceived it.

Apart from Gobi dust, there was no hint of these properties in Peking. Here it was green tea that flowed in people's veins. Philip had a theory that a comparative study of tea would go far to elucidate the Chinese character. Russia linked China to the rest of Europe ; the samovar acting as a buffer between the thin, clear infusion of leaves like cicada's wings which is wont to be sipped by moonlight or amid the fragrance of flowers, and the thick brown brew which Britishers dilute with milk and sugar. Each of these varieties accounted for certain pronounced national traits. The buttered brick-tea relished by Mongolians was closer to Anglo-Indian tannin than the Slav infusion with its slice of lemon, hence Captain Gulley's predilection for the descendants of Genghis Khan.

What would Elvira do next ? After creation, that was the ever-recurring problem. Already she could look back on an output that would absorb a considerable proportion of space —a prolific family of hulks that required powerful cranage. No Tanagra statuettes for Elvira ! It was her ambition to strew the world with Behemoths. Wherever they went they would extract their toll of human energy. " Gnosis," biggest in circumference of all her works, had been likened to the Tarpeian Rock, and at first Elvira had been puzzled and looked it up in a dictionary. Tarpeian Rock ? There was evidently more in it than met the eye, but what ? Reality, whence man had often flung himself in despair, surging above the unknown strata of the psyche, crystallized from the remotest geological epochs ? An unfortunate accident solved this enigma. One of the men who had been engaged to remove " Gnosis " from her studio had died of hernia shortly after, and Elvira was sued by his widow. The affair had got into the newspapers.

Elvira was filled with awe to think that she, still under forty, and looking so much younger than her age, had been responsible for such a diversity of suggestive shapes, the nature of which herself had seldom foreseen. Even in those rare moods when her interest in sculpture flagged, there seemed something god-like about the process which made her proud and humble by turns. Who had said that sculpture is the greatest of the arts because one has to move around it ? The saying had stuck in Elvira's memory. To make people move about one's own creations and keep them moving, brain and muscles braced, long after one was dead and buried : was not that a good stride forward in the direction of immortality ? " Frustration," too, stood every chance of enduring the wear and tear of time. If nothing else, the critics would have to respect its dimensions. Art-critics, she had noted, were usually short of stature.

Notwithstanding these considerations she was eager to register a few critical reactions. Alas, with the possible exception of Cedric and Veronica, there was nobody's opinion here that counted. Elvira was the only ultra-Modern in Peking. As such, one embarrassing doubt assailed her. New beauty, as Jean Cocteau had said, cannot have a beautiful air : it should not seem or appear to be beautiful on first acquaintance. If it had a " beautiful air " it would flatter human indolence, evoking all sorts of memories. Did " Frustration " possess that fatal air ? Elvira wondered. In Peking it was so easy to lose one's sense of values. " Every day and in every way one has to keep a sharper eye on oneself," as Sheila Mascot said.

# Frustration

Was this due to the climate, or to the constitution of the foreign community ? Behind their façade of solidarity the foreign residents had few interests in common. Each went his primrose way in an ever-waxing aura of self-esteem, each a Victor Hugo on his Isle of Guernsey. Nobody questioned that Rosa Hawkweed was a great novelist, Hector Pilchard a great authority on fecundity symbols ; the high quality of their attainments was passively taken for granted. The community accepted them, in fact, without scrutiny, at their own inflated valuations, and would continue to do so as long as they footed their bills and contributed their quota to the social gatherings chronicled in *The Peiping Star Bulletin*. Nay, they were even proud of these second-rate " personalities " of theirs and smiled indulgently at their second-hand eccentricities ; at Rosa's interminable cigarette-holders and audaciously tinted cigarettes ; at Hector's lapses of memory while buttoning his nether garments. For they had a definite publicity value. As well as being the erstwhile Capital of a mighty Empire, it was hoped that Peking would vie with Florence and Munich as a City of Manners, a centre of attraction for the intellectually refined, and, more materially to the point, a draw to those international pretenders to culture who had leisure and money to spare. It could not be said precisely to vie at the moment. The floating population floated far too much. And ominous clouds were floating from the East. Hence any fixture with a fetish, like Philip Flower with his Manchus, could soon become a leonentity on the strength of it. Thanks to Philip, Peking was winning an Oxfordian dignity as home for " lost causes and impossible loyalties."

In so complacent a community Elvira found it easy to measure herself with Praxiteles, and " Frustration " with that stale old Hermes of his. In those days there was no photography. Praxiteles didn't have to worry his noddle about pure abstract form : mere representational skill could turn the trick. . . .

In the midst of these comforting cogitations, Elvira had forgotten that it was her At Home day. She was still wearing her sober Soviet overall when Philip Flower was announced. Bumping into a protuberant limb of " Frustration," " How clumsy of me ! I beg your pardon," he said, half to the statue and half to Elvira. " I hope I haven't injured your latest child."

" Come and sit ye doon, oh saucy boy ! Since you've run straight into it I want your first reaction."

Philip attempted to make excuses. " You know I know nothing about sculpture. It's no good pretending I do. We have always been honest and above board with one another. . . . That's a dream of a batik turban, but where did you get that proletarian overall ? "

" Cut that out," said Elvira. " I'm entitled to your candid opinion."

" It might offend you."

" I am only offended when I feel I'm being cheated of reactions. By all means be honest and above board and tell me how you really and truly react to my latest child, as you call it. So long as you *do* react I'm satisfied."

Philip almost cowered before the menacing shape that rose above him.

Elvira prompted him. " Well ? "

Philip wriggled. " Fond as I am of you, Elvira, I am not qualified to appreciate your work. I could never grasp what modern sculptors are driving at, and you are so appallingly modern."

Elvira prompted him again. " I'm waiting."

" All I can say is that it strikes me as uncannily depressing."

" Thank you, Philip. You should have been a professional art-critic. Your reactions are always right."

" Don't be sarcastic. You asked for my honest impression and you have extorted it against my will. Perhaps you'll tell me now what that unwholesome form is supposed to represent."

" Half-close your eyes and concentrate. One, two, three, four, five." She counted the minutes. " Now what does it remind you of ? "

" I'm jiggered if I know," said Philip with unwonted asperity. How tiresome Elvira was today ! He was sorry he had come.

" You had better consult an oculist. Look at that spheroid and that ovoid. Take a squint at those flowing cylindrical rhythms. What is it they combine to accentuate ? "

" What indeed ? "

" A Nigerian nigger could answer that in a trice."

" No doubt he could : I am afraid I haven't his advantages."

" Where are your instincts ? Granted that, like all my work, it's a geometrization of visual experience, it obviously becomes a middle-aged woman with a cigar in her mouth. Now is the problem solved ? "

" I'm still in the dark," said Philip.

" Frustration, you duffer ! What else could it possibly be ?"

" That accounts for my failure to recognize it. I'm finished with frustration. At least," he added with a wistful smile, " I hope so."

" Cheers. You must tell me all about it. How refreshing that we can have the whole afternoon to ourselves."

" But isn't this Thursday ? "

" Oh dear ! so it is ! I can't possibly let people see me like this. I never display the creative side of me."

She hurried out of the room just before Mrs. Mascot tiptoed in, fancying herself, as usual, a ray of sunshine.

" What a lovely surprise ! " she chirruped.

" To see me here ?   Oh, thank you ! "

" To see Elvira's sculpture, I meant." Mrs. Mascot peered up with a vague expression of malaise. " I suppose it is hers ?   There's nothing else quite like it in Peking. . . ."

" Heaven be praised," said Philip.

" Do be an angel, Mr. Flower, and tell me what it means. I feel utterly lost."

" Really, Mrs. Mascot !   I should think that the meaning was as plain as a pikestaff.   Frustration, of course."

" So that's what it is !   I suppose it's tremendously new and original.   It makes me feel behind the times.   Where's Elvira ?   I seem to be rather early. . . ."

" It's the early bird that catches the worm ! "

" My word, Mr. Flower, you do say the most cryptic, devastating things !   But underneath I'm sure you've a heart of gold.   Why don't you marry Elvira ?   I believe you two would get on like a house on fire."

" I dare not compete with Captain Gulley's moustaches."

" Oh, that reminds me——"

Extracting a bright red envelope from her bag, she attempted to tie it round a piece of the statue, but the latter was too bulky.   " Not a word ! " she cautioned, and stuck the envelope on a jutting convexity.   As soon as Elvira entered, Mrs. Mascot flung her arms about her.   " My darling," she exclaimed, " you've hit off Frustration to the very life.   Who could believe it possible ?   Let me kiss you."   Effusively she pecked her.

" Admire the superiority of feminine instinct ! " said Elvira.   " Sheila knew at once ; she did not have to be told."

Philip grinned.   Elvira was wearing trousers of black velvet, an orange cummerbund and a lemon silk shirt which revealed her Rossetti-ish throat.

" Genius ! " cried Mrs. Mascot, unabashed by the many creases in her neck, so wizened by contrast.

" Hello, what's this ? " Elvira caught sight of the red envelope. " An invitation to a Chinese wedding ? I do hope Fêng and Yi are going to be married. I'm getting worried about that pair."

She tore it open. A sheet of typewriting stared at her. " *To Elvira,*" she read :

> *If I'm too passionate, forgive*
> > *A soldier-dreamer pale with love—*
> *If there were else that I could give,*
> > *I fear it would not be enough !*

> *I'm grateful that you are not kind,*
> > *For kind words stab more sharp than spears.*
> *Be cruel, Darling ; then my mind*
> > *May melt its sorrow with the years.*

There was no signature.

" What is this nonsense ? " she asked Mrs. Mascot.

" How should I know, dear ? "

" Is this a prank of yours, Philip ? "

" Certainly not."

" Methinks he doth protest too much," said Mrs. Mascot, with a wink that would be roguish at Philip.

Elvira scanned the words for a clue, an anagram, but they would not yield one. Too passionate ! Alas, she had not noted any particular evidence of passion since she had settled in Peking ; and the fact was beginning to perturb her. Despite her apparent languors there was nothing deciduous about Elvira : her senses were still awake to all enjoyment. Sculpture could never absorb the gross of her Canadian energy.

" Come back ! " her Parisian friends implored her by every post. " You're losing touch with the normal outside world. . . ."

But was the " outside world " normal. A glance at the

P

newspapers, and she decided that it wasn't. (Paris. Mme. Guigne, 25 years of age, has been sentenced to two years' imprisonment for killing her husband by shooting him because he failed to come home to dinner. As, however, she is granted the benefit of the First Offenders' Act, she will not have to serve the sentence. . . . Elizabeth, New Jersey.— A twenty-six-year-old dancer died here in a hospital, after collapsing on the floor of the Bayonne Opera House, where he had danced continuously in a marathon contest for 1,147 hours, or forty-seven days and nineteen hours. . . . Geneva.—A man arrested at St. Gallen for alleged theft became ill and was taken to the local hospital to undergo an operation. The surgeons found in his stomach two broken silver spoons, five pieces of iron 2 in. long, two sash window-fastenings, a safety pin, a wood screw 1½ in. long, and two nails. An X-ray photograph showed several other metal objects. *Und so weiter.*)

Nay, the newspapers made her feel that Peking was stagnantly normal. Normal, banal. She remembered how she had been driven to China by a febrile spirit of unrest. But she had not discovered calm. She was still awaiting that apparition or event which she could not define, yet of which she had a powerful premonition. There was something more which China had to give her, something valuable which China tantalizingly withheld. What an admission of defeat if she returned to Paris now !

"The trouble is that there is too little passion in Peking," said Elvira. "There are so few vibrations to draw upon for my sculpture. I think I shall go away, before it is too late. Sometimes I hate Peking, I can see nothing but dull black patches ; and all its charm turns sour."

"That is a propitious sign," said Philip. "Such a revulsion is only a prelude to a deep love-affair. I hope it will be a lasting one, like mine."

" Ah, Philip, all was plain sailing for you. Yours was love at first sight. Your anima found her animus in Peking. My animus, on the other hand, has never found his anima. He's just drifting about, aimlessly. I'm getting tired of it."

" I'm not sure that I can follow your jargon," said Philip. " But if you talk like that your animus, as you call it, will never find his anima. You've got to rid yourself of your cosmopolitan self-consciousness. Then things will start happening. It's like Ch'an Buddhism : the master must not make things too easy for the novice. You arrived here with all sorts of questions. Peking, like the Ch'an teacher, has replied inconsequentially, if indeed she has replied at all. Without completing your novitiate, you could not understand. It is no use trying to force an answer. One day you will hear it and be grateful : I envy you that wonderful moment, that flash of ecstatic comprehension ! You will become aware of another, richer dimension, and it won't matter whether you stay or leave, for you will have attained to Sudden Enlightenment."

" That remains to be seen."

" You're talking miles and miles above my head," said Mrs. Mascot. " Let's come down to earth. What about the *billet-doux* ? Can you guess who wrote it ? "

" A soldier-dreamer pale with love. . . . The only soldier I know is Captain Gulley, and I haven't set eyes on him since the opening of *The Whoopee Hop*. Maybe I'm wrong, but he doesn't fit in with my notion of a dreamer, and he certainly isn't pale—couldn't be even if he tried, poor dear, with that brick-red face of his."

" Poetic licence," said Mrs. Mascot.

" Mind you're thoroughly brutal to the perpetrator of those lines, whoever it is. They're an obvious plea for sadism."

" I believe, Mr. Flower, you are jealous."

Perhaps, mused Mrs. Mascot, he really was in love with Elvira in his own peculiar way. They were birds of a feather. Why had she never thought of it before? Behind all that highbrow patter there might be passion, of a perverted kind.

"Can you see me brandishing a horsewhip while the pale soldier crouches at my feet?"

"I can see you whipping the Captain. You always said there was something doggy about him."

Pallor, emaciation, suffering: why should Venus and Cupid mix such drab colours on their palette? Why should love be associated with agony? Poets were largely responsible for this state of affairs. Elvira thought of Yavorska reciting Musset in her studio: "*J'aime et je veux pâlir; j'aime et je veux souffrir.*" After which it was Elvira who had suffered, for Yavorska had given her such a bite that she couldn't face the dressmaker. She smiled at the recollection, but the smile became a frown when she remembered Captain Gulley. She had not come to Peking for anything so banal. Ah, males apostrophized by D. H. Lawrence, " palpable, invisible nearnesses in the dark, sending out magnetic vibrations of warning, pitch-dark throbs of invitation," where, oh, where can you be? The irony of it all! Every morning she woke up with a new wrinkle, and the Chinese with their faces of porcelain and ivory made her morbidly aware of it. Even Yi.

"Does Fêng write poems to you?" Elvira asked her.

"Of course," said Yi, " in China it's *de rigueur.*"

"Are they anything like this?"

She handed her the typewritten sheet, and after reading it Yi giggled like a schoolgirl. "I wish they were," she said, "I like that dash after love, and the semicolon after darling is sweet. Fêng's poems aren't nearly so amusing."

"You surprise me, dear. Doctor Li conveyed the impression that Fêng was an ultra-modern."

" He writes in *pai hua*, that is to say the vernacular, and he's fond of imitating Shakespeare's sonnets—I suppose that's what Doctor Li meant by ultra-modern. But his images are older than the hills."

" What sort of images ? "

" All clichés. My soul, for instance, has ' the tranquillity of a river in autumn,' my bones are 'fashioned of purest jade,' my cheeks are 'tinted like the hibiscus flower,' my eyebrows have ' the elegant curves of willows ' ; perhaps I am ' an Immortal from the Jasper Lake ' . . . "

" Darling, how very delightful ! And how true ! If Fêng sends you poems like that you have not much to complain of. I wish we could exchange. He must adore you."

Then Captain Gulley swaggered in. " I apologize for my kit. It flashed across me that today was Thursday, Elvira's Thursday, plumb in the middle of our gymkhana."

" And what might that be ? " said Philip.

Captain Gulley ignored him. Trying to be funny, he supposed. Elvira gave a sudden gurgle of laughter for no apparent reason. " What's the joke ? " he huffily inquired. Mrs. Mascot covered her embarrassment with two sharp separate little coughs.

" I'm sure this will amuse you," said Elvira. " Do read us the poem of passion, Philip. You have just the right voice for it."

Philip dropped down on his knees before Elvira and pressed a hand against his heart. Then pitching his voice in a higher key, he began :

> " *If I'm too passionate, forgive*
> *A soldier-dreamer pale with love. . . .*"

During his ordeal the Captain's face was, as Mrs. Mascot subsequently described it, a study. Jowl upwards, it was inundated, octopus-wise, with an angry bluish colour. The veins bulged out of his forehead like tentacles. But his voice, when he spoke, was steady.

"So that's what you were all sniggering about? You would. Let me tell you this : you are dead to all decent feeling."

"Our standards of sensibility may not be the same. Explain yourself, Captain. If you'll expound your philosophy of behaviourism I can promise you an appreciative audience."

"Sheer waste of honest breath. I made a huge mistake. Thank God, I've realized it in time. I thought you were a lady."

"Don't, oh please don't torture us, I beg ! Do you want us all to die of laughing ? I know I shall have a stroke. It's hardly fair," Elvira gasped.

"Encore !" said Yi. "I should like to learn that lyric by heart. *C'est vraiment un bijou !* "

"Oh dear, oh dear," said Philip. "I believe you wrote it, Captain. That can be the only explanation."

"Christ, how I hate Art !" said the Captain, and marched abruptly out of Elvira's house.

Polo tomorrow ; and tomorrow ?

"Exit the soldier-dreamer," said Philip wistfully, as if it were autumn and the leaves were falling.

Now that he had left her, Elvira was repentant. After all, he was the only man who had even attempted to make love to her in Peking, and he had not bored her half as much as she had pretended. Perhaps he was not so stupid as she had supposed. . . . She turned to Yi. "I think we've been too hard on him," she said. "I didn't realize it at the time. One never does."

"Be cruel, darling," Philip reminded her. "He got just what he asked for."

" Where is Fêng ?  I wish you'd make up your mind about him, Yi.  This dangling can't be good for either of you. And he is such a pet as soon as he takes off his glasses."

" He may go the same way as your Captain," said Yi. " I'm finished with him."

" What has come over us ?  Are we in for a total eclipse ? Here's Philip finished with frustration, you with Fêng, and I with Captain Gulley."

" And I," Mrs. Mascot announced, " am through with *The Whoopee Hop*.  I've had my fun out of it, and now that it's a going concern I'll hand it over to Cedric.  When he's had enough, I can always pass it on to Mr. Mascot."

" Do you know, Sheila, I believe this is the first time I've heard you mention your husband. . . ."

" I trust it will be the last."  Dramatically Mrs. Mascot paused.  " Lancelot Thistleby has proposed to me so often that I'm on the brink of accepting."

" Take my advice and retain your identity," said Elvira.

" That's just what prevents me from coming to a decision. Everybody in Peking knows Sheila Mascot.  I don't want to be thought of merely as a novelist's appendage, even if the novelist happens to be as famous as Lancelot.  What's in a name ? say some.  A lot's in a name, say I ; and I don't take to the name of Thistleby.  If I marry Lancelot, it will be on condition that I remain Sheila Mascot."

" Why not hyphen the two ? " said Philip.  " Mascot-Thistleby, or better still, Thistleby-Mascot."

" Plain Mascot's good enough for me."

" How did it all come about ? "

" It was love at first sight," she explained.  " I had read *Yashmak* in the toilet at Cheltenham.  Yes, it was through Lancelot that I was first drawn to the Orient.  Of course he's old enough to be my father, but I always preferred men older than myself.  We both agree about nature : we share the same response. Would you believe it, as soon as he saw my temple he burst into tears. Let me drink it all in, he said. Then he closed his eyes and recited Robert Browning :

> ' *Oh, world as God has made it, all is beauty !*
> *And knowing this is love and love is duty ;*
> *What further may be sought for*
> *Or declared ?* '

His voice rang out like a glorious challenge in the mellow afternoon. As for me, I had a lump in my throat."

" Has he recovered from the nervous breakdown ? "

" Thanks to me," said Mrs. Mascot, " since I gave him a gleam of hope. He has entirely re-written *The Thirteenth Concubine*. It is simply dedicated : ' To Peking—in superfluous words—to Sheila Mascot.' His favourite lines from Browning come just underneath."

" You'll have to marry him on top of that," said Elvira.

" What happened to that chapter which began with the frogs croaking in the Jade Canal ? "

" When in doubt, cut it out, said I. My suggestion was that it should begin like this "—Mrs. Mascot paused, as if to change gear, before she intoned in a contralto voice—" ' A threatening calm brooded over the Purple Forbidden City ; a calm which was the precursor of a storm. Along the dusty *hut'ungs*, in the stately courtyards . . .' I have forgotten how it runs on, but it grips you right away. Lancelot promptly adopted it. I'm sure it will create a sensation. There's a lot of little me in *The Thirteenth Concubine*. I gave him some real inside stories, you know. . . ."

" Why didn't you bring him along this afternoon ? "

" He's at work on a new novel. It is to be entitled *The Jade Thumb-ring*. He declares that I provided the inspiration."

All this had taken the wind out of Elvira's sails. " Frustra-

" It sounds as if they wanted to rest their legs. You're welcome all the same."

" Sure," said one, " this is the studio Danny Frieburg told us about, piano and all. I certainly like a piano. Say, who can strum around here ? "

" My," said another, " you've got swell premises."

" Yeah," said the cheeky one, " it sure is a fust-class establishment you keep here."

Wang arrived with a tray full of bottles and tumblers. The men helped themselves while Elvira wondered which of her neighbours was wont to entertain marines at this late hour.

" Whew, I'm all of a lather," said the Viking. " This climate certainly takes it out of a person." He tossed a handful of salted peanuts into his bountiful gullet and drowned them with a liberal slug of Scotch. Another turned on the gramophone.

It was a Balinese record. " Hey, what's this ? " he exclaimed. " Is this the stuff you jazz to in Bay-ping ? "

" Aw, take that off, it gives me the jitters, and just as I'm wantin' to cool off."

" Jeez, it's hot ! I guess I'll switch to beer. Boy, bring me six bottles of lager straight off the refrigerator, and nuts to the Scotch ! "

Elvira did not succeed in learning more about her guests than that they were newcomers to Peking. A lousy dump they called it. It was mainly the absence of amenities that irked them. Peking society was too snooty, too " highhat." They preferred Shanghai. She asked if they had visited *The Whoopee Hop*, and it transpired that none of them had. Nor had they yet encountered Mrs. Mascot. Elvira assured them that if this was the case they were not qualified to dismiss Peking as a dump, and she proceeded to paint an idealized picture of all they had missed, of all the fun that awaited them round the corner, of the ravishing girls they would find at *The Whoopee Hop*. She boosted the place as if she had shares in it.

The marines began to yawn and kick their heels.

" Well, lady," said the Viking, " it's mighty agreeable sittin' talkin' to you, but where are your girls ? "

" Yeah," said another. " We didn't only come to say hello. Are all the girls busy or what ? This ain't Saturday night, is it ? If they don't show up mighty soon we better be quittin'."

Elvira was too much amused to take umbrage. " You've come to the wrong address," she said sweetly, " but I dare say my Boy will be able to give you the right one."

The four marines, crestfallen, stammered apologies and wished to pay for the drinks they had consumed.

" Don't mention it. You must look in again. I'll renew my stock of records in the meantime."

Elvira told Wang to direct their rickshaw coolies to Mrs. Mascot's abode. He was to send someone along on a bicycle to make sure that they got there. What a revenge, she thought, and what an escape ! But was it ? These lads were rather lovable : they represented the wholesomeness for which she had been craving. If only they had not drunk so much. " Good-bye," she held out her hand to each in turn.

" You've been pretty darn good to us," said the Viking.

" You're a real decent lady and I'm tellin' you," said another. " More power to your elbow ! "

" I hope you'll find what you're looking for," said Elvira. Which disconcerted them. The Viking gave her hand a good long squeeze. " You're a regular peach," he informed her.

The compliment went straight to her solar plexus, and for a moment she devoutly wished that the others would slip away and leave her alone with this bold young Aryan

Bacchus. Unfortunately that was out of the question to-night ; for she remembered that Yi was in the garden.

" When will you come to see me ? " she murmured in spite of herself. " Alone," she added.

Lowering his voice, a furry baritone, " Tomorrow night," he said, " if I can make it, but gee, I wish I could stay right now. I've not felt so grand since I left Manila. I'm sittin' on top of the world."

As they were near the door Elvira turned out the electric light, and he caught her in the grip of his powerful arms. Brutal but how refreshing the kisses he showered and burst upon her ! They flooded her veins with a thick and ting-ling nectar. She all but fainted away. " Tomorrow," she whispered, " just ourselves."

" You bet."

Elvira sat half-stunned in the darkness, chaotic emotions mingling with her thoughts. This brief adventure should have been distasteful : it had been delicious. Those men were ready for anything. . . . How easily it might have developed into an orgy ! But for Yi . . . She was pricked by pins and needles of regret.

Elvira was aware of a blissful metabolism. It was years since she had felt like this. An American marine—she had not even asked his name—had aroused in her a new kind of interest.

" Yi," she cried, " what have you been doing all alone in the garden ? Talking to the pixies ? "

The chorus of cicadas had died down, and the garden seemed cooler than it was in consequence. " Yi, where are you ? " The moon had risen, varnishing the freakish foliage with silver, converting the rugged rocks into glistening quartz. Elvira raised her voice : " Where are you, child ? "

Complete stillness. She peered into the Pavilion of Longevity and called again. No answer, no echo. Behind the pavilion there was a grove of trees. Why surely—Elvira gaped, unable to believe her eyes. The figure of Yi appeared to be dangling from a branch. As Elvira drew closer she uttered a long loud shriek. Tentatively, Wang crept out of the house with an electric torch in one hand, a heavy stick in another. Two servants followed close behind with kitchen-choppers.

It was no phantom, no optical illusion. Yi was hanging from a girdle, with glazed eyes and protruding tongue. She had climbed up with the aid of a chair which she had kicked from under her as soon as her neck was secure.

Immediately Wang jumped up and released her, the others assisting. Elvira telephoned for a doctor in the meantime. When she returned Wang reported that Yi was still alive. The cook, a scullery boy and an amah had joined the first-aid party. While Wang supported Yi's limp body these bent her knees forward and the amah massaged her stomach. Two of them clutched Yi's behind, in order, they said, to prevent any gas from escaping. Her neck was fearfully swollen, but she did not appear to have lost any blood. The pendulous tongue was what chiefly appalled Elvira : it was like an excrescence, reducing her delicate face to a monstrous mask. How could she ever forget that protruding obscenity ? Would it never stop lolling ?

It seemed an age before Doctor Kuo arrived, an alert young Cantonese from the Rockefeller Institute. He rapped out various orders and sent the servants running in all directions. Very gently Yi was moved on to a chaise-longue and carried indoors. " There is a fair chance of recovery," he concluded after his examination. " She had better remain here till tomorrow. Have you got in touch with her family ? No ? They will hold you responsible, if anything happens. . . ."

"I'll tell them to go to hell," Elvira retorted. "It was they who drove the poor girl to suicide."

Doctor Kuo looked scandalized. "It is your first duty to summon her parents," he cautioned.

Wang had anticipated this contingency, and Elvira was somewhat taken aback when Mr. and Mrs. Tu appeared with their own physician. At first they were so incensed to find a "foreign-style" practitioner in attendance that they made a scene the purport of which was lost upon Elvira. It was evident, however, that high words were being exchanged and Elvira, overwrought by such an accumulation of dramatic incident, butted into the fray. Unfortunately for her Yi's parents were monolingual : her tirade was wasted as on desert air. "Will you be my interpreter ?" she appealed to Doctor Kuo. "I would like you to point out that they are to blame. This is what comes of forcing a girl to marry against her will."

"I am sorry," said Doctor Kuo, "but that is none of my business. In China we mind our own business."

"Well, kindly inform them that such is my opinion." The doctor's silence exasperated Elvira the more. "Very well," she said, "I'll try to *make* them understand." She set about it with a repertoire of extempore gestures and grimaces whose variety could only be accounted for by the presence of that "funny blood" in her veins of which she sometimes boasted. On the other hand, her entire Chinese vocabulary comprised two words : *hao*, good, and *pu hao*, no good, *ergo* bad. Shouted by Elvira in sharp crescendo these two words became as effective as a whole glossary of vituperation ; and her harangue, culminating with three *pu haos*, each more spiritedly aspirated than the last, was punctuated with a clenched fist which she shook at the shrinking, blinking elderly couple.

"As for you," she turned upon Doctor Kuo, "you're a

contemptible little coward. I don't know how you wormed your way into the medical profession. You look as if you should still be in the kindergarten."

The doctor shrugged his shoulders. " I should advise you," he said laconically, " to go to bed."

" Easier said than done, my little man ! "

Their dismay subsiding, Yi's parents took no more notice of Elvira than of a coolie shouting in a *hut'ung*. Mrs. Tu knelt down beside her prostrate daughter. Sobbing, she smoothed Yi's hair again and again, as if she imagined that she could thereby restore her to consciousness. Mr. Tu stooped over her with a haggard mournful stare ; in a steady voice he questioned his private physician, who had felt each pulse for an eternity. Mr. Tu declined on principle to listen to any doctor from the Rockefeller Institute. Satisfied with the diagnosis of his physician, he asked Wang to show him where the accident had occurred. Wang conducted him to the sinister tree behind the Pavilion of Longevity. Ghastly it appeared in the cold light of an electric torch. Yi's girdle still clung to a twisted, evil-looking branch, and the chair which had served as accomplice stood underneath it. Wang was explaining that the looseness of the girdle, the comparative lightness of the branch and its nearness to the ground had probably saved Yi from immediate strangulation, when he started gibbering " *hao ssŭ, hao ssŭ* "—" it is good to die " —and slipped the girdle over his own head. It required the combined strength of all Elvira's servants to drag him away, raving like a madman. Then he collapsed.

To everybody except Elvira the solution was obvious. The garden was haunted by a *Tiao Ssŭ Kuei*, or " hanging ghost." There are plenty of that ilk in the nooks and byways of Peking, ever lying in wait for those who are weary of this mortal coil. Eager to play the prompter's rôle, they will even go so far as to fix the rope in position : in this case it had been Yi's girdle. The amah swore she had beheld the spectre, an innocuous-looking oldster in white, beckoning from behind a tree. Wang was equally emphatic when he recovered, still badly shaken and all of a tremble, from his swoon. He declared that the ghost had kotowed to him several times, muttering " *hao ssŭ* " in an extraordinarily persuasive tone. " But you muttered it yourself," said Doctor Kuo, saddened by his countryman's display of superstition.

" I ?—never !—I'm far too fond of life. In worshipping the Old Man of the South Pole I'm as zealous as the First Emperor himself."

" That is the trouble," said Doctor Kuo, " you're suffering from over-zealousness. Your eyes saw nothing at all. . . ."

" What about mine ? " interjected the amah. " Who else has white whiskers here ? I saw the ghost as distinctly as I now see you, and I've never had to wear spectacles yet."

" Superstition's as infectious as diphtheria," sighed Doctor Kuo. " These cases should be isolated and rigorously dealt with."

Wang decided to fetch a Taoist wizard to exorcise the ghost. The tree was sentenced to be cut down. It was hard on four in the morning when Elvira retired, but the Viking's ravenous lips blotted every other image from her brain, and his baritone uttering crude syllables of desire dissolved her body in delicious slumber.

# CHAPTER XIX

## Passing the Torch

PHILIP had only one matter to complain of : Hsing-chieh was badly bitten by the West. He did everything within his power to counteract this obsession. He had him vaccinated, and took him on excursions to historical sites in Peking and its vicinity. But all the wonders of the Forbidden City and Summer Palace combined failed to evoke more than a momentary, supercilious interest. America was the land of his heart's desire : he panted for the skyline of New York. In his room he treasured a picture of the Empire State Building : one hundred and three stories, twelve hundred and fifty feet high, nearly a quarter of a mile of vertical distance, the scale of it impressed him far more than the Great Wall and the hoary antiquity of China's past. Philip was frequently tempted to confiscate this picture and destroy that bundle of *The Illustrated London News* which had wrought so much havoc, but on second thoughts he refrained. For Hsing-chieh might resent it ; persecution might aggravate this obstinate disease.

Guiding him through temples and palace halls, Philip was most painstaking in his efforts to stimulate the patriotic pride of his protégé : he would tell him about Kublai Khan who laid out the capital " with long wide roads through which horsemen could gallop nine abreast," about Yung Lo who rebuilt and magnified it, some said according to the secret plan of a Taoist priest, and of the city's vicissitudes and splendours from that time until 1928 when the Nationalist Government degraded it and altered its name. Hsing-chieh's

256

indifference was crushing. Though Mr. Tun reported that he was making progress in his studies—Hsing-chieh possessed the retentive memory of his race, reinforced by his early discipline under Mr. An—Philip guessed it was chiefly due to the Kodak he had promised him on his conquest of the *Three Character Classic* and *Catalogue of Surnames*. For Hsing-chieh made no bones about it : his Chinese teacher bored him, and he longed to study English.

Philip did his best to discourage this hankering. " How will you ever master a foreign language when you have not mastered your own ? You'll have plenty of time for English later on. . . ."

But Hsing-chieh was so importunate that Philip had to give way. Eventually their evenings were dedicated to English grammar and the ABC.

This Occidental mania, rather than a confused conception of *meum et tuum*, explained the boy's reluctance to wear his own clothes. At first he had the excuse that he had pawned them to help Mr. An. But when Philip redeemed them, buying him quite a trousseau besides, and Yang still persisted in wearing the old pepper-and-salt Norfolk jacket, this excuse was no longer valid. Perhaps, thought Philip, he will come to change his ways when he sees that I adopt his native garb in preference to mine. Philip henceforth discarded his serge and grey flannel.

A double transformation thus took place : while his Chinese protégé was striving to Westernize himself, Philip was gradually turning into an extinct type of Oriental. To cultivate a queue was out of the question, but he grew a moustache which he trained to straggle downwards with a special comb, and he let his nails develop into scholarly talons. Nor was he ever without a trio of polished walnuts which he revolved in his hands, to increase tactile sensitiveness rather than to cure rheumatism. He made a gallant effort to addict

s

himself to a strictly Chinese diet, but in this case though the spirit was willing the flesh was weak. So long inured to homely British fare, his conservative stomach revolted. He could not mortify the flesh to the extent of forgoing his morning porridge or the seed-cake which invariably accompanied his afternoon tea (with sugar and cream). He compromised by having his meat and vegetables minced and served in little saucers, and by substituting chopsticks for a knife and fork. In lieu of Swedish exercises he daily wrote a hundred characters and practised painting mountainous landscapes according to the recipes of the sublime Tung Ch'i-ch'ang.

"The painter," said Chuang Tzŭ, "divests himself of his raiment and sits cross-legged." Philip took this saying so literally that he caught a chill. In searchings after the requisite spirit-resonance (*ch'i-yün*) he lost flesh. Everything else could be acquired by earnest application, but if the spirit-resonance were lacking he would never be more than a dauber. Mr. Tun had praised his mists and dissolving clouds. Unfortunately Mr. Tun was afflicted with cataract.

Granny Yang had become a household institution. Established in the eastern wing of the compound, she devoted her time to eating, sleeping, and gossiping with the old women of the neighbourhood. Philip's extravagance—as such she saw it—alarmed her. Granted that barbarian victuals were more costly and that foreigners were made to pay more for everything on the strength of being foreigners, it chafed her, as Kou-êrh's grandmother, to know that Philip was being so grossly overcharged. And the knowledge that Ning pocketed so much "squeeze" in which neither she nor her grandson had any share was like an acid corroding her rusty brain. She watched Ning like a lynx. She tried to keep tab of his daily purchases. She waylaid Mr. Tun, and extracted from him that he had to hand over to Ning not ten but twenty per cent. of his salary. She discovered that the cook had equal cause to be disgruntled. But she bided her time. Too prudent to broach these matters to Philip directly, she fomented the general dissatisfaction with Ning, yet nobody dared to take the initiative. Kou-êrh's marriage seemed the one and only solution.

" Now that this unexpected good fortune has come to us," she remarked to her grandson, " I shall be able to find you a bride."

" Have you consulted my father ? "

" It's been on my mind these last few days, so much so that I haven't been able to sleep."

" What prevents you from seeing him ? "

" The trouble is this : as soon as I come in sight of those popping eye-balls and that big beak of a nose like the God of Thunder's I get so panicky I'd run away if only I knew whether my legs were carrying me backwards or forwards ; the tongue cleaves to the roof of my mouth. I think you'd better do the talking. You can say that I spoke to you about it, and that being a peasant woman without much knowledge of the world I couldn't presume to approach him."

" Let's wait a bit. It's only a month since I've been eating his rice ! "

" The sooner the better. With a wife under my super-vision to keep an eye on things less money will go astray. At this rate of expenditure there will be nothing left over for your sons and grandsons. Though the master may be rich, we mustn't mistake him for ' a money-shaking tree.' "

" There's a saying : if it is your destiny to have sons, what signifies early or late, provided they do but live."

" There's another saying much more to the point : sons should be born early, not late ! "

" Just now it's rather too early. Besides, I do not want to

marry yet. Foreigners choose their own mates : why shouldn't I ? "

" *Ai-ya*," sighed Mrs. Yang, " my worst fears are coming true. As soon as I stepped over this threshold I said to myself : This is all very fine so long as the boy keeps his head, but there's a danger that this devil from across the sea will cast a spell on him. I came too late to prevent it. You must have looked into a mirror and been bewitched. Before you know it you'll turn into a barbarian yourself with whiskers round your mouth just like a monkey. Now you're what we used to call a Secondary Hairy One when I was young— dressed up in that silly suit ! It's a very sad case and I'm sorry I lived to see it. Well, well, it must have been deter- mined in a previous incarnation ! "

Hsing-chieh was indignant but respectful. As for Granny Yang, she never despaired. Was it not a fixed principle that " an orphan boy will have sons and grandsons galore " ? She quietly pursued her private investigations. A go-between by instinct, she already had her list of virgins, but the final choice rested with Philip. The money was there all right ! From the average of his monthly expenses she deduced that he could afford a first-rate wedding. Her be-all and end-all was to bring this about as soon as possible. Dreaming of the feast and procession of gifts and Western-style band (her one concession to modernity), Mrs. Yang dismissed her grandson's unfilial objections. The bride-to-be stepping down from the scarlet chair, the envious eyes of those who had slighted Mrs. Yang in the past—all the élite of Pei-an-ho should witness the festivities—these were what the dame looked forward to with such excitement that she felt she would burst if she contained it any longer. Speak to Philip she must. It was not in her nature to keep her thoughts to herself. Screwing up her courage she finally sent him a message that she had a matter of the utmost importance to discuss.

Philip was sitting cross-legged in the nude preparatory to painting a sprig of plum-blossom. "Don't disturb me," he said, "I'm waiting for the divine afflatus."

"Mrs. Yang says it's urgent."

"What a nuisance!"

Philip's mind still dwelt on yesterdays more fascinating than today when Granny Yang appeared. She had pinned a bright red flower of chenille in her imitation nape-knot and looked positively skittish, as if, by sympathetic magic, she had become the bride her brain was full of. "It must be something to do with the Tuan Yang festival," Philip surmised. "We're already in the fifth month.[1] Good gracious, how time flies!"

Consequently when he inquired if she was preparing any *tsung-tzŭ*, the glutinous rice-cakes which appertained to this season, Mrs. Yang misunderstood him.

"*Sun-tzŭ*! (Grandsons!)" she exclaimed with a chuckle. "What a coincidence, for that's precisely what I've come to consult you about. It's time Kou-êrh was married. I can find him just the right mate, thus saving you all the expense of a professional matchmaker. Will you leave the arrangements to me?"

"You did not hear me correctly," said Philip. "I said *tsung-tzŭ*. I happened to be thinking of the Tuan Yang festival. What is this nonsense about marriage?" Forgetting that he had been born in England by mistake, he frowned as he continued: "Hsing-chieh—(I wish you'd stop calling him Kou-êrh)—is far too young to marry. He hasn't been a month inside my house, and he is now trying to master the *Catalogue of Surnames*. A wife would distract him from his studies and probably impair his health. He has a great deal more to learn before we talk of nuptials."

"Are you going to make a monk of him? 'To marry

[1] According to the Chinese (lunar) Kalendar.

boys and girls is the cardinal rite of rites ; how can parents refuse to perform this duty ? ' Rearing sons for old age is more important than book-knowledge."

" You evidently did not think so when you sold him to Mr. An. Which reminds me that Hsing-chieh should observe some sort of mourning for his departed teacher. This haste is most indecent."

" If I hadn't sold him we'd have had nothing but wind to eat. One can't subsist on swallowing saliva ! Given the same circumstances you'd have done likewise. As for that teacher of his, why should he go into mourning for an opium-sodden good-for-nothing ? A young unmarried man, says the proverb, is like a vicious horse without a bridle. Ponder this thrice, my lord ! "

" Let us discuss it in a year or two," said Philip. " His education comes before all else."

" If you leave the arrangements to me, I'll pledge my word that marriage won't interfere with his education."

" Enough ! If you so much as mention the subject I'll send you back to Pei-an-ho. I won't have you putting foolish notions into the boy's head. Time will show whether Hsing-chieh is worthy of the fatherly affection I have bestowed on him. I would remind you of the proverb : ' If you have only ten taels don't buy many clothes ; if you have only one hundred dollars don't marry a wife.' The blunder of a moment may poison a lifetime : remember that ! We are now in the fifth month and the season of heat is advancing. You had better turn your thoughts to warding off disease and evil influences. Have you got plenty of calamus and mugwort to hang outside the doors ? "

Granny Yang retreated in confusion. Strange that Philip, Chinese in his ways where so much else was concerned, should have this one blind spot ! She knew that Ning, eavesdropping as usual, had witnessed the failure of her mission.

How he would gloat over her loss of face ! She would appeal
to Kou-êrh : even if it meant humiliating herself she would
make him listen to reason. The doting foreigner would
surely give way if Kou-êrh set about it in the right manner.

" Stop ! " shouted Philip. " Did Hsing-chieh put you up
to it, or did the idea of this hasty marriage spring from your
own misguided brain ? "

" I really don't know," said Mrs. Yang slyly, " but it's
not to be wondered at if a boy of his age should think of
settling down."

" I must see him at once," said Philip. " At once ! "

Mrs. Yang fled.

Hsing-chieh, however, was not to be found. He had
stolen off to see the Marx Brothers.

Philip paced his study with folded arms, deliberating what
he should say. He was seriously perturbed. Was he being
unreasonable about Hsing-chieh ? Funny that the boy had
not confided in him if it was marriage he desired. No
doubt it was due to an innate delicacy. . . .

Philip had avoided sexual topics. He had never asked him
if he had slept with a woman, though he had often been on
the point of sounding him on the subject, of warning
him about the attendant risks. Venereal disease was said to
be sadly prevalent in Peking, and Philip himself had been
more than once deprived of sleep by a wicked little pimple.
So morbid had he become with regard to spots that he
scrutinized himself in the mirror with all the assiduity of a
professional beauty and, at the slightest rash, rushed off for a
blood test. It therefore behoved him to embark on an explanation, but he lacked the courage : the whole thing was
too distasteful. He might only do harm. Hitherto he had
consoled himself by noting Hsing-chieh's lack of curiosity
in the other sex. What if he should ignite that curiosity by
drawing attention to it ? Perhaps he had been wise to

refrain. He wanted to get his mind away from it, but he could only do that by seeing him. What did he know of Hsing-chieh's temperament ? He realized immediately that he knew very little, apart from a few rough indications, a certain wilfulness and perversity, an odd streak of feminine vanity, as when one day he had kissed his own photograph. All his memories, beginning with that afternoon in the Chi Hsiang Theatre, seemed far too flimsy for adequate understanding of his character.

Granny Yang had wakened Philip from his trance. It was a rude and chill awakening. Just when he fancied he had shed his old body and soul to assume that of a Chinese scholar, she had reminded him that he was British after all—a sentimental Englishman fantastically floundering outside his own stratum of humanity. Elvira was right : he was far too self-centred. Completely shut off from every foreign distraction, surrounding himself, as it were, with Chinese spirit-screens, he thought he could impose an exotic design on his existence and finally, through the adoption of a Chinese boy, live himself into the traditional life of Peking, severing every link with that other planet England. He had been too meticulous, too conscientious : in his preoccupation with the details of his design he had lost sight of the essential spacing, the distribution of parts. He had lost, in fact, his visual grip of reality. Instead of accepting Hsing-chieh as he was, he had tried to remodel him in accordance with preconceived theories : come to think of it, the projects he had formed for his education were almost as bad as the English Public School system ! Naturally this had produced an opposite effect to that which Philip had intended. Disappointed as he was, Philip was forced to admit his self-deception. Hsing-chieh, alas, was not such stuff as Confucians were made of. The irony consisted in this ; while trying to fortify himself in one of those rare precincts of the past at which the present has kept battering in vain, Philip had unwittingly opened his door to the present, personified by the boy he had adopted. As an experiment it was beginning to prove expensive. Hsing-chieh would have to be married sooner or later, and then he would have to find him a job. Philip possessed a tidy little income, but not what are known as means.

Ning appeared. " Have you found the young master ? "

" No, *Lao-yeh*. Ma *T'ai-t'ai* wishes to see you."

Philip hesitated. " Tell her I'm not——" But no, in his present mood he might as well face her. It would take his mind off his troubles.

Mrs. Mascot simpered in like an imitation of her usual self, spurting words like a geyser.

" Oh, my godfathers ! You've grown a walrus moustache ! Whatever induced you to do that ! You remind me of Old Bill in Captain Bairnsfather's cartoons—Old Bill dressed up as Doctor Fu Man Chu. Well, well, some say that a kiss isn't a proper kiss without bristles. It makes you look more manly, I declare. I wish more men would grow moustaches ; they're getting too like women altogether. But science is taking such strides these days that soon I dare say another sex will be evolved. I hope I live to see it. What a cosy little den you've got here. And to think that this is the first time I've tracked the lion ! What a very strange place the world is ! But really you have no right to shut yourself up as you do, depriving us of your genial company. There are duties you owe to society, you know, and duties you owe to The Chow Club. Which reminds me I've a bone to pick with you. Don't be alarmed : it isn't a big one ! Why didn't you attend our last meeting ? "

" I'm so sorry. As a matter of fact, I . . ."

" Don't trouble to make excuses ; *tempus fugit*, and it's only a waste of time. We managed somehow to jog along without you. Sharks' fins with pickled bamboo shoots and cassia sauce were the speciality, and oh, nyum-nyum ! pig's trotters, roasted and boiled, and the tastiest chicken-skin soup. Don't I make your mouth water ? All the same your absence was commented on. We put a cross against your name in the roll-call and fined you a dollar. Next time we'll fine you two dollars, but that's not what I'm here for. As the mountain would not come to me I decided I'd go to the mountain. I'm not afraid of losing face, not I ! " Mrs. Mascot paused to refill her magneto. Her eyes sparkled and rolled, busily scanning, recording, challenging the objects around and calculating the cost. " Do you know," she continued, " there's something about this house of yours I like. It's certainly got a something. But it needs a few feminine touches—a divan, a few splashes of colour. Keep your hair on : I don't mean anything new-fangled ! I wouldn't change its Chinese character ; on the contrary I'd underline its quaint Chineseness—that flavour of dragons and vanished dynasties and the glamorous nevermore. Why don't you let me do it over for you ? I wouldn't charge you a sixpence, honour bright ! I'd take that jolly rug as the basis of my colour-scheme. The key is pitched just a trifle too low—your timidity line again ! I'd take it cranny by cranny, nook by nook—please let me change the position of that table !—and by the time it emerges from its nap, you'll scarcely recognize it ; it'll be a perfect darling of a place. We'll give a party in its honour, lots of parties, and I vow they'll acquire a reputation all their own. Whoever comes will want to come again. Mind you, our invitation-list must be very exclusive. No climbers shall be asked, but we won't insist on social position. All we shall demand of our guests is that they be worth-while. Oh Phil, I'm so glad I looked you up this afternoon. It's given me bushels of ideas, all piping hot ! But I'm wandering off the beaten track :

that's not what I've come about." Mrs. Mascot fanned herself, fluttering her eyelids. Philip waited.

" What about our partnership, Phil ? Have you made up your mind ? "

" That's asking a good deal," said Philip. " As you yourself remarked, you have so many fish to fry. There's the Costume Salon, the tea shop, the lending library, The Chow Club, The Whoopee Hop, the Hopei Crafts and Arts : if you think I could cope with all these you're a poorer psychologist than I imagined."

" We women are like butterflies. We must always be fluttering from flower to flower, taking a sip here and a sip there. A single flower soon palls. I should never expect any man to cope with all the blossoms in my garden. I flatter myself few women could. I only meant the curio facet of my activities."

Philip was thinking about the future of his adopted son. It suddenly struck him that this might give Hsing-chieh an opening. If he had only himself to consider he would snap his fingers at such a proposition, but his recent interview with Granny Yang had turned the scale : " a change came o'er the spirit of his dream." Philip retained a poker-face the while.

" You must know my aversion to tourists ! "

" Fiddlesticks ! You can get on with them famously when you make up your mind. The Pomfret party have never stopped singing your praises. Why, Lady Darkling was asking me only the other day, ' Who was that most engaging man I sat next to who specializes in Manchus ? ' She was most impressed by your mystic manner as she called it. . . . Besides, circumstances alter cases. Mrs. Mustang begged me to let her take my house. She's never given me a moment's peace since she set foot inside it. Always at the telephone, beseeching me on her bended knees. My house, as you know, has always been sacred to me, an inviolable part of my innermost essence. I believe I lived and loved there in a former incarnation. What tales it could tell! What a multitude of associations, bitter and sweet, all steeped in history and mystery! But Mrs. Mustang bullied and nagged at me so, I finally had no alternative but to yield. Not without shedding tears, I must confess. In the meantime I'd accepted Lancelot, and we both decided we needed a change. This is a dead secret, Phil: we're going to be married on the Pacific Ocean. Our reasons would appeal to you, they're rather subtle. We've chosen the Pacific because of its symbolic name, also because blue happens to be Lancelot's favourite colour. Besides, the ocean is boundless —but mum's the word! Thus altruism has its compensations. Everything fits into the pattern if one's a philosopher, and China makes one that. Mrs. Mustang has turned out to be very appreciative and understanding, and I've had lots of fun doing the place over for her. At first the furnishings promised to be something of a problem—a bathroom to every bedroom, yet everything with a distinctive Eastern quality, even the taps. Just now it's a regular shambles— all colourful confusion—but as soon as it's shipshape and in apple-pie order I'll invite you round. You'll be surprised: it's entirely rejuvenated. Lancelot will announce our engagement at the housewarming. We hope it will coincide with *The Jade Thumb-ring's* last full stop. It's Lancelot's masterpiece beyond the shadow of a doubt, even more gripping than *The Thirteenth Concubine*. I won't attempt to describe it, for it utterly beggars description. Here I am wandering again! The tragedy of my life is that I've got too much to say and never the time to say it in. I'm always forced to be brief. To return to the question of our partnership. I'm seizing the bull by both horns and opening a shop."

"Surely," said Philip, "you've had one ever since I've known you."

"Not a curio shop. I've only dealt privately and with people who came to me with letters of introduction—people with an established social background. Of course I can't do that with Mrs. Mustang in my house. I shall have to carry on at *The Whoopee Hop*. Cedric's come over queer since Veronica gave him the slip : he's lost all interest in the management...."

"I shouldn't think it was exactly the right place," began Philip.

"Of course I'll change the name of the premises. In future it will be known as *The Mascot Galleries*. Not suitable ? Why it's absolutely ideal ! "

"And where do I come in ? "

"Don't flurry me ! One thing at a time. I'm always shy when it comes to talking business. My whole spirit revolts against the petty material details. Sheer agony, though you might never guess it—practical as I may strike you on the surface, I'm absurdly sensitive when it comes to mentioning money. Money, always money ! The clink of coins, the minted round of metal ! The drab necessity of this vale of tears ! I often wish we could barter as in the good old days, embroideries for velvets, peaches for pears. . . . Well, well, as I was saying, I'm removing my collection to The Mascot Galleries. Everything will be arranged so as to create a series of pictures illustrating the glamour and grandeur of past Cathay. I'm representing the Han period by a miniature stable of pottery horses ; the T'ang by a caravanserai of clay camels on the one hand—(they were introduced into China by Captain Gulley's Mongols)—and by picturesque groups of dancing girls and musicians on the other, all fresh as paint ; you'd never dream they were dug up out of age-old tombs. It's no good my asking Cedric to give us dance-music in his present frame of mind ; I'll have to put in a concealed gramophone to complete the

illusion. You'd swear the figures were actually moving
when I turn on the light. Celadon is the keynote of my
Sung section. But I've never been much of a historian, Phil,
and sometimes I get a wee bit wonky about the fundamental
facts. Ch'in, Tsin, Kin and Ch'ing, for instance—I always
get those dynasties mixed up. Now *you* can put me right.
I've had to sense my way through the epochs by dint of sheer
instinct. This is where I need your advice and co-operation.
You who've read everything about Cathay can come in as
my historical expert. Things Chinese demand for their
appreciation a certain initiation, a certain special sense. I
want you to help me prepare a little brochure which will
serve as an intellectual cocktail to the uninitiated. My clients
often complain that blackwood chairs aren't comfortable :
we must counter this with a hearty dose of uplift. Comfort
and beauty very rarely click. Which has the greater inspira-
tional and spiritual value ? Beauty. ' A thing of beauty is
a joy for ever.' You can't have your cake and eat it. . . .
Now I'm going to make you a very generous offer. Mine's
the capital and mine's the spadework, but I'm ready to offer
you a twenty-five per cent. commission on everything sold
in the shop."

" What will happen while you're away ? "

" We can discuss that later. The question is, are you
agreeable ? "

" I've had so little experience in this sort of thing."

" You can leave that to me. I'll provide the experience.
But it needn't be a one-sided affair : there's a lot we can learn
from each other. ' We mortals lend each other life, and
parch—(excuse me) *pass*—the torch from hand to hand '—
that was one of my father's favourite quotations. I'm passing
you the torch, Phil. Now do come out of your shell and
be a sport ! You'll soon get into the swim."

It was half-past four and Ning brought in the tea, thick

brown Ceylon, a jug of cream, Demerara sugar, buttered toast, scones, a substantial seed-cake and a pot of Crosse & Blackwell's bloater paste.

" Will you please pour ? " said Philip.

" You make me feel I'm in England. What a spread ! Really, Phil, you'll never hoodwink me. It's no earthly good your pretending to be a Chinaman : I've caught you out. Where do you get your seed-cake ? " she continued. " I've never tasted better."

" It's home-made."

" True blue caraway ! We used to have it on Sundays at the vicarage. You must have taught the cook how to make it. Now I've got you in my clutches, Mr. Flower. If you reject my offer, everyone in Peking shall hear about your solid English teas. You won't be able to put on any of your Celestial airs after that ! "

" What makes you think I'll reject it ? I merely have to be cautious. I have my adopted son to think of."

Hsing-chieh chose this moment to return from the cinema. Philip introduced him.

" You old humbug ! "—Mrs. Mascot wagged a forefinger at Philip. " So Poppy Trumper was not far wrong after all. Do introduce me to the Manchu Missus. Something told me this wasn't a bachelor's abode : I felt it in my bones, I couldn't say why. I'm sure she's responsible for the seed-cake. Does the son and heir speak English ? "

Hsing-chieh's eyes glittered. He had managed to understand the last sentence. " I speak little," he said. " I just begin. I love English language. I love speak English any time, all time. I velly happy speak with you."

The ardour and breathless rapidity of this little speech left Philip stupefied. He could not have believed it possible.

" That's very nice of you," said Mrs. Mascot.

Philip twisted his fingers nervously.

Hsing-chieh laughed gaily at his personal triumph. " I hope I see you many times," he said.

" So do I—I'm sure we'll have lots in common." Turning to Philip, she said : " He's irresistible. Such sympathetic eyes ! You'd never think he had an English father. I suppose he takes after his mamma. He's as pretty as a girl. You ought to dress him up. And he'll fit beautifully into the shop. I foresee his success as a salesman. Have you any other additions to the family circle ? No ? That is a shame. My word, it's time for Lancelot to take his drops. Don't keep me waiting : is it to be yes or no ? "

" Have you brought a contract with you ? "

Mrs. Mascot gasped. " In a purely friendly arrangement of this kind, why bother with a contract ? " she exclaimed. " Surely my word is sufficient ? "

" No doubt it's the fad of a fogy, but I prefer things cut and dried. When arrangements are in black and white I know where I stand."

" How like a man ! I've always abominated legal documents—the niggling little clauses and fussy complications. Materially they're an extra expense ; spiritually they're so squalid and degrading—you'd think honesty was as extinct as the dodo. A contract nips romance in the bud."

Philip had caught the rhythm of Mrs. Mascot's rhetoric. " It needn't in our case ! Just a slight formality," he said suavely. " I wouldn't insist if you were not going away."

There was nothing else but to submit with a good grace. " I appreciate your point," she said. " I'll have the contract ready by tomorrow. And now I must return to Lancelot. This has been a real red-letter day. Together we'll open up new channels, new areas of beauty. . . ."

Granny Yang had been listening at the door, and Philip turned the handle before she had time to retreat.

" Aha," crowed Mrs. Mascot, " the famous Manchu Missus ! How-do-you-do ! "

Mrs. Yang smiled, but her eyes peeped full of panic from their wrinkles. Nobody had ever shaken her hand before.

" She's Hsing-chieh's grandmother," Philip tried to explain.

" Your mother-in-law ! I hope she keeps you in line."

" I assure you I adopted Hsing-chieh as an orphan. . . ."

" Tell that to the horse-marines ! "

Mrs. Mascot left Philip spluttering. What had he let himself in for ? At any rate the contract was not signed. . . .

He felt considerably better after shaving his moustache. That evening he asked his adopted son if it was true that he wanted to marry.

" Loans without interest should be paid as soon as possible," said Hsing-chieh ; " benefactors should be rewarded at the earliest opportunity. I shall marry whenever you require me to."

" Would you like to marry soon ? "

Hsing-chieh said nothing, but his face was clouded.

" Whenever you wish," he repeated with a resignation that sounded none the less dejected for being polite. " But before I do that, oh please, take me to see at least one foreign country ! "

A weight was off Philip's mind ; such trifling considerations as his partnership with Mrs. Mascot were swept aside in the torrent of his relief.

" You shall," he promised fervently. " You are a filial and a "—(he hesitated, embarrassed by a sudden surge of emotion, but every carnal thought seemed an impiety, and he ended on a tamer, triter note)—" a very *sensible* boy."

An extraordinary radiance shone from Hsing-chieh's jet-black eyes. He clasped Philip's hand and shook it with all his might. " I love my Daddy," he intoned in English.

Philip did not attempt to restrain his tears. This was the

T

most wonderful thing that had ever happened to him, the moment he had waited for all his life. The very air was almost too sweet to breathe. He felt he would, nay must, be happy ever after.

# CHAPTER XX

## A Puff of Cloud

M RS. FÊNG had been snoozing on the sofa. Hearing her son's familiar footstep she opened her eyes and smiled. That smile was the consummate expression of a devotion which had never been demonstrative despite its depth. Chung-han was her favourite child : she would have spoiled him had she possessed the means. He had given her twice as much trouble as her other children and was therefore twice as dear. She had studied his passing moods, so that he did not have to tell her what was on his mind. She knew that Yi had played with him and cast him off. The crisis was over now. The painful intentness of his manner, his nervousness of gesture, had given way to a refreshing calm. His face had set in a definite and gathering expression of resolution, and Mrs. Fêng's hopes had lately begun to revive. He had promised to go back with her to Amoy. He had been very pliable, realizing that he must get away from the place where he had been so unhappy. Yes, he had been brave ; she was proud of the self-control he had shown throughout these long and bitter months.

" I had only intended to lie down for a short rest," she said, " and I must have fallen asleep at once. How long have I slept ? Already four o'clock ! Alas, the body gets the upper hand as one grows old and feeble. Where have you been ? "

" At Doctor Li's, as usual."

" Has he accepted your resignation ? "

" He has given me three months' leave to reconsider it."

" You told him that I wished you to resign ? "

" Yes. He said : ' You cannot be faithful to the demands both of filial piety and loyalty to your country at the same time.' "

" What arrogance ! So he identifies himself with China."

" It is an open secret that he will soon be appointed Minister of Education."

Mrs. Fêng did not appreciate Doctor Li Ssŭ. He illustrated Confucius's saying : " Men of old learned for their own sake ; the men of today learn for show." She considered his influence pernicious : but for the Doctor, Chung-han would never have met Tu Yi.

" So much the worse for us," said Mrs. Fêng. " That charlatan ! It was an evil day that brought you two together. I read in this morning's paper that he was sailing for Japan. What is he going there for ? "

" He was going to Tokyo for a conference ; but he's suddenly changed his mind. He leaves for Shanghai tomorrow. I gather there's likely to be another ' incident.' He's shutting up house and sending his family south. The archives of our institute are all ready for removal. It seems that General Hu's last speech ' The Time for Sacrifice ' has provoked the militarists of ' a certain nation.' They're making new demands, so it's just as well to be prepared for the worst."

" We're leaving anyhow," said Mrs. Fêng.

Chung-han was not so certain. Already he repented of his decision. He dared not tell his mother he had also called on Yi. Elvira had sent him word that Yi had been at death's door, and he had gone directly to the Tu mansion for news of her. Yi was recuperating but he had not been allowed to see her. Perhaps that was fortunate : he wanted to forget her. But the mere mention of Yi upset Mrs. Fêng : all her anger flamed out against this unnatural minx who had held her dear one fawning on a leash of futile hope.

" Have you written to your sister ? "

" I haven't had time. I'll write her now."

He sat before his roll-top desk. " What am I to say ? "
He had tried to coax his mother to stay longer, but she felt she
would serve no useful purpose by doing so. In Chung-han's
house there was not enough for her to do ; he was absent
most of the time. Her recent ill health had been mainly
due to ennui : in Amoy there was always something to
engross her attention. True, she had enjoyed the nursing-
home. Chung-han had persuaded her that a rest-cure was
what she had been needing ever since her arrival, and that a
nursing-home with a quiet garden and comfortable rooms
could guarantee her that. But it was chiefly the company
and conversation of valetudinarians like herself for which she
languished, and the nursing-home had provided her with
these simple healthful distractions. The patients were always
ready to discuss their ailments ; the doctors their treatments ;
and the nurses seemed to have been especially selected for
their gift of sympathy. One of the nurses, a Miss Hsü, had
made a particularly delightful impression on her. They had
become great friends in spite of their disparity of age. Even
Chung-han had been susceptible to her charm. Mrs. Fêng
said nothing to influence him ; she would let nature take its
course ; but she knew that as a daughter-in-law Miss Hsü
would prove ideal.

" Just a short letter will do," said Mrs. Fêng. " Tell your
sister the time we're due to arrive, and so forth."

He looked up and laughed. " Are we really leaving next
Saturday ? "

" Next Saturday ! " she exclaimed. " I thought we had
decided to leave on Monday."

Postponing and procrastinating, he resembled his father, for
all his revolutionary tendencies. Wherefore this sudden
reluctance to leave Peiping ? Could it be due to Miss Hsü ?

She had noticed his anxiety to engage her in conversation ; his face had lit up when she came into the room. They had talked of Tolstoi, of Gorki—Miss Hsü had the modish mania for Russian novels : that was the only fault she could find with her. Mrs. Fêng checked the joy that was bubbling in her heart. It did not do to be over-sanguine.

Chung-han read the sentences aloud as he wrote. " Is there anything else you would like me to add ? "

But Mrs. Fêng's thoughts had been straying to her clandestine interview with a soothsayer. Her amah had prevailed upon her to consult one, against her better judgement. And against her better judgement she had been comforted by his assurances that all would come right in the end. Within eighteen moons she would be blessed with a grandson. . . .

" Please read it again."

" DEAR SISTER,—Mother has now decided to leave on Saturday——"

" You mean *you* decided, you rascal ! "

" The steamer is due to arrive on the 30th at 9 a.m. You had better hire Lao Li's sampan to meet us. If that has already been taken, the Ch'êng's is the next best choice. Tell Wang Ma to give the furs a thorough airing. The weather is getting hotter every day. Yesterday it was 99° in the shade . . ."

" Is that your modern way of writing a letter ? "

" Of course. A letter in the living language. Here I've been sending you *pai-hua* periodicals all these years and you haven't digested the fact that nowadays we write as we speak ! "

" It sounds ridiculous, but I suppose it'll pass muster. Go on ! "

" Mother has been feeling ever so much better since her rest-cure, but I fear she is disappointed with the result of her mission.

Three months have gone by and still no indication of a daughter-in-law ! I tell her not to fret. The girls of Peiping are as ' the blossoms filling the spring palace of Yüeh ' ;  maybe I'll pluck a branch in the midst of a dream.  No doubt the news will soon take Mother by surprise, as indeed it will myself."

—Isn't that so, Mother ?  Don't get huffy ! ' "

Mrs. Fêng, her brow contracting nevertheless, replied : " You're quite mistaken.  Your marriage, as I've often told you, is entirely your own affair.  But your health I do feel responsible for, and you're terribly reckless.  So long as I have a word in the matter Doctor Li will not work you to death.  Whatever he says you're coming with me to Amoy."

He stuck and stamped the envelope, then went over to the sofa where his mother was reclining.

" Mother, you are altogether remarkable," he said, " a remarkably good woman, and a remarkably wise parent. Unfortunately, in this particular case . . ."

" You had better send that letter by air mail," she retorted.

Chung-han's encomiums embarrassed her.  He inevitably spoiled them with an anticlimax about her being old-fashioned, thus evoking a past she preferred not to think about : unreal to Chung-han, it was all too real to her—the persecution she had suffered from her relatives, the sporadic hysteria during the first years of the republic, which had driven her from place to place for the safety of her children, her constant anxiety and struggle to make both ends meet. Only a woman could understand what she had been through. She could confide in Miss Hsü as she could never confide in her sons.

Chung-han still stood beside her.  " Well, well," she said, continuing her private train of thought, " no modern girl would care to follow in my footsteps.  From the modern point of view, I'm nothing more than a dull domestic drudge."

" That's fishing for compliments. Of course you know that Miss Hsü admires you immensely. When you two get together she scowls at me, and if I say anything she asks me not to interrupt."

" I wouldn't call Miss Hsü a modern type of girl."

" Did unmarried women work in hospitals when you were young, nursing male patients, taking their temperature, and washing them all over ? Of course they didn't ! Miss Hsü is playing her rôle, humble as that may be, in the national renaissance. She is keenly aware of her social obligations, and fully able to hold her own in the battle of life. If everybody had her willingness to submit to a practical training and much fatigue, I would feel more optimistic about the future ! "

" Do you think there were no women with moral courage and strength of purpose in the past ? Before the word modern you stand agape like the proverbial country bumpkin ; dazzled by dreams of lady athletes, lady lawyers, lady magistrates and professors, you forget your history. Have we any women today who can rival the political genius of Empress Wu, the poetical genius of Li Ch'ing-chao, the masculine courage of Mu Lan, the scholarship of Pan Ch'ao ? "

" Those were all prodigies," said Chung-han, " I was thinking of ordinary women."

" It is true that the average woman did not work in a hospital when I was young. That she was, as you moderns say, a purely domestic person, is also true. Her interests were limited to the family circle. But you must remember that the average family circle was infinitely larger than the number of patients in the care of a hospital nurse, and required more thoughtful handling. A woman did not only have her husband to look after ; there were usually a mother and father-in-law, brothers and sisters-in-law with their wives and children—apart from concubines and unmarried members of the family—sometimes ill, often needing advice, encouragement and comfort, not a few of them jealous, wishing to curry favour with the mother-in-law, the mistress of the house, and all of them living under the same roof. A woman had to be supremely skilful, dutiful, tactful and self-sacrificing to please so many people and win their respect. Besides housekeeping and a certain amount of needlework, she had to attend to the elementary instruction of her children—there was very little time for relaxation. Wasn't this a practical training? Would you deny these ordinary duties of an ordinary housewife any social value?"

" It seems to me that a great deal of practical ability was wasted. The modern world demands more of its women : we should take domesticity for granted, not make a cult of it."

" Until the world ends it will remain the most natural cult of all. The modern girl has gained a certain independence, but she has lost the qualities that make it worth possessing."

" Even Miss Hsü?"

" Miss Hsü is a rare exception. She promised, by the way, to visit us this afternoon."

Chung-han hastened to tidy his desk ; he upset the contents of an ash-tray into a spittoon and ran a comb through his dishevelled hair—trivial preparations which his mother observed with a twinkle in her eye.

The amah soon announced the young woman in question. Chung-han admired the way she walked into the room. So light and graceful, so free from affectation, she was verily " like a puff of cloud emerging from the hills." He had tried to struggle against this attraction : would it not lead to further misery? For Miss Hsü loved her independence ; and her work at the nursing-home supplied this independence. . . . So pure and clear her voice, it was a pleasure merely to listen. He had thought of it in retrospect, and now it grew upon him, and it thrilled him quite apart from anything she happened to say. This was the first time he saw her without her uniform. She looked slighter, standing not much higher than Chung-han's elbow.

Unlike Yi, who would have sat anywhere, in contempt of traditional etiquette, Miss Hsü stood hesitating while Mrs. Fêng urged her to sit beside her on the sofa. "Don't let's stand on ceremony," said Mrs. Fêng. But Miss Hsü insisted on selecting a stiff-backed chair ; even then she sat demurely on the edge. Throughout this little comedy, while her words floated along in a current of conventional courtesies, Chung-han became increasingly conscious of her charms. Not only the charm of her voice ; her face, shaped like the melon-seed and entirely free of cosmetics, had the smoothness of frozen lard and the glow of peach-blossoms ; her eyes were like bright ripples in a deep dark pool ; they brimmed with humour beneath eyebrows which he could not help— hackneyed as the simile was—comparing to the spring willow leaf. Surely he must have been blind not to notice these before ! When he first met her at the nursing-home she had seemed to him rather dowdy, rather countrified, and almost plain in her starched white cap and uniform. But then it was Yi who held him in thrall. Ah, he must not think of Yi— already he could feel the tears coming back. Yi's image was fading. He had ceased to love her, yet the tears came back. Not tears of anger or frustration or self-pity. It was that her mere name had become a symbol of suffering, commanding tears as hunger commands saliva.

"I had intended to come earlier," Miss Hsü explained. "Just as I was ready, another patient turned up. I was so upset—I thought I'd lost my only opportunity of seeing you before your departure. Fortunately it was nothing very serious—a hysterical girl who had tried to commit suicide. Her nerves are bad but otherwise not a scratch—the pistol went off in another direction. It's the suicide season just now ; the heat has much to do with it. . . ."

Chung-han stifled an exclamation. It couldn't be Yi since she was recuperating in the Tu mansion. But the question lingered on the tip of his tongue.

While Mrs. Fêng renewed her expressions of gratitude for all Miss Hsü's attentions, Chung-han fell into a contemplative reverie. He regretted that Miss Hsü had had her hair waved, for it did not suit her. On the other hand it betrayed that she was not above the vanities of fashion, and this amused him. Miss Hsü appeared unconscious of his scrutiny. Her bare arms, lightly tanned, showed a warm yellowish brown against her blue-speckled creamy dress, and the sight of them, soft and firm at the same time, was peculiarly soothing. She inspired him with her own self-confidence. She made him strong and clever. To be honest with himself, he had to admit that he loved her. Could she love him in return ? He would have to postpone his departure for Amoy.

" I would have invited you before, but I know how busy you are, and why should you waste your precious leisure with a stupid old woman ? Hadn't you been able to come today, I'd have gone round to the nursing-home ; it is thanks to you I am feeling so much better."

" You are far too considerate. Have you fully recovered your appetite ? "

Once on the subject of health, Mrs. Fêng's monologues became as inexhaustible as those of Chinese actors at the beginning of a play. She proceeded to explain that she had not really been ill ; but for Chung-han it would never have occurred to her to enter a nursing-home. . . .

" Mother was very sceptical," said Chung-han, " she never had much confidence in doctors, and when it comes to nurses . . ."

" You shouldn't say such things. You know I've changed my mind."

" Thanks to Miss Hsü," said Chung-han. " Now she adores the whole profession."

" We know that we're much criticized," said Miss Hsü, " I suppose it's only natural, for most patients have little else to do. But it's not only the patients "—Miss Hsü glanced mischievously at Chung-han—" it's their relatives who come and pester us, trying to draw us into conversation, and coax us away from our duties."

" You have my deepest sympathy," said Chung-han. " If they are only men it's not so bad, but if they happen to be women, what a bore ! "

" In any case you're an exception," said Mrs. Fêng. " The other nurses may be as competent, but they're certainly inferior as to charm."

Miss Hsü poured the tea and handed the sweetmeats ; she refused to be waited on.

" Why don't you prolong your stay ? Peiping is surely cooler than Amoy."

" I feel I'm needed at home. Besides, my son must have a change. He never gets a real holiday, and lately he has been talking in his sleep, which is a very bad sign. And he eats even less than I do. If he stays on, he'll be the next one to enter your nursing-home ! "

" I should like nothing better, provided that only Miss Hsü looks after me. I wouldn't allow another nurse in the room."

Miss Hsü coloured. " Then you'd have to go elsewhere," she said. " If I neglected my other patients I'd get the sack."

" Better still ! Then you could come here and devote yourself to me."

" I've come to see Mrs. Fêng, and not to listen to your idle chatter."

" I've never been more sincere," Chung-han protested.

Mrs. Fêng cackled with delight. For Chung-han had spoken the truth : he had never so gaily and frankly declared himself before. He was advancing into love with shining eyes. Nor was it all so sudden as it appeared.

" Ah, Mr. Fêng said in his letter that you wanted my photograph. I've brought one with me."

Mrs. Fêng was taken by surprise. " When was that ? " she blurted.

" You must be losing your memory, Mother mine ! "

Miss Hsü, pretending not to hear, produced a little brown photograph from her bag. " I'm afraid it isn't a very good likeness," she said.

" I've always thought you pretty," said Mrs. Fêng, " but your photo is even prettier ! "

Chung-han seized the photograph and examined it. " I can't think what has come over you, Mother. Usually you say the proper thing. In this case you should observe that lovely as the photo is, it does not render justice to the original."

" I'm telling the simple truth," said Mrs. Fêng.

" If you'll forgive me," said Chung-han, " I'll go and fetch a frame."

All he had left of Yi was a snapshot and a bundle of her letters. The former he had framed ; scarcely more than a suggestion, a silhouette, it had played a tremendous rôle in his recent life. Often, like Mr. Chu who passed through the painted wall in the *Liao Chai* story,[1] he had joined Yi through medium of this snapshot : it had afforded him a bliss the real

[1] *Strange Stories from a Chinese Studio.* Herbert A. Giles. *The Painted Wall*, p. 6.

Yi had withheld, encouraging him, invoking luxurious visions. So potent once had its magic become that he had only to hold it for Yi to materialize in his arms. But this magic soon departed : perhaps he had abused it by excessive cerebration, demanding too much, as if it could turn to flesh at any hour through mere intensity of gazing. Sometimes he had felt he was going mad because it stood there solidly yet utterly out of reach, looking at him—was that a mocking smile ?—and refusing to move. Like a poem too often recited, it had lost all evocative power. On it he now fixed his eyes, fresh from admiring Miss Hsü. Would the figure step forward ? Would Yi beckon and make one last appeal ? He removed it from the frame, still questioning intently. But he could discern no more than an anonymous dummy, featureless, almost formless, melting into shadow, the more he gazed, the more indistinct. His fingers tightening on it furiously, he tore it up and threw the fragments into a spittoon.

Miss Hsü's photograph fitted the frame to perfection.

" I have a pleasant surprise for you," said Mrs. Fêng when Chung-han returned with his trophy. " Miss Hsü is coming with us to Amoy."

" I hope she'll never leave us," said Chung-han.

" I'm only going so as to look after your mother," said Miss Hsü. " I'd be afraid to leave her to your tender mercies. Just think of it, she comes from afar to visit you and you allow her to pine away."

" Don't scold him. The fact is I'm getting too old for travel."

" What nonsense, Mother ! Miss Hsü is quite right. I'm shockingly careless and unfilial. I promise to do better in future. By the way, Mother, have we a thermometer ? "

" No. Is there anything the matter ? "

# A Puff of Cloud

"I believe I've got a temperature. Miss Hsü, would you please feel my pulse?" Chung-han held out his arm.

"Your face is neither flushed nor pale. I can see," said Miss Hsü, "that you're only pretending."

"Dear Miss Hsü, it can't harm you to feel my pulse, and it will give me such exquisite pleasure!"

"Don't be naughty, Chung-han. Do you want your mother to beat you?" Mrs. Fêng playfully tapped him with her fan.

"You shouldn't waste so much energy," said Miss Hsü. "Let's go to the Pei Hai and see how the lotuses are blooming. Mr. Fêng will have to row us round the lake as a penalty for fraud."

"I'm ready to row you round the world so long as you sit facing me."

Mrs. Fêng was all in favour of an outing. "Well," she said, "if we're going to the Pei Hai I had better change."

A few minutes later she heard a startled cry.

Mrs. Fêng and the amah peeped in. "Why, what has happened?"

Miss Hsü had covered her face with her hand. Chung-han was bending over her.

"Where did it sting you?" he asked with great presence of mind.

"Sting? What stung you, dear?"

"A wasp," sighed Miss Hsü. It was a sigh of relief. Her eyes were sparkling with love and gratitude.

"Well, well, it's scarcely surprising," said Mrs. Fêng. "Seeing such a delicate figure a wasp might easily sting you by mistake. Has nobody at the nursing-home given you 'Wasp' as a nickname?"

Amid laughter they got into rickshaws.

# CHAPTER XXI

## Elective Affinities

AFTER Mrs. Mascot there was perhaps no busier body within the purlieus of the Legation Quarter than Freddie Follicle, social editor of *The Peiping Star Bulletin*. While Mr. Beevy, the editor-in-chief of that same estimable journal, sat stirring his cocoa over tomorrow's sermonette—Mr. Beevy was a Seventh Day Adventist with archæological leanings, and his editorials were couched in the phraseology of the pulpit—Freddie was sedately threading his way from hotel lounge to lobby, from embassy to club, from bar to Y.M.C.A. Springing into and out of his rickshaw like a jack-in-the-box, Freddie collected gossip as Mrs. Mascot collected curios, with an indomitable smile. And he would approach the lobby of the Peiping Palace Hotel in the same spirit in which Mrs. Mascot would enter a Chinese curio shop, eyes a-bulge. For him, too, life was earnest. Just now, in the coppery heat— (one was only too grateful for the breeze of a passing tram) —it was rather a strain. He could never resist a film-star, and Paquita Gossamer's parties on the Palace Hotel roof had kept him up too late. But they had been worth it. She had promised him an autographed " study " of herself in *Semiramis* by Cecil Beaton. Of copy he had garnered enough and to spare, but Freddie Follicle knew not the meaning of satiety ; though ready to faint from fatigue he paused at the French Bookstore for a few preprandial words with Monsieur Vetch.

Bother ! He should have known it. Doctor Pilchard again ! Vetch was looking more tousled than usual and no wonder, hemmed in between the pertinacious gas-bag and new-piled mounds of *In Search of Old Peking*. No chance of getting a word in edgewise with Pilchard in proximity. Doubtless they were discussing that new edition of Pilchard's *Intimate Symbols*. They had discussed it for the last half-decade. I'd better slip away, he thought, when he chanced to overhear : " They cut off one of Gulley's ears and threaten to lop off the other if the ransom isn't forthcoming within ten days."

" And *la belle Véronique* ? "

" Oh, she's all right. I believe the bandits themselves escorted her to Kalgan, and parked her at the Mount Sinai Mission. Aspergill has already gone to fetch her. Very decent of him, considering the way she's behaved. I'd have left her to shift for herself."

" *On pardonne tant que l'on aime*. I suppose he loves her."

" Apparently her type didn't appeal to the bandits—they're said to be homosexual."

" *Tiens, tiens !* "

" Trumper has offered to make contact with the kidnappers and negotiate for Gulley's release. It appears that their chief was one of his *mafoos*—I wouldn't be surprised if they divided the dough between them. I'm sorry for poor old Gulley : looks as if he's in for it up to the neck."

None of this had got into the newspapers ! Freddie Follicle rushed back to the *Bulletin* office, inventing lively headlines all the way. Outside the social columns there had been a singular dearth of news. It was an ill wind that blew nobody any good.

Had it been a missionary, Mr. Beevy might have reacted to the news with some excitement. He viewed Mongolia as a missionary preserve : unless travellers went thither as messengers of the Gospel of Peace he could see no valid excuse for pitching a tent on the Mongolian steppes under present disturbed conditions.

U

"It serves him right," said Mr. Beevy. "This is an excellent object-lesson to others of that kidney. I've no patience with these flat-footed fools who go where they've no rhyme or reason to be, just stirring up trouble for honest Bible-workers. Apart from the annoyance to our embassy, it puts the Nanking government in a most embarrassing position, and it makes one's heart bleed to think of all the wicked expense that's involved. As an officer and a gentleman Captain Gulley should have known better. But is he a gentleman? What was he doing with another man's wife, I'd like to know? The whole business is discreditable. In my opinion the Captain ought to be cashiered."

"But Mr. Beevy, just think what he's been through! They've cut off one of his ears!"

"Providential retribution," said Mr. Beevy. "Worse punishments have been meted out to those who commit adultery. These bandits have their virtues. Often they rob the rich to help the poor."

The face of Freddie fell. "But Mr. Beevy!" he stammered.

"No, Follicle! The less said the better. It would be more dignified to maintain a discreet silence. We have the prestige of the community to consider. The *Bulletin* shall not be laid open to the charge of sensation-mongering. We'll leave that to the *cloaca* press of the treaty ports."

"But our subscribers are diminishing, Mr. Beevy. The general complaint seems to be that our news is stale. If we are the first to publish the facts of this outrage, our circulation will rise immediately. Two prominent figures in the community captured by roving bandits! That's news, Mr. Beevy, and we can't afford to disdain it."

"From what I've heard of her, Mrs. Aspergill is far from popular. She never comes to the Dorcas or helps at sales of work or Mission Fund Bazaars, and though her father was a canon she's a very poor churchgoer.  By their activities shall ye judge them.  Have some cocoa.  You're looking a bit green about the gills."

Freddie felt aggrieved.  Whenever he walked in with what he considered a scoop Mr. Beevy dropped down on him like a wet blanket.  But for the social section, *The Bulletin* might aptly be styled *The Missionary Gazette*.  Not long ago Mr. Beevy had delivered himself of a vehement editorial on "Military Protection for Missionaries."  Apparently the military themselves were not entitled to such protection.  It was useless trying to argue.  "I must be going," he said curtly ; " my lunch is overdue."

"Wait till you hear what I've got up my sleeve," said Mr. Beevy with a benevolent smile.  " Archdeacon Twining has unearthed another Nestorian tablet and the fragments of a fine Nestorian cross.  It is one of the most significant archæological discoveries of recent years, and it is bound to have far-reaching repercussions.  This tablet, which puts the other in the shade, proves up to the hilt that Christianity flourished in China long before the T'ang dynasty and had an even greater success in the sixth than in the seventh century.  Not only were there churches in every prefectural city, but all the great families had private chapels and, just think of it, Follicle ! the emperors of the Han dynasty attended services on Sundays.  The implications are tremendous, and I have no doubt of a great Christian revival in the near future.  The Archdeacon concludes that of all alien creeds in China Christianity has had the biggest following—until the persecution in 843.  Here is his article—I don't know when I've been so moved.  It is more than scientific : it is a spiritual message, an earnest of the extension of Christ's Kingdom, a stirring prophecy that the true faith will prevail.  And here are the photographs.  Note that the tablet is quite intact : it might have come fresh from the mason's."

"Perhaps it has," said Freddie ; "it looks to me like a fake."

Mr. Beevy gave a sharp choking sound. "Who are you to impugn the Archdeacon's scholarship ?" he fumed.

"Just now I'm a journalist. As such I think I have a sense of values. Captain Gulley's ear is news. And bandits are news. And damsels in distress are news. But a Nestorian tablet—well, it'll feature nicely, of course, in our Sunday edition. . . ."

Mr. Beevy was mollified. The Sabbath edition was his ewe lamb.

"I believe you're right, Follicle. We'll make a special Sunday feature of it. I suppose there's no escaping Captain Jenkins's ear—I'll leave it to your discretion."

Follicle's tact had won, but his cærulean shirt was sopping and the spring had gone out of him. He considered resigning, not for the first time, as he returned to his vegetarian meal. Mr. Beevy was wearing him out.

A glass of hot malted milk restored his optimism. It had been a triumphant morning. During the last fortnight the social page had related mostly to summer-resorts (echoes from Peitaiho shells) ; while he was sweltering in a dusty office, others were off to wallow in the briny. There had been the usual number of entries to hospitals " for treatment " —how few constitutions the Peking climate agreed with !— and several births (mother and infant in each case doing well). Freddie had been quite depressed : his daily prowl had brought him in so little. He had had to rack his brains for items about Dame Nature. " The watermelons this year " . . . " visitors to the Pei Hai will observe " . . . " three shooting stars were seen to alight in the vicinity of the Mormon Mission. . . ." Among the misprints there had been, as usual, some happy inspirations. Mrs. Obadiah Z. Pomfret, for instance, was " *rusting* in Peiping after an *expensive* tour of the Orient." And now the capture of Captain Gulley and this glut of engagements! The cockles of his heart were warmed again. Mrs. Mascot was an exacting friend; she knew the value of publicity and often made use of Freddie to get it gratis, but Freddie could not help admiring her. She had put him in touch with several celebrities. It was thanks to her that Thistleby had autographed his copy of *Yashmak*. "To Mr. Frederick Follicle, yours sincerely, Lancelot Thistleby"—such teeny writing that one had to look at it through a magnifying glass. And, thanks to her, he had met Paquita Gossamer. The thought of tomorrow's harvest added a dash, as of paprika, to his plate of insipid greens. The social page was brimming. He had secured snapshots of (*a*) Mrs. Mascot smirking on the arm of suave Lancelot Thistleby, (*b*) Elvira MacGibbon drooping on the arm of truculent Mr. Robert E. ("Tarzan") Dixon, of the U.S. Marine Corps, and (*c*) "a chic Chinese wedding": Mr. and Mrs. Yü Wang-shu (the bride, *née* Miss Tu Yi, was formerly associate professor of Western literature in the Mo-têng University, and the only full-time lady member of the faculty).

Freddie's youthful ambition to become a professional tap-dancer had been diverted rather than thwarted; never entirely forsaking his ideal, he tap-danced on the typewriter, with Ginger Rogers and Fred Astaire in front of him as an inspiration. Hastily swallowing the slippery segment of a canned California peach he returned to his desk or bureau as he called it. The urge to be tapping was upon him again; Ginger and Fred were beaming encouragement. Cupid, he tapped, has been busy, he tapped, in Cathay's old Capital . . .

\*     \*     \*

"Those yellow roofs," wrote Lancelot Thistleby, "glinting over the horizon, row after row." He paused. "Row after row . . ." Were they yellow or orange? Which led to the question he had not yet succeeded in solving to his satisfaction. What was the precise colour of the walls of the Forbidden City? Salmon-pink, terracotta, dried blood—it never seemed the same. He mopped his forehead. The scenes of violence and passion flowed staunchlessly from his pen, but when he came to the details of local colour it was ever thus : perplexed, he had to pause. For Lancelot Thistleby, that past-master of coloured narrative, was really colour-blind.

Mrs. Mascot had crept up stealthily behind his chair. She covered his eyes with her fingers, having previously sprayed them with lavender water. " Naughty !" she said. " Still ruminating phrases ! I've just booked two cabins de luxe on the *Empress of Ruritania*. Everything's straightened out. Mrs. Mustang has handed in her cheque. She decided to take the temple with the house, as it has such a wonderful effect on her guru. He has experienced all sorts of mystic revelations since he stepped into it. I said he would. I've had them myself, though mine weren't exactly mystic. Philip Flower will look after the shop. And Paquita has offered us ' Phœbe's Folly,' her Elizabethan cottage in the Beverly Hills. You must see that she has the film version of *The Thirteenth Concubine*. She has bought up the entire Costume Salon, lock, stock and barrel ! Poppy Trumper is taking over the tea-shop and beauty parlour, and Rosa Hawkweed has taken the bungalow at Peitaiho and promised to keep an eye on the Lhasa lions : if Rosa knew half as much about human beings as she knows about dogs she'd be one of the great Victorian novelists. But what am I saying ? Some dogs are more than human. The psychology of my Tibetans has often struck me as quite uncanny. Their souls are in their eyes. And they're so knowing. It makes one sit up and think. But to go back to my original theme : everything's arranged ; we've nothing to worry us.   It all pans out so pat I can hardly believe it."

It seemed superfluous to add that having chatted Mrs. Pomfret into a pair of jade phœnixes—pure Ch'ien Lung— the whole journey was more than paid for in advance.

"There is nobody like you."   He clasped her hand and planted a kiss on it.   Other women he had known had always seemed fragments of other women : Sheila was entirely herself.

"Base flatterer ! "   So far she had blurred over the only obstacle.   Now that had been removed.   Mrs. Mascot's philosophy (never face unpleasantness even if you have to : just blur it over !) was justified.   Dick Mascot had been carried away by a stroke in Harbin.   And the last vestiges of Deborah had died with Dick.   Long live Sheila ! She was all ready to set out on her career as Lancelot's better half.

"I have been puzzling," said Lancelot, "about the rightness of this paragraph : ' Those yellow roofs, glinting over the horizon . . .'   Would you say they were yellow, Sheila ? "

"I'd say they were gold, pure gold."

" ' Those golden roofs, glinting.'   That's a fine alliteration. You should turn author, my love."

"I'm thankful to say I know my limitations."

They understood each other well, these two.   Or as Sheila put it to her friends and clients : " We have found a something on which to base our harmony."   This was the will to glamour.   By joining forces they could form an effective bulwark against the invasion of old age.   Both made the most of themselves and the least of their burden of years.   With his dyed hair and tight pink skin and fastidious wardrobe the novelist, now sixty-three, looked little older than Sheila, now fifty-five.   Massage gave him a cherubic air.   Of course Sheila had the greater vitality, the richer " capacity for life." In certain respects it looked as if the novelist were getting the best of the bargain, for she was ready to act as his secretary, his banker, his business agent and, above all, as his sentry. She would continue to guard him against intruders. Gratefully he kissed her hand again. "You are a marvel," he exclaimed. "My Lady Peking!"

At the moment, however, her thoughts were not of Peking, but of Hollywood. Bali could wait awhile. The missionary spirit, ever burning within her, yearned to convert the decorators and dressmakers of America to an exclusive faith in Things Chinese, and Hollywood, ever hungry for Messages, promised to be a fertile field for her dynamic operations. She would titillate their yearning to be among the Initiated : she would make that Eldorado dragon-conscious, lacquer-conscious—jade-conscious. With Paquita paving the way she could preach her Pekinese crusade : Hollywood would be turned into a second Peking, Peking into a second Hollywood. . . . From Hollywood she would proceed to New York, then forward to London and Paris, making new contacts, extending her connections. The price of porcelains had become so exorbitant in the local market that it would more than remunerate her to replenish her stock in America and Europe. The cost of shipping included, they would yield handsome profits in the history-mystery-hallowed aura of their native environment.

"I can't think what has come over me lately," she confessed. "For the first time since I've been here Peking seems a trifle stale, and I don't feel tempted in the least by Peitaiho. You've stirred up the vagabond soul in me, just as you did with *Yashmak* years ago. It's more than a holiday mood. I can't think why I've stayed in China so long without a change. I feel I've been wasting my youth. I want to be up and away. East of the Sun and West of the Moon!"

"I've been a little off colour myself," said the novelist truthfully. "We'd better elope before I'm sued for alienation of affections. Peking won't be Peking without you, Sheila."

"I'll feel parting with the place, of course. And the dear ' Old Curiosity Shop ' will miss its *Ma T'ai-t'ai*. But absence makes the heart grow fonder. There now," she dabbed her moistening eyes, "I mustn't begin to get soppy. We won't tell a soul when we're leaving. I could never abide farewells. I know I should break down at the station. Why don't we fly to Shanghai ? It's time I became air-minded, and the journey's so much cooler."

Next morning Mrs. Mascot was on her virgin voyage through the air. Alas, she felt too queasy to enjoy the panorama quivering below, a vast walled pleasaunce rather than a city, the familiar white dagoba rising above the lawns of lotuses, the shady arbours and forsaken temples, patches of old gold, and beyond the walls green fields of *kaoliang*, the parched plateau, the incandescent undulating hills. Once, twice, she waved a damp little lace-edged handkerchief at the glittering diagram of the Forbidden City, the lapis lazuli bead of the Temple of Heaven, then : woo-oops ! dizziness was stealing over her with startling rapidity and she had to shut her eyes. It was like her first experience of the lift at Selfridge's, prolonged and intensified. Would she never, never set foot on solid ground ? No : the air is not my element and I was not meant for soaring, she regretfully concluded, but I won't, I won't, disgrace myself ! The effort not to be sick absorbed all the attention she had wished to devote to scenery. Enveloped in such noise it was impossible to look at clouds with silver linings or listen to the music of the spheres. Dimly, though, she remembered Elvira and her vibrations. A plane would knock some of that nonsense out of her, she thought vindictively ; and the picture of an agonized Elvira vomiting through the empyrean took her mind off her own predicament. She became more cheerful ;

she began to get acclimatized to the sky. Perhaps I'm not so terrestrial, she mused. But I mustn't jump to premature conclusions. Woo-oo-oops ! I believe I'm going to be sick after all. Oh, my poor, poor tummy ! This is absolute torture. Why was I ever so rash as to suggest it ? She gritted her teeth, which sent a sharp shooting pain right through her head ; two of them felt loose, they seemed to be wobbling about in the gums. Supposing she swallowed them ? It's like a super dentist's drill, she decided.

"How are you feeling ? " Lancelot scribbled on a page of his notebook which he passed her with a pencil. " Ethereal," Sheila scrawled. "It's loads of fun." Loads was twice underlined.

Far below, among those courtyards embowered in trees, Yang Pao-ch'in, alias Hsing-chieh, peered at the purring, shimmering machine until his eyes could follow it no longer. Still he stood there transfixed, staring into the hyaline, and all that day he was haunted by the vision of those wonderful wings ; he could think of nothing else. He now had a new obsession ; and Philip Flower sighed, for he knew that he would have no peace until he permitted his protégé to fly.

# CHAPTER XXII

## Towards Nirvana

WITHIN the next few days the visitations of aeroplanes became more and more frequent, but these were of a distinctly different type and nationality from that which had borne Mrs. Mascot on the first stage of her journey towards Hollywood, and they contained more bombs than passengers. In roaring fleets they circled over the city, to the vast irritation of the dragons that regulated the rainfall.

Mrs. Mascot had calculated her departure to an exquisite nicety. For the ominous cloud which had long been gathering on the eastern horizon could control itself no longer. It chose this moment to burst, at a distance of seven miles west of Peking. Lu Kou Ch'iao, which is known to foreigners as Marco Polo Bridge because the Venetian traveller paid it a memorable tribute, was the actual scene of its explosion. One of the Eight Famous Sights of Peking is the reflection of the moon at dawn on Lu Kou Ch'iao ; and like most beautiful things it has had to suffer. That it was destroyed by a flood in the seventeenth century ; and that several of its arches were washed away since K'ang Hsi rebuilt and Ch'ien Lung repaired it, may seem incredible, for now it spans a shrunken muddy stream. A mutiny at this bridge led to the capture of Peking by Genghis Khan in 1215 ; the manœuvres of Japanese infantry near the same structure led to the occupation of Peiping by Japanese troops in 1937.

It never rains in North China but it pours ; and the thunder of machine-guns, accompanied by heavy artillery and rifle-fire and exploding bombs, ushered in the rainiest of rainy seasons and mimicked the thunder in the firmament.

Yes, Mrs. Mascot had done well to pay heed to that intangible and indefinite sense of something impending which had come to her repeatedly of late. For by no stretch of the imagination could Peking be associated with fun, as Mrs. Mascot understood it, since the Lu Kou Ch'iao " incident." Martial law was declared ; all the gates of the city, except Ch'ien Mên, were closed ; sandbags were piled at the corners of thoroughfares. Peking was wrapt in gloom. No shopping " to freshen one up and relax the mind," for most of the shops were closed. In Jade Street, Lantern Street, Silver Street, Embroidery Street, nothing doing. The curio market, like the social merry-go-round, was at a standstill. Paomachang was evacuated, ponies and all ; the temples in the Western Hills were left to a few decrepit bonzes.

On the twenty-eighth of July the Embassies sent notices to their nationals living outside the Legation Quarter that it was advisable they move into it before noon. Most of them, begirt with their national flags as an extra precaution, had already moved in, a scuttle only less dignified than the common attitude of the so-called " interested Powers "—if to crouch like yokels peeping at a rape through a fence may be designated as an attitude. It was but natural that all Chinese who could afford to should seek asylum elsewhere : what could they gain by lingering ? Had not the commander of the Japanese garrison in North China declared that his mission was " to chastise the outrageous Chinese " ?

The foreign community, who had not been threatened with such chastisement, behaved as if they had. Panic herded them together within the toy fortress walls of the ugly little international settlement. The hotels were crammed, yet rather than go back to the comfort of their homes these poor whites preferred to stew in stuffy tents within their Embassy compounds.

Rumour throve on the hothouse air and general uneasiness. Poppy Trumper had heard " from one who ought to know what he was talking about " that the Forbidden City was on the verge of being blown to perdition by Communist agents. According to Rosa Hawkweed the imperial halls were being refurbished for the ex-Emperor's return : the whole place, she declared, was positively humming with eunuchs, two of whom she professed to have seen, in brocades that were " temptation personified "—(a pity Sheila Mascot wasn't here : she would have turned green with envy !)—dusting the Dragon Throne with a plump live peacock, or rather, to be more accurate, a sort of phœnix, a cross between an argus pheasant and a peacock. . . . It had uttered the strangest cries : you'd think you were in a Chinese theatre. Some said that there was a new movement afoot for the restoration of the pigtail and dragon flag. Doctor Pilchard claimed that it was for the last scion of the Ming dynasty that the Forbidden City was being swept and garnished.

Ming or Manchu, what did the dynasty matter ? Viewed from the Legation Quarter, China was a perennial panto-mime. Wouldn't it be grand to witness the age-old customs and costumes, the dragon flags a-flying, the revival of quaint symbolical ceremonies ? Simply grand. History in the making. Something to tell the folks at home about.

But no rumour surpassed the monstrous fantasy of realities, such a reality, for instance, as Japan's sincere effort to promote Sino-Japanese friendship.

At last the Aspergills made good. Of all the guest-houses open to English " refugees " theirs had the most personal touch : scented sachets in the wardrobes, charades and sherry in the evenings, records of the Savoy Orphean and " The Beggar's Opera," and Cedric ever ready to oblige at the piano. And for the first time tasting the sweets of popularity, they began to enjoy Peking. They blamed Mrs. Mascot for their domestic troubles, decided that she had the evil eye. Henceforth they referred to her as The Witch of Endor. Cedric composed a lyric about her which kept their guests in fits of boisterous laughter.

*In Pekin there is a witch*
*Who'd queer anybody's pitch . . .*

None the worse for her Mongolian misadventure, Veronica did a great deal of sewing for the wounded and, to quote from Freddie Follicle's column, " displayed a friendliness and hospitality that warmed the heart of guest and stranger alike." It was generally voted that the community had misjudged her. The community made amends by forgetting her escapade. Cedric took up sewing to keep Veronica company and declared it to be a most delectable vice. After a brief stitching stage he turned to knitting, which led him to try his hand at embroidery, for which he discovered an instinctive talent. His ambition was now to master the intricacies of *petit-point*. Heliogabalus had changed sex and was going to have puppies. Captain Gulley was convalescing in a Tientsin hospital : to such an extent had he bored his kidnappers that they had been content with one ear and a mere fraction of the original ransom demanded.

Elvira's engagement to Mr. Robert E. (" Tarzan ") Dixon was off. As the wife of an American marine she would have been ordered to evacuate, and much as she enjoyed her Viking's embraces she had no intention to return to God's Own Country, whether 'way beyond Rockies line or below the Dixie one. There were new realms of experience for her to conquer. Tarzan had reconciled her to Peking : his straightforward attitude had been a tonic. But he had set her body tingling, not her brain. After a while the need of intellectual stimulus began to gnaw. Would she never achieve the perfect fusion? The itch to mould recurred. She remembered a phrase about the Russians being the strongest kinetic force in Europe, and she suddenly saw the light. The U.S.S.R. had been her destination all along! Peking had merely been an interlude, a temporary purgatory to test her mental discipline, before she was fit to emerge into the new state of awareness she yearned for. Now everything was clear. She was meant for Russia, and Russia was meant for her. Colossi were in vogue there: was not Stalin himself a plastic inspiration? Granite or bronze? Already she visualized him in the abstract, at least forty-five feet high, as tall as a four-story building. Why not taller? Preferably bronze. The biggest job of casting ever handled. Elvira drew a deep breath and clutched her bosom. Energy was the only life, the modern necessity. New canals, new embankments. Commissars, concrete, steel towers, the hammer and sickle. Collective farms and factories, factories everywhere! Moscow beguiled her merely as a name. She determined to try it out. First she must get in touch with the toilers' vibrations, contemplate the muscles among the machines, join, perhaps, one of the shifts in one of the factories. . . .

Again Elvira took French leave, and caught the Trans-Siberian express without a word of farewell. "Frustration" she had foisted on Yi as a wedding present. It stood in the front courtyard of the deserted Tu mansion, deserted but for the door-keeper and his family who, not knowing what to make of it, decided to use it for hanging out the laundry.

Philip Flower was one of the few who stayed at home in his *hut'ung*, a detached and pessimistic observer behind his spirit-screen. The world was again one seething torrent, as in the age of Confucius. In describing that age Mencius might have been describing ours: "The world had fallen into decay, and truth had faded. Perverse doctrines and violent deeds had arisen ... Confucius was afraid." And Philip, like Confucius, longed for silence. But that was impossible with artillery fire in the offing and fleets of bombers roaring overhead. They drowned the matin songs of his birds ; they shattered the gracious stillness of his study. It was deplorable, yet he did not entirely blame the Japanese. The West had shown them the way ; the West had forged these weapons of destruction. Had not the Occidental nations been the first to insist on commercial intercourse with a reluctant Japan ? Had not Japan, like China, suffered from the bombardment of foreign navies ? She had learnt her lesson earlier, that was all. This meant the elimination of foreigners and their treaties, no more " open door policy " : Asia for the Asiatics. Bulldog and Boston terrier had had, like every other dog, their day. As if to corroborate this *The Peiping Star Bulletin's* social column was little more than a catalogue of departures. Not a globe-trotter left. The shrewder sharks were pursuing their prey to other climes. A good riddance, thought Philip. Whatever happened, he was resolved to remain. In his heart of hearts he hoped the Manchus would return, and that Peking would be reinstated as capital of a mighty empire.

Hsing-chieh's enthusiasm for aircraft soon subsided. He was rapidly impregnated with a new spirit of patriotism, and longed to go and fight the Japanese. Instead of studying the classics he pored over the newspapers and the *San Min Chu I*, a copy of which he had procured just before it was banned by the new régime. He picked up a smattering about the League of Nations and the Washington Conference. He bought maps of China and tacked them on his wall over the views of Manhattan and the Empire State Building and the reproductions culled from *The Illustrated London News*. These maps filled him with an ancestral feeling he had never known before. The space above his bed was adorned by a triangular Kuomintang flag. He lectured Philip very seriously about the abolition of unequal treaties.

" Has any treaty ever been equal ? " said Philip with a smile.

All the same he was worried as well as startled. Hsing-chieh was getting a bit above himself. His tone had been a little arbitrary on more than one occasion. It was fortunate that the gates of the city were closed. There was no telling what this *enfant terrible* would be up to next. Philip's peace was slipping away from him. Then, just as he was about to curse his folly, he realized that his destiny was intermingled with that of this young man. He had nobody else in the whole wide world to be fond of.

Nank'ou had fallen.

" Where are all the English and Americans ? " Hsing-chieh broke out pathetically. " Why don't they come over and help us ? "

" They have a saying that God helps those who help themselves."

" We are doing our best. I do not understand."

" China is very far from Europe ; Japan is even further. If they were nearer it might make a difference, but I doubt it. For the foreign nations are consumed by jealousy and hatred ; at present they are much too frightened of each other to move in this direction."

" But America ! She has always been our closest friend. . . ."

" When will you learn that it is the foreigners, beginning with their Protestant missionaries, who have been responsible for all China's misfortunes since the T'aip'ing rebellion ? After a long and stormy voyage China's ship of state was sailing serenely into broader, smoother waters. Both pilot and crew were congratulating themselves, as well they might :

305

x

they had overcome thirst and seasickness and briny drench-
ings ; they had contended with monster billows and been
miraculously delivered from at least one typhoon. The junk
remained intact ; the worst of the journey was over. But
for some time rats had infested the bowels of the ship. The
crew, perhaps because of their Buddhist heritage, had been
far too lenient to those rats ; some they had even tamed for
their amusement. One day they awoke to their danger : the
junk was leaking, and soon it began to sink. The ships of
certain Western states happened to be cruising in the vicinity.
Their captains saw that the junk was in distress and responded
to her signallings with messages of heartfelt sympathy. But
their ships sailed on."

" Is that all ? "

" Their ships sailed on. Sustained by messages of spiritual
sympathy, let us hope the junk's pilot and crew may keep
afloat."

" Is there nothing I can do ? "

" You can help to keep it afloat."

" How so ? By going to fight the Japanese ? "

" By studying the classics. By cultivating your mind.
The intellect can also be a powerful weapon. And you have
so much to learn ! You have only begun. . . ."

Hsing-chieh's moments of depression were fugitive as the
shadows of clouds, and they were diminished by the gift of a
radio set. Every night at eleven his ears were cocked for the
latest news from Nanking, while Mr. Tun recited the Diamond Sutra from the opposite end of the courtyard.

> *Like a dream, like a vision, like a bubble,*
> *Like a shadow, like dew, like lightning . . .*

The words, phonetically transcribed from the Sanskrit, were
chanted to the beat of a skull-shaped block of wood.

Hsing-chieh's tutor had taken refuge in Philip's house with

his wife and children, since Japanese soldiers had occupied the
school next door to his lodgings. The serenity of this old
scholar had long been a source of wonder to Philip. He was
going blind yet refused to consult an oculist, though Philip
had offered to pay the fee. His smile, tolerant, charitable and
aloof, disquieted Philip ; it was as if the dim eyes were
finishing a prayer while the mouth murmured : "To what
purpose?" It was the smile of an ancient civilization which
knew how to wait. Did not all Chinese have it? Had he
not seen it even on the faces of coolies? How subtle this
co-operation of lips and eyes beside the heavy obvious grin of
Europeans ! He gazed at Mr. Tun with a certain awe. Life
had surely not given him much to smile at. Or had it?
Was Mr. Tun a humorist *sui generis*? Still Philip was disquieted. Perhaps I'm romancing, he thought, but I can't
help it. It struck him that he stood before China as Walter
Pater had stood before Mona Lisa. Behind Mr. Tun's
smile he fancied he discerned a sweet philosophy, a blessed
peace that he envied. And as Hsing-chieh had turned to
Philip, so Philip now turned to Mr. Tun.

"I wish I had your peace of mind," he said.

"You let yourself be worried needlessly," said Mr.
Tun.

"Perhaps. But how can one avoid it in the midst of
all this madness?"

"Everything is passing away. Once you accept that fact
you can be freed."

"Who doesn't accept it? But I don't see how this can
prevent one from worrying."

"You do not really accept it. For that you need deliberate
practice—meditation and prayer."

"I thought you were a Confucian," said Philip.

"Confucianism does not exclude Buddhism, neither does
Taoism for that matter. 'The three roads are different, but

they lead to the same source : the three doctrines are the whole doctrine.' "

Mr. Tun offered to lend Philip some Buddhist scriptures and tracts ; among them he said there was one in particular, the Diamond Sutra, whose wisdom transcended all other knowledge known to philosophy. Philip accepted them with diffidence, for he felt that he was too much of an individualist to pursue his' inquiries into the Buddhist realm of thought with any profit. Mr. Tun assured him that Buddhist teaching had brought an entirely new estimate of the individual to the Chinese masses.

" If one conquer in battle a thousand times a thousand men, and if another conquer himself, he is the greatest of conquerors," [1] he quoted. "Again we have a saying : ' Well-sinkers lead the water whither they will ; fletchers bend the arrow ; carpenters shape the log of wood ; but wise men mould themselves.' This conquest of self, and this moulding of self, is it not the true meaning of individuality ? Pre-Buddhist China scarcely recognized the individual : each was submerged in the family, the clan. But Buddhism gives every individual a distinct place in the great wheel of the law, and enables him to reach the highest goal of salvation."

Philip still had misgivings. A creed which held that human life and the sensuous world were deceptive phenomena could surely produce no literature that was not arid. Yet once he began to read he was astonished. The poetry of these phrases was as moving as their wisdom. It was as if the beautiful scenery amid which Buddhists invariably built their temples, the wooded hills and valleys, the streams and pools of lotuses and carp, had entered into the spirit of the words and taken possession of them.

" The scent of flowers does not travel against the wind, neither that of sandal-wood ; but the scent of good deeds

[1] Translation of Max Müller, in *Sacred Books of the East*, Vol. X.

travels even against the wind." "Long is the night to him who is awake ; long is a league to him who is aweary ; long is this life to the fools who know not the Law." Such phrases haunted Philip like the temples in the Western Hills, and they were the more potent insomuch as he could learn them by heart. Above all Philip was stirred by the purely spiritual concept of Buddha which had inspired the writer of the *Yüan Chiu* Sutra : " Drifting clouds, waning moon, ships that sail the seas, shores that are washed away—these are symbols of unending change. But the blessed Buddha, in his essential, absolute nature, is changeless and everlasting."

Studying the sutras with all the delight which accompanies intellectual discovery, he did not hear the roar of aeroplanes ; he forgot the rage of destruction outside the city, the dismal headlines of *The Peiping Star Bulletin*. Hsing-chieh occupied a pleasant niche in the background of his consciousness and ceased to worry him. Philip applied himself strenuously to the art of sitting in meditation, but the ecstasy did not come. Mr. Tun encouraged him, introducing him to several pious monks. " You are still confused by ideas," they told him, " ascribing to them a reality they do not possess. . . ."

It would take him years to reach any degree of mystical enlightenment ; it was only with faltering steps that he could enter the path which leads to Nirvana ; but he could leave, at any rate, the " burning house " of this world by joining Mr. Tun in reverent recitals of the Lotus and Diamond Sutras. He did not have to subject himself to exceptional austerities or sacrifice any fingers and toes to achieve mastery over the flesh. Materially there were few stumbling-blocks to his spiritual progress. A vegetarian diet suited him ; he had always been abstemious. But for Elvira he would never have touched a cocktail, and Elvira had departed, nor was it likely that he would meet her again. He closed The

Mascot Galleries.  He became a confirmed recluse.  Gradually that " conscious blessedness of perfect peace " for which he had envied Mr. Tun descended on Philip : he too hoped for nothing more than to become another bubble floating on the great ocean of Bodhi—spiritual enlightenment.

> *Like a dream, like a vision, like a bubble,*
> *Like a shadow, like dew, like lightning . . .*

He chanted the Sanskrit syllables with Mr. Tun.  Granny Yang might be wrangling with the servants ; Hsing-chieh's radio might whistle and bray ; the hawkers might scream themselves hoarse in the *hut'ung* : Philip, " transfused with the mellow light of imperishable truth," did not hear.

## Other books made available in Oxford in Asia Paperbacks